# BREAKING GLASS

## TRINITY OF MIND
## BOOK 2

### WRITTEN BY
# J. ABRAM BARNECK

Breaking Glass

Edition 1, Version 1.5 (November 17, 2024)

ISBNs
  Paperback:  978-0-9898109-3-7
  Hardback:   978-0-9898109-8-2
     Ebook:   978-0-9898109-2-0

This book has met the rigorous quality standards needed to earn the Certificate of Quality Publishing in 2020.

These Quality Publishing Standards are intended to raise the quality of small press and independent works.

For more information see this site:
http://scififantasyreaders.com/services/certificate-of-quality

# DEDICATION

For Aiden, who inspires my imagination each day.

# OTHER WRITING

## BY J. ABRAM BARNECK

## TRINITY OF MIND

Fire Light  Book 1
Breaking Glass  Book 2
Torched Heart  Book 3
† *untitled*  Book 4

## SHORT STORIES & NOVELLAS

† Drindél the Winged One
Winged Ones (In DKC Anthology)
* Future 7, Inc
* Mud in the Gutter

† Release forthcoming

* Available at:
www.jabrambarneck.com/writing/short-stories

## POETRY

* Post-millennial Sonnets
* Fantasy Poems
* Free-verse Poems

* Available at
www.jabrambarneck.com/writing/my-poetry

# CHAPTERS

Chapter 1 Clean Dirt.................................................................1
Chapter 2 Proposal .............................................................11
Chapter 3 Indecision ...........................................................17
Chapter 4 Parking Lot .........................................................24
Chapter 5 Teeth ...................................................................31
Chapter 6 Eldra ...................................................................39
Chapter 7 Kiss .....................................................................46
Chapter 8 Dream ..................................................................52
Chapter 9 Broken .................................................................60
Chapter 10 Nerves ...............................................................66
Chapter 11 Sis......................................................................77
Chapter 12 Visitors ..............................................................86
Chapter 13 Eldra ..................................................................92
Chapter 14 Bedchamber ...................................................100
Chapter 15 Servants ..........................................................107
Chapter 16 Visitor..............................................................112
Chapter 17 Zombie .............................................................120
Chapter 18 Practice ...........................................................126
Chapter 19 Scarlett............................................................132
Chapter 20 Rescue..............................................................139
Chapter 21 Severed.............................................................150
Chapter 22 Survivors .........................................................156
Chapter 23 Connected ........................................................161
Chapter 24 O'Brien.............................................................172
Chapter 25 Rope.................................................................182
Chapter 26 Mundane Tasks ...............................................189
Chapter 27 Druid Cache ....................................................193
Chapter 28 Driving East.....................................................199
Chapter 29 Hanna ..............................................................206
Chapter 30 Waking .............................................................214
Chapter 31 Warning............................................................222
Chapter 32 Rhoades............................................................231
Chapter 33 Cavern..............................................................241
Chapter 34 Roped ...............................................................247
Chapter 35 Dreamspeak .....................................................254
Chapter 36 Released ...........................................................259
Chapter 37 Coyote ..............................................................267
Chapter 38 Only One ..........................................................272
Chapter 39 Spirits ..............................................................279
Chapter 40 Certain Death ..................................................285
Chapter 41 Exiting..............................................................298
Chapter 42 Heading home ..................................................304

# CHAPTER 1
# CLEAN DIRT

Eldra is forcing us to write a journal about how the Trinity of Mind affects us. She warned us that sharing thoughts at our age could get awkward and embarrassing quickly. It first got old quickly. Kendra misses drill team. Again. Alexis is trying to clear her mind and hiding thoughts from us. Again. Now, the awkward and embarrassing topics arrive unexpectedly. There is so much in a girl's mind that a guy should never know. I know them now. —Jake

The car lurched to a stop, and I snapped awake. I couldn't believe I'd fallen asleep in the car despite Lexy's fast driving. Usually, I needed very little sleep. Growing back most of my epidermis sapped my energy.

I glanced toward Lexy, catching her lithe, leather-clad form exiting the car with angelic grace. I unbuckled, opened the passenger door, and nearly tripped and fell on my face. But I clung to the door and my dignity, barely staying on my feet. I was no longer the athlete I once was. Kendra snickered behind me. OK, maybe I hadn't clung to my dignity.

North Salt Lake stayed plenty warm in August, but late at night, the air reached a comfortable, cool temperature, which did nothing to hide the stench of the nearby oil refineries.

The cheap burner phone that Mr. Espinoza had lent me rang as I swung the door closed. I answered, ignoring the mental reprimand from Alexis. It was Sis. I had to answer. Kendra approved, so, two against one.

"Hey, Sis." I hoped to hear her tell me all about her days at Disneyland with Dylan. Any trip that alliterated so well had to have been magical. I needed some good news.

1

No such luck.

"Jake," Sis's voice sobbed through the phone. "Those . . . people. The ones who tried to kill us," Sis sniffled. "They murdered John. The police think Mom did it. They think she might have been involved in," another sob, "in your murder, too."

"I know," I felt a pang of guilt. A few days ago, I had made the difficult choice to rush after my sister and leave my stepfather unprotected. I'd make the same choice again, but that didn't absolve my guilt. I glanced at Lexy and Kendra, who waited willingly but impatiently in the darkness. Their faces reflected yellow from the dim, bug-infested porch light that failed miserably at fighting off the night's darkness. The front of the building had bright neon signs—one in the shape of a pinup girl—and two light poles stood on each side of the parking lot, but neither those lights nor the city's ambient glow came to the pathetic porch light's aid. The light switched back and forth from dim to dimmer, the flickering failing to match the beat of the music inside the establishment.

Sis and Dylan were the only two *uninvolved* people who knew that O'Brien had faked my death.

I wished Luiz hadn't told Dylan and Justine that it was safe to come back. They could have stayed at Disneyland for a few more days.

"You have to tell them, Jake," Sis pleaded. "You . . ." her voice caught. Being my sister, I'd seen her chin quiver often enough to know it quivered now.

I really wanted to help. I wanted to tell someone that Mom was innocent. Unfortunately, it was two in the morning, and there was nothing I could do at this hour. Even if it were daytime, I was supposedly dead. If I revealed that I was alive, I could become a target again. That could endanger Sis. Even if I took that chance, what could I say? That three nightwalkers and two druids killed my stepdad, John. Neither the cops nor the judge would believe the truth.

"Justine, I can't." I pressed my knuckles against my head as I squeezed the phone. "We can't tell anyone. Everyone needs to keep believing that I'm dead. If you say different, people will think you're crazy."

Lexy tapped her separation stone, and her mind joined mine. She wore a necklace with two pendants. The first, a pear-shaped black diamond pendant, was enchanted to be both a healing and a protection stone—spells Lexy and I had cast on the stone

2

together. The second pendant, a two-carat diamond enchanted as a separation stone, sat in the center of a silver trinity symbol.

*Tell her that I have already called a lawyer*, she thought to me. *He will be here tomorrow.*

She tapped the separation stone again, cutting off her thoughts. I also heard a few other thoughts before she tapped off our connection—thoughts such as, *Keagan is waiting*, and, *Hurry, Jake. This is neither the time nor the place.* Other memories slipped out, ones that I'm sure she would have preferred to keep secret. It wasn't by her choice, but at only eighteen, Lexy was no stranger to the type of dancing that went on inside this building. Keagan's desire to kill Lexy provided me with something to distract my mind from such thoughts. Keagan hungered for power.

"Sis, it will be OK." I tried to assure her. "I have a rich friend. She has a lawyer coming to help Mom tomorrow. You'll be fine staying at Kendra's house tonight, right?" I asked. At Kendra's request, her parents had left their Bear Lake trip early to come home and take care of Justine.

"Kendra's not here, Jake. Do you know where she is?"

I glanced over at Kendra, who stood right next to me. She also wore a necklace with a protection stone and a separation stone, though both were mounted on one pendant. Her separation stone, a trinity symbol with a two-carat diamond in the center, differed from Lexy's only in the diamond's cut. Lexy's was princess cut while Kendra's was Asscher cut. For Kendra's protection stone, Eldra had enchanted a small Burmese ruby, Kendra's birthstone, and mounted it to the top arch of the silver trinity symbol pendant. In crystal lore, a ruby represents emotion, and Kendra excelled at emotional magic. I had a hunch that Eldra had enchanted that stone with more than just the protection spell.

"Yes, she's fine," I said, trying to avoid lying to my sister. Inside the building, the music had switched. Hopefully, Sis couldn't hear the muffled thumping of the increased bass. "Sis, I gotta go. Don't tell anyone that I'm alive, and don't mention anything weird to anyone, OK?" I hung up, not giving Sis time to argue.

Kendra didn't give me any time to shift from talk-to-sister mode to daunting-meeting-with-Keagan mode. She stepped forward under the yellow porch light, which accentuated her short, golden brown hair, and pressed a button on a card reader next to the metal door. The faint sound of a buzzer fought its way to our ears over the muffled music.

My skin, white as an albino where it didn't appear road rashed, must have looked hideous while reflecting the yellow porch light. I pulled my hoodie on and tightened it to hide my face. My skin's lack of healing left me disappointed. I looked exactly the same as when I had woken Tuesday night. It had only been twenty-eight hours since I had woken, but I had slept three more times, so I expected some progress. The healing progress had stalled. What if my skin had finished healing and the result of the damage I'd done to my deeper layers of skin had caused it to heal hideously? What if I was going to be a road rashed albino forever?

Lexy shifted her stance and elevated her chin, her long neck somehow making her more royal. She knew exactly how to own her new title as Princess of the New World.

"Positions!" she ordered verbally, with a pronounced, regal tone.

As her newly dubbed generals, Kendra and I had to maintain formal positions. Kendra stood to her front and I stood just at her rear—which, by the way, gave me the better view. Yes, Lexy wore her usual tight leather pants and bustier that left her ribbon-bow tattoo exposed on her lower back. Being a few inches shorter than Lexy and drill-team thin, Kendra wore borrowed leather pants that didn't stretch around her backside like Lexy's did. They hung loose, allowing for bunching below her pockets and at the back of her knees.

They both disabled their separation stones and our three minds became one, while my eyes still focused on their lower curves.

*Oops.* They caught me looking.

*Seriously?* Kendra didn't turn back and glare at me because she didn't have to. Her mind scolded me with both her thoughts and feelings. That didn't make much sense to me because just over a week ago, she had worn a white, string bikini with every intention of me noticing. I didn't get how she didn't want me to notice her now when she was dressed far more modestly.

*Things are different now!* Kendra answered my thought.

I caught a hint of guilt from her as she remembered wearing a bikini for me.

*You tempted me to wear it!* she accused.

Great, now she blamed me for breaking her usual modesty standards.

*I didn't ask you to wear it,* I reminded her.

*Focus!* Princess Alexis ordered, half her mind on Keagan and the other half fixated on my memory of Kendra in her white bikini juxtaposed against her own memory of Kendra demanding to wear a modest leather outfit. She formed a single thought: *Hypocrite.*

The metal door opened halfway, letting out the beating music and cutting off Kendra's mental protest. Lexy breathed in a thousand different scents from inside while ignoring the oil-refinery stench in the outside air.

I'd imagined the door would be opened by a six-foot-six bouncer with a metal chain hanging from his front pocket to his wallet, or maybe some thick-necked bodyguard with a gun on his hip. Instead, a short, white guy in slacks and a white, button-up shirt stepped into the half-open doorway. He didn't even look creepy. He looked completely normal. In fact, he looked like he'd just stepped out of church, tie removed and top button undone. He stood in front of a hallway with doors on the sides.

Lexy picked out the guy's thoughts. His brain consisted of only simple, all-business thoughts. We were as young as he'd been told we would be, but he'd been ordered to ignore that. Honestly, I felt the same way. We were young and had no business going into such an establishment, but we were also ignoring that.

"Welcome to Club Exposed." The man smiled. "Mr. K is inside." He opened the door the rest of the way, stepped aside, and gestured with his white-sleeved arm for us to enter.

*Two Salt Lake City Mormons and a vampire—Half-dhampir, Lexy interjected—walk into a strip club. What's a good punch line?*

*We get caught,* answered Kendra. She imagined herself sitting on the bottom bleacher in our school gym, her drill team instructor standing over her and shouting the words, "You are off the team!" Kendra clenched her teeth and gulped.

She reached her hand forward, stretching it across the threshold. I'd argued that checking for a threshold would be a waste of time because how could a strip club have built up a threshold? As soon as Kendra's hand crossed it, however, I knew how wrong I'd been. The magic refused her.

*I told you not to judge,* Lexy's thought came through strong and clear.

There was little truth to the whole threshold myth. It wouldn't keep bad things out. It wasn't a force field that monsters couldn't cross. You couldn't revoke an invite and have some dark creature of night expelled from your home. But the truth that *did* exist regarding the threshold myth actually mattered. The energy we use for magic is sentient. Inside a threshold, magic refuses to work for those who are not invited in. Even magic you bring in immediately stops working if you're not invited over the threshold.

"Invite us in!" Kendra ordered, trying to be as regally demanding as Princess Alexis, but her voice just came out loud and breathy.

The man pulled at his collared white shirt. His five o'clock shadow extended halfway down his neck. "No invitation necessary." He waved one hand toward the dimly lit hallway leading inside. "The door is open."

*He was ordered to avoid inviting us in,* Lexy read his mind. Eldra had warned us that they might try that. Lexy's nerves hit me as strong as Kendra's, only Lexy's were less about our current situation and more about the *protector*—me—who stood so close behind her. I tried to pry into her memories to find everything she knew about what a protector was—what I was—but I couldn't find anything. She'd created a lockbox in her mind where she could hide away the thoughts and memories that I most wanted to access.

Kendra consciously clenched her teeth, trying hard to come across as ferociously angry. "I said: Invite. Us. In." This time, her voice sounded low and creepy like the demonic presence that inhabited Linda Blair in *The Exorcist.*

"My apologies." The man looked down guiltily. "Please, come in."

Kendra's hand still hung in front of her, extending into the doorway. Hearing the clear invitation, I immediately stepped forward but neither Kendra nor Lexy moved.

*Wait,* Kendra warned. The magic across the threshold still refused Kendra.

The still-healing skin on my legs stretched painfully as I tried to stop my momentum, but I couldn't. I lost my balance. I would have fallen forward but Lexy stood in front of me, so my body leaned against hers. She tensed her back at my contact, and shivers ran up her arched spine. She didn't want to, but her mental lockbox exposed an image—an ancient painting really—depicting a man standing above a young woman who was strapped to a stone table. Some metal instrument forced her mouth open, and the man dripped blood into it from a cut in his wrist. She was screaming.

Lexy forced the image away and focused. She shrugged her shoulders back, pushing me off her. I wobbled back and managed to keep myself from falling.

Both Kendra and Lexy tried not to worry for me, but they couldn't stop it. After only exerting the effort to stand straight, my leg muscles burned as if I were at the gym working out. If the girls had lost fifty pounds of muscles and had to regrow their epidermis, they'd be weak, too.

*We should have left him home,* Kendra complained.

*We already argued over this,* Lexy responded. *Keagan specifically demanded that both of my generals attend this meeting.*

*Being weak physically doesn't mean I am weak magically,* I defended myself.

Then Kendra's and Lexy's bad thoughts from yesterday repeated. The thoughts that Eldra demanded that we push out of our minds and never repeat. It had started as part of their constant catfight. Kendra apologized to me again. Alexis snapped at her, but she had been involved and had added to that thought as well.

*It was only an unfiltered thought,* Kendra defended.

Still, she couldn't *unthink* it, and as any Leonardo DiCaprio fan knows, "an idea is like a virus. Once an idea has taken hold of the brain, it's almost impossible to eradicate."

*This man,* Lexy thought, changing the subject, *does not belong to this establishment. He has no right to invite us in.*

*You're right,* Kendra agreed.

*Demand that he send another!*

"Your invitation is inadequate," Kendra spoke the formal and demanding words that Alexis provided her. "Send another." Alexis managed to lend Kendra her regal tone that demanded obedience.

I watched the man's Adam's apple drop toward his unbuttoned collar and rise back up. His lips quivered as he spoke. "Yes, of course." He turned, closing the door behind him.

As we waited under the dim, yellow porch light, I felt a slight tremor reverberate in the space between my muscles and my newly grown skin. I'd recently learned that I could sense evil like a retired NFL player's joints could sense a coming storm. I considered whether a nightwalker was near, but were that the case, my muscles would have been pole dancing under my skin.

Had my muscles just responded to the strip club's corruption? Or perhaps the corruption didn't so much come from the strip club as those who frequented it. Or was it Keagan I sensed? I assumed it was one of those and ignored my body's warning system, a mistake I hope to never repeat.

 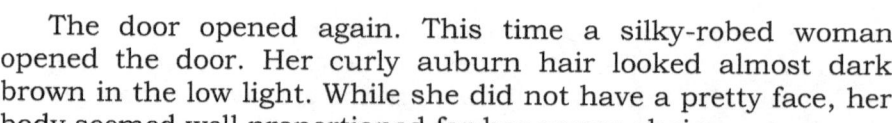

The door opened again. This time a silky-robed woman opened the door. Her curly auburn hair looked almost dark brown in the low light. While she did not have a pretty face, her body seemed well proportioned for her career choice.

With our three minds joined, Alexis and Kendra had a background thread of consciousness in a continual catfight—at least they tried to keep it in the background. They paused their bickering long enough to snap at me for noticing the way the stripper's too-short, silk robe clung to the woman's voluptuous figure.

"I's told to invite y'all in," she spoke with a rural, southern accent that suggested she'd grown up somewhere in the south, not from Utah. "I'm Scarlett—" she paused as her eyes moved from Kendra's face to Lexy's and then to mine. I doubted she could make out my hideously re-growing skin underneath the shadow of my hoodie. Despite it being two in the morning and despite the perfectly cool shorts and T-shirt weather, I started to sweat under my hoodie beneath her gaze. I pulled a layer of magic around my skin to cool myself.

"Y'all sure ya belong here? Aren't ya a little young to be meeting Mr. K-Creepy here?" she asked.

"Yes. Yes, we are." Kendra answered for us.

I laughed inside. If there were a hundred and four days of summer vacation, there were a hundred and four nights too. And, no, this was *not* a good way to spend them.

Alexis ignored my chuckle and stayed focused. Mr. K-Creepy meant Keagan. Lexy found it very interesting that this woman could call him that. Keagan's allure should have kept her from finding him creepy.

Kendra hesitated. She didn't want to be invited in.

*Don't worry. We won't go in front,* I reminded Kendra. *I won't see anything.*

We'd argued against coming here, but Princess Alexis was forced to obey the rules of a challenge, and by rule, the challenger picked the meeting place. Alexis was certain he had picked a strip club to play against the insecurities of her less-than-glamorous upbringing.

"Would you please be so kind as to invite us in?" Kendra's voice heightened to a friendlier tone.

Scarlett seemed to hesitate. She took another look at each of our faces but then nodded. "A'ight, y'all. Come on in."

Kendra reached her hand forward again. The magic tingled as it flowed into Kendra and up her arm.

Scarlett raised her eyebrow at Kendra's outstretched hand, clearly calling her weird with her eyes. Kendra took offense. She didn't know what kind of woman worked at a strip club, and naturally, she assumed the woman had to be a creep herself. My unfiltered thoughts joined in. I called her *slut* in my head. Kendra followed up with *dirty whore.*

*Stop it,* Princess Alexis scolded us.

Neither Kendra nor I would have allowed such negative thoughts to leave our lips. We would have filtered them out, but with the Trinity of Mind, there was no filter.

Alexis focused her red eyes on Scarlett's green ones and reached deep into her mind.

Scarlett's real name was Jody. Office assistant by day, exotic dancer by night. Her autistic son, Carl, recently started locking himself in his closet to play video games. Jody—a foster-system kid turned adult—struggled to pay his special school's tuition. A few years ago, she'd prayed for months to get enough money for her son's school. As if a blessing from God, the money she made by dancing at Club Exposed covered the monthly tuition exactly. This job was the answer to her prayers.

*I told you not to judge,* Lexy slapped both Kendra and me with her thought.

Kendra and I both felt our hearts open to Jody. At church, both Kendra and I had been taught to love others and not to judge, but by bad example, we had also been taught *to* judge. I had cousins in California that always complained about Utah Mormons. They claimed that religious cities, like Salt Lake City, can sometimes be overly judgmental places. Funny how the truly righteous, those who *might* have the right to judge, never did; but those who have no right to judge, like me, still judged indiscriminately. I made a goal to work on that.

*Wait, who's watching Jody's son while she works?* I asked. Kendra's interest also piqued at my question.

*It is impolite to pry.* Lexy stopped reading Jody's mind. We reluctantly agreed. Who were we to turn Jody's thoughts into our personal reality TV show?

*What about her?* Kendra asked, eyeing a younger woman who just entered the hall from the front of the establishment. She wore the same scanty, silk robe—a company uniform perhaps? Having just finished her routine, the young woman was just now tying it closed as she walked down the hall toward us. Her thin, dark-brown hair, just a shade lighter than Lexy's, hung perfectly straight and tapered at her chin. With Lexy's hair currently chin length, the girl and Lexy looked surprisingly alike.

Alexis focused on the girl's mind. Here at the club, she went by Layla, but her real name was Gina Godard. She studied English Literature at the University of Utah and had a rich daddy. She worked here simply because she liked it and because she looked forward to the day her father would find out and be humiliated.

Gina turned into a doorway halfway down the hall.

*You still should not judge,* Alexis argued. Never underestimate the effect of daddy issues.

*Or in your case, granddaddy issues,* I responded.

*Touché.* Nobody had granddaddy issues as bad as Lexy's.

"Well," Scarlett spoke loudly, interrupting our Trinity of Mind. "Y'all come'n on in or what?"

"Yes," Kendra answered, following her extended hand inside. Lexy and I stepped in perfect unison, staying close behind.

# CHAPTER 2
# PROPOSAL

*If I have to give up drill team, at least it is so I can use magic. I love magic. I don't like the Trinity of Mind so much. The separation stone makes it bearable. Alexis calls me the worst names. Jake keeps suggesting I ignore her. It isn't that easy. She is so good at hitting me with the most hurtful thoughts. —Kendra*

Scarlett—er, Jody—led us past the small entry room and into the hallway. Jody's robe wasn't long enough, so I tried to keep my eyes on Kendra and Lexy. This time neither girl complained that I kept my eyes on their tight leather pants. They preferred my eyes looking at them than allowing my eyes to wander. I couldn't avoid glancing around to assess the place, though.

The hallway floor looked to be nothing more than cement painted like a red carpet, only years of stilettos had worn away the paint down the middle, but the floor was still clean. The walls were painted greige, part gray and part beige, which is a color a guy like me would never have thought of. But with two women in my head, I found I now knew a lot more color names. The first poster on the wall showed a modern rendition of Rosie the Riveter, featuring her flexed bicep and the phrase, "We can do this!" This modern rendition differed from the original. It was a long, full-body picture. Below her shirt, the woman dressed as Rosie the Riveter flaunted bare legs and wore high heels and a bikini bottom that matched her bandana. I tried not to look at the other posters on the walls. White trim surrounded white doors. Neither the doors nor the trim was fancy but were surprisingly clean. White, foam tiles, the kind with hundreds of tiny holes in them, hung in a grid from the ceiling.

We passed by a changing room where a half-dozen exotic dancers prepped. Nakedness did not seem to be a source of embarrassment—at least, not for the women in the rooms. I had

11

assured Kendra just seconds ago that I wouldn't see anything. I'd
been wrong. My cheeks flushed. The women glanced our way but
otherwise ignored us. It wasn't so much the women's nakedness
or my natural response to it that forced color into my cheeks; it
was Lexy's and Kendra's unrestricted access to my mind as I
experienced my natural reaction. My hooded sweater saved me
from flashing my red cheeks.

I missed my tan. I missed not being hideous.

The hallway smelled like cinnamon. I located an air freshener
plugged into one of the hallway's outlets. A hint of alcohol trailed
in from the front of the establishment. Or maybe only Lexy
smelled it, as her dhampir nose sensed much more than mine
did. Being completely joined to two other people really caused
havoc with our senses.

"Keagan's wait'n on y'all in here." Jody stopped at a door with
a glass panel and knocked. "I'm headed on stage next, so I'll be
leavin' ya here."

Jody gave us a nervous stare, clearly worried for us, then
turned and headed toward the front of the establishment.

*Can you try harder not to imagine Jody's performance?* Kendra
snapped at me, annoyed by my imagination, which was aided by
images I'd seen on internet sites I should have never browsed.
Guilt swelled throughout my chest. Sharing everything about
myself with Kendra and Lexy, especially my sins, just plain hurt.

Through the glass in the door, we saw Keagan lift his head
and look at us. He sat behind a large table. Two dark, female
forms stood on either side of him. Their eyes also turned our way.
The woman on his left had a look that screamed Whoopi
Goldberg, especially her hair. But her weak chin and small nose
weren't at all like Whoopi's. The other woman would have made
a long twig feel short and fat. She also had skin almost as dark
as a nightwalker's, yet she still managed to have dark circles
under her eyes.

*Haitians.* Lexy gulped. The fear she had directed at me,
because I was a protector, was redirected toward the two women
and increased tenfold. I hadn't noticed before now, but Lexy's fear
gave off a musty scent. A couple of memories flashed from Lexy
into Kendra and me, and we both shared a tingling sensation that
rose from the base of our spines and past our necks before
stopping to dance around our hair follicles.

I brought up a mental world map with my almost-but-not-
quite photographic memory. I located the island just southeast of
Florida. Haiti shared that island with the Dominican Republic.

Haitians don't hang out in Utah very often. At least, neither Kendra nor I had ever met one. Since most of the state is white, Hispanic, Native American, or Polynesian, a black person sticks out like a sore thumb, so we Utahns usually notice them. We probably stare. Most Utahns are not prejudiced, though. Sure, the reason we stare has to do with skin color, but I think there is a huge difference between bigotry and just noticing somebody because they stick out like a sore thumb. Bigotry requires taking negative judgment based on the race, and while Utah probably had people like that, I didn't know any. We probably get a bad rap for staring, though.

I won't lie; I felt some negative judgment toward the two women standing next to Keagan; however, their skin color had nothing to do with it. Besides hanging out with Keagan, whom I'd just as soon erase from existence, my muscles had started that pole dance I'd mentioned earlier, and these two women had inspired it. Turns out the institution wasn't causing any of the crawling under my skin. It was all coming from this room—some from Keagan, but mostly from the Haitians. The small round one had a miniature metal skull hanging from her neck, and the beanpole one—well, she didn't have a creepy object on her. She just exuded creepy. In addition to my crawling skin, their magic had a . . . I wanted to say stink, but I don't sense magic with my nose, it is a feeling. Maybe *taint* was the right word. I can also see magic, a rare ability. A murky haze of tainted magic surrounded the Haitians. Kendra, Lexy, and I suddenly wanted to shower.

Though a vampire, Keagan didn't have magic, and as far as I knew, he wasn't a Jedi, so someone else must have been in the room near the door because it opened at the motion of his hand.

Kendra hesitated to enter.

*Lead us inside,* Princess Alexis ordered.

Kendra stepped inside first, then Lexy and I followed. I could have sworn that I could smell dirt and cow manure the second we walked in—except, again, Lexy smelled it, not me. I glanced left at a short man in overalls. Kendra stood five foot six, though the black combat boots Lexy wore lent her an extra two inches. Even had she not worn those boots, the man that had opened the door would have had to look up to meet Kendra's eyes. The guy's vacant eyes told me there was something off about him. But we weren't here to see him, so I ignored him. We came here for Keagan. If all went well, I'd get to erase Keagan from existence and revel in the pleasure of it. I didn't really expect Lexy to feel remorse at the thought of me erasing Keagan, but she did. Her emotions had felt mixed and confused all day.

13

"Please. You sit." The short, round woman spoke with a jumpy accent.

The room extended about twenty feet wide and stretched about fifteen feet long. I had no idea why a strip bar needed a conference room, but that is where we found ourselves. Unlike the cement hallway, the conference room floor had thin, hard carpet that extended halfway up the walls. Between two tall windows, a large panoramic photo of over thirty bikini-clad women stretched the length of the wall behind Keagan and his voodoo witches. I spotted Jody on the poster, third woman from the center. On the walls to the right, left, and behind me hung various photos and posters that were not age appropriate.

"We will stand," Kendra responded. Lexy had already prepped us that under no circumstances were we to sit down. She wanted us ready to move at any moment.

*Sports position!* I imagined my football coach's loud voice.

"Will you address your princess?" Kendra spoke forcefully to Keagan.

I'd remembered Keagan having some nasty claws, but tonight his hands looked completely normal.

*Like our teeth, his claws retract,* Alexis explained.

Her mind shuddered as she thought of how, unlike fangs, which grew in within hours of being turned, it took a long, painful process to grow claws: it involved the repeated removal and regrowth of one's fingertips. Kendra shuddered too. Lucky for Lexy, dhampirs didn't have vampire claws, or her grandfather would have found great joy in repeatedly cutting off her fingertips.

Keagan stood—he maybe had me by an inch, but since losing my skin and muscles, I cowered in my hoodie, making him seem even taller. Like Alexis, he dressed in black leather—clothes that doubled as body armor. He looked every bit like the Vampire King's strongest general. However, Alexis felt a hint of vulnerability coming off him. To my annoyance, both Alexis and Kendra found him extremely handsome. I'd blame his vampire allure, but along with their separation stones, both girls wore protection stones, which dimmed a vampire's allure.

Keagan eyed both Lexy and Kendra hungrily—except his eyes were blue not red, which didn't make sense.

*He is wearing contacts,* Lexy informed us. *He is hiding the fact that he is a vampire. I often wear similar contacts for the same reason. Vampires are not exactly welcome inside the line.*

*What line?* I asked.

*Utah's border.*

There was a history to her answer but now wasn't the time to delve into it.

Alexis liked the way Keagan's eyes looked in blue. I didn't like the way Alexis's breath and heartbeat increased at seeing Keagan, I didn't like it at all. Her jumbled thoughts and emotions confused me. I didn't like that either. I would have been less confused if our minds weren't joined.

"Of course, I shall address my princess." Keagan bowed low over the conference room table, but his eyes never left Alexis's. He waited in a bowed state for what seemed like a long time before Princess Alexis lifted her hand. She'd forgotten that, by custom, since she was a princess now, etiquette required that he wait for her to motion for him to rise. She hoped he hadn't noticed.

"Princess Alexis," Keagan continued. "I have been waiting for you for quite some time." His words held a double meaning; I just couldn't decipher the second meaning yet. He leaned over the table and extended his hand. Alexis stepped to the table and stretched her hand out to his. He took it and managed to kiss it over the conference table without looking awkward at all.

Protection stone or not, she shouldn't have let him do that. Kendra and I got a montage of images of all the recent times she'd been specifically *gifted* to Keagan. Lexy's grandfather, the Vampire King, had made a practice of "gifting" out his granddaughter to entertain special guests or to reward those who pleased him. I still regretted not erasing the incestual bastard. Keagan, as the Vampire King's general, had been the one steadfast and regular man in Alexis's life. And recently, he hadn't exactly treated her poorly. While some had used Alexis in ways so evil and corrupt that I couldn't even begin to describe them, Keagan's treatment of her had improved each time her grandfather gifted her to him.

"You may speak," Princess Alexis addressed Keagan herself.

"Do you know why I am here?" Keagan started. I hadn't remembered his Scottish accent.

"You are here to issue a challenge for the rule of the New World." Princess Alexis spoke calmly.

"Quite the contrary." Keagan laughed. "I betrayed the Vampire King. I left him the moment it looked like his side would lose." He glanced at me, and I knew immediately that despite my hideous skin providing me an unwanted disguise, he recognized me. "I have not survived over four hundred years by fighting on the losing side. Yet you foolishly let him live. That puts me in a precarious position."

"The precariousness of your position does not concern us," Alexis stated flatly, but inside, her mind danced in turmoil. She could almost sense what was coming.

"I am afraid I cannot return to the Vampire King, lest he kill me. Even if I hadn't betrayed him, I witnessed his defeat. I have spoken with your mother. The king's defeat will remain a secret, and I threaten that secret. But enough about me, how have you been?"

"I have been well, thank you," Alexis answered.

I tightened my muscles nervously. This conversation had turned somewhat pleasant. Of all the possible ways I'd imagined this going, pleasant was not one of them. Whatever he was preparing for was going to be big. Unexpected. Something that neither Alexis nor Eldra had thought of. Kendra shared my concern, but I couldn't read Alexis. Trying to hear one of her thoughts or feel one of her emotions was like trying to pick out one single gust of wind from a raging hurricane. Her tormented emotions ripped at the Trinity of Mind. Kendra and I fought to keep our own minds from being ripped and pulled into Alexis's emotional maelstrom.

Keagan gave off a strong musk scent. All vampires gave off different scents with different emotions. I didn't know Keagan like I knew Alexis, so I didn't know which emotion that scent indicated, but Alexis knew Keagan far too well. I didn't like that he felt *that* emotion.

"Just tell her why you're here," I spoke through clenched teeth.

Keagan looked my way a second time.

"Do you plan to challenge me for the New World or not?" Lexy asked.

"I do plan to rule the New World, Alexis," Keagan continued. "Only, I plan to do it by your side." He dropped to one knee, and I guessed his words before he said them. His hand stretched out, and as he spoke, he opened a little square box revealing an extremely large, black diamond ring. "Alexis Kaloyan, will you marry me?"

# CHAPTER 3
# INDECISION

*The Trinity of Mind is a bit difficult to navigate. I have knowledge that my grandfather has forbidden me from sharing. Knowledge even Eldra is unaware of. I dare not think such thoughts. That is not all I would like to hide, either. Eldra promised to help, but she had conditions. I reluctantly agreed. How long can I keep my secrets? How long can I keep Jake and Kendra safe? —Alexis*

"**H**ell, no!" I shouted. There was no question that Keagan and his freaky-looking voodoo witches heard my answer loud and clear. However, they completely ignored me as if my shout hadn't exploded through the conference room and down the hall.

If that wasn't bad enough, Alexis didn't back up my answer. Her usual pumpkin spice scent augmented and wafted powerfully through the conference room, mingling with Keagan's strong musk. If Keagan's proposal had caught me by surprise, Alexis's reaction to it blindsided both Kendra and me like a left side defensive end unabated to the quarterback. The maelstrom of emotions pounded against mine and Kendra's mind. She needed our minds to keep her emotions from tearing her sanity apart.

Of course, when she needed us most is when Alexis tapped her separation stone, shutting off our connection to her mind.

*What's she doing?* Kendra asked.

Eldra had given us a single solitary rule: Until the meeting ended, we should never separate our minds. Alexis had just broken that rule.

Before she'd closed us off, I had gathered as many thoughts as I could discern from the raging storm that was her mind. I started to piece together the thoughts thrashing through her head.

17

It might sound freaking nuts that Alexis might love the same man that had killed and turned her dhampir mother into a full-blown Vampire. The same man that had requested Alexis as a gift for tracking down both her and her mother. The same man that, every year on both his birthday and hers, requested the Vampire King gift Alexis to him. Only, I'd seen in Alexis's memories, at least in the more recent ones, how each time she'd been gifted to Keagan, he had treated her like they were two lovers having an affair.

Alexis *loved* him.

I tensed what muscle I had left. Her protection stone blocked her thoughts, but it didn't fully block her emotions from me. I could feel her love for him rolling off her. Only it wasn't exactly love as I knew it. She couldn't see that her love for him had a taint as putrid as that of the Haitians' magic. If her love for Kendra and me were a clear stream, then her love for Keagan was a stagnant and murky marsh, where mold grew around the pumpkins and the spice smelled stale.

Alexis probably didn't notice the taint because she had so little love in her life to compare it to. Kendra and I had loved a lot in our lives. Kendra had such a huge family who all loved each other that I couldn't even name them all. I didn't grow up with near the love Kendra had, but I'd grown up with much more than Alexis had. I loved Sis and she loved me back. My grandma had loved me thoroughly until passing away when I was eleven. I loved my mom, and despite her faults and the unfortunate circumstances of my arrival in her life, she eventually loved me back. Alexis never had any of that. She'd supposedly been loved by her mother and grandfather, but both those loves were just as tainted as her love for Keagan.

*Oh, my heck!* Kendra thought. *Alexis has Stockholm syndrome.*

It took me a second to remember what Stockholm syndrome was. I'd never taken psychology, so I only had a few movie references that hinted at what it was. Kendra had read a book about it, so after a brief brain dump from her mind, I agreed with her diagnosis. Stockholm syndrome is where the abused begins to love their abuser—especially after the abuser shows kindness. Keagan had shown Alexis kindness. In fact, I'd seen a memory in Alexis that showed her looking forward to Keagan's last birthday. I cringed. That memory would haunt me forever.

I stepped to Alexis's side.

"Tell him no," I growled into her ear.

"Silence!" she shouted back at me. An angry scent of copper instantly replaced that of pumpkin spice.

Her eyes fixed on Keagan. I could feel and smell her emotions change as she considered her answer. I just couldn't believe she struggled with this choice.

A large, white, analog clock hung on the wall to the left and its tick-tock became the loudest sound in the room—slow and stressful.

"Keagan," Alexis finally spoke. "I need more time to answer."

Keagan's scent changed to the repelling stink of citronella oil. Having closed off her mental connection with us, Alexis couldn't tell me what emotion he was feeling, but I didn't need her to. His eyes changed to a much lighter shade of blue. It was hard to tell through the blue contacts, but I was pretty sure they'd turned white. I'd learned recently that a vampire didn't only change scents with extreme emotion, their irises change color too. While emotional scents varied per vampire, the way their irises changed was uniform. Black meant anger. Black with red lightning streaks meant hunger. White meant fear.

Keagan's eyes flicked to Voodoo Whoopi on his right and then to Stick Witch on his left. Then his eyes focused on Alexis. His pupils widened invitingly. Keagan was letting Alexis read his mind. Alexis's mind-reading capabilities were not exactly common—rare, in fact, among both vampires and nightwalkers. Only those closest to her knew she could read minds.

"I need more time," Alexis confirmed.

"Is that your final answer?" Keagan shifted nervously in his stance.

"Yes. For now." Alexis's voice quivered vulnerably as she spoke.

"Well, then," Keagan spoke, and he literally gulped. Keagan's fragrant fear set off warning bells in my head. If the Vampire King's strongest general feared something, you could bet it was scarier than hell.

*Protect yourself,* I shouted into Kendra's mind, but she'd already brought up a containment around us. Sure, containments wouldn't stop anything physical, but if any of them attacked us with magic, we could surprise them and hit back.

"The decision is yours to make, Lexy," Keagan continued; "however, while I am happy to give you more time, my colleagues here will only allow you to walk out of here alive if you say yes."

I'd filled my body with magic long before we entered the back of Club Exposed. I could form a magic missile and release it in about half a second. My only question was this: Which of the three should I target first?

I *so* wanted to erase Keagan. If I'd hated him before, Alexis's Stockholm syndrome–induced love made me hate him even more. And where did he get off calling her Lexy? I told myself it had nothing to do with jealousy; it just had to do with his pure evil. However, lying to myself didn't change the fact that it was the two witches, not Keagan, who had my muscles joining Scarlett for a pole dance.

"I need time," Alexis spoke more firmly.

"Then you may have more time," Keagan answered, "if you survive."

I caught movement to my left. The short, little farmer lunged at me with a knife. I twisted but not fast enough. The knife embedded itself into my upper arm and I felt the point hit bone. I lurched away, but my legs, still weak from my recent massive muscle loss, gave out. I fell to the floor. The thin office carpet did nothing to pad my fall.

Dark semi-solid shadows, which reminded me of the nightwalker's mist, rose from the floor like swords and lashed at Alexis and Kendra but shattered against the containment. The magic in the room trembled, and the girls' containments shattered too.

I rolled away from the shadow blade that swiped at me, and still lying on the carpet, I launched a magic missile at Stick Witch. My missile never reached its target. A second shadow blade redirected from its target—my head—and intercepted the glowing orb like a poorly thrown Brett Favre pass. Then the blade of darkness and my magic missile both faded and disappeared.

Alexis jumped forward, pulling a rune-covered dagger from the sheath belted at her thigh. She swiped at Voodoo Whoopi's neck but missed by an inch as the witch stepped back and leaned away. Before Alexis could take another swing, a shadow lashed around her like a whip and then tightened like a boa constrictor.

I kicked up into the farmer's groin. I connected, but as if pain didn't matter to him, he continued toward me, knife in hand, stabbing down at me. He put his weight behind the knife and tried to thrust it into my neck, but I twisted away. The blade's tip hit the floor to my left, an inch from my carotid. I didn't have anywhere near the strength needed to fend off the farmer. It didn't matter if he stood only five foot four with shoes. Farmers are tough as nails, and this farmer seemed hellbent on using every ounce of his strength to kill me. I missed the fifty pounds of muscles I'd burned off the other day.

The farmer elbowed me in the face, knocking the back of my head to the floor. His eyes found mine, and they were as hollow as death. A Caradoc thought flashed in my mind, and I didn't hesitate to react. I dropped the containment I'd been trying to imagine around my body and imagined a complete seal around the farmer, encapsulating everything—magic, thoughts, emotions, smells, spirit. He went limp and dropped weightlessly on top of me.

I struggled to roll him off and came to a sitting position.

I must have looked weak to the two Hagathas because they ignored me and focused on Kendra and Alexis. Alexis stood frozen in a trance with the tendrils of blackness wrapped around her. She wore her protection stone. Would it help her against the voodoo darkness? Kendra hadn't really mounted any kind of offense, probably because the shadow blades attacked her from all sides and somehow snaked their way into her containment and she kept having to push them out.

*Water.* It wasn't my thought; it was Kendra's. Her eyes glanced at the ceiling, and sure enough, a line of three fire sprinklers stuck out from the foam-tiled ceiling. I'd felt the power in water, so her thought didn't make complete sense. Eldra had been so sure of what she'd told her that I went with it anyway.

*Fyr Leoht!* I thought, and focused the magic, not on a spot above my palm, but on the spot near the ceiling. Fire erupted in a ball just below one of two sprinkler heads in the room. The flame rose, wrapping around the metal and dancing against the ceiling.

If this were a movie, the instant the fire hit the sprinkler head, every sprinkler in the entire building would have gone off. Unfortunately, this was real life, so I would have to wait a few seconds for the sprinkler head to reach one hundred and sixty-five degrees, and only the one sprinkler head that reached that temperature would spray water.

I glanced at Alexis. What was happening to her? Why did she close off her mind? Why didn't she tell Keagan to go to hell? Unfortunately, between increasing the heat of the fire and thinking of Alexis, I had neglected to keep the containment—my special *everything-seal*—on little old McDonald. I'd forgotten about him completely until I felt the knife enter my left calf.

"Gaaaahhhh," I shouted in pain, jerking my leg away from the blade and then scooting away.

Sitting on the floor with a zoned-out farmer holding a knife was probably not the best time to notice that there was an insane amount of gum stuck to the bottom of the conference room table. *Gross.*

I didn't scoot fast enough. The farmer lurched at me and stabbed again, hitting my left front pocket. My burner phone gave a plastic cry of death as it shielded me from a second cut.

The sprinkler reached the needed temperature. I heard a small pop, like a shattering light bulb, and water sprayed out in an umbrella shape from the single sprinkler head and began spraying all of us as well as the conference room desk between us. This establishment had not hooked the sprinklers to the fire alarm, because it didn't go off. Eldra had taught Kendra that water would disrupt magic, but in the shower and in the hotel pool, I'd felt the power in water. It seemed to me that the water would augment a spell's power. But just as Eldra had told Kendra it would, running water dissolved everyone's magic.

My hoodie covered my forehead, shielding my eyes, but the cold water hit my mouth and chin and dripped down my neck, causing me to shiver. Alexis stood in a trance, letting the water splash over her face and hair. Kendra stepped to the side after the initial spray.

The witches weren't prepared for the spraying water. They each stood on one side of Keagan, and both turned their heads away from water, covering their faces with both hands. That's when Keagan, ignoring the water spraying on his face, turned and punched Stick Witch in the side of the head, sending her head crashing into and cracking the glass covering the panorama of the bikini-clad workers. He simultaneously kicked backward, his boot connecting with Voodoo Whoopi in the center of her round obliques, causing her to stumble and fall against the left wall. A clay bottle on her waist broke and an ethereal substance, smoke-like but very real, slipped out.

Keagan smiled at me, still oblivious to the water spraying on his face. "Brilliant rescue, lad." Then without further hesitation, he leapt over Stick Witch and dove headfirst out the tall, closed window, shattering the glass on his way out. The outside air filled the room, as did the scent of the oil refineries. The moving air made the water even colder on my lips and chin.

Out of the corner of my eye, I caught the smoky substance from the clay bottle hovering over the short farmer where it slowly seeped into him. Still sitting, I turned to get a better look. His eyes, previously hollow, filled with a hazel color and blinked away the water dripping into them.

*Jake,* Kendra called. *Lexy still won't move.* Whatever the voodoo witches had done to her, the water hadn't washed it away.

I tried to stand, but with a cry of pain, my left calf refused. I took a breath. *Suck it up,* I told myself and forced myself to my feet despite my bleeding pain. I took a step and fell back down.

Old McDonald—OK, the farmer looked to be only in his mid-thirties—stood up and put one hand over his eyes, shielding them from the man-made rain, and offered me the other. "Let me help you up?"

I'll be honest. I thought the guy would stand up, freak out, and be useless. I should have known better. He was a farmer. I grabbed his hand, and it didn't matter that I rose a foot taller than him or that slippery water covered our hands. His grip felt like a vice, and he lifted me to my feet with ease. I barely had to put any weight on my left leg.

"Let me try to—" All of a sudden, the water shut off, causing me to cut my sentence short. Voodoo Whoopi—she'd fallen outside the spray of the ceiling sprinkler—had sent a tendril of darkness up the far wall—the one that wasn't getting sprayed with water—and somehow it had shut the water almost completely off. All that remained was a trickle of dripping water that fell to the conference room desk.

# CHAPTER 4
# PARKING LOT

Have you ever been addicted to something? Wanted to do something because it is the best feeling ever, but you know that doing it is wrong? I think I'm going to hell. I sure look like hell. Could I be any uglier? Maybe I'm already in hell. I'm certainly being punished. —Jake

Using the wall for balance, Voodoo Whoopie struggled to her feet across the room from me. I considered sprinting over and form-tackling her, but my bleeding calf muscle wouldn't let me.

"Hey, farmer guy, carry her." I pointed at Alexis. The little farmer stepped around Kendra and grabbed Alexis at the hips. He lifted and turned her, sitting her on the conference table. Then, with both hands, he lifted her over both his shoulders as if she were a baby calf.

Voodoo Whoopi raised her arms and sent a tendril of shadow magic coming our way. I formed a small magic missile and hurled it at her, again forcing her to redirect her dark shadow to intercept my tiny orb of light and disappear with it. That gave the farmer the moment he needed to carry Alexis out through the conference room door. Neither Kendra nor I waited for an invitation to follow.

As I stumbled painfully out of the conference room, I pulled the door shut behind me. I'd never done this before and didn't even know if it would work, but I focused an extreme amount of heat into the lock, more than a dozen times what I used to cast fire light. Then I told it to stay there. Best case, the doorknob would melt and stop working. And if I got lucky, one of the Hagathas would burn her hand.

Farmer guy tripped and would have fallen, but Kendra put her hands under Alexis to help stabilize them. Kendra glanced

24

 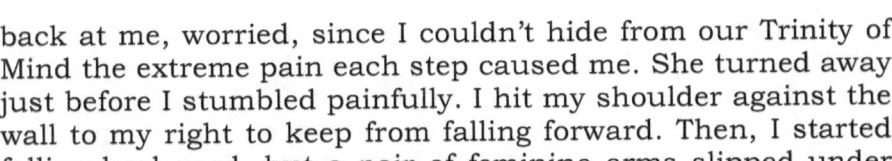

back at me, worried, since I couldn't hide from our Trinity of Mind the extreme pain each step caused me. She turned away just before I stumbled painfully. I hit my shoulder against the wall to my right to keep from falling forward. Then, I started falling backward, but a pair of feminine arms slipped under mine and kept me from hitting the ground.

"Somehow, I knew y'all'd end up like this," Jody spoke calmly in my ear. "'Cept for being wet. I didn't expect that." It was a good thing that she was behind me, because she had just finished her dance routine, and while I'd never been to a strip club before, I was pretty sure she hadn't ended her routine dressed.

"Where're ya hobblin' to?" she asked.

"Our car," I guessed.

"Out back?"

"Yes."

"Can ya stand for a sec?" she asked.

"Uh, huh."

"A'ight, don't glance back unless ya have a crisp twenty for me," she humored.

I sensed her wrapping herself in the silk robe she'd worn earlier. Then, the good Samaritan that she was, she slipped her head and shoulders under my left arm and started helping me down the hallway.

I heard a high-pitched scream come from the conference room. I grinned, imagining one of the Haitian witch's palms burning as she gripped the doorknob. Kevin McCallister would be proud.

We walked past the changing room where a few girls were getting ready for their routines. They had noticed the noise and stood as far from the door as they could get. Still, they stared at us from the corners of their eyes, their bodies stiff with a mix of fear and curiosity.

"Y'all know the drill. Stay inside. Don't get involved," she told them. Jody kicked the door closed. I wonder what they thought of Jody getting involved.

I didn't really notice if the girls were undressed this time or not, which was very un-guy-like of me. But when the girl I love was helping some random farmer carry a catatonic Lexy, who happens to be the other girl I love, who just got proposed to by a vampire general, and I had a knife wound in both my arm and my calf, and I could only walk because a silk-robed stripper was holding me up, and I was running from two Haitian voodoo witches, I was just too distracted to notice.

Kendra opened the back door. The farmer had to turn sideways to get Alexis out. A few seconds later, Jody and I reached the door, too. Jody slipped out from under my arm because we wouldn't both fit through the door at the same time. Unfortunately, even if we did fit through the door, I no longer wanted to go outside. I grabbed Jody's shoulders. There was no way I was letting Jody outside because Kendra's fear was burning into me. Her pupils hadn't adjusted to the darkness yet, but even still, through her eyes, I could see a number of ominous silhouettes that awaited us.

"Stay inside," I urged Jody.

I grabbed the door frame to keep from falling, and despite the chills that ran up my spine to dance that pole dance under my skin, I hobbled out into the darkness.

Like Kendra, I couldn't see much until my eyes adjusted. The yellow porch light hadn't improved. It took long seconds before I could see the silhouettes myself. I started counting them from the left. One. Two. Three. Kendra counted a few to our right. Four. Five. Six. My eyes adjusted, and I noticed a few silhouettes separated into two. Seven. Eight. Nine. Kendra counted the last three. Ten, Eleven. Twelve. Huh, I would have assumed thirteen. How *un*cliché of them. Thirteen seemed a more appropriate number for the voodoo witches to have chosen. Of course, the farmer had been a voodoo zombie. Never mind, these witches *had* met their cliché expectation. I almost called the hags pathetic, and I would have if not for their impressive shadow blades. With those as weapons, they might have won. Who was I kidding? We hadn't escaped yet. Depending on what these silhouettes planned for us, they might still win.

Despite the tantalizing entertainment at this establishment, the rear parking lot only had two rows for cars and many stalls remained vacant. Of course, there was a second parking lot out front where all the patrons parked, and with all the modern transit and ride-sharing options, few drove their own cars to places like this.

The air had been the perfect temperature before we entered the building, but now, it chilled my skin, giving me goosebumps. I blamed the chill on my damp hoodie.

I heard some movement around the corner of the building. The twelve silhouettes just stood around, not moving toward us at all, so I risked looking away from them. A tall form stepped out from around the corner of the building, followed by a short chubby form. Stick Witch and Voodoo Whoopi. They must have taken Keagan's exit out the window and come around the outside of the building.

Stick Witch raised her hand and six of the silhouettes stepped methodically toward us. Voodoo Whoopi raised her hand next, and the other six came toward us, too.

Kendra froze and her mind sort of locked up—I could still feel her mind, or at least the fear that completely encompassed it, but she wasn't responding. She'd frozen in fear just like this the other morning when Mr. Espinoza, newly turned and hungry, had woken her in her bedroom. We'd have to cure her of this incapacitating fear if she planned on staying alive.

*Come on, Kendra. We need you.* I prodded her mind as best as I could, urging her to push past her fear and act. Except I recognized her paralyzing panic for what it really was. I'd experienced the same in the days after fighting the nightwalker. Post-traumatic stress disorder. My time holding the healing stone had mostly cured me of it—at least the physical symptoms of it. I wasn't sure if the mental symptoms could be cured.

"I should've taken your advice and stayed inside," I heard Jody whisper behind me.

"Hey, farmer," I called. "Why don't you set down Alexis and accompany Jody inside. Jody, why don't you take him in front and let him buy you a beer?" It was an order, not a suggestion, but they didn't move. If Alexis had given them the same order, they'd have obeyed instantly.

I found myself free of the pain in my calf muscle. God bless adrenaline. I helped the farmer set Lexy down on the asphalt and ushered him to Jody. They seemed to hesitate to go back inside.

"I said, go!" I shouted. The silhouettes only had one more row of cars to walk through, so I wanted Farmer Joe and Jody to hurry. "Don't come back outside," I added. Jody stayed put, ignoring me, so I pulled a cheap shot. "Your son Carl needs you."

She blinked at me and threw her head back, tossing her red hair. She hadn't told us about Carl, and I could tell she wanted to know how I knew about him, but having been reminded of her autistic son, she also remembered she had a duty to stay alive for him. After the farmer set down Alexis, Jody grabbed his hand and took him inside.

I had considered sending Alexis inside, but I acted on hope that she would shake off her trance.

While I was glad that Jody and farmer went inside, I realized that my interaction with Old McDonald had unknowingly ruined my attack plan. See, a couple of minutes ago, he was a voodoo zombie. Not the come-back-from-the-dead type that I hoped wasn't real. The real-life type. A person who'd had his mind tampered with—a puppet to the Haitian witches. Once the zombies' magic—the puppet strings—were cut, he was once again himself—a regular person. The twelve other zombies walking toward me were also regular people. So far, I could only cast two offensive spells: fire light and a magic missile. I couldn't use a magic missile and kill—let alone erase from existence—innocent people who'd done nothing wrong except allow themselves to get voodoo mind-jacked. I probably shouldn't burn them up either. Why hadn't Eldra taught me lightning yet? Perhaps because I'd only been awake for just over a day.

As the silhouettes stepped between the cars, I started to see their faces. Their heads hung down, and to look left or right, they seemed to look with their chins, not their eyes. Seeing them pass between the cars gave me an idea.

"*Fyr leoht*," I whispered and focused my energy about two feet inside the frame and down a bit from the right side of an SUV, where I imagined the gas tank would be. It took about a second before . . .

BOOOOM!

The gas tank in the SUV exploded with a ball of flame shooting from under its frame. It lifted a few feet into the air and then fell back down. Four zombies had been walking near the SUV, two on each side. The explosion threw their bodies against the adjacent cars. They slumped to the asphalt and didn't try to get back up. I hoped I knocked them out without killing them.

Unfortunately, the other eight zombies kept walking toward us. I needed to stop them. I could blow up another car, but three of them had moved passed the parked cars, and the other five were in vacant stalls, so blowing up the nearest cars wouldn't do much good.

Except maybe the zombies were the wrong targets to begin with. The Haitian witches walked between the strip club's outside wall and a little car, maybe a Ford Focus. I didn't look their way. Instead, I looked at a car near the other group of zombies, looking them off like a quarterback looks off a free safety. But out of the corner of my eye, I focused on where I thought the little Focus's gas tank would be. Let's just say I was double *Focus*ed.

"*Fyr leoht*," I whispered again, before . . .

BOOOM!

The little car exploded just like the SUV had. It lifted higher off the ground than the SUV had, but that was probably just because it didn't weigh much. The explosion knocked Stick Witch into Voodoo Whoopi, and both went down hard.

Without hesitation, I cast a magic missile their way, but to no avail. Even as they fell to the ground, a tendril of darkness whipped up to absorb the attack.

I heard something break when they'd hit the ground, and it wasn't until five ethereal forms lifted like luminescent mist and floated toward the zombies that I understood what had broken. I've seen a person's spirit before, and these looked like spirits, sort of. Something wasn't exactly right. The mist seemed to be less than a full spirit—perhaps just a small part of it. I watched as three of them settled into crumpled forms by the SUV. Only two of them settled into the zombies that still came for me.

OK. Down to six—er, seven. The one zombie puppet by the SUV that didn't get its spirit back stood up and whipped its chin and vacant eyes my direction.

I took a deep breath. Alexis lay catatonic on the pavement. My hope that she would wake soon remained unfulfilled. Alexis had spent the past day intentionally teasing Kendra by promising to fulfill all my hopes and dreams. Well, Kendra could now torment her by telling her she'd already failed to keep that promise. If only Alexis had not closed off her mind, this wouldn't have happened. Had Keagan's proposal been part of the Haitian witches' plan? Could they have known she would separate her mind from Kendra and me to think?

The two still-awake people whose souls had returned looked around, disoriented. One was a woman with short hair and a business skirt. The other was a man in jeans with a polo shirt. I couldn't see much more of their features. Neither noticed the zombies behind them or the way those zombies opened their mouths menacingly. Honestly, it wasn't exactly their mouths that were scary. They were normal, everyday, regular people mouths. But combined with the way their bodies drooped, the way their arms hung awkwardly, the way they seemed to turn their head with their chins, and the way those mouths seemed to target the two helpless former zombies standing vulnerably in front of them, those zombie mouths made me want to turn around and run screaming like a frightened four-year-old.

I hesitated, unsure whether to attack or not. I decided to attack, but my decision came too late. The zombies dropped their open mouths onto the shoulders of the two confused once-zombie people. They didn't care that they were biting through shirts; they just bit. The man twitched and shouted; the woman let out a

29

bloodcurdling scream. Then both fell to the ground, thrashing. Of course, the two zombies that had bitten them no longer had white teeth. They'd bitten into flesh, and they'd each come away with a chunk. I could tell because they chewed with open mouths. My body shivered as one of them swallowed then shifted its chin as it licked its blood-darkened teeth.

I didn't want to kill these zombie people, but three of them were only steps away from us. I noticed the Haitian witches were back on their feet, also walking toward us. They must have risen while I watched the once-zombies get bitten.

I grabbed Kendra and physically moved her behind me. She managed not to collapse in fear, and her mind seemed close to fighting off her paralyzing panic, so I left one hand gripping her arm behind me.

*I need you,* I reminded her. I brought up the memory of our first kiss. Between the memory and the feel of my hand, her mind gained the last bit of courage she needed to snap out of it.

I glanced down at Alexis, who still lay catatonic in front of us. I considered dragging her behind me, but I didn't have time. If we survived this, I was going to take away her separation stone until she learned to follow the plan. I thought about slapping some sense into her, which I'd never actually do since I would never hit a girl.

*I'll slap her for you,* Kendra cut in.

Kendra's mind hovered on the edge of falling back into paralyzing fear. She needed some direction and some hope to keep from freaking out. The idea of slapping Alexis gave her more hope than I expected it to. Unfortunately, we had no time for her to fulfill her catfight hopes and dreams.

The zombie-people stepped too close to us. Kendra shivered and asked, *What do we do, Jake?*

I so wished I had some direction or some non-catfight-related hope to give her.

*I don't know,* I answered.

# CHAPTER 5
# TEETH

*If two girls on drill team hated each other, our drill coach forced them to hang out for two weeks straight. They had to do trust exercises. She would say, "Hating is not allowed on our team!" Well, I'm trying not to hate Alexis. I guess we are on the same team permanently, with the Trinity of Mind. And she is the princess, and I'm her general. Weird. If we hadn't fought monsters at the cabin at Bear Lake, I wouldn't believe any of this. If I didn't truly believe I'd endanger my family, I'd just go home. —Kendra*

"**H**ave I mentioned yet that I really, really wished I still weighed over two hundred pounds? A week ago, I could probably have knocked out the zombies with one punch each, but now I could barely stand. I could punch about as hard as an eighth-grade geek. I knew because, well, I once was an eighth-grade geek.

Was I only a geek again? Had I burned off the jock part of me when I burned off my muscles? Being a jeek—part jock, part geek—used to define me. I had attended my own funeral recently. I wasn't in the coffin, of course. Still, everyone at my funeral thought football defined me. Football had never defined me. But by dying, fake as my death was, I'd lost football. I'd lost what everyone who used to know me thought defined me. But they were wrong. Football never defined me. From my point of view, being a jeek defined me. Having the jeeks as my friends defined me. Having a sister whom I loved defined me. It seemed I'd lost everything. Sis knew I was alive, but if I didn't stay away from her, would she ever be safe? I'd lost her. Of my three jeek friends, only Luiz knew I was alive. I may never hang with all the jeeks again. Everything that had once defined me was gone.

Had I somehow been undefined?

It was probably the wrong time to think about all this, but maybe instead of seeing my life flash before my eyes before I died, I became introspective.

Kendra listened to my mind and didn't interrupt, at least until I either had to act or let one of the zombies bite me. I'd seen zombies in movies, but zombies in real life sucked so much worse. Why did they have to be regular people that I couldn't just erase or torch? I'd much prefer the undead, spiritless, half-corroded, corpse kind of zombie.

The closest zombie had to be the biggest one, too. He stood four inches taller than me, and I was six-foot one. He also looked like he weighed about two-fifty, which meant he had me by a hundred pounds. Of course, most people didn't realize it, but until I became the star running back last year, I'd played both ways: offense and defense. Fortunately, the jeek in me had demanded I study and practice until I had mastered the perfect form tackle with which even a David could tackle a Goliath.

All at once, I lowered my shoulder and exploded forward, hitting the oversized zombie below the belt buckle with my right shoulder while I grabbed behind his knees and used my legs, injured calf and all, to drive my momentum through his hips: a textbook football tackle. The large zombie fell back hard, his head whiplashing back against the asphalt. His body padded my fall.

I tried to roll off smoothly and come to my feet. I rolled all right. My attempt to stand failed. Instead, I stumbled and fell at the feet of two other zombies. One was a gray-haired, aging woman in a business skirt. The other was a short, stocky guy that had to be an accountant or something. The way their chins already pointed down at me, mouths halfway open, I expected them both to fall on me and start biting. Instead, they each took another step and tripped over me. Being controlled by a voodoo witch didn't do much for their coordination. Their four legs draped over my supine body and pinned me down, a pair of legs over my thighs and a pair over my upper chest. I looked up in time to see another hungry face. The woman had to be in her mid-forties. Her mouth hung open and her wide, vacant eyes refused to blink. If that weren't creepy enough, she had yellow teeth. *Yuck.*

She was thin, which I was grateful for, because she dropped on top of me, or more precisely, she fell on top of the two pairs of zombie puppet legs already on top of me. Indifferent to my thick hoodie, she tried to force those yellow teeth into my chest. I managed to get my forearm under her chin and somehow had the strength to keep her from biting me as she thrashed on top of me.

She stopped trying to bite my chest, giving me a moment of relief. Then her hollow eyes focused on my face and neck, the only flesh she could see. The stench of too many cigarettes exuded from her breath—that explained the yellow teeth. She pushed harder against my forearm and clacked her teeth together, but I had four zombie legs pinning me down, and the leg highest on my chest braced my forearm and aided me in keeping her teeth a few inches from my throat. Her saliva dripped down onto my neck.

Kendra backed away as two construction-worker zombies sought her out. One was a tall, white guy with an ugly baseball cap. The other was a short, Latino guy. They had paint spots all over them—the same color—so they must have worked together. Their mouths opened and their tongues licked hungrily. Kendra's fear burned inside of me. I gulped with her, even as I tried to keep businesswoman zombie from making a meal out of me. Why was I willing to die before I was willing to kill these zombies to save myself?

*Because they are just normal people,* Kendra answered my thoughts.

I'm such an idiot. I could do something else. I had already done it to the farmer. I brought up my everything-seal containment around businesswoman zombie and she went slack. I rolled her off me and that also freed the two pairs of legs lying on my chest. The two zombies connected to those pairs of legs—the ones that had tripped over me—twisted their bodies toward mine. I escaped the man's legs first. But the prostrate zombie woman's legs lay directly over my chest. It had been one of her legs that had helped hold my forearm propped up to protect my chest and neck.

I twisted and slid out from under the old zombie woman and accidentally pulled her skirt down around her knees. I tried to ignore the gross sight of pantyhose over granny panties as I struggled to stand up.

The zombie I'd tackled didn't move. I remembered all the zombie movies I'd seen. They always said to go for the head. Was that true in real life? When I'd tackled the zombie, his head had whiplashed back onto the pavement. Alexis probably knew.

"Ahhh!" I screamed, jerking my leg away.

I'd repeated my previous mistake. I'd dropped the imagined containment around businesswoman zombie, just like I'd done earlier around the farmer. She'd bitten my leg. Fortunately, my denim jeans kept her from really doing much damage. All she'd accomplished was pinching me with her jaws.

Maybe my moral compass kept me from killing these people, but I had no problem dishing out a concussion. I kicked businesswoman zombie in the head—probably too hard. Her head twisted awkwardly to the left and she went still. I cringed and hoped I hadn't broken her neck. Hadn't I just said that I'd never hit a girl?

Accountant zombie grabbed my left arm. I punched him with my right, but I didn't hit him hard enough. The punch hurt me more than it hurt him. My knuckles screamed in pain, but he didn't look fazed at all. Grandma-panties zombie grabbed my right arm. Her fingers gripped me with unnatural strength. I tried to pull free, but they just gripped harder.

Kendra's back bumped against the door, and she grabbed the knob and tried to open it, but it was locked. Her fear erupted inside her, so overwhelmed that her mind started to shut down again. The tall, construction-worker zombie grabbed her shoulder, mouth open wide.

*Kick him,* I shouted into her head, trying to get her to act before she shut down.

She didn't kick, but she brought her knee up hard. The zombie didn't react to her knee at first. He continued pulling at Kendra. His mouth tried to bite into her shoulder but failed to penetrate the leather body armor Kendra had borrowed from Alexis. She brought up her knee again. And again. And again.

Finally, as if the pain in his crotch just registered with his brain, the tall construction worker zombie squeezed his legs together and dropped to the ground.

*I guess hitting a guy zombie in either head works,* I thought to Kendra.

Grandma-panties zombie and accountant zombie pulled me closer. My arms weren't strong enough to pull away. I jumped and kicked with both feet, one foot at each zombie. I managed to break away, but that left me horizontal and falling from a few feet above the concrete. My back hit the asphalt hard, knocking the wind out of me. I tried to breathe but couldn't get air to come in. I fought for a breath that wouldn't come as I scrambled away from the three zombies in front of me. Then my breath finally returned, and I sucked in air desperately.

Just then, pain exploded from my hand. "Aaaahhhhh!" I screamed. I looked at my hand, but nothing was wrong. It wasn't my hand that had been bitten; it was Kendra's. I'd felt her pain like it was my own. A snakelike darkness slipped into Kendra, and I felt it push at our connection. Kendra tried to fight back, but the darkness took her. Her mind shut off. I could no longer hear her in my head.

I stumbled as fast as I could over to Kendra. The zombie bent over, his head low, biting her hand. I kicked the Latino, construction-worker zombie in the temple, knocking his head to the side, which jerked Kendra's arm since his mouth still bit down on her hand. A second kick to the head did its job, and the Latino zombie's mouth flew open as the man collapsed, allowing Kendra's hand to swing free from his mouth. Blood poured freely from a bite-shaped wound.

A black tendril of magic grabbed me. *Oh, crap!* I'd forgotten about the Haitian witches. The blackness had a similar power to the nightwalker's scream. It tried to control my mind and bring me into darkness. My protection stone flared to life, dimming the attack, but it didn't dim it enough. The darkness hit my mind with far more power than I had expected. The despair was palpable. It beckoned my fears and inadequacies from the darkest parts of my mind. Never had I felt more worthless. Never had I had felt more certain that everyone would be better off were I dead. The shadow blades burrowed inside and laid eggs into that thought. If I hadn't already survived the nightwalker's scream, I would have been overcome, but I had practice fighting off just such an attack. Still, it took a far greater effort than it should have to make like Peter Pan and find my happy thoughts. Somehow, I found them, and my mental shield formed. I ignored the fact that the thought remained infected.

Unfortunately, I couldn't fight the zombies physically and the voodoo witches mentally. Three zombies were left, but that was three too many. Worse, if a zombie bit me, my mental shield of happiness would collapse. I couldn't mentally fight off both the witches' shadow blades and the snakelike darkness of a zombie bite. Game over. I felt fingers pull at my left arm. Some part of me watched my hand as grandma-panties zombie pulled it toward her open mouth.

But the bite didn't happen. My arm dropped free.

The black tendrils dropped me and moved away. I found myself free to think. Had the zombies turned on each other? It seemed so. A stocky, black-haired man stood behind grandma panties. As he bit her neck, blood dripped down onto her blouse.

Had I miscounted the number of zombies? Where had this zombie come from? Why were the witches attacking their own zombie with their black tendrils?

The man stopped biting and raised his head, and his red eyes looked past his long nose at me.

"Mr. Espinoza," I shouted.

He flashed me a bloody grin, his fangs hanging menacingly. I never thought I would be grateful that my best friend's dad had been turned and bit someone, but at that moment, I was. The shadow blades lashed at him but had no effect on him, perhaps because he had just fed?

"And me," shouted Luiz, who hit a thick zombie man in the chest with the butt of his twelve-gauge shotgun, knocking the zombie down. Then he flipped the gun back around, pressing the butt against his shoulder and fired a shotgun blast at the two voodoo witches, who dropped defensively behind a car. The shadow blades dropped with them, disappearing. Luiz then turned and swung his shotgun like a bat at the same zombie he'd just knocked down as it tried to stand and attack. This time, he hit the zombie in the head.

Mr. Espinoza jumped to the remaining zombie and bit down. I breathed a sigh of relief. Mostly. A small part of me felt that the zombies, being regular people, needed protection from Luiz's dad. If only I could find a way to shatter all the clay containers entrapping the partial spirits of the zombies.

*Brecan glæs.* The words echoed in my mind—a memory embedded in Caradoc's blood. Old English for breaking glass. With the words came his experience of casting the spell. I didn't hesitate. I used his experience as if it were my own and launched the spell at the Haitian witches.

I felt the air vibrate and hum. The magical energy fueled a high-pitched sound that I couldn't exactly hear but only felt through the magic. I didn't think any dogs would be around in an industrial area like this, but dogs began to bark and howl from miles in all directions. The car windows all shattered but at slightly different times, like a chain reaction in a minefield. Club Exposed didn't have any rear windows, but the yellow porch light exploded with a pop, and what little light it had provided disappeared.

I never heard the witches' clay jars break. Still, they must have broken or cracked because I witnessed the luminescent semi-spirits expand from the darkness where Stick Witch and Voodoo Whoopi had been standing. Providing as much of a glow as the porch light had, the remaining eight partial spirits floated back to rejoin their corporeal forms. From the spirits' light, I vaguely saw both witches running in the opposite direction where

they disappeared around the corner of the building. Distant sirens joined the dog's howling.

"*¡Alo!*" Mr. Espinoza spoke, his mouth inches from my ear. I jumped, and he laughed. "I will carry the girls to the car." He spoke with a thick Spanish accent, rolling his Rs and saying *wheel* instead of *will* and *geerrls* instead of *girls*. He lifted Kendra in his arms, and I heard his mouth make a sound. Vampire saliva heals, and even though I couldn't see, I was certain he hadn't passed up the opportunity to lick the blood off the half-circle bite-wound on Kendra's hand.

"*¡Maldición!*" Luiz commented. "What happened."

I couldn't see Luiz, and I didn't have the energy to answer.

What would happen to the twelve zombies? Except for the two who were bitten, they were awake and lucid, if confused and disoriented. Surely, they wondered what they were doing hanging out in the dark parking lot behind Club Exposed. Maybe they would just assume they had drunk a few too many?

Our BMW doors were locked. Alexis had the key. I walked to where I remembered setting her down and felt my way in the darkness with my hands on the asphalt, trying to find Lexy's body.

"A little left," Mr. Espinoza suggested. I couldn't see him, but I could hear him. I moved left. My hands found soft leather.

"Those aren't her pockets." Mr. Espinoza laughed.

I moved my hands much lower on her body and found her hips. Her leather pants were so tight that it took some effort to fit my fingers into her pocket and get the key out. Annoyance that Alexis had never woken and anger that she enabled her separation stone were both as strong as my concern for her.

"I can carry her," Mr. Espinoza spoke, his mouth inches from my ear, again, causing me to jump, again. He must have set Kendra down by the car. In the nearly complete darkness, I could vaguely see him lift Lexy. To him, she didn't weigh anything. I clicked a button on the BMW's key and even though I was a couple dozen feet away, the car started up. To my relief, the headlights turned on. I could finally see again.

Luiz stood a dozen feet away, holding the shotgun tight to his shoulder, still pointing at the confused people who had recently returned from their zombie state. He glanced around before easing up on the shotgun and making his way over to me.

The BMW stood out as the only car without broken windows. Bulletproof and spell-proof. I hustled to the car and opened the back door. Mr. Espinoza set Alexis inside the back seat and buckled her in. Her head flopped to the side as if she were simply asleep. Her chin-length hair fell over her face. Mr. Espinoza picked up Kendra and put her beside Alexis. As I started toward the passenger's side, I tossed Mr. Espinoza the keys. He tossed them back.

"I drove *la motocicleta.*" He smiled, flashing his canines at me. His extended much longer than Alexis's.

"I drove the Sonata," Luiz shrugged.

They both started off toward the front of the building. Good thing or Luiz's car windows would have been shattered.

"*Luego,*" Luiz called back over his shoulder.

I didn't have a driver's license, and the sirens sounded much closer. Still, I jumped in the driver's seat and put the BMW in gear. I turned onto Beck street. I almost didn't notice them as I accelerated, but a handful of transients walked toward the Club Exposed. They looked like homeless people, but I could sense they were more than that. I expected them to chase us. Last time I encountered these creatures, they'd chased O'Brien and me. A Caradoc memory popped into my head. He stood in the darkness explaining to a fellow druid as he pointed out a group of transients that followed. "We know little about them. They only hunt those with magic who are also weak. If you show any strength, they will avoid you."

Perhaps I had shown enough strength because, this time, they didn't chase me. One of them nodded at me. The rest just stood there, watching me drive away.

# CHAPTER 6
# ELDRA

*I have never been free before. It is new. Different. Jake and Kendra do not understand. They have always been free. I have been a slave my whole life, though I did not understand that until I was thirteen. Jake's thoughts are different because he is a ~~boy~~ man. He is a different gender. Kendra and I are the same gender, but we are so opposite. Her hair is light while mine is dark. Our thoughts are as different as our hair and in the same way. —Alexis*

Eldra leaned on her runed staff, waiting for us in the garage. Her gray braid hung over one shoulder. As soon as I opened the back door of the car, she eyed the cut and bloodied left sleeve of my hoodie. Her gaze held a combination of disapproval and worry, which reminded me of my grandma.

Mr. Espinoza had pulled into the massive ten-car garage right behind me and was already lifting the catatonic Kendra out of the back seat.

"I shouldn't have let you go alone," Eldra noted regretfully.

The garage sported a few concept cars as well as a couple bullet bikes. The floor, painted gray with decorative specks and clean enough to eat from, reflected the eyeball lights that illuminated each car.

Eldra shook her two-century-old head in disgust. Her long, gray braid swung behind her like a cobra preparing to strike. She couldn't hide her emotions—she didn't wear them on her sleeve so much as she wore them in the deep wrinkles around her eyes that look like frozen lightning bolts, only they were made of shadows not light. Still, the fierce wrinkles energized her eyes in

39

such a way that suggested she could strike us down with an angry blast from her pupils.

Eldra was the only official druid left. O'Brien wasn't officially a druid, just a druid bodyguard. An unknown *they* assassinated the rest—over a thousand people—in an organized attack infamously known as The Day of a Thousand Deaths. We didn't know who *they* were, but our best guess was someone had organized the many lesser secret societies to participate in the druid genocide.

The druids had been a powerful secret society. Perhaps the most powerful. Most druids had held political offices, high military ranks, or revered executive titles for top companies.

Eldra and her husband survived The Day of a Thousand Deaths because Dane—a vampire—had taken control of them with his allure instead of assassinating them. They were under his influence until a few days ago when Dane used the old couple to try to kill us. Kendra and I had blasted the old druids with magic missiles. We hadn't erased their existence, but we thought we'd killed them both. Hours after the battle ended, Eldra unexpectedly woke up. Alexis had unknowingly freed Eldra when she charred Dane to ash with her sunlight spell.

Eldra and I now shared one thing in common. Almost everyone, present company excluded, thought we were dead, and both of us wanted to keep it that way. If word got out that Eldra was alive and not under vampire control, she'd become a target, which was why Eldra chose not to come with us to meet with Keagan. It was also why she dressed like one of Alexis's servants. If any unexpected visitors showed up—and with Lexy's princess title, many would come—Eldra would go unnoticed.

"Take them and lay them in the containment ring in Jacob's room," Eldra told Mr. Espinoza. Mr. Espinoza now held both girls at the same time, one on each shoulder. He carried them with ease. Of course, he still had to twist and turn to fit through the door from the garage into the mansion. I cringed when Lexy's head smacked against the door frame.

My mind felt unusually empty. I couldn't feel Kendra's or Alexis's thoughts or emotions at all. Under normal circumstances, the silence in my head would have been more than welcome. Having my mind permanently connected to both Kendra and Alexis drove me crazy. Sure, both girls wore separation stones which allowed them to disconnect their thoughts from mine, but their emotions, though dimmed, came through. I felt lost, as if drifting alone in the vast cosmic space,

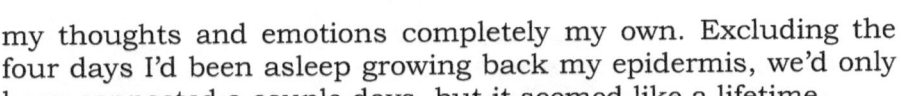

my thoughts and emotions completely my own. Excluding the four days I'd been asleep growing back my epidermis, we'd only been connected a couple days, but it seemed like a lifetime.

As we walked—well, I limped—down the hallways to my room, we passed Carolyn, the youngest of the servants. She was in her twenties. She saw us coming and stood to the side against the wall, making it easy for Mr. Espinoza to pass her while packing the girls. Carolyn had auburn hair that her servant's bonnet partially covered. Yes, the servants dressed like you'd expect a servant from the 1800s to dress. Bonnets. Dresses covered with a white pinafore. Certainly, the word "pinafore" hadn't come from my mind.

I paused just after stepping by Carolyn and turned back to her. My left calf needed a break from walking anyway. I don't know why, but I hated the fact that Alexis had servants. They weren't paid, except with room and board. They were here because some vampire had used his influence to force them to be here. I'd made a choice to treat them like normal people, not servants.

"Carolyn," I called her back.

She came reluctantly.

"It didn't go well. A pair of Haitian witches ambushed us." I wasn't certain whether she knew where we had gone or why, but I suspected the servants knew more than we thought they did.

"Thank you, Protector." Carolyn curtsied to me, then hurried off.

Carolyn had started calling me by the title of Protector just yesterday. How the servants knew that I was a protector before anyone else did, I couldn't be sure. Alexis wondered that as well. Unfortunately, I had no idea what being a protector meant. The title alone seemed obvious. I would protect something or someone. What or who, I wasn't sure. Alexis wouldn't talk to me about it. We hadn't told Eldra yet, but with the servants using my title freely, she was bound to find out soon enough.

I had assumed that I had inherited my quick healing from my estranged biological father, but perhaps I'd been wrong. Perhaps it came from being a protector. Had my biological father been a protector as well? I couldn't believe that the man who raped my mom—yes, that was how I was conceived—could possibly be a protector. I couldn't imagine that someone who felt the overwhelming urge to protect others could ever do something so horrible.

I limped into my room. Mr. Espinoza smelled of soap. Not an off-putting chemical smell, but the kind of soap that makes a woman want to hug their man and breathe in the deep scent. All vampires had attractive smells, except when they were afraid. I'd started taking notes about their scents. Mr. Espinoza's soap scent exuded from him with extra enticement. Most vampires' scents increased when they were hungry. I should have worried whom he would feed on, but instead, I worried for Alexis and Kendra.

Mr. Espinoza had already laid the catatonic girls on the floor in the middle of the silver Star of David circle. The ring was the most powerful containment I'd ever seen—not that I'd seen many—but Caradoc had, and his memories confirmed that this containment was world class. The first time I'd ever been in this room, I'd woken chained to a bed inside the same circle. Somehow, even though it was supposed to be impossible, I could poke holes in most containments, but not this one.

Alexis stirred. Even though her protection stone annoyingly blocked her thoughts, I felt her groggy emotions seep into my mind, ending my mental alone time. A minute ago, I felt too alone in my own head; now, I instantly wanted my alone time back.

Alexis sat up, and her blinking red eyes searched the room until they settled on me.

"What happened?" Her red eyes interpreted the anger in my thinned, lashless eyes, and she swallowed.

I shook my head. Anger—my own—rumbled inside me as I remembered how Alexis had shut off her mind at the worst possible moment.

"You actually considered Keagan's marriage proposal!" I accused. Could Alexis feel my rage as easily as I could feel her confusion? Kendra had promised to slap her for me. I looked at Kendra, hoping she'd wake up so I could remind her of her offer.

Alexis touched her separation stone. *You are vexed with me.*

*Duh! Miss Awkward. Try using a contraction sometime!*

Alexis never used contractions. She didn't swear either. My accusation brought up her memories as to why. I watched a montage of memories where an abusive vampire tutor whipped such habits out of her bare back.

*Isn't my past so fun? You insensitive ass,* Alexis forced out both a contraction and cuss, as well as sending out the coppery scent of blood.

My mind responded with a few harsh words before I could stop it. I have a hard enough time controlling what I say, let alone what I think. I have a lot of wild thoughts, many of which are just junk that I discard. Most thoughts never reach my lips. Choosing what to verbalize is usually a natural and effective filter. Except Alexis had unrestricted access to my mind, so I didn't get the chance to filter anything. It wasn't just swearing, it was all my thoughts and emotions. It goes both ways, though. Her thoughts are just as unfiltered.

"Out loud, please." Eldra interrupted us. "Just as it is rude to speak in a foreign language with others in the room," she tossed an accusing look at Mr. Espinoza, "it is rude to converse in front of us through the *myndtiegan*."

Eldra and her late husband had been joined in their own *myndtiegan* for over a century. Over the past few days, Eldra had proven especially adept at noticing when we were thinking to each other through our own. Only, we called it our Trinity of Mind.

Alexis touched her separation stone, and her thoughts cut off. Her tumultuous emotions remained. I could feel her heart ache, but whether it ached for me or Keagan, I couldn't be sure. She also felt spite and fear, both directed at me. Spite didn't have a scent, but her mild fear came out all musty.

"Speaking of foreign languages, ¿Como es que no habla español?" Mr. Espinoza asked, breaking the ice that filled the air between Alexis and me. "In two centuries, you should have learned." His red eyes gleaming mischievously at Eldra.

"I'm so sorry," Eldra feigned a frown. "I only learned French, German, Italian, Latin, Swedish, Gaelic, Welsh, Cantonese, Hindi, Navajo, and Ute. Oh, and Old English. I was never assigned to Spain or Latin America."

"Eldra," I interrupted the aged druid, trying to ignore Alexis and her hurricane-like emotions. "Why isn't Kendra waking up?"

"I don't know," she answered. "I powered the containment before they entered the circle. The spell on Alexis couldn't cross into the containment with her. It seems Kendra is inflicted with something other than magic. Maybe you should tell me what happened. Keagan should have honored the rules of the challenge. I find it hard to believe that he attacked." She turned her wrinkled eyes toward Alexis. "Your grandfather will have his head for this breach in etiquette."

"Keagan did not challenge me," Alexis answered, offering no further explanation.

"He didn't attack either," I explained. I glanced at Alexis—OK, I glared at her. She didn't seem to want to speak more, so I continued to explain to Eldra what had happened. I told Eldra about Keagan's proposal and how Alexis disconnected her mind from Kendra and me. Eldra glared at Alexis too. I told her about the Haitian witches, their attack, and the regular-people zombies. I didn't really mention Jody or the farmer, or anything else about the strip club, figuring all that was irrelevant.

"If Mr. Espinoza hadn't shown up, we would have been goners," I confessed.

"Well, well." Eldra grimaced with her wrinkled face. Sometimes, she looked too old to be alive. "Perhaps I was wrong to think a newly turned vampire would just cause problems." Her words were probably as much of an apology as Mr. Espinoza would get.

"*Si.* I resolve *los problemas.*" Mr. Espinoza grinned wide enough that the sharpness of his retracted canines showed.

"Yes, yes. You've proven you are at least as useful as a calculator," Eldra tried to joke, smiling at Alexis then at me as if expecting one of us to laugh. "A calculator? It solves problems," the queen of bad jokes explained, annoyed. If Luiz had been here, he'd have laughed. He got a kick out of Eldra. Disappointed, she shook her head and continued. "It would be better if you were a problem preventer."

I had no patience for their lackadaisical conversation.

"Eldra!" I cut in sharply, my voice elevated. "What's wrong with Kendra?"

"I said, I don't know." Eldra turned her eyes toward Kendra. In seconds, her pensive stare turned into a glare. The hate in her eyes proved that she hadn't forgotten that Kendra and I had killed her husband of nearly two centuries.

"What do you mean you don't know?" I shot back.

"Jacob, it may come as a shock to you, but in two hundred years, I haven't once dealt with a voodoo witch or zombies."

"But you're going to help her, right?"

Eldra's eyes thinned, replacing hate with anger that focused on me like a pair of lasers, which for her was probably possible. For half a second, I considered raising a containment around myself for protection.

"Of course, I'll help the girl," Eldra growled.

"I know you hate her!" I accused before I could stop myself. Would Eldra take this opportunity to get back at Kendra? Would she leave Kendra like this forever out of spite?

Her hating eyes turned to me, and she smashed her thin lips together in a way that somehow made her look even older. "Yes," she agreed. "I'll hate her until my dying breath. But my hate is neither her fault nor mine. I am a healer, Jacob. I can heal even those I hate. I healed you, didn't I?"

Nobody likes to be hated, but I preferred Eldra pointing her hate at me instead of at Kendra. Alexis's emotions turned to pity for Eldra. I used glaring at Alexis as an excuse to break eye contact with Eldra. I took a breath—Alexis's musty fear was probably half the cause of the tension in the room—and forced my jaws to unclench, but my shoulder muscles wouldn't relax. The pain in my arm and calf significantly added to my agitation.

"I'm not healed yet!" I countered, interrupting the tension.

She pursed her lips and scanned my face under my hoodie and then grabbed my left hand and looked at the skin. "Hmph!"

That grunt meant my skin, which had grown back quickly enough while I was in a coma, wasn't clearing up. It was still white, road rashed, and flaky, with no healing progress since I'd woken. She had been certain that I would heal, but now she tightened her wrinkled eyes in doubt.

Eldra blinked the doubt away and turned and knelt over Kendra, placing her palm on her cheek. Silence filled the room as we all waited. Then Eldra stood.

"I think you and Alexis will have better luck healing her than I will," Eldra suggested.

"What's that supposed to mean?"

She pointed to Kendra. "I'd suggest removing her separation stone. Then pry into her mind yourselves."

Alexis jumped into my mind. *Permission to touch your girlfriend?* she asked.

I unleashed a few negative thoughts at Alexis that I couldn't filter out in time, before voicing out loud. "Yes, Alexis, you can remove Kendra's necklace."

*It is not "you can." It is "you may."* Alexis's memory of her brutal tutor whipping her bare back returned.

"You *may* remove Kendra's necklace," I corrected, trying not to be an insensitive ass again.

She reached over and slipped her hands under Kendra's neck and unfastened the silver chain. She stretched her arm to set the necklace just outside the containment.

"So, what do we do?" I asked Eldra.

"What else? Go inside her mind and get her back." With that, Eldra turned and left. Mr. Espinoza followed her.

# CHAPTER 7
# KISS

Whenever the Trinity of Mind is on, Kendra and Alexis have a non-stop catfight going on. It usually isn't the forefront of their thoughts. It's an ongoing noise, like a background buzz of a bad cell connection. They're trying to stop. I think it is my fault. They both like me. Or at least, they both used to like me. I'm too ugly to like now. Kendra's and Lexy's bad thought made that perfectly clear. Trying not to focus on that. Anyway, their background-noise catfighting is really getting to me. —Jake

"Wearing Alexis's clothes had changed Kendra's appearance dramatically. The clothes hid her cute innocence. She looked dark, mysterious, and more like Alexis than I expected. The left side of her face had some smudges just below the tips of her boy cut hair, probably from the asphalt. Her hand had a white half-circle patch of skin where the zombie had bitten her. Vampire saliva makes cells regenerate rapidly. It nearly eliminates scarring. It doesn't cause pigment to regenerate, however.

The small circle around her palm reminded me of what my entire body looked like. Where I didn't still have scabs, my skin was dry and flaky, like road rash after the scab falls off.

I limped into the circle and sat on the floor on the other side of Kendra from Alexis. I took Kendra's healed hand in my own. Her palm felt icy and limp. A nervousness settled deep inside my gut.

*What if she doesn't wake up?*

*She will,* Alexis answered, despite knowing my question was rhetorical. *We just need to find a way to wake her up. It almost seems like she is just sleeping.*

46

I had to laugh as a certain Disney character flashed in my head. Could it be that easy?

*You should try, Prince Charming,* Alexis urged, despite the bubble of jealousy the idea ignited.

I leaned down over Kendra and put my hand behind her head. I lifted her head slightly and kissed her. I poured as much love and passion into the one-sided kiss as possible. I felt Alexis's jealousy flow freely into me. Sure, as a protector, she feared me, but she still wanted me to kiss only her—which didn't make sense because I looked hideous. In fact, it was my hideousness that caused Kendra's and Lexy's bad thought, the one we weren't supposed to repeat.

Trying not to be distracted by Alexis or the fact that even monsters looked cute compared to me, I let my lips gently press against Kendra's. I held the kiss long after I knew that it wasn't working.

Despite suggesting that I try, Alexis hadn't believed the kiss would work. I wasn't shocked that Alexis hadn't seen Disney's *Sleeping Beauty*. Alexis had grown up without TV, except for a few short weeks just before she turned thirteen when her mother, Carina, had taken her on the run. Her grandfather had told her a much different version of Sleeping Beauty—a vampire version. I'd never heard it myself, but I got the cliff notes straight from her brain. In the vampire version, there was no such thing as true love's kiss. Instead, it was a blood kiss—a vampire French-kissed a dying woman while biting his own tongue to bleed into the woman's mouth. The woman woke because she turned.

*No one is giving Kendra a blood kiss,* I shouted the thought angrily.

*Of course not!* Alexis shook her head at me. *It was just a memory of a fairy tale.*

*Your version sucks!*

*My version? You mean the vampire version. I am not a vampire. I am only half-dhampir, remember?*

I tried to shake off my defensiveness.

*Well, the kiss didn't work, anyway. Do you have another idea?*

*We could yell for her,* Alexis suggested.

I didn't think yelling was a good idea. For all we knew, it would freak Kendra out more and send her mind deeper into wherever it was hiding.

*What would you have us do, then?*

I thought about it for a minute. *Remember things to her.* The idea came to my head all at once. I started bringing up memories

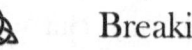 

of Kendra. With them came memories of my sister, which interrupted my thought process immediately. Sis had come home from California to find Mom arrested for my stepdad's murder. Three nightwalkers and two vampire-influenced druids had slaughtered him.

*Focus!* Alexis urged.

I brought up memories of Kendra and tried my best to prevent thoughts of Sis from distracting me again. I remembered a night when Kendra was eleven and had a sleepover with Sis. I was thirteen. I snuck into Sis's room while they brushed their teeth and hid under the bed. I waited patiently until they finished brushing and both had sat on Sis's bed. Mom turned their light out and told them to get to sleep. I don't remember what they were giggling about, but I slid slowly out from under the bed, stretched my fingers out as if I had claws, grabbed them, and growled. Sis and Kendra screamed and jumped off the bed and ran to the door.

*So, you think a memory of you scaring her will wake her?* Alexis cut off my thought. *You are stupid.*

*I don't know. I'm just grabbing memories at random here.*

*Try something more extreme, more memorable,* she suggested.

Another memory popped into my head. Kendra had been at my house playing with Sis most of the day. We all sat down to dinner. It was spaghetti night. Kendra didn't seem hungry. "Eat something, honey," Mom urged. "I don't want your mother to think we don't feed you." Kendra looked up and said, "Mrs. Stevens, I . . ." but she didn't finish because she threw up all over the dinner table. I remember jumping up and knocking my chair over.

*No!* Alexis cut my thoughts off. *You are pathetic, Jacob. Kendra's mind is in the darkness and you go with throwing up? Try something more recent. Like this.*

Alexis brought her own memory. My arms wrapped around Alexis and our lips pressed together. The darkness made it difficult to see the trees forming the druid grove, where Alexis and I had first connected our minds. We searched through each other's thoughts and memories haphazardly. Alexis found my memory of Kendra. She witnessed me walk into the dimly lit living room at Kevin's house. I placed Kendra's cheeks in my palms, and without waiting, I kissed her. The kiss had tasted like vanilla mint ChapStick mixed with her salty tears.

*OK. I should have gone with that memory first,* I conceded. Maybe I'd subconsciously stayed away from that memory for

Alexis's sake, but now that she brought it up, I dove in. Kendra had formed an emotional bond with me that even Eldra didn't fully understand. Whatever she'd formed, it was like a rope of emotion that connected us. Except the rope of emotion could only be felt when flared up by proximity and passion. I couldn't feel that rope now, but it must still be there waiting.

Alexis hated that I'd somehow connected that deeply with Kendra. I ignored her jealousy, mostly, though I sort of enjoyed it, and focused on the emotional thread, trying to bring it to life, but it didn't work. I needed more passion.

I cupped Kendra's cheeks, mimicking the buildup to our first kiss, which was difficult since she lay supine and motionless. I leaned over and kissed Kendra again. More jealousy exploded from Alexis, and she looked away. This time, I didn't try to wake Kendra's mind; I tried to pour passion into the missing rope of emotion. If I could bring it to life, I could use it to connect to her mind.

I felt something between Kendra's heart and mine, but it wasn't exactly a rope. More like a thin thread. It was weak. I tried to pull at the thread, to use it to wake Kendra's mind, but the thread faded away.

*Kiss her again,* Alexis suggested coldly. She hated thinking those words and hated worse that I obeyed. I felt Kendra's lips with mine. This time Alexis watched, so even though my eyes were closed, I watched my kiss through Alexis's eyes. Our mind connection could be trippy. Seeing it didn't help. Having just regrown my skin, I didn't exactly look good. We'd gone from Sleeping Beauty to Beauty and the Beast. Scratch that, the beast was way better looking than me.

I felt awkward keeping my lips against Kendra while she lay limp, but the thread of emotion returned. This time I pulled on it while I kept kissing her and this time the thread didn't fade.

*Try harder.* Alexis shook her head. *That is not passion. Kiss her like you mean it.*

I tried to add more passion, but passion requires two, and doing this without any response from Kendra just wasn't working.

*Kiss her like you kissed me.* As my lips pressed against Kendra's, Alexis once again brought back the image of us in the druid grove. She pushed the memory of our arms wrapped around each other into my mind. In the druid grove, we'd pressed our bodies against each other. We wanted to be closer. We needed to be closer. The desire had escalated to a level beyond anything I'd ever felt.

The rope of emotion between Kendra and me thickened, only the one emotion that strengthened it wasn't love, it was jealousy. Were Alexis's and my memories making their way across the emotional bond? They certainly were. At the moment, jealousy was the only emotion thickening the rope, so I needed to increase Kendra's jealously by a lot.

I pulled my lips away from Kendra's. I suddenly knew what to do. I *could* wake Kendra with true love's kiss. Only it wasn't her I needed to kiss. The kiss had to be with . . .

Lexy turned her red eyes and stared into mine. I could hear her chest rising and falling in anticipation under her string-tied bustier. Despite wanting to kiss me, she gulped and her back tensed. Can I survive kissing a protector? *Can I survive kissing you?* she questioned.

*You've already kissed me,* I reminded her, but I didn't need to. Fear wasn't her dominant emotion because pumpkin spice replaced any trace of mustiness in the room.

How could she be attracted to me in my current state? She couldn't hide that she thought I was ugly, but she didn't see me as some ugly, albino, road-rash-skinned monster. She'd been with ugly often enough that she had long since become desensitized to it. She could be passionate for ugly—for me. But it was more than that. When she looked at me, she saw the man who killed the nightwalker. The man that had nearly given his life to save her from her grandfather, the Vampire King. She saw me as her savior. It was a bond that would never go away. A bond my hideous looks had not broken. Yet.

I reached across Kendra's body for Lexy's hand, holding the memory of the druid grove in our minds. She almost pulled her hand away, but she let me take it and pull her toward me. She crawled over Kendra's legs nervously. Then I grabbed her around her waist and pulled her in. Our lips met. Unlike Kendra, Lexy reciprocated my passion. Her lips moved with mine. Her arms wrapped around me, though she was careful to stay away from the blood on my shoulder. She reached her hand up and slid her fingers into my hair.

I almost forgot about Kendra and the growing emotional connection between us.

Lexy let go of my hair and put both hands on my chest and pushed against me, forcing me onto my back. She crawled on top of me and straddled me, pinning me to the floor. She let her body press against mine as she kissed me again. I could feel the stiffness of her leather shirt on my chest. She slid her left hand

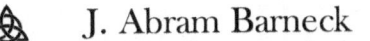 

down to my hip, then slid it back up under my hoodie, leaving her palm on my exposed ribs, the epicenter of the wave of chills that swept over my body.

Lexy did a good job taking my mind off my inadequacies. Just a few days before, I'd had a muscular, athletic figure, but that was gone. If Lexy could still kiss me like this, my self-esteem might survive being the ugliest person I'd ever seen. I forgot how I looked and lost myself in this kiss.

The protection stone hummed warmly against my neck as if begging me to remove it so I could get the full effect of her allure as she kissed me. If my hands were free, I would have done it. But my right hand was locked on the bare skin of her lower back—right where her ribbon bow tattoo would be. I tried to pull her closer. Not that she could get any closer.

"What the hell!" Kendra shouted.

# CHAPTER 8
# DREAM

*Alexis's grandfather made her ... well, I don't want to write it. Alexis isn't shy about sex. I guess after five years of being gifted, it becomes normal. I'm only sixteen. A virgin, of course. But with the Trinity of Mind, I remember her memories. All of them. I know things now because Alexis knows them. They are her memories, but with the Trinity of Mind, they feel like mine. I am not sure how her memories will affect me, but because of them, I feel like I'm not a virgin. —Kendra*

**K**endra sat inside the containment, propped up on one arm. Lexy sat up and pushed off my chest, standing quickly. Kendra's eyes bored into her with the fury of a woman spurned. I smiled sheepishly back at her, ecstatic that our little plan had successfully awakened her, yet partially ashamed.

Lexy and I didn't try to say anything because we didn't have to. We both smiled at her and let her read our thoughts. Reading our thoughts didn't exactly help as much as it should have because while our thoughts explained how we'd used jealousy to ignite the emotional connection between us to wake her up, it also gave her a front-row view of where Lexy and I were headed. We hadn't wanted to stop. And even now, I couldn't stop thinking about kissing Lexy.

Lexy stood and held out Kendra's necklace with her protection and separation stones, offering it to her. Kendra snatched it from Lexy's hand. I tried to keep my mind from hearing the mental name calling between the two girls.

*Those are unfiltered thoughts,* I reminded myself.

Lexy took the brunt of the name calling and returned plenty herself, but she also consciously forced an image of herself kneeling with her head bowed as if submitting to one's master, or begging for forgiveness.

Kendra grabbed the two ends of the necklace and hooked them together behind her neck. Her thoughts shut off. Lexy shut her mind off, too. Like always, I could still feel their emotions. Kendra's chest went from an exploding volcano to simply bubbling and flowing lava. Knowing why we'd kissed didn't slow the way her body trembled in angry jealousy or cool the flame in her usually soft, blue eyes.

"Welcome back," I said with mostly a smile.

She looked at me and her eyes dampened. Her quivering lips caught the first two tears. She stood up, took a few steps, then looked back. She tried to speak but her chin trembled. She gulped and then continued out of the room.

"Wait," I called and jumped up to start after her.

"No." Alexis grabbed my arm. "I'll go."

"Like she wants to see you right now!" I shot back.

"If she refuses my company, then I shall send Carolyn." Lexy's eyes burned into me. "Get some sleep."

"You think I can sleep after . . ." I gazed into Lexy's eyes. Cheeks flushed, I glanced at my bed a few feet to the left of the silver Star of David circle. I couldn't help but imagine Lexy joining me in that bed, but I also didn't want to hurt Kendra like that. It was better if Lexy left before I did something foolish.

I sighed. "I'll try to sleep."

Lexy smiled knowingly at me as she turned away. I watched her leave, my eyes fixed on her ribbon bow tattoo until the door closed.

It hurt to take off my hoodie. My left arm had soaked the sleeve with blood that had now dried. The wound had already started to heal but was still open at the center. A piece of my hoodie stuck to the beginnings of a scab at the end of the cut. I gritted my teeth as I yanked the material from the knife wound, making it bleed again. Taking my pants off wasn't a joy either. My calf screamed in pain with every movement.

A knock came at the door as I stood there in my boxers. My heartbeat increased. Was it Kendra or Alexis? Well, only Kendra would have knocked. I considered putting something on but didn't. I stepped to the door and opened it.

A short, dark-haired man stood there. His nose was too long for his face. I remembered Dr. Stewart. He had treated O'Brien.

"I was informed that you have some wounds that need to be stitched." He held up a plastic case that read University of Utah Hospital on it.

I let him in. I heal quickly, not instantly, so I could use some stitches. I sat on the bed and he injected my wounds with

53

lidocaine before cleaning and stitching up both the cut on my arm and on my calf. It took a half-hour. He didn't say anything and neither did I. However, as he got up to leave, I had to ask.

"How is O'Brien?"

He looked up at me, which emphasized the length of his nose. "Who is O'Brien?"

"The man you treated here last week," I explained.

"I've never been to this house before in my life," he answered.

My breath caught.

As Dr. Stewart let himself out, he mumbled something about never making house calls, and how he wasn't sure why he decided to take this one.

I let myself breathe. I don't know why it freaked me out that he had no memory of treating O'Brien. Perhaps I hadn't understood the extent to which vampires could mess with memory. I had to wonder if all my own memories were accurate. My hand instinctively reached up and touched the protection stone. No, all my memories were still here.

I considered doing something with my bloody clothes. Instead, I left my hoodie and pants on the floor and slipped into bed. Even with the stitches, I would probably get blood on the sheets. I probably should have showered first. Of course, as much as I didn't like the idea of servants, I liked the usefulness of having them. They'd clean everything up for me.

The knife wounds and the use of magic combined with my healing skin quickly allowed sleep to overcome my racing mind. Unfortunately, I felt pulled into a dream that I didn't really want to enter.

⚜ ⚜ ⚜

I didn't know where I was. I stood before a little shack. The bright morning sun lifted above the roof, lighting up the blue sky, forcing me to squint. The exterior was painted bright green with the shutters and door painted bright yellow. A dirt path led to the door. The windows weren't exactly windows; there was no glass, just metal blinds. The door didn't have a doorknob, just a latch and an unlocked padlock.

The warm, humid air seeped into my skin. Of course, I only wore boxers. My albino white skin felt the morning sun burning it. To the left of the yellow door, a tall man stood silently watching me. His excessively dark skin contrasted with the white shirt he wore. He smiled, and his teeth contrasted with his skin as much as his shirt had. He gestured with his hand to the door.

I opened it, but I couldn't see inside. The bright sun had shrunk my pupils, and it didn't seem that the metal blinds let in much light. I stepped inside and blinked the darkness away. As my eyes adjusted, two figures, one short, one tall, came into focus. They stood on the dirt floor, and behind them, a three-burner gas stove sat on a makeshift wooden table with a propane tank below it. The floor, despite being made of dirt, had a perfect pattern of lines—broom lines. Who sweeps a dirt floor?

"*Bonjou*," Voodoo Whoopi spoke. "We be expecting . . ." She hesitated as if just now recognizing me. She glanced at the tall, thin woman and then returned her dark eyes to me. "We be expecting someone not you."

If they hadn't been expecting me, who had they been expecting?

"I be Atabei, and this," she pointed to Stick Witch, "be Manouchka."

I preferred calling them Voodoo Whoopi and Stick Witch.

"Why are you in my dreams?"

"These be not your dreams, young man." Atabei smiled, showing a few missing teeth. "They be his." She pointed behind me.

I whipped around. The yellow shack door no longer led outside. Instead, it opened into a long room that extended some thirty feet. A man sat at the end of a long table. The room and table looked very similar to the dining hall at Lexy's mansion, with notable differences. The table, while still dark, was a slightly lighter shade of wood, and instead of a single large chandelier, three small chandeliers lit the room.

I glanced back and the rest of the shack had completely disappeared. Atabei and Manouchka stood in the exact same position as before; only now, they stood in front of a well-decorated, cement wall.

"Who are you?" the man asked as he rose from his high-backed chair. I recognized his face because it matched my face, only with a hint of wrinkles at the eyes. I wished this were a sci-fi movie and the man was the older version of me who traveled back in time to fix some wrong decision in my life. But I was pretty sure this was my biological father. The creep responsible for my not-so-immaculate conception. He had visited my dreams many times, but this dream felt far more real than any of my prior dreams.

"Who are you?" he repeated, "and why are you visiting my dream?"

I didn't answer. I didn't understand how he didn't recognize me. He'd always recognized me in my other dreams.

"You look captivatingly hideous. You're not albino? What are you?"

Still, I didn't answer. But he'd reminded me why, in my currently monstrous and self-loathing state, he wouldn't recognize me. Since I had last shared a dream with my biological father, I lost fifty pounds of muscle; my skin went from tan to albino with road rash splotches and white flakes; my hair, which used to hang almost to my eyes, was now stubble; and I had barely any evidence of eyebrows or eyelashes. I was unrecognizable.

"He be one of Princess Alexis's generals," Atabei offered. "We tried to capture him'n de girl—a youngling." Atabei's Haitian accent was thick. "But this be no youngling. His power be great."

The man—I didn't want to call him father, so I decided to stick with "the man" for now—looked at me with interest. "So, this boy is your excuse for failing?" The man tossed his eyes at Atabei and Manouchka. "And the athletic one. My lost son. What of him?"

My biological father's words confused me. What did he mean by calling me his *lost son?* Hadn't he found me in my dreams?

"Your boy did not come," Atabei answered.

"He didn't come?" the man growled. "Keagan gave his word. I've been searching for him for almost two decades!"

"Keagan lied." Atabei pursed her lips.

"Then kill him! I'll not be lied to!"

Atabei lowered her eyes, unable to meet her master's eyes.

"Don't tell me. You let Keagan escape?"

Atabei and Manouchka both nodded.

"Did you find the place of power?"

"We did," Atabei answered.

"Was it outside the line?"

I had no idea what the place of power was or what "outside the line" meant. To me, outside the line meant I was a half-yard short of a touchdown.

"Yes."

The man turned back to me. "Well, you don't say much." He paused as if thinking. "We can't have one of Alexis's generals interrupting my dreams again. Atabei, Manouchka, do you think you can rid us of his problematic spirit?"

I glanced back at the Haitian witches. The shack had returned. The witches again stood in front of the three-burner gas stove. The makeshift table and the dirt floor had also returned. I glanced back to where the man—my biological father—had been and instead saw the shack's yellow door leading outside.

I heard the Haitians muttering and I turned back to them. Their eyes went dark—not just the irises, the sclera went black, too. Manouchka—Stick Witch—pulled out a clay bottle and held it while Atabei—Voodoo Whoopi—sliced her palm and dripped blood into a bowl that already had giblets and other nastiness in it.

"So nice of you to be offering a piece of your soul," Atabei cackled.

A coldness wrapped around me. It gripped me and pulled. I could feel the clay bottle as if it surrounded me. But it didn't have me yet. Stick Witch gave me a wicked grin that I didn't like. I couldn't stop myself from moving toward the clay bottle. My spirit—or at least the part of my spirit that had somehow entered this dream—was about to be bound in dark magic that I didn't understand.

I looked around, trying to think of a way to escape. I only knew two offensive spells. Since I was in a wooden shack with the Haitian witches standing directly in front of a propane tank that sat under the makeshift wooden table, it was obvious which spell I'd choose.

I smiled at the witches even as my spirit started to contort and stretch toward the bottle.

"Fyr leoht," I whispered, directing the heat of my fire into the center of the propane tank.

The propane tank exploded in fire. Metal and wood flew away from the shack as fire consumed everything that remained—including me.

This was no ordinary dream. My spirit weighed down in agony as the flames did real damage. My spirit would burn away, like I'd erased the nightwalker and others. My body would be left an empty shell, comatose and braindead.

Pain pierced my left calf muscle but not from the fire. Something bit me just above my ankle. An animal, not a monster. It dragged me from the flames, saving my spirit. I couldn't see what type of animal it was, but still, I knew it was canine. It spoke to me, but I was in too much pain to hear its words. The accent was not Haitian. It was Native American.

I jerked awake and sat up in my bed. I could see light outside my windows. I'd slipped into bed just past four, and the red digits on the desk clock now read 8:58 A.M. I'd slept more than my usual four hours, so I guess it was time to get started on the day. For half a second, I thought it was Friday because we'd fought the witches at the strip club on Thursday morning, but it was still Thursday morning, just later.

I almost forgot about the dream, but it rushed back to me as I stood. I felt pain in both my left calf and my arm as I stepped out of bed. My left calf had a cut, not bite marks. Lexy's healing stone hung around my neck. She must have slipped in and traded her protection stone with mine while I slept. We'd been trading our protection stones day and night. Her protection stone was also a healing stone. She used it during the day, as it protected her from the sun. I used it at night when she didn't need it to heal more quickly. I already healed fast, so between the stitches and the healing stone, both the cut on my arm and the cut on my calf looked to be almost a week old. No change on the rest of my skin though.

I didn't have to limp much as I stumbled over to a new stack of clothes laid out for me on the desk chair. I glanced around. My blood-soaked hoodie and pants had been removed. As expected, the servants had also slipped in while I slept.

"I have been waiting for you to wake up," Alexis spoke in my ear as I was putting on my pants.

She startled me, and I jumped. Yes, I jumped with my pants only partially on. Yes, I stumbled and fell. My hip and elbow broke my fall. The cuts on my arm and calf shouted at my brain with pain.

"Alexis!" I complained, pulling my pants the rest of the way on while on the floor. I stood up and picked up my shirt. "This shirt is still black, and you know I want a hoodie."

I threw the shirt at her face. Alexis snatched my shirt from the air before it hit her. Despite our little make-out session last night, I scowled at her. I hadn't forgiven her for not telling Keagan to go to hell. She'd told him she'd think about it. I still couldn't believe it.

Today, Alexis wore a black leather shirt that I hadn't seen before. This one was simple, pretty much like a t-shirt, except leather and skintight. Normally her leather pants were indistinguishable, but today the black leather had large rivets lining the top seam all the way around her waist and down the outside seams of her pants, each rivet exposing a quarter-inch circle of skin. She wore tall, black heels instead of boots that made her at least as tall as me.

"I don't want to talk to you right now!" I snapped.

She tilted her head and grinned mischievously. "Would you like to continue where we left off last night?"

"No. I, uh," I stammered. I wanted to say yes. Fortunately, her separation stone remained active or she'd have known. Who was

I kidding, she didn't need the Trinity of Mind to know I'd just lied. Her smirk brought an angry grunt out of me. "I only kissed you to wake Kendra. Otherwise, I wouldn't have done it. You didn't deserve it after . . ." I finished my sentence by gesturing with both my hands in frustration.

She hid her emotions on her face, but they slipped through her protection stone and directly into me anyway. My words cut her like a knife—I could feel it. Surprise mixed in with her emotions. She either hadn't realized or she'd forgotten how much trouble she was in for the Keagan thing.

I unlatched the necklace holding her healing stone and tossed it at her face. She caught it just as easily and threw my shirt at my face. Unlike Alexis, I didn't react quickly enough.

The doorknob clicked, and I heard Carolyn's voice.

"Breakfast. We made your favorite dozen-egg omelet."

It wasn't four dozen, just one, but hopefully, it would help me grow roughly the size of a barge. Again.

I pulled the shirt off my face and noticed Carolyn glancing at my chest. I used to have pecs that stuck out and attracted girls' eyes. Now where my pecs used to be, my ugly white skin on my chest rippled around the shapes of my ribs, repelling girls' eyes. Carolyn's eyes flickered toward Alexis and then she lowered them. Had Alexis somehow reprimanded her for looking at me?

I hit the restroom. As I washed my hands, I checked myself out in the mirror and confirmed that despite wearing the healing stone, my skin hadn't healed at all from last night's sleep. My skin's complexion showed no progress whatsoever, casting yet more doubt that I would ever look normal. For the second time, I wondered whether my skin was as healed as it was going to get. I moved to the scale and watched the digits settle on my weight: 149.8. Before the Cabin Battle of Bear Lake, I weighed 202.4. I had burned off fifty-three pounds.

I walked back to my room and my eyes settled on the dozen-egg omelet.

"Eat quickly," Alexis suggested. "We are going to see O'Brien."

# CHAPTER 9
# BROKEN

*Jake worries about everyone. Kendra, O'Brien, me. No man has ever treated me as well as he does. I do not care if he looks ugly forever. I shall never forget how he killed the nightwalker. The power that comes off him when he casts magic is greater than anything I have ever seen. Also, despite the Trinity of Mind, Jake does not know yet. Eldra's training is working. —Alexis*

The last time I was in a hospital, I thought I had died. I wasn't very fond of hospitals. They have an inescapable smell brought on by a war of modern medicine and chemicals against sickness and death. Both sides of the war won their share of the battles, but the war—like the smell—would never end.

Kendra stood on my left as I looked down at O'Brien. Seeing him unconscious in a hospital bed was becoming annoyingly commonplace. I hated the hum of medical equipment and its random beeps almost as much as I hated the hospital's smell.

I'd ordered Carolyn to find me a thin cotton hoodie, which looked odd for a hot August day, but not as odd as my . . . I didn't want to think about my skin as it would remind me of Kendra's and Lexy's bad thought. I no longer had the self-esteem necessary to fight off that thought.

Standing over O'Brien, I felt so safe that I lowered my hoodie. I shouldn't have felt safe, because he looked weak and vulnerable. He had two tubes down his throat and an IV in his arm. I couldn't see it, but supposedly he had eleven inches of stitches on his back. The surgery had repaired his spine but hadn't restored movement to his lower body.

He also looked thin. Before Alexis's grandfather broke his back, O'Brien had weighed at least as much as I had. I took a tentative breath. I hadn't understood that someone could atrophy so quickly. In just five days, his legs had thinned enough to make the joints look knobby. He weighed less than I did now. Somehow, regular life was stranger than magic. I'd somehow burned fifty pounds of muscle off my body in a few seconds by converting my own mass into magic, and that had seemed crazy impossible. Yet O'Brien, with a snapped L3 vertebra, had lost the use of his legs and had burned just as much muscle lying in the hospital bed.

I thought about that Saturday. Lexy's grandfather had touched a crystal on his neck and thrown O'Brien into the sheetrocked wall. His lower back had wrapped around one of the studs before he collapsed. He hadn't moved his legs since. One more reason for hating Alexis's grandfather. Again, I regretted letting him live—even as a slave under Carina's control.

I couldn't imagine what it would feel like to find out you may never walk again.

Alexis stood just outside O'Brien's room. I could see her through the glass wall. She was speaking to two doctors, a man and a younger woman. I grinned at Lexy's outfit. She'd changed into a white shirt—yes, white—and a pair of maroon jeans with gray boots. Kendra had taken Alexis shopping at Aeropostale yesterday morning. They had made a deal. Kendra would wear Alexis's leather body armor while acting as the princess's general, and in return, Alexis would dress like Kendra when we went to normal places during the day.

Alexis hadn't lost her own style, though. The front of her white shirt flared up showing her navel, and her low-rise jeans exposed the top of her tattoo. With the healing stone, she didn't need to protect her skin from the sun—she just got hungry more quickly, mostly for food. Her thirst for blood increased slightly, too, but it wasn't anything she couldn't handle.

I turned back to O'Brien. He had a significant amount of facial hair. He normally shaved. I wondered if I should ask the nurses to clean him up, but the nurses weren't Alexis's servants, so I just kept my mouth shut.

Alexis glanced at me through the door. Then she tapped her separation stone, allowing me to listen in as the doctors explained that enough days had passed that spinal shock may no longer be a factor. His paralysis could be permanent.

"We want to try to reposition the backbone in a few days when all the swelling has gone down," the young doctor said. "We feel that, in O'Brien's specific situation, we have a good chance of repositioning the broken L3 vertebra, which will offer him one last chance to walk again," the woman glanced at the older doctor as if asking for his approval to continue. Was she an intern? "Of course, there are risks," she added.

"O'Brien will have to make that decision," Alexis told the doctors, but she couldn't hide from me her hopeless belief that he would never walk again.

*I know he'll say yes,* I thought, irritated at her lack of hope.

A part of me felt lucky that O'Brien wasn't awake. How do you talk to a new paraplegic? How do you look them in the eyes and tell them everything will be OK? How does one lie like that? He'd never be OK again. Who was I to tell him different?

O'Brien had been a badass military sniper turned bodyguard with minor druid powers that made sure he never missed. Now, what was he going to be?

My lower lip quivered. I tried to blink away the dampness in my eyes, fighting off the tears. I didn't want to cry. I didn't want to be vulnerable in front of Kendra and Alexis. Alexis tapped her protection stone, and I could no longer hear the doctor. I hadn't intended to feel like this. Seeing O'Brien broken hurt so much more than I'd expected. It didn't matter that he had freaking shot me just over a week ago. Sure, it had been part of his desperate plan to fake my death and recruit me as a druid. Wait, how did he win me over after that first impression? He'd taught me to be a druid. We'd survived the nightwalker together.

Kendra reached over and grabbed my hand. She'd been watching my face. She pulled me in for a hug. My tears fell onto her shoulder.

She had either moved past last night's anger and forgiven me or set her anger aside to comfort me.

Alexis and I had argued about healing O'Brien the whole way here. Despite my protests that we should at least try, Alexis adamantly refused to try the healing stone on O'Brien. She maintained that once the backbone is out of place, enhancing his healing wouldn't put the backbone in place again. Rapid healing would only make the backbone fuse in the wrong place sooner, making it harder for the doctors to try to reposition the vertebra. She offered to turn him, assuring me that the symbiotic virus responsible for turning a human into a vampire could repair spinal damage. I hadn't responded kindly. Swear words got involved.

I let go of Kendra and wiped my eyes, trying to pull myself together.

Until today, only Alexis had visited him. I would have visited him yesterday if we hadn't been forced to spend the day preparing to face Keagan. We didn't learn any new spells but instead worked on not going insane with three minds joined. We worked on understanding unfiltered thoughts, not judging unfiltered thoughts, and not believing unfiltered thoughts. Alexis's and Kendra's minds spent the day trying and failing to not catfight. If I had to hear them mentally call each other names one more time, I might go insane.

With me, it was different. From the very beginning, I understood the concept of unfiltered thoughts. The moment we'd first joined minds, I'd stopped their bickering with just such a lecture. I could usually ignore their unfiltered thoughts—when those thoughts weren't about how ugly I was or when those thoughts weren't like Kendra's and Lexy's bad thought. The one I wasn't supposed to repeat. I wasn't doing a good job of ignoring that thought. Still, having their minds around gave me something to do. It gave me something to browse since I didn't have my phone or laptop and couldn't browse the internet.

I didn't feel nearly as comfortable sharing my unfiltered thoughts as I felt browsing theirs. Many of my thoughts embarrassed me. Guys think very differently than girls. And we think of certain things more often.

According to Eldra, the three of us should have gone insane. She hypothesized that joining our minds under a life-and-death situation forced us to focus, saving us from insanity. She further surmised that my collapse into a coma and Lexy's dying—though we brought her back, and she hadn't stayed dead long enough to turn—gave us all a reprieve from the mental onslaught once the life-and-death situation had ended. Alexis could also read minds, and she had experience sharing thoughts. Only the combination of all those unusual circumstances helped the two girls stay sane until Eldra gave them the separation stones that had belonged to her and her husband. She claimed that without the separation stones, I would have woken to two insane girlfriends. I wasn't so sure, but I didn't argue.

Alexis turned and tapped her separation stone again so I could hear that O'Brien might be comatose. The doctors said he hadn't woken yet. When he did wake up, he'd find out he couldn't move his legs. I wondered about how backbones function. What about the spine made a person paralyzed? Sure, trauma was the obvious cause, but modern medicine hadn't figured out why some people recovered while others didn't. The doctors might feel they repaired one backbone exceptionally well, but the person never walks again. Their next repair might be nearly impossible to get right, but the person walks. It could take decades of more research to figure it out.

Not knowing why, I pushed magic into my eyes to enhance my sight. The world came to life and exploded into bright color.

I could see the white glow of electricity flowing through the cables to the medical equipment. I could see Kendra's spirit, dimmed by her clothes. Her protection stone and separation stone radiated more light than I expected. I could somewhat see through walls. At least I could faintly see the spirits of the two patients in the next room and that of a person—perhaps a nurse or doctor—talking to one of them.

I focused on O'Brien's spine. The thin white hospital gown hardly dimmed my view at all. I didn't really know what I was looking for, but I looked anyway. O'Brien's spirit shone around his backbone just as it did throughout his whole body. I didn't see anything wrong, but then again, I didn't have anything to compare it to. Wait, yes, I did. Kendra stood right next to me.

"Turn around." I grabbed Kendra's shoulders and spun her so I could see her backbone.

Kendra wore a red t-shirt with a wide frilly neck that now had damp tear spots on it. Under that, she wore a black camisole. The two layers—especially the black camisole—dimmed my view of her backbone, making it hard for me to see.

OK. How was I going to ask Kendra to take her shirt off? Would she believe that I was asking in the name of science?

"I want to look at your backbone . . . with magic," I explained. "Don't move." I turned her so her back was to me and I lifted the bottom of her shirt up. Kendra stiffened, her modesty instincts kicking in, but she let me raise the back of her shirt up. A hint of embarrassment and naughtiness trickled from her. Lexy found it quite fun. I did my best to ignore the fact that I could see the clip of her bra and focused on the inner light in her backbone. I could see a motion to the light. A slight current, flowing up and down. The backbone didn't just hold up the body, it provided a conduit for the spirit as well.

Lexy divided her focus between the doctors and what I was doing. Her curiosity matched my own.

I scanned O'Brien. I could see it now. His spirit didn't move up and down the backbone, but instead, it flowed to the lower back and then fell back, like ocean waves. Perhaps I'd found the difference between someone who would walk again and a paraplegic. Perhaps the trauma had as much to do with the spirit as it did with the body. That might explain why despite all the effort and research on how to repair paralysis, the best a surgeon could do was to try to repair and restructure the broken vertebrae and hope. Modern medicine has yet to embrace the fact that healing requires knowledge beyond the physical.

I lowered Kendra's shirt. She turned around and blinked at me with wide, confused eyes above reddened cheeks. If she wanted details, she could tap off her separation stone; I was too busy thinking to answer her questioning look or address her embarrassment.

It didn't help at all that I knew about the problem with O'Brien's spirit. I couldn't fix it. He was still just as paralyzed as he was before I'd examined him. I guess I'd just wasted my time. I pulled the magic from my eyes and the world returned to normal.

I felt helpless. Alexis felt the same. We couldn't do anything for O'Brien. What if he never woke up?

On a whim, I pushed magic—pure energy—into him. O'Brien stirred. His eyes blinked open and he looked at me. I could tell he didn't recognize me. His eyes flashed to Kendra, and I think he tried to smile. O'Brien's right arm twitched, and he mouthed out a name, "Rachel." Then his eyes closed, leaving Kendra and me to wonder whom he meant. He'd never mentioned her before.

"Let's go," I suggested. The doctors had left the area or I would have told them that O'Brien had briefly woken.

I let Kendra wrap her hand in mine. Alexis didn't seem to mind.

We walked past the next-door room where I'd seen two patients and a doctor. This room was empty, so I must have confused where I was looking and looked at the room on the other side of O'Brien's.

# CHAPTER 10
# NERVES

The Trinity of Mind went too far today. Kendra is late. Yes, I am talking about girl stuff. Her period. She was supposed to start on her birthday. She just noticed this morning. I remember fifth-grade maturation class, where an awkward video taught me what a period is. I've never thought much about it. Once last year, Teresa, my ex-girlfriend, asked me to hold her jacket and a pantyliner fell out. She'd picked it up and winked and said, "Don't tell anyone." I didn't because it was awkward. I realize now how naïve and immature I'd acted. Well, the Trinity of Mind just wiped my naïvety away. I know things now. Kendra started having periods at eleven, a month before turning twelve. Her mom hadn't even talked to her about it yet. I know that she prefers tampons over pads. I know the brand. Tampax Pearl, to be exact. Sis uses the same brand. But that isn't even the worst of it. I share her mind, so I know everything. Ugh! I shouldn't know this girl stuff. —Jake

Alexis slipped smoothly into the driver's seat. I offered Kendra the front seat, but she declined and jumped in back, so I took it. The parking garage consisted of gray concrete and black asphalt. The few signs and white parking-stall stripes and numbers provided the only other colors. We'd parked in stall twenty-seven.

"Jake," Alexis said as she put on her large black sunglasses. "We are going to visit your sister at Kendra's house. Would you like to give her a call and tell her we are on our way?"

"We can't just go to Kendra's house," I argued as I buckled my seatbelt. "Someone might recognize me."

"Not likely," Kendra cut in. "My parents definitely won't recognize you."

If Kendra thought her comment comforted me, it didn't. Her parents wouldn't recognize me as Jacob because they would freak out at the sight of me. Come to think of it, Sis would freak out at the sight of me too. She hadn't exactly reacted well the last time she saw me. How would she react to me now as one giant, recovering skin disease?

"Everything will be fine. Just call your sister," Alexis added. "Do not use O'Brien's old phone—"

"I can't. It took a knife last night," I interrupted.

"—we have a different one." Alexis continued, ignoring me. "Kendra, the phone."

"Here, Jake." Kendra handed me a phone from the back seat. Only it wasn't her phone. She handed me a new phone that had a blue-ribbon bow wrapped around it.

"It is yours, Jake." Lexy smiled.

"I slyly asked Kevin which phone a genius geek would design for a spy," Kendra explained. "He said his dad's company just started selling secure phones last year."

I almost said jeek to correct her, but I'd consumed the jock part of me. For the second time I wondered, *Was I only a geek again?* Thankfully, the phone was just awesome enough to keep me from spiraling into a depressed abyss.

"Slyly?" Alexis challenged. "Hopefully, he does not guess for whom you were asking. Or that the purchase order placed the next day was a direct result of your question."

"We already argued over this," Kendra responded.

Alexis looked like she was about to challenge Kendra further but didn't. Instead, she turned to me. "It arrived this morning."

"We thought we'd give it to you after you saw O'Brien," Kendra added.

"How did you hide this from me?"

"I let Alexis hypnotize me. She made me forget until she used the phrase, 'Kendra, the phone.'"

I remembered Dr. Stewart's confusion earlier. I wasn't sure Kendra should be letting Alexis mess with her mind. Neither of us felt the need to ask Lexy how she had hidden the surprise from me. We weren't sure if we were annoyed that she had a mental lockbox of thoughts or jealous that we didn't know how to create our own.

"How is it safe to call my sister with it?"

"It just is," Kendra answered.

"It switches carriers every hour," Alexis explained. "It works with or without a SIM card. We can discuss all the awesome features later."

"Wow, I would have thought your grandfather already had a way to get secure phones."

"He does," Alexis responded. "However, I want our phones to be secure from *him* as well."

I held my brand-new cell phone in my hand. I couldn't believe it. I swiped my thumb across the screen. It had all the latest features. Lexy and Kendra had completely caught me by surprise. I clicked on the contacts button and found a short list of letters with numbers by them: A, E, K, L, M, S. For half a second, I wondered who the letters were for.

"Do these letters stand for Alexis, Eldra, Kendra, Luiz, and Mr. Espinoza? But there is no J for Justine, so is S for Sis?" I asked. The phone numbers for each contact was the same, which meant the phone routed through a secure line, then was forwarded. My calls couldn't be tracked.

"Yes, and technically, the M is for Miguel, Mr. Espinoza's first name," Lexy explained.

I selected S to call Sis, and immediately, a computerized female voice asked me for a voice or fingerprint identification. I touched my fingerprint to the screen. The female voice confirmed my identification and promised to connect me.

I didn't expect my gut to wrench as I listened to the first ring. My mouth felt dry. Sis and I hadn't seen each other since I'd erased a vampire with a magic missile right in front of her eyes. The horrified look she'd given me flashed in my mind, increasing my nervousness. We'd talked on the phone last night—actually, it had been this morning at two—but that hadn't exactly gone so well for me or the burner phone I'd used.

I listened to the second ring. What was I going to say? How could I make everything all right for her? The third ring. Alexis hadn't started driving yet; she just sat in the driver's seat looking at me. Kendra eyed me from the back seat as well.

I detected a hint of repulsion coming from Kendra that reminded me I hadn't covered my head with my hoodie.

The fourth ring.

"Hello," Sis answered.

"Hey, Sis," I answered back.

"Hey, Jake," Sis spoke hesitantly. I could tell that talking to me made her nervous.

*Tell her not to say your name,* Alexis suggested. Of course, both Alexis and Kendra would choose this moment to enter my head. Who needs speaker phone when you can simply share minds, right?

*I need to get my own separation stone so I can shut you out.*

*That wouldn't be any fun,* Kendra thought. Alexis agreed.

"Are you still at Kendra's house?" I asked.

"Yes," Justine replied.

"We're coming over."

"You said *we*," Sis noted.

"Yes," I hesitated. "I'm with Kendra and a friend you might not know. Her name is Alexis."

"Oh, I know Alexis. We met at," she hesitated, "at your funeral. She visited a few days later, too," Sis replied.

From Lexy's mind, I witnessed both memories. In the first memory, Lexy talked to both Sis and my mom at the funeral. Before Lexy had met me, she had used her allure on my mom to give her the courage to move out and leave John. I hadn't known until seeing this memory that Lexy had helped Mom make that decision. Gratitude swelled up from my chest, and I was forced to blink away some watery eyes.

In the second memory, Lexy visited Sis and Mom at the new apartment she'd set up for them where she'd used her allure to take control of them. I'd known she'd visited Luiz and Kendra, but I hadn't realized she'd messed with Sis and Mom, too. How had I not seen this in her mind before now?

"Great," I told Sis, though I didn't mean it. "We'll be there in about half an hour," I added.

I gave Alexis the eye. I wasn't sure whether to thank her for helping Mom finally leave John or hate her for controlling Mom and Sis.

*Why do you keep so many secrets?*

*To protect you,* she answered.

*How do you keep them when our minds are joined?*

*Discipline,* she answered.

*Eldra told us that even with connected minds, it takes a long time to fully know someone,* Kendra offered, making an excuse for Alexis.

*You're defending Alexis?* I couldn't believe it. I pressed my knuckles of the fingers that held the phone to my ear against my temple.

*She also said that if we knew how, we could share everything at once, but there is a risk we would lose who we are,* Alexis added, choosing to ignore that their presence in my head was putting me on edge.

*Can you both get out of my head, please?*

*No!* They both responded.

"OK," Sis replied. "I'll see you in a few minutes then."

The formality of the conversation—the phone conversation with my sister—was not lost on me. Sis and I were never formal. Our relationship would never be what it once was, would it? I didn't believe either Kendra's or Alexis's mental assurances that my old relationship with Sis would survive.

"Sis," I had to tell her before she hung up, before she saw me. "I don't look the same. No one will recognize me."

"What do you mean?" she asked.

"I had to . . ." I started but couldn't finish. How could I explain to my sister that I could convert matter to energy and that I'd converted my hair, skin, and fifty pounds of my muscle into fuel for a magic spell? Oh, and by the way, I grew the skin back, mostly, in a few days but not the muscle, so I looked like a scratched-up albino? I could also heal quickly, but despite that, my skin's healing had stopped progressing.

"I did something to myself . . ." I started again but couldn't figure out where to go with that line either. "Just be prepared for me to look thin and ugly."

"Thin and ugly?" Sis questioned.

Would Sis agree with Kendra's and Lexy's bad thought? Alexis scolded Kendra again for starting that thought and Kendra's mental apologies started again, while at the same time, she scolded Lexy back for adding to the thought. I had to focus on Sis, which was OK by me, as Eldra didn't want me repeating that thought, anyway.

"Yeah. And albino," I added.

"Albino?"

"Well, with scabs, flaky skin, and splotchy red patches."

"Oh, my gosh, Jake. Are you OK?"

"No, I'm not OK. I'm dead, remember. Don't tell anyone it is me who is coming to visit. Pretend I'm someone else." Yeah, because asking my sister to pretend I wasn't her brother wasn't awkward at all. "We'll see you in a bit," I finished and hung up, and Kendra and Alexis both tapped their separation stones, annoyingly separating their minds from me.

I had to fix this between Sis and me. Our relationship couldn't continue like this. I couldn't be ugly *and* lose my relationship with my sister.

"Sis gets to know everything," Alexis spoke with her princess-of-the-new-world voice, using it as if she had the right to make decisions for me. Well, princess or not, she didn't make decisions for me.

"But I don't want her involved. She—" I tried to argue, but Alexis spoke over the top of me.

"Kendra and I decided earlier."

I glanced at Kendra.

"Justine is already involved," Kendra confirmed. "You, her brother, and me, her best friend, are druids. Nightwalkers brutally murdered her stepdad, and her mother was arrested for it. Besides, we know how close you two are. You don't keep any secrets from each other."

"Even secrets told to her best friend," Alexis flashed her grin into the rearview mirror for Kendra to see. She pulled the car out of the parking lot and turned onto North Medical Drive, which quickly turned into North Campus Drive.

"We're not talking about that secret again," Kendra exclaimed, her cheeks going red.

"What are you two talking about," I asked, frustrated that I could feel a taunting coming from Alexis and a large amount of embarrassment coming from Kendra.

"Practice," Alexis teased Kendra.

"What practice?" I asked.

"Stop it, Lexy," Kendra urged, her voice raising a bit.

"What?" I asked again.

"Kendra and Justine liked to *practice*," Alexis emphasized.

"Practice what?" Did she mean drill team?

I sighed. I really had no clue what they were talking about, but I felt like I should know. It did, however, remind me of something else.

"We talkin' about practice? Not the game?" I gave my best Allen Iverson impersonation. "We talkin' about practice, man."

Neither girl had a clue. I laughed. I could leave them on the outside of an inside joke, too.

"Do you know what you are going to say to Sis?" Kendra asked, clearly trying to change the subject.

"Just let me think about it," my words ground out, revealing more frustration than I intended.

After driving a few blocks, Lexy commented, "Do not turn around, but we are being followed."

"What?" I snapped to attention, having to fight off the urge to turn around.

"A black SUV pulled out of the hospital with us," she added. "It is about five cars back."

71

"Can we lose them?"

"I have taken a few abnormal turns, and yet they are still on our tail. I have not tried hard to lose them. That would make it obvious that I have spotted them." The corners of Lexy's mouth were turned up in a half-smile. To her, being tailed meant the start of a fun game.

"If someone is following us, there is no way we can visit Sis."

"No. We are visiting Sis. You need her!" Alexis assured as she stopped at a red light. She waited until the black SUV stopped, still five cars behind us.

Alexis turned the steering wheel and hit the gas. The BMW's engine roared and threw me back against the seat and then to the right as Alexis pulled into the lane of oncoming traffic, but with the red light, there were no cars on this side. She ran the light, barely missing being t-boned by a blue F-150, before swerving back into our lane. She gunned it to the next light, turned right, and zig-zagged our way toward the 600 North freeway entrance. She pulled into a back alley and stopped.

"If they find us, then they are tracking us," Alexis grinned.

"This car doesn't have GPS, I responded."

"Our phones shouldn't be trackable," Kendra added. "Kevin's dad's company is too good."

Kevin's dad owned a private tech security company. Every computer in his company ran on OpenBSD, one of the most secure operating systems in the world. Over the past two years, he had gone from a small startup to a hundred-million-dollar company. Since his company built this phone, it was probably more secure than we needed.

"Maybe they put a tracker on our car."

"Maybe," Alexis answered.

I wondered if I could sense a tracker. The tracker would be sending a wireless signal, which was energy, and to me, energy is magic that I can feel. I reached out, but the engine was the dominant energy source. The pistons hammered up and down. The alternator gave off electricity.

"Turn off the car," I suggested.

Both girls jumped into my head to find out why. Asking with words was too hard now. Of course, they immediately started a verbal catfight, just barely above the subconscious level, like a buzzing background sound in a failing pair of earbuds.

The engine didn't stop being the dominant energy provider simply by being turned off. It now only gave off heat, but heat is energy. I examined it for a second and wondered: if I pulled all the energy away from the engine, would it freeze?

I ignored that thought for now and tried to find a wireless power source. I moved from energy source to energy source, sensing that they were joints or bearings that had warmed with friction, before finally finding a faint energy source that pulsed every ten seconds just above and behind the rear passenger wheel.

Alexis slipped from the car to investigate and was back in the car with a tiny device the size of a micro-SD card. It had a small, round battery and an antenna that arched to a point on one end. The device had an LED with a plastic cover, but light seeped out faintly around the base. It had a small on/off button. Alexis clicked it off. The light didn't dim.

*Give it five seconds,* I suggested before she tried to click it on again. My geek came out as my mind shared with Kendra and Alexis how technology can run for up to thirty seconds after being powered off. *That is why when you call tech support for a wireless router,* I explained, *they ask you to turn the device off and leave it off for a minute before turning it back on.* Alexis was strangely interested. Kendra, not so much. Their catfight moved to the forefront of our minds.

"Tap them off, already," I suggested.

They glared at me but consented.

We drove in silence. It took twenty minutes to drive from that alley in Salt Lake to my old neighborhood in West Jordan. That wasn't nearly long enough. I dreaded seeing Sis. I spent the better part of the twenty minutes stressing out about seeing her. Would she recoil from me again? Would she find me too hideous to look at? Would she ever forgive me? Assuming she even believed it was me. I'd put her through so much lately, getting her involved in all this. Putting her through my fake death and funeral. Crashing her date with Dylan, after I was supposed to be dead, to save her from a couple gunman and some freakishly fast vampires. Then killing the vampire in front of her—with magic.

Who were those gunmen? If Alexis's mother, Carina, hadn't warned me with magic, my faked death would have become all too real that night. If the gunmen weren't with Carina and the vampires, who were they with? If I weren't so focused on seeing my sister, I might have thought about that a bit more. But nothing could distract me from reliving how Sis recoiled from me the other day, the memory on a loop in my mind.

As Alexis drove through my old neighborhood, we passed what used to be my house. My house had always stood out from all the rest. Mom inherited the house from Grandma when I was eleven. According to my late grandma, it was the only house for miles back when she and Grandpa bought it. Now it was the only *old* house. It did have the only huge tree in the neighborhood—an oversized apricot tree. The apricots flattened the grass underneath it now. The grass always grew sparse under that tree. But my house stood out now more than ever. Unfortunately, it wasn't the age, the lack of upkeep, or the large tree ringed with moldy apricots in the grass that made my house stand out. It was the yellow police tape that read: Caution! Do not cross!

I hadn't saved my stepdad that night. Did it make me a bad person that I didn't feel regret? I felt guilt but not regret. I felt responsible because the nightwalkers and the druids went to my house because of me. I felt responsible because I did nothing to protect him. However, I didn't regret my decision. Perhaps the lack of regret was due to the fact that had I tried to save him, I'd be dead and so would Justine and Dylan, and probably everyone else, too.

Sis . . .

I gulped once again as the image of Sis recoiling from me into Dylan's arms came back, again. The almost-healed cuts on my arm and leg itched. Being a minute from seeing Sis once more had my nerves so on edge that I welcomed the itching. The two cuts had healed enough that I would remove the stitches before I showered next, but for now, my stitched wounds were a welcome distraction.

My house faded behind us as we drove past the newer homes and their perfectly edged grass. Alexis drove on to Kendra's house. The houses on Kendra's street weren't as new or as big as those we'd just passed, but they were still newer than my house.

Anxiety spilled from Kendra. I glanced at her tense form in the back seat. I had no idea why going home stressed her out. I thought about asking her, but I didn't. I could feel her stress, and it added to mine.

I'd visited Kendra's house a thousand times but had never really studied it before. Four windows reflected the day on each side of the front door, two on the ground floor and two on the second floor. The roof cut down in a V between the upper windows. A brand-new door, painted red, stood out from the tan, stucco exterior. That night when the nightwalkers had killed my stepdad, they'd also come to Kendra's house. Eldra and her husband had been with them. Alexis had rescued Kendra, and using her allure, sent her parents to a hotel for the night before the creatures had arrived. I'd felt the ripple of the spell's magic. Had Eldra and her husband destroyed the front door? That would explain the new one.

Alexis pulled into the driveway and turned off the car. I just sat there. Alexis opened a contact case, and using the rearview mirror to see, put in a pair of blue contacts. She finished, and I remained sitting.

*Are you OK?* Alexis asked.

*Yeah, are you?* Kendra chimed in.

*I don't know,* I answered back after a sigh, and I wasn't lying. Ever wished you could be in someone's head when they answer with "I don't know" because you don't believe them? Well, usually, a person in turmoil really *doesn't know* because their mind and emotions are a mess. Reading a teenager's mind doesn't provide a better answer; it just exposes the hurricane of emotional and mental confusion.

I covered my head in my hoodie even though the August sun blared down. A normal person would sweat buckets in this hoodie. A thin layer of magic kept me cool.

I grabbed the door handle but didn't open the door. I held the handle as if that were enough to build up my courage. Finally, I popped open the car door and stepped onto the driveway. My feet led me to the red door far too quickly.

The color of the door touched on Alexis's desire to feed. Why did it have to be so obviously the color of blood? Perhaps they chose crimson, blood red, because Alexis had taken control of them and her desire for blood influenced them through that bond.

Sis had to have been waiting right by the door because before my knuckles struck a third time, the door swung open, and there she was, standing in the doorway in front of me.

She looked at me. Her eyes widened.

If things were all right with the world, Sis would have joked something like: "Hey, I knew we had different dads, but I didn't know yours was Deadpool."

Instead, she sucked in a quick, high-pitched breath, put her hand to her mouth, and swallowed.

No, things are *not* all right in my world.

*Great. She noticed I look like a monster,* I thought to no one because Kendra and Alexis had chosen to grace me with a moment of mental privacy. Of course, what did I expect? That she wouldn't notice for a few minutes? That I would have time to build up to tell her?

Sis recovered quickly. Her face firmed up; her expression resolute. She scrunched her eyes together as if trying to recognize the brother she used to know hiding behind the version of me that was now ugly.

All at once, she smiled, and her embarrassment dimple appeared on her right cheek.

"Jake?" she whispered my name questioningly. Then she lunged forward, her arms reaching for me like the zombies from the previous night.

I jumped back quickly and brought up my right arm to hold her off. Fear shivered through me. Why would she lunge at me like that? Had the voodoo Hagathas gotten to her? My armbar caught her in her sternum, and she made a small grunt. Her smile faded. I looked into her eyes, expecting to see a vacant expression and empty irises. Instead, I watched her green eyes lose the glitter of happiness and switch to confusion as they glanced from my arm that held her back to Kendra and Alexis behind me. Her arms remained extended out on either side of her body like she had been trying to do nothing more than hug me.

*Oh.* She had simply lunged forward to hug me, and I'd ruined it. My recent experiences had affected me so deeply that I'd flinched away from my sister's hug. I dropped my forearm.

"Sorry, I—" but instead of talking, sadness overcame me. My eyes dampened. My chin quivered. I could shake off the overwhelming fear that accompanied a nightwalker's scream, but the fear of losing my sister broke me.

# CHAPTER 11
# SIS

*Eldra was teaching us how not to go insane with two other people sharing our thoughts when I realized I hadn't started my period. Jake got all awkward, which I expected. Alexis laughed at me because I'm a virgin, while at the same time, she felt so jealous. Then she cleared her mind like she was hiding something. How? I want to hide stuff, too. —Kendra*

Acknowledging my fear kicked me into action. Or perhaps I just didn't dare let this moment go by. I reached forward and wrapped my arms around Sis. I hugged Sis and she hugged me back. I am sure my eyes dampened her blonde hair a little because a few strands stuck to my cheek. She'd started crying too. Her tears dampened my hoodie. She didn't smell like I remembered. She usually smelled like citrus, but instead, I breathed in the chemical aroma of hotel shampoo and lotion. I didn't feel any hesitation in her hug. It felt as if the other night had never happened; as if she had never recoiled from me.

Her strands of blonde hair peeled away from my cheek as we stepped apart. She brushed those strands behind her ear.

"Jake, what happened to you?" she asked. "Did you challenge Deadpool to a who's uglier contest?"

I smiled and then chuckled. I was with Sis again. Maybe, amidst all my hurricane-like turmoil, everything could be all right with the world, even if only for a moment. Or perhaps I was just in the eye of the storm.

"Yes. I won. Ryan Reynolds has been swearing about it for days," I answered, wishing, not for the first time, that my life was just a movie so I could rewrite the script. But this was real life, and there was nothing I could do to change my looks. In fact, I had chosen this myself.

"Seriously, though, Jake?" she asked, all humor gone.

"Long story," I answered. She started to protest, but I cut her off, "Which I will tell you as soon as you hug Kendra."

I stepped aside, and Sis's moist eyes looked behind me.

"Kendra," Sis said as she wiped her cheeks.

"Hey, Sis." Kendra smiled back and hugged Justine. I'd never heard Kendra call Justine "Sis" before. I wonder if that somehow transferred to her from me. "Are you OK?" Kendra asked in her ear.

Hugging Kendra, Sis lost her composure. "I don't think so," Sis sobbed out. She glanced at Alexis then at me. Her lower chin quivered. "I just don't know what to do. And Jake. What happened to Jake?"

I put my arm around her. I almost told her everything would be all right, but I didn't like lying to my sister, so I just kept my mouth shut.

"Oh, Kendra," Justine lifted her hand and touched Kendra's short hair as they ended their embrace. "I can't believe you cut your hair?"

"Not by choice," Kendra's eyes flickered to me and back.

Sis followed her eyes back to me.

"Jake, can you tell me what happened to you now?" Sis turned to Kendra. "Would you mind if I spoke to my brother in private?" She gave Kendra an apologetic look and pretty much disregarded Alexis all together.

The answer to her question came crashing into me like an oversized nose tackle who shed his block early. Nothing I ever did or said would be private again. The Trinity of Mind between Kendra, Alexis, and me, though currently dimmed, was permanent. Life was making a valiant effort to get me to lie to my sister.

"We're pretty much as private as we're ever going to get," I answered. "Let's go inside. We've got a lot to tell you."

Sis pursed her lips and blinked at me. Her eyes again flickered to Kendra and Alexis. She took a deep breath that lifted her shoulders and expanded her diaphragm enough to show that she didn't approve of either Kendra or Alexis sharing what should be a private conversation between brother and sister.

"Kendra, how come it feels like I am supposed to invite you into your own home?" Sis asked, eyeing Kendra with unexpected displeasure.

Kendra blinked and bit her lower lip, not answering. I didn't need her facial cues to feel through our dimmed connection how that question had stung Kendra. Had Kendra been wondering, as I have, whether coming home would ever be possible? Despite having just hugged, a new tension existed between the two friends. A tension very similar to the one starting between Sis and me.

"You two better not start fighting like you did in ninth grade over Tyler Earl," I reminded them.

"Hey," Sis shot back as she stepped across the threshold into Kendra's house. "You promised never to bring him up."

"Ugh. I'd forgotten about Tyler completely," Kendra added. "Why'd you . . ." she stopped as the magic in the house accepted her. She realized she hadn't been sure it would. She'd been worried. "Why'd you have to remind us?" she continued, trying to hide her pause.

I stepped aside to let Alexis go in first. But she stopped abruptly at the doorway, causing her baggy white shirt to flare, showing a little bit extra of her pale but smooth-skinned midriff.

"Kendra," Alexis called out with her soft, yet commanding voice. "Jake and I are invited in as well, are we not?" She had intended to ask Sis to invite us in, but since the magic accepted Kendra, she went ahead and asked her instead.

Kendra glanced back, the corners of her mouth lifted in a mischievous half-smile. I could almost hear her wondering if she could get away with not inviting Alexis in. Then she sighed, and her smile fell.

"You're both invited," she said, tossing her head to motion us inside. Her boy-cut hair barely moved despite her exaggerated head motion. I missed Kendra's long golden-brown hair and the way it used to move with her. Eldra had taught Kendra a spell to speed up her hair growth, which is why she didn't have stubble like me. She'd have her long locks back soon enough.

Alexis put her hand inside the door and stopped. Kendra's invitation had not been enough. When had her ability to invite people in stopped? At some point, this had stopped being Kendra's home. Kendra had wondered, feared this was the case, but when the magic had accepted her, she momentarily thought it wasn't. But now she knew. She gulped away her smile as she realized what this meant. The magic had accepted Kendra not because this was her home but because she had an open invitation to come home anytime. She was always invited, but this would never be her home again.

"Aren't they invited in, Justine?"

"Huh," Sis turned back around. "Uh, yes, come in," she looked confused.

The house accepted us. More importantly, the magic accepted us. In the real world, thresholds can't keep anything out, but magic is somewhat sentient, and it chooses not to work for those who are not invited in. With that thought, Alexis let a piece of information slip. The microbial organism that creates a vampire—often incorrectly termed a virus but is a multicellular, symbiotic protist—couldn't live more than a few hours without magic. It could handle a visit, but it would be holding its magical breath, so to speak. Kendra and I filed that knowledge away, with a mental reminder from Alexis that her grandfather would kill anyone who knew as much about vampires as we'd learned from her.

Kendra's front door led to what her mom called the pretty room. It had a matching couch and love seat, expensive-looking, and a fancy wooden chair. A curtain hung in the opening between the pretty room and the rest of the house, which was messier. Messier was a relative term. The messier part of Kendra's house was cleaner than my house had ever been.

Kendra sat in the love seat, which annoyed me because it forced me to choose between sitting with her or with Alexis. She subconsciously acted in ways that forced me to choose between the two. Being a month from turning eighteen, I had no intention of choosing between them, now or any time in the near future. I sat in the wooden chair.

Sis took one end of the couch while Alexis took the other. The couch had a high back and firm cushions, which seemed to fit Princess Alexis's posture perfectly.

I noticed a folded paper sitting on the end table. It had my stepdad's picture on it and his name, John Braen. His funeral program. I quickly glanced away.

"Jake, what happened to you?" Sis asked for the third time.

"You really want to know?" I asked, but it was more of a general question. Did she really want to hear my story? Just hearing it would make her more involved and she knew that.

"Yes," Sis replied with a hesitation that contradicted her answer.

"I got in a fight. You should see the other guys," I laughed. But the joke also gave her one last chance to change the subject and avoid getting more involved.

"Ha, ha!" Sis cut back, not amused. She blinked her green eyes and pursed her lips. "Did the, uh, you know," she paused, "the magic you use," she stopped again, "do this to you?"

I glanced at Alexis, not sure how to answer. She just smiled at me. *Should I really tell her everything,* I tried to ask Alexis, but she annoyingly had cut herself off from our Trinity of Mind with her separation stone. *Fine,* I thought.

"Sort of. *I* did this to me."

"But what I saw you do . . . your magic, it was involved, right?" Sis seemed certain that my magic was to blame, not me.

"Do you remember the two men who came after us?"

"They weren't men. What were they?"

Alexis chimed in, "You already know *who* they were. You saw their fangs and pale skin."

Sis nodded and swallowed nervously but didn't respond.

"Sis, they are real. I fought their king and a few of his minions last Friday night," I explained. "And no, his minions are not as cute as Gru's."

Sis grinned. "So, they did this to you?"

"I did this to myself," I repeated. I waited for Sis to look at me. She did, but then looked quickly away. Oops. I'd forgotten that I was too ugly to look at during a conversation. "I was out of magic, and it turns out I can convert matter to energy and the only matter available to me just happened to be my own. I sort of used up a bunch of my skin and muscle in the fight."

Sis nodded as if she understood, but her green eyes refused to meet mine. The way she looked down and to the left suggested she didn't really understand. She sat there quiet for some time. None of us interrupted her.

Sis turned to Kendra. "I know I told you that you should date my brother, but now I am not sure it's safe. Maybe you shouldn't."

Kendra looked at Sis with wide eyes. Then a huge smile cracked the seriousness of the moment.

"There is already too much between us," Kendra giggled. "We—"

"Kendra," Sis interrupted. "If you saw what I saw Jake do . . ."

Kendra sighed and stretched one hand toward Sis, her palm up.

"I *have* seen what he can do," Kendra responded, then whispered under her breath, "*Fyr leoht.*" A small flame flickered to life above Kendra's hand. "I can do it, too."

Sis twitched and slid back. She recoiled from Kendra, similar to how she had recoiled from me. Sis gulped and pulled her hair behind her ears. Kendra closed her hand, and the one-inch flame disappeared.

Sis glanced at me accusingly, as if this were my fault. What, did she think I had infected Kendra with a disease?

"Hey, she could use magic before I could," I defended, not hesitating to throw Kendra under the bus because I needed Sis to keep being Sis to me.

Kendra nodded, confirming my statement.

"Remember the end of last school year when I thought I had a fever for four days?" Kendra asked. "Mom took my temperature and it was completely normal, so she thought I was faking."

Sis thought about it for a moment. "Was that when your mom accused you of trying to dodge your geometry exam?"

"Yep," Kendra answered. "You were dating Jason and caught him kissing Heather."

"Ugh." Sis frowned. "First Jake reminds me of Tyler, and now you remind me of Jason."

"Well, Jason had you so sad and angry that I came over to cheer you up," Kendra continued. "I just wanted you to be happy again."

Sis smiled. "I remember. You pulled off the best cheering up job in the history of the world. I . . ." Sis stopped, suddenly aware of what Kendra was going to say next.

"That was the first time I used magic. That warmth that made me think I had a fever, well, it warmed my happiness up like a fleece blanket. I willed that *blanket* onto you that night, and it worked. Eldra says I have a way with emotions."

"Who's Eldra?" Sis asked.

"There's so much to tell you," I cut in.

"You should show her," Alexis suggested. Her fake blue eyes caught me off guard. Despite her blue contacts, the blue didn't look uniform.

"Show her? How?" I asked.

"Blood memories," Alexis answered. Despite her contacts, I detected the change in her eyes, which turned black with red stripes. She was fighting off a wave of hunger, probably brought on by talking about blood.

"But Sis doesn't have any magic," I argued.

"Blood memories can be seen by relatives with the simplest of magic. Justine is your sister. She will see the memory."

"Wait," Sis cut in. "I don't like the sound of blood memories. Kendra, can't you just give me the cliff notes version like usual?"

Kendra started talking fast. "Jake, Lexy, and I fought the Vampire King, a bunch of his minion vampires, a few flesh-eating obsidian creatures—part grim-reaper, part banshee—called nightwalkers, and an old druid couple under vampire control. Jake joined our three minds permanently, so we will forever share each other's thoughts. Jake used his skin and muscles as magic fuel for a spell that we used to kill all the nightwalkers and vampires, except Lexy's mom and the Vampire King. Then he helped Lexy and her mom overpower and take control of the Vampire King. Only one of the old druids survived. Eldra. When the vampire controlling her died, his control faded, and she is now on our side, mentoring us."

I jumped in, trying to talk as fast as Kendra. "You forgot to mention that O'Brien shot me to get Caradoc's blood transfused into me, kicking off my druid powers. He pretended to be a nurse, gave me a spell that faked my death, and stole me from the morgue. Then he taught me to use magic. We went to my own funeral, then nearly died fighting a nightwalker. We recovered at Lexy's until we rushed into hiding at a cabin in Bear Lake when what Kendra just told you happened."

"Kendra is still faster," Sis confirmed. "She wins again."

Kendra could speak faster than most auctioneers. We always used to try to beat her and never could.

"Give me a second to let the," Sis made quotes with her fingers, "'you're so full of crap' thoughts go away." She closed her eyes and took a deep breath, trying to take this all in. It would be hard. She fought off the moisture in her eyes, trying not to lose her composure again since she had just teared up a few minutes ago while hugging Kendra.

"Also, some voodoo witches attacked us last night. We don't know why they are involved, yet," Kendra added, interrupting Sis's breathing.

"Oh. And Mr. Espinoza is now a vampire," I dropped that bomb like it was an afterthought.

"I am supposed to go to his funeral on Saturday," Justine sounded confused. "My third in two weeks."

Luiz and Alexis had filled me in about how Mr. Espinoza and Alexis had orchestrated his death. He'd returned home Sunday, while I was still in a coma. He *died* that night. At least he lay in bed, stiff and cold. Luiz calmed his mother, prevented her from calling 911, and instead called the mortuary. Alexis used her allure on a mortician, who picked up Mr. Espinoza and returned him to Lexy's mansion. Luiz's mom was a mess, and Luiz had to keep fake crying for his mom's sake.

The room stayed silent for what seemed like an hour, but I checked my phone and only two minutes had passed. The three of us waited for Sis to absorb everything we'd just shoved at her.

Lexy's lips seemed pursed with worry, and her eyes remained fixed on Sis. Her chin-length hair emphasized her face, which is probably why seeing her fake blue eyes caught me off guard again.

"Is Luiz OK?" Sis asked, her voice soft with legitimate concern.

"I think so. Did you know his dad had lung cancer?" I asked. "Luiz seems happier than he used to be. His dad had been days from death, but now he'll live forever."

"Or will he *un*live forever?" Kendra quipped, sounding like Luiz. And Justine almost cracked a grin, but then her chin wavered. Her grin faded before it started, and she started crying.

"Vampires are not undead," Alexis rolled her hungry eyes.

"I stole that joke from Luiz," Kendra defended.

Sis ignored them. She didn't seem to be absorbing the cliff notes version very well.

Kendra stood up and stepped over to the couch and sat between Sis and Alexis. She wrapped an arm around Sis and leaned her head on her shoulder and kissed her cheek.

Suddenly a memory hit me, and I started laughing. "Practice. I remember now." I grinned, glancing between Kendra and Sis. Suddenly Sis's embarrassment dimple became her most prominent feature.

"I'm so sorry, Kendra," Sis said the words despite half crying and half laughing. "I didn't mean to tell him."

"So, how does a girl get in on this practice?" Alexis grinned mischievously. "Or is this just a best-friend-only thing?"

Sis's eyes widened and her mouth sort of just hung open.

"You're both only practicing on me, now," I cut in smiling. Only neither of them laughed. In fact, Sis scowled and glanced between Kendra and Alexis. Now that I'd said it, I could see how it wasn't funny.

"So, uh . . ." I searched for anything to break the awkward silence, "Mom will be fine. We know she didn't do it. The lawyer will get her off because there won't be any evidence," I assured Sis.

Alexis glanced at me and pursed her lips. I sensed a lack of certainty seep through our dimmed connection, which concerned me. I felt uncertain too, but I didn't want to seem uncertain in front of Sis.

We heard a noise come from the kitchen.

"Mom!" Kendra shouted and jumped up and ran through the curtained entryway.

Justine, Alexis, and I remained seated in the pretty room as Kendra celebrated seeing her mom for the first time in days. We listened awkwardly as they caught up. We didn't talk. Instead, we sat quietly. Time ticked by slowly. I was almost grateful when a hard knock at the front door echoed through the formal room.

Lexy's alert level hit def-con four somewhere between the first and the second knock. Fast but graceful, she stood and pulled a rune-covered blade from somewhere under her billowing white shirt. She held the knife behind her back as she approached the front door.

"Who could that be?" Kendra asked, as she parted the curtains from the kitchen to the pretty room and headed for the door. She froze, seeing Alexis holding her blade. She could probably sense the magic that I'd just absorbed, too.

"Positions," Alexis commanded, like the princess she was.

Kendra stepped between Alexis and the front door. I stood and hurried over to cover Alexis's rear. It was probably the wrong time to realize that this was the first time I'd covered Alexis's rear while she wore jeans. She had fleur-de-lis-stitched pockets. It was the stitching on her pockets I noticed. I promise.

Kendra formed a protective containment while I gripped the pebbles that I now kept in my front pocket. I powered up a bullet-protecting spell and spread it over all our clothing.

The knock came again. Five rapid beats that seemed to shake the house. It could be anyone out there. The knocking had been a solid pounding, not friendly at all, so it definitely wasn't just one of Kendra's friends or a neighbor just popping in for a visit. This was a serious, no-nonsense knock. I briefly thought of Keagan. Had he tracked us down? But it couldn't be him, not in the middle of the day. What about Stick Witch and Voodoo Whoopi—could it be them?

I cursed under my breath because this new, blood-red front door didn't have a peephole. The old door had had one.

Kendra's dad volunteered as one of the local leaders at her church. The Elder's Quorum President. The church has weird titles for some of their positions. O'Brien had once told me that a religious leader had power. I hoped Kendra's dad had blessed their house, and if so, that that blessing made this house safer—perhaps strengthening its threshold. I stretched my magical senses past the thick threshold, which pulsed as I crossed it. It was far stronger than the threshold at Lexy's mansion.

I stretched my senses to the porch, where my magic quickly detected two human-shaped figures. Both men.

Kendra and Alexis tapped their separation stones, and our minds once again became one. Kendra lifted her hand slowly and grabbed the doorknob, turning it ever so slightly, as if trying to hide the sound from whoever had just knocked.

The bright midday sun stood high in the sky. How bad could daytime visitors be?

The new doorknob didn't even click as Kendra turned it. She gave us one more questioning glance then jerked the door open.

# CHAPTER 12
# VISITORS

*The Trinity of Mind has significant benefits beyond tormenting Jake and Kendra with my life experiences. They can feel when I desire blood. If I lose myself in the Trinity of Mind and become one with them, then my hunger is basically only one-third as strong. —Alexis*

Two police officers stood just outside. The one on the left had a manila envelope in his hand, while the one on the right had a wallet open, displaying a badge. Behind them, the blue, late summer sky hardly held a cloud. The air felt warm. The leaves fluttered from a light breeze on the few visible trees. The midday light lit up the world outside the door. Something about the officers darkened the day, and it didn't feel right to blame it on their dark blue uniforms.

My focus fixed on the officer on the right. A scar cut vertically above and below his right eye.

*I've seen Scarface before,* I shared with Kendra and Alexis. *Twice.* Before my untimely yet very fake demise, Scarface had shown up wearing a Forest Ranger uniform the day Sis and I went wakeboarding with Dylan. He'd also been dressed as a cop at the hospital. Whatever he'd said to Mom, she'd come back into the hospital room in a fury. *I don't know who this man is, but I know he isn't any more of a cop than O'Brien was FBI,* I added.

Scarface had to be forty-something. A hint of gray lined the sides of his hair. His hard face reminded me of O'Brien, except if his and O'Brien's hard faces collided, I wasn't so sure that it wouldn't be O'Brien's that would break. His badge read Officer C. J. Connelly, but the only part of that name that was even close to accurate was the first syllable of the last name.

Alexis tried to read Officer Connelly's mind but ran into a brick wall that surprisingly wasn't powered by magic, just by mental toughness.

A *Skull Shadow,* Alexis thought. *They are trained to have closed-off minds.*

She exposed what she knew of the Skull Shadows with us. They were a secret society made up of military members that split away from the Skull and Bones. Over the past half-century, Skull Shadows became mercenaries, doing work other secret societies couldn't do on their own. Skull Shadows handled all issues too sensitive for the average Skull and Bones members to know about.

*They have ties to almost every secret society. Even my grandfather answers when they call.*

*We know the other cop,* Kendra and I added simultaneously. We let our memories of Officer Weekes flow into Alexis. He'd been a cop in West Jordan for years. He'd come to school a few times and presented about drugs. His youngest son Mike—yes, the one I punched—started at quarterback for West Jordan High. What was Officer Weekes doing hanging out with a Skull Shadow?

"Is Justine Bennett here?" Officer Weekes asked.

I glanced over at my sister, who still sat on the couch. She blinked her eyes nervously. I didn't like how he used her whole name. He knew Justine. Sis and I had sat at his dinner table with him and Mike on a few occasions. With his son starting as quarterback, he'd had the whole football team at his house after the season ended last year.

"Why do you ask?" Alexis demanded, allowing her vampire allure to exude out in her soft voice.

"We have a warrant to take Justine Bennett into custody. Is Mrs. Duncan in?"

"Mrs. Duncan is occupied," Alexis's voice came out with an added edge.

Officer Connelly reached out with one hand and grabbed Kendra's upper arm, "Step aside so we can come in and do our job."

"Get your hands off of Kendra," Alexis's voice grated as she spoke, and her command dripped with her allure, "or I will demand that Officer Weekes charge you with assault of a minor."

Officer Connelly blinked and took a second look at Alexis. His eyes widened as he dropped Kendra's arm.

Officer Weekes glanced nervously at his scarred partner. "It might be best if you don't make physical contact."

"Show me the warrant," Alexis commanded again. She pulled out her phone as the officer removed the warrant from a manila envelope.

*It looks official,* Kendra thought. The warrant had a nice, official seal and a judge's signature. I had no doubt of its authenticity. If he was a Skull Shadow, he had the resources to get a very real arrest warrant.

"Mr. Brandt?" Alexis spoke into her phone. "I have at least one police officer here," she grinned mischievously at scar eye guy, "with a warrant for a minor." Alexis listened for a second. I heard the other side of the conversation through Lexy's mind. "Yes. I can have them show me the warrant again." She turned to Officer Weekes. "Would you mind showing us the warrant again?" Alexis's voice shifted from demanding and harsh to the soft urging of a beloved daughter, as if she were the perfect child no one could say no to.

Officer Weekes held up the warrant.

Click. Alexis snapped a picture of it with her phone. With a few taps to her screen, she forwarded the picture to Mr. Brandt.

"Mr. Brandt is the family lawyer," Alexis explained, with a smile. "Would you mind waiting for him to examine the validity of the warrant?"

"Just step aside," the scar-eyed man growled and started forward again, but Officer Weekes put a hand on his chest, stopping him. Fake Officer Connelly looked down at the hand with fury in his eyes, and if I didn't know better, Officer Weekes was in danger of losing his hand.

Officer Weekes turned back to us and spoke slowly and kindly, "I think we can give the young lady and her lawyer a minute. As long as Justine stays right there on the couch." Even though he couldn't see Justine, he nodded toward his right as if looking through the exterior wall into the pretty room.

Justine flinched at the sound of her name.

*He can't see Justine from there, can he?* I wondered. *How did he guess where she's sitting?*

*He knows because the moment he mentioned Justine's name, both of you glanced at her,* Alexis reprimanded.

"Yes, Justine is here," Alexis answered Mr. Brandt. "No, she never ran away. She is right here." Another pause. "Yes, we are at Kendra's house." Pause. "Mrs. Duncan is in the kitchen." Pause. "It will be my pleasure." Alexis turned to me. "Jacob, go get Mrs. Duncan."

I turned and walked through the curtain and into the kitchen. The kitchen looked a few decades old, with Formica counters and oak cabinets, and a linoleum floor. The sun brightened the kitchen from a large window that hung over the double sink, which was full of dishes.

Mrs. Duncan stood at the kitchen island making sandwiches. Not for the first time, I wondered if Kendra had inherited any of her father's features. Kendra's mother was a thin, healthy woman who looked pretty much identical to Kendra, except for deep wrinkles at the corners of her eyes and around her mouth that seemed to be in a permanent half-smile. Her hair, while the same healthy golden brown as Kendra's, was shorter—well, shorter than Kendra's hair used to be. She had what I would call a mom hairdo. She was tending to three plates with a single sandwich on each and one plate with two sandwiches. Had Kendra told her mom to make two for me? My mouth watered just seeing them, but lunch would be delayed. My sister was more important than food.

"Can you come to the door?" I asked.

Mrs. Duncan glanced up, noticing me for the first time. I suddenly remembered that she didn't know I was Jacob Stevens. I didn't look anything like the Jacob Stevens she remembered. He had been two hundred pounds of muscle, but now I was lucky to be a buck fifty soaking wet. I also didn't have much for hair or eyebrows. The flaky texture of my skin would hide any resemblance the bone structure of my face offered.

Through Alexis's control of Mrs. Duncan, I felt the questions surface in her motherly mind. She wanted to know who I was, what had happened to me, and how I knew Kendra. Fortunately, a nudge from Alexis to ignore me stifled her questions.

"Is someone at the door?" she muttered more to herself than to me. She stepped around me as if I didn't exist. Perhaps Alexis's suggestion to ignore me had been more powerful than just a nudge.

I followed Mrs. Duncan back through the curtain. Alexis and Kendra's bodies held enough magic that I could see it glowing inside them. I glanced at Sis, who had her hands over her face. She was crying in worry. I walked over and sat next to her and put my arm around her shoulder.

"She's here," Alexis spoke into the phone. "Of course, I can put you on speaker." Alexis touched her phone's screen and Mr. Brandt's voice echoed from the phone's surprisingly loud speaker.

"Mrs. Duncan?" Mr. Brandt asked. His nasal voice had a flatness to it that made him sound as bored as Ferris Bueler's economics teacher.

"This is Mrs. Duncan," Kendra's mom replied. Her voice seemed a little nervous. Alexis could have calmed her down and brought her into a state of indifference, but it seemed that Alexis controlled her passively—only using her control to steer Kendra's mother when the situation required it.

"Mrs. Duncan, is the minor Justine Bennett currently under your supervision?"

"Yes."

"Has she ever run away?" Mr. Brandt asked.

"Of course not," Mrs. Duncan responded, confused. She adjusted the bottom of her blouse nervously.

"Officers Weekes and Connelly," Mr. Brandt addressed them through the phone. "Thank you for your time and your service, but this warrant is not valid."

"Of course it's valid," Officer Connelly shot back, his voice gruff and angry.

"Really?" Mr. Brandt challenged. "The last known location of Justine is listed as unknown, and the reason for taking Justine into custody states: 'Justine Bennett has left the custody of the person or agency vested by the court with legal custody and guardianship without permission.' Both fields are mistakes. Justine clearly did not leave the custody of her mother without her permission. Is it not true, Officers Weekes and Connelly, that you arrested her mother?"

"I am afraid we can't answer that," Officer Weekes replied.

"No need to answer. I am also Annie Stevens's lawyer. I am on my way to meet with her. Also, were you aware that Annie Stevens has Mr. and Mrs. Duncan listed as Justine's guardians, should anything happen to her?"

Officer Weekes chuckled just a little, then glanced at his partner whose lower jaw clenched so tightly we could see his muscles twitching near his cheekbones.

Mr. Brandt continued speaking through the phone. "It sounds like the minor Justine Bennett didn't flee the custody of her legal guardian. She's sitting right there in the house with her legally designated alternate guardian. I am calling Judge McGhie right now about this warrant. I probably won't file a complaint against those who provided mistaken information leading to this less-than-valid warrant." Mr. Brandt's voice paused. "Unless I find out that it wasn't a mistake. Surely the judge was not intentionally provided false information?"

Officer Connelly turned his icy glare toward his counterpart, demanding he do something. Officer Weekes sighed. "Surely you are not talking on the phone while driving, Mr. Brandt?" Officer Weekes challenged back feebly.

"You mean in the back of my limo?" Mr. Brandt cut back. "I think you and Officer Connelly better be going before I change my mind about filing a complaint."

"Step aside," Officer Connelly demanded. "We are going to take her in. We can clear this up at the precinct." He grabbed Kendra's arm again and moved her out of the doorway. Officer Weekes put a hand on his shoulder, but he shrugged it off.

I raised the arm that wasn't around Sis and pointed it at Officer Connelly, hitting him with a blast of magic wind. Both Alexis's chin-length hair and Kendra's boy-cut hair raised with the wind. The air cycloned around the pretty room. The curtain to the kitchen made noise as it fluttered nearly horizontal, as if an American flag in the wind. The *Ensign* magazine on a side table next to the love seat flipped open. A picture depicting the second coming of Christ fluttered on the wall, and across from it, a family picture fell to the ground.

The magic caught Officer Connelly off guard. The force drove him back out the front door. I dropped my hand, ending the magic-propelled wind.

Alexis jumped to fill the doorway, her face fierce and glaring at Officer Connelly. She pointed the phone screen at him as if it were a gun.

Mr. Brandt shouted through the phone's speaker, "Now, I am not only filing a complaint, but I'll be filing an assault charge against Officer Connelly!"

I wrapped both my arms around Sis and rubbed her back as she stared at the door, confused.

"Sounds like we'll be going," Officer Weekes spoke. He took a few steps back, shaking his head, as confused about what just happened as Sis was.

I felt a wave of relief that wasn't wholly my own, but Kendra's and Lexy's, too.

"Goodbye, then," Alexis said, not waiting for them to respond before shutting the door in their faces.

"It is all going to be OK," I whispered into Sis's ear. I shouldn't have said that. I never lied to my sister. Why had I started now?

# CHAPTER 13
# ELDRA

Alexis and Kendra are making it more awkward for me all the time. Alexis doesn't dress modestly, and I noticed her cleavage. Kendra mentally lashed out at me while simultaneously jealous that Lexy has a bigger cup size. Then Alexis, who wanted me to look at her chest moments earlier, snapped at me for looking and blamed me, saying their fight was all my fault. I just want to forget all this and go back to playing football and running over linebackers like I used to. —Jake

It didn't feel right leaving Sis, even if she was with Kendra's parents, but we were late, and Eldra would not be happy. We said our goodbyes and started the half-hour drive back to Lexy's mansion. Team voodoo nearly had their way with us last night, and coach Eldra wanted us to work on our magic in case we faced them again.

No more than five minutes into the ride, I fell asleep again. Maybe it was because the car ride was a bit longer, but this time I dreamed.

       🔯    🔯    🔯

I saw two dark figures walking through a dark cave. I could only see hints of their silhouettes, enough to know there were two of them but nothing else. I tried to follow them, but a dog—no, a coyote—jumped in my path. It howled and then disappeared.

I heard a voice say, "The ice melted. Their dreamwalk ended. You are needed."

I turned my head back and forth, trying to find the source of the voice but saw no one in the dark cave. Just walls of rock and dirt and damp earth under my bare feet. Why was I in a cave and only wearing boxers?

A hand touched my shoulder.

"Have they changed with the seasons?" The voice whispered the question into my ear with a distinct Native American accent. I twisted around to see whose hand touched my shoulder.

Lexy hit the brakes and swung the car into the garage, jolting me awake, cutting the dream short. I wasn't sure what the dream meant. It didn't involve my biological father, but it still felt like more than a dream.

Neither Kendra nor Lexy were in my head, so they missed out on this vignette of a dream. I was sure they'd catch up later.

By the time I shook off the grogginess and exited the car, Kendra and Alexis stood at the door to the house, waiting on me. Alexis's red eyes indicated she'd removed her contacts. I followed them inside, and we made our way down the hallway. The hallway to the garage had a wooden floor and two modern, yet dark, concept paintings: one all black with swirls around an eye; the other red-and-black line art that could be either a red-outlined vase or two women's faces with blood spilling from their necks to their breasts. I hadn't noticed the second possibility until just now.

I remembered standing in this hall the previous week, talking to Alexis, who held a thin red cape around her otherwise naked body. Thankfully, Kendra's separation stone was in full force. I glared at Alexis as she continued down the hallway. Why had she considered Keagan's offer! I clenched my right fist and felt my fingernails dig into my skin.

We turned a corner and headed to the library. The library consisted of a square room, and all four walls had built-in, floor-to-ceiling shelves of books, even above the door. The ceiling was easily ten feet high. The old encyclopedia set I had used to look up the chemical formula of the crystals we had enchanted took up the length of one shelf on the left wall. The center of the library had six chairs next to small tables, all sitting on a square, fifteen-foot, decorative floor rug. Perhaps this is what a designer would call *feng shui*.

Eldra sat in one of the high-backed, brown leather chairs, knitting a reddish, pinkish something. I couldn't tell what. Her fingers moved with the needle at a speed that looked magical but wasn't. I can see magic.

"Nice thneed," Kendra offered with a cautious, half-grin. I felt her awkwardness exude into me. Joking with the aged woman a few days after killing her husband felt awkward. Who'd have guessed?

To our surprise, Eldra chortled so hard she started coughing. At her age, it didn't look like she could possibly survive such a fit, but eventually, she got her breath under control. She calmed herself and set aside her knitting needle.

"Unfortunately, my thneed is not a thing that anyone needs," she quipped back. "Shut the door, please," she requested of me; then she continued, "I never have been good with a needle. I blame my mother for never teaching me.

Seeing how fast her fingers moved, I was left wondering what she considered *good with a needle* to be.

"Why didn't she teach you?" Kendra continued.

Eldra thinned her wrinkle-outlined eyes. Kendra should have been satisfied with one joke because whatever she had just stepped in, it brought out Eldra's hateful eyes in full force.

"The bloody cholera got mum in 1831," Eldra spat. A thick British accent slipped into her words. "The crewmen tossed her corpse overboard with a dozen others without so much as a ceremony. I arrived at Ellis Island alone." Eldra's eyes reveled in her hate for Kendra. The old druid enjoyed sharing a truth so heart-wrenching that Kendra had no choice but to tremble into tears.

The room silenced. I glanced from Eldra to Kendra before shrugging to Alexis. Someone had to interrupt the sudden onset of awkward silence. Might as well be me.

"We're here, as promised."

"You are late!" Eldra's voice struck like a cobra on her last syllable.

"So?" I didn't apologize. "We had to prevent my sister from being falsely accused and joining my mom in prison," I added, reminding her that while she had tragedies in her past, I had tragedies happening right now. I tried to stare down her hateful eyes, but she just turned them away, ignoring me. How did she look away and still win my eye challenge? Annoying.

"How about you show me how to use that lightning spell that you pounded us with the other day," I suggested.

Her lightning spell was a marvel to behold. A rune on her staff had lit up with blue light and then the lightning had shot at us with enough strength to strain our containment. A spell like that could come in handy.

"How about we start with learning how to check whether you three are completely still here. Last night, a soulwisp escaped this house's mantel, and I want to know whose soul the caplatas have grabbed a piece of." Her eyes returned to Kendra, but the hate had been replaced with determination. "Let's start with our joking little Dr. Seuss here. Did you have any strange dreams last night?"

As my dream came rushing back to me, Kendra answered, "I don't remember any dreams, but what's a caplata and a soulwisp?"

"It wasn't Kendra," I defended her. "It was me."

Eldra's eyes turned to mine, and I almost wished I hadn't spoken. Her irises turned pure white and the glowing magic in them burned into me.

I shuddered as her stare penetrated me, exposing everything about me—like she could see through me and took in my entire existence in a second. Having recently joined minds with two females, I'd felt exposed enough, but at least they had to search my mind and memories or listen to my thoughts to get to know me. Whatever magic Eldra used, it exposed my entire existence to her in a brief second. I felt violated.

Then it was over.

Her eyes widened, and her jaw dropped, stretching the wrinkles at the corner of her mouth. "Magic in a dream," she whispered. "It can't be you."

"What do you mean by," I made quote symbols with my fingers, "'It can't be you'?"

Repeating her own words back to her in a question startled her. She shook her head, which made her wrinkly skin wobble, then gathered herself. Alexis hadn't wanted Eldra to know I was a protector, and I had a feeling the old druid had just found out. Now, if only I could find out what a protector was.

"Well, it seems your spirit is quite intact." She intentionally ignored my question. "But you got lucky. You can't keep using the same magic tricks and expect to survive long. Blowing up gas tanks has worked twice for you now. I wouldn't suggest trying it again. It probably only worked the second time because you were in a dream."

"How about lightning then?"

"No," Alexis cut in. "Not lightning. Teach them daylight."

"Agreed," Eldra nodded. "Shadow blades are best defeated by daylight. Training has officially begun?" Eldra ventured, looking at Alexis as if waiting for her to acquiesce. Alexis nodded, and a shiver of magic rippled in the air. Eldra nodded back and then pursed her lips in a way that reminded me of my mom when I got in trouble.

"We'll practice casting daylight." Eldra continued. "But not here. I want you to cast it in complete and utter darkness. Anyone know a place nearby that is utterly dark?"

"There is a cave by Bear Lake where they turn off the lights . . ." Kendra started, then stopped. She followed Eldra's eyes to Lexy's, which had widened around her fearfully white pupils. The library started to smell musty, and no, it wasn't the books. I wanted to leave.

"Yes. A cave," Alexis recovered. "There are closer caves than the one in Bear Lake. I know of a cave near the druid grove that no one else knows about. It is closer than driving to Bear Lake."

Eldra whistled loud and long, and the hate had returned to her eyes, only her eyes fixed unexpectedly on Alexis.

"So, you lied. You didn't tell them," Eldra hissed. "I thought as much."

"He does not have any of them enthralled yet," Alexis spoke, and I could see the instant moistness in her eyes. She looked more vulnerable than I had ever seen her. Part of it was the billowing white shirt she wore. She took strength from her usual black leather outfits, as if her leather protected not only her skin but her emotions, too. The confidence her leather outfit gave her was noticeably absent.

"Lead the way!" Eldra spat at Alexis.

A tear dropped from Lexy's cheek, and her eyes glanced to mine, then down. "They will hate me," she whispered. Then she gulped.

"Eldra," I shouted the aged druidess's name.

"Save your shouting," Eldra grimaced. "You'll be doing plenty of it shortly."

"Do not make me do this!" Alexis stammered.

I hadn't known Alexis very long, but with the Trinity of Mind, I felt I knew her deeply. I'd never seen a side of her this emotionally vulnerable.

"You will do this," Eldra demanded. "You have made an oath of obedience during training to your *magister*." The last word came out with a very clear Old English accent.

I wanted to ask what a *magister* was, but I couldn't stop glancing from Alexis to Eldra, wondering what was going on between them. Eldra just turned and started walking.

"Come, children," she beckoned, her words dripping with condescension that reached all of us, despite being directed at Alexis. "Lexy's bedchamber *is* a cave."

Alexis hesitated then followed reluctantly behind Eldra.

*Any clue why Alexis doesn't want us to see her bedchamber?* Kendra asked. I didn't have any more of an idea than she did, which left Kendra wishing Alexis would turn off her separation stone.

Alexis had offered to show me her bedchamber once. Had I taken her up on the offer, she'd have led me straight there. I *did* want to see her room, even if I wasn't ready to do more in her room than just see it. It didn't exactly make sense that she didn't want me to see it now. What had changed since then? Why would she not want me to see it now?

*Good thing you didn't take her up on that offer,* Kendra scolded me mentally. She followed it up with a few nasty names for Alexis, but her outburst faded more quickly than usual. She felt protective of Lexy and resentful toward Eldra. Her mental abuse quickly turned Eldra's way.

What did it mean that Kendra felt defensive of Lexy? We explored the question together for a few seconds, but neither of us came to a conclusion.

Eldra took the hallway that led to the garage, but before we reached the garage, she turned into a small square room; a sitting room, with nothing but four chairs, one in each corner. A tall bookshelf rose to the ceiling between two of the chairs.

*A receiving room,* Kendra explained. *You know, for receiving guests.*

Eldra walked directly to the bookshelf, reached behind it, and pulled. The bookshelf moved easily from the wall, revealing a hidden closet. The closet had no floor. A slide—old-school, metal-playground style—descended into the darkness. We could either take the slide or climb down the slide's ladder.

"You have a slide to your room?" I blinked into the darkness, trying to see how far the slide led.

"I'm jealous!" Kendra added, ignoring Alexis's obvious emotional turmoil.

"And a ladder," Eldra gestured to the ladders top, black-steel rung, "but I prefer the slide." Eldra smiled, also oblivious to Alexis's whimpering. "Follow me," she ordered. Then as if she were a little girl, she sat on the slide and pushed off, letting out a rough, gargled squeal.

"Did she just shout *weeee* or was that a death cry?"I mocked, wondering, not for the first time, how Eldra could change emotions so quickly.

"That's the oldest *weeee* I've ever heard," Kendra answered.

I sat down on the slide.

*Let's make a train,* Kendra thought, then sat behind me and wrapped her arms around me.

"Are you coming?" Kendra, to my surprise, asked Alexis.

*First defending Lexy and now inviting her to slide with us? Are you and Lexy becoming besties?* I teased.

*Doubtful,* Kendra responded, thinning her irritated blue eyes at me.

Despite the anxious displeasure that exuded from her, Alexis wrapped her arms around Kendra and the three of us slid down. It was a grade-school moment, except the slide was about thirty feet, so the ride lasted much longer than a grade-school slide.

I almost shouted *weeee* myself.

At the bottom, Eldra stood holding a candle. A real one.

"Never use magic unnecessarily," Eldra stated in answer to my raised eyebrow. Eldra's wrinkles cast odd shadows over her face, making her look like some evil witch. Alexis's almost all-white eyes reflected the candlelight's glow. Her fear seeped into my skin like a winter breeze.

*You can still feel her emotions,* Kendra looked wide-eyed at me, her blue eyes barely visible in the candlelight. Alexis had her separation stone on, but Kendra didn't. I tried not to think about the fact that I could also feel Kendra's emotions when she had her protection stone turned on, but of course, trying not to think about something meant I thought about it.

Kendra gasped.

I had hoped to keep that a secret longer. Still, I hadn't tried to keep it a secret. It was just that I had only thought about feeling their emotions when their separation stones were blocking out their thoughts.

*Alexis, your room rocks!* I thought, trying to change the subject.

*Alexis isn't listening in,* Kendra reminded me.

*I knew that. I just forgot to engage my vocal cords.*

"Engage my vocal cords." OK, Captain Piccard, Kendra teased. *You're such a geek.*

"Alexis, your room rocks!" I repeated out loud. *And it takes a geek to make that joke,* I countered to Kendra.

"This is only the hallway," Alexis replied in a nervous but monotone voice.

*You mean cavern-way? Any idea what we are walking into?* I asked Kendra.

*Ask Eldra?* she responded.

I took one look at Eldra. The candle lit her face mostly, but her wrinkles created a pattern of thin shadows that left her face demonic. *You ask her.*

Eldra turned away and walked down the tunnel.

*We'll know soon enough,* we both thought simultaneously, which usually would have made us smile, but not this time.

When the Vampire King had this mansion built, the plans included a manmade cave. Perhaps *man*made wasn't the right word. Or maybe it was. I didn't question Lexy's humanity, despite being half-dhampir. I did, however, question the humanity of her Vampire King grandfather and his minions. What about her mom, Carina? What about Luiz's dad? Did I consider either of them human?

*Luiz's dad is in Lexy's bedchamber,* Kendra remembered. *Alexis is staying in the room next to mine.*

*That's what changed.* I realized. *When Alexis had invited me to her bedchamber last week—Slut,* Kendra interrupted with an unfiltered thought that I tried to ignore—*she still slept down here alone. Now, Mr. Espinoza is staying down here.*

*Why does Eldra want to show us where Luiz's dad is staying?* Kendra asked.

*Why is Alexis scared and ashamed?* I answered with a question.

Kendra and I shared a sinking feeling, and it swept away any curiosity we had to see Alexis's room.

# CHAPTER 14
# BEDCHAMBER

*Alexis grew up unbelievably lonely. Once her mother fully turned, nobody loved her. At least, not real love. She wasn't literally alone, because there were always others around, but they didn't love her. I shouldn't be so mean to her. She's had enough meanness in her life. I just can't stop responding to her mental insults. We constantly shout mentally at each other. Jake hates it. The Trinity of Mind will connect us forever. I can't handle a forever fight. Besides, I like Alexis. A lot. It's just Jake that we fight about. What do we do about Jake? —Kendra*

K endra and I tried to prepare ourselves for Mr. Espinoza's sleeping form to shock us in some way. I tried to imagine his cold corpse on Alexis's bed. What could he look like that would be so bad? To not think about it, I started counting steps, because I liked to count when I wanted to control my thoughts.

We walked at a downward angle into the mountain under the house for about seventeen steps, which I roughly estimated to be about fifty feet.

The tunnel didn't look as much like a cave as it looked like a mine. The Rocky Mountains are mostly granite, and someone had cut through the sturdy rock to make this tunnel, leaving me to wonder how they made the walls so smooth. Had they used technology or magic or something else?

I stared at Alexis, trying to read her mind. I pushed at Alexis's separation stone as if it were a containment that I could poke a hole in. I felt the stone's magic falter slightly and a single thought slipped out where I pushed.

*What will they think of me when they see them?*

Kendra heard the thought too. Her mind did a nice little drill team dance, literally. *Left face,* she turned and focused on me.

*How did you just do that? Right face,* she turned and focused on Alexis. *When Alexis said "them," who did she mean?*

*Which are you more worried about? Who she meant by "them" or drill team starting on Monday?*

*Is drill team even an option in this new life?* she responded, and a homesick feeling flooded through her, dampening her eyes to a point just shy of tears. Despite the question, she clung to the slightest hope that drill team practice might still be possible.

We stopped at an oak door, hinged directly into the stone wall. The cave continued on into the darkness. No, the long iron handle didn't need a brass key, but if it had, I would have been worried a little dwarf would run out of some stairs and steal my golden egg.

*You're a geek, Sir Graham,* Kendra mocked me.

*That's twice now that you've made a joke only another geek could make,* I countered.

She knew geek stuff because I knew about geek stuff. How many times had she been staying over at my house, visiting my sister, and had watched Star Trek with me, or watched me play video games? She'd had a crush on me long before I noticed her as more than my sister's friend. She hadn't seen Star Trek or played video games with me because she liked them. She'd done it because she liked me. Hundreds of memories that we had both shared permanently merged. They would now forever be memories with both our points of view.

She looked into my eyes as we shared our memories.

We had only been joking because we knew we weren't ready for whatever bad stuff we were about to see when the oak door opened. We hadn't expected it to be a meaningful moment. I hadn't expected to explore the beginning of her crush and find it started when I was still scrawny; before I'd moved from geek to jeek.

Now, I was only a geek again. There was no *jock* side to me left to shift *geek* to *jeek*. I had coined the term *jeek* for myself and my three friends, Kevin, Ethan, and Luiz, because we were geeks who started playing sports. After we all played varsity football last year, we weren't geeks anymore. But we refused to identify with jocks. Becoming a jeek, a hybrid of both, was natural and effortless. Two of the jeeks, Kevin and Ethan, didn't even know I was alive. Was I betraying Kevin and Ethan?

Alexis grabbed the long iron handle on the door, then flashed her eyes at us. They were no longer white but had turned black with red lightning streaks extending into her sclera. Her canines extended to her bottom lips. I breathed in the thickened scent of honey that filled the cavern hallway. Shivers traveled up my spine to dance around my hair follicles. Alexis barely had control of her hunger. Her desire to feed overpowered her separation stone and flooded into me. Both Kendra's protection stone and my own warmed on our necks.

Alexis pulled on the door, and it swung open.

Kendra stood behind me and couldn't see into the door, but even still, she closed her eyes and waited, not wanting to look inside herself, preferring to see inside through my eyes. Eldra followed Alexis inside. I trailed behind them. Eldra's candle didn't show much. I could see the outline of a large king-sized bed and the shape of someone sleeping in it. Wait. Not just *one* someone. I counted multiple clumps.

Eldra tapped her staff on the floor and two candles flickered to life, adding to the dim yellow glow of the one in her hand. The candles orchestrated a shadow dance on the ceiling. The room had been carved straight into the granite mountain, as the cavern hallway had been. The ceiling curved into the walls, making the room appear as one continuous wall.

Two steps, also cut into the granite, led up to a dark-wood, four-poster bed. We faced the left corner of the foot of the bed. A crimson canopy draped from the four posts. Mr. Espinoza slept in the middle, with two thin forms sleeping on his left and one on his right. The black-and-red comforter partially covered the two women closest to him. Both the girl on the right and the first girl on the left, closest to Mr. Espinoza, had black hair. The second girl on the left, closest to us, looked ready to fall off the edge of the bed. She had blonde hair and lay on her stomach. An edge of the black sheet stuck out from the comforter to barely cover her from her lower back to her knees. Dried blood clung to her neck and wrists.

I heard a step behind me. I reached a hand back to stop Kendra from coming into the room. She pushed my hand away and looked in. Kendra's body stiffened, trying to avoid emotion as she scanned the room. I watched her eyes go from the bed to the far corner of the room. Two more girls slept in a reclined sofa chair, huddled together as if protectively, a dark blanket wrapped around them.

Alexis lowered her eyes, refusing to meet our eyes, and swallowed nervously.

Nobody said anything for at least a minute. The scent of blood called to Alexis. Her hunger growled its way through to me.

Kendra felt it, too. How could she bear the desire without feeding? Each time she licked her lips, which seemed often, I could see her extended canines.

"Tell me they aren't dead?" Kendra snapped, breaking the silence.

"Of course not," Alexis defended, still looking down.

Kendra breathed a sigh of relief, but that was the only outward evidence of her inner turmoil. Inside, her mind went crazy with unfiltered thoughts that mingled with mine. She considered killing Mr. Espinoza and Alexis in a dozen magical ways. Strangely, I did not. My thoughts froze.

"Mr. Espinoza, it seems, likes to play with his dinner." Eldra laughed bitterly. She eyed us like an angry grandma about to scold disobedient grandchildren. "Didn't you know? Surely you must have thought about this. These are to be his thralls. Miguel is not like Alexis. He is not a dhampir. He must feed daily to survive."

"There are seven. Two runaways, three homeless drug addicts, and two prostitutes," Alexis explained. "They are better off than they were," her voice came out soft and sincere. "I promise!"

"I only see five," I responded.

Kendra spotted two sets of naked feet that stuck out on the far side of the bed, and my eyes followed hers.

*Why hadn't I thought about this?* I wondered to myself. I sort of expected rage to swell up inside me, but it just didn't happen. My overwhelming desire to protect these girls didn't flare to life, either. If it had, I don't know what I would have done. Would I have killed Luiz's dad?

Alexis's shame rolled into Kendra and me.

Fury with Alexis shook Kendra, then turned on me because I didn't share her anger. She started a mental tirade and blasted me with unfiltered thoughts. My emotions dampened her anger. Alexis's vulnerable fear softened her anger, as well. After a few final, shouted thoughts, her fury changed focus and targeted Eldra instead of Alexis.

"OK, so what?" Kendra glared at Eldra. "We can't even practice casting sunlight in this room with Mr. Espinoza in here. You only brought us in here because you want us to hate Alexis for this," she shook her head. "You're," she hesitated, and words that I didn't think Kendra even knew echoed in her mind as unfiltered thoughts. She filtered those words out before speaking, "You're not very nice."

I expected Kendra to revel in anything that made Alexis suffer, but instead, she defended her. That was twice now. *Interesting.*

Eldra pursed her lips, and it appeared she was about to lash back when a red light flashed on the bedchamber wall, which grabbed her attention. Even Mr. Espinoza stirred.

"The doorbell," Lexy explained, her voice held an edge of confidence that was likely the result of us not hating her after seeing Mr. Espinoza and his future thralls. "We have an unexpected visitor."

"Permission to postpone—," Lexy started but was interrupted.

"Help me," a desperate woman's voice whispered. The woman on the floor at the far side of the bed sat up. She gripped the corner bedding enough to keep from collapsing. Her thin, pale hands trembled. She wasn't dressed. Her ribs stuck out under her small breasts. Her ratty blonde hair hung down in knots past her shoulders. She scratched at the discolored crooks of her elbows. Had Mr. Espinoza fed on the inside of her elbows? Usually, vampire saliva healed, hiding puncture wounds within a minute.

"I need . . ." she pleaded.

Her plea ignited me. I felt my protector magic flare to life. I willed my anger to life with it. A few seconds earlier, I had wondered if I could kill Mr. Espinoza. Now I knew. I could kill Mr. Espinoza to protect her. If she wanted my help, I stood ready to offer it. Magic flowed into me. Luiz's father or not, if she asked it, I'd do it.

"Help me," she repeated. "I just need one more," she mumbled. "Just one more." She adjusted her grip on the dark comforter at the corner of the bed and tugged it nervously. "Just one more. Please. I have money. I can trade."

The marks in the crooks of her elbow were needle marks. My need to protect the woman fizzled, as did my magic. The protector magic, which I was just learning to recognize separately from regular magic, stayed strong.

I didn't know fully what it meant to be a protector. I understood that she was a drug addict, but didn't she need to be protected? I asked the protector magic why. My breath caught as, unexpectedly, that protector magic proved its sentience and answered me with magic that wasn't mine; magic that I couldn't tap into at will.

The protector magic delivered visions to me of what would have been all seven women's short and terrible lives. Kendra shuddered as she experienced my visions with me. The younger of the two runaways would have died of exposure this winter. Two of the drug addicts would have died of an overdose within two years. The third would have lasted ten. One of the prostitutes would have died gruesomely at the hands of a patron, his only punishment an extra payment to an angry pimp. The other prostitute would have taken her own life after fifteen years of abysmal treatment. The last girl, the second runaway, would survive twelve terrible, schizophrenic years on the street, malnourished and homeless, before spending forty years in a mental hospital. The reason my protector magic didn't kick in is because these seven were already protected. As thralls, Mr. Espinoza would protect them. He would keep them alive. He'd free their various issues: addiction, mental illness, or despair. They had the potential to live to old age serving as his willing blood donors.

The sentient power on the other side of the protector magic disappeared. I breathed out, and chills caused by these visions started at my lower back and rose to my scalp. While the answer came in a vision, the answer was clear. Alexis had been honest. They were better off as thralls than they were before. I didn't want to believe they could be better off. That didn't jive with my religious beliefs. But I couldn't deny it.

In life, we don't always get to choose between good, better, or best. Sometimes, the only options are bad, worse, or worst. Maybe becoming a thrall was like choosing bad instead of worse or worst. Or maybe being a thrall wasn't good or bad, but instead was somewhere in between, like neutral or indifferent.

Mr. Espinoza sat up and seemed to either yawn or flex his fangs. He wasn't wearing a shirt, and his lightning red eyes proved he'd woken famished. A hint of attraction tingled from both Kendra and Alexis. Mr. Espinoza's vampire allure seemed to be in full force. A vampire's allure was supposed to affect everyone regardless of gender, but his didn't affect me. Honestly, his hairy chest grossed me out.

"*Discúlpame,*" he nodded at us. "Por favor. *Permítanme ayudarla.*"

"English, Miguel," Eldra spoke, smiling at him, his allure clearly affecting her as well.

Mr. Espinoza looked at Eldra and blinked. The red light flashed again on the wall.

"Never mind," Eldra frowned, obviously breaking out of the allure, "We have a visitor ringing the doorbell to attend to." She turned from the room, and staff in one hand and candle in the other, she strode out the door and down the cavern hall.

Both Kendra and I hesitated, morbid curiosity locking our feet in place as we watched. Mr. Espinoza beckoned to the drug addict, and without hesitation, she crawled up onto the bed with him. Her bony hips and legs looked even thinner than her arms and torso.

"Come!" Eldra called back to us. "Alexis, training is postponed" I felt a hint of magic release with those words. Alexis's hips swayed differently as she walked away. She raised her shoulders and lifted her head. I hadn't noticed before, but her posture had been that of a depressed teenager as we came down into the tunnel, but after Eldra announced the training postponement, she stood tall and regal, a full-blown princess again.

# CHAPTER 15
# SERVANTS

*The empty box in my mind is working. If I think about the box, Jake thinks I have secrets hiding in there. They are hiding outside the box, but if he keeps prying at the box instead of rummaging around my mind, he won't learn the things that could get him killed. Kendra does not pry like Jake does. She is trying not to hate me. She is far more complicated than I realized. She is not just a brainless, teenage girl on a drill team. I've never had a friend. Is she my first? —Alexis*

"**H**e is waiting in the parlor. He says his name is Porter," Carolyn spoke as we walked. She kept her eyes lowered, avoiding Lexy's face. Carolyn wore her usual servant's outfit, complete with bodice and apron over a dress. No bonnet, though. "He says he must speak with the Princess of the New World."

Kendra and I walked on either side of Princess Alexis. The hallways looked as rich as the rest of the house, lined with paintings and other expensive decorations. Eldra hadn't followed us.

"Did he use that title? Did he actually call me 'Princess of the New World'?" Alexis questioned.

"Yes, he used those exact words," Carolyn answered, still avoiding Lexy's eyes.

Alexis stopped. She looked down at her billowing white shirt, her jeans, and gray boots. She didn't feel like herself in those clothes. She'd picked them out for herself, but she still considered them Kendra's clothes.

"Wait for me here," Alexis ordered and turned to leave.

"Lillian has a new wardrobe on the way," Carolyn spurted out.

Lexy stopped. I took note of the name Lillian. Except for Carolyn, I didn't know the names of the other servants. I had started calling one Thirty-Something and the other Grandma. But I hadn't even given nicknames to the other three servants yet.

"She should be here shortly," Carolyn added, her eyes on the floor.

"Excellent." Alexis nodded and then grabbed the bottom of her billowing white shirt and pulled it over her head. She wore a white lace bra underneath. Lexy popped the button on her jeans and . . .

Kendra grabbed my chin and turned my head. "You don't need to watch," she chided. She also turned her back as well.

"After all we have been through," Lexy's voice held a hint of humor in it, "there is no need to turn your backs on me."

"Modesty is always important," Kendra cut back sharply. She glanced at me and rolled her eyes.

"Remind me again the color of the string bikini you wore for Jake," Lexy retorted.

"Gah!" Kendra growled. "I wore a bikini. One time. Are you ever going to let it go?"

The servant that I'd nicknamed Grandma—she must be Lillian—walked in carrying a pile of folded black leather. Lexy's usual attire.

"Let it go? Definitely not!" Lexy laughed. "It was white, was it not, Jake?"

"Shut up!" Kendra shouted back.

Carolyn twitched noticeably at Kendra's words, and the older servant, Lillian, was so startled that she dropped Lexy's leather clothes and stared at Kendra, her mouth open in shock.

In less than half a second, Lexy pinned Kendra up against the wall with her left forearm pressing into her sternum and her right hand wrapped around Kendra's neck. The whole thing happened so fast that it caught me off guard. Both girls' minds joined mine, causing a brief second of disorientation. I took a step toward Alexis to try to separate her from Kendra but they both joined my mind at the same time.

*Jake, wait,* they both thought to me, and I stopped.

*This is a show for the servants,* Alexis tried to explain, her mental voice coming out rushed and desperate. *We cannot forget that these servants are not mine. Two are my Grandfather's thralls. I don't know which ones. I do not know who the others belong to. They report all activity to their masters. My mother*

*believes that you two are only safe from those who assassinated
the druids because they believe you are under my control. I cannot
have you challenging my authority in front of them.*

The intense scene froze my nerves. Alexis's forearm was
nearly crushing Kendra's chest, and her fingers, gripping tight at
Kendra's neck, barely allowed her to breathe. Lexy's tall form
towered over Kendra. Her white lace underwear matched her bra.

*Stop looking,* Kendra scolded me.

"I have given you my friendship," Alexis spoke firmly, "and
you have betrayed it." Then only to Kendra and me, she added,
*Kendra, I need you to apologize. Look at my feet and talk in a
whisper, but speak loud enough for the servants to hear.*

Kendra and I had not forgotten that we weren't safe. However,
we hadn't understood that the servants weren't Alexis's. Who did
the servants belong to? Their minds were unusually well-
protected. Alexis couldn't read their thoughts. Their master, or
perhaps masters, had to be strong.

*We could ask Carina?* Kendra suggested.

Carina's words came to mind. "Lexy and I are rivals.
Remember that. Perhaps one day, I will meet you again as a
friend. Until then, you are my enemy." No, despite being Alexis's
mother, Carina couldn't be trusted.

At the cabin, we'd been part of a real-life battle of wits, part
of a mental chess match between Alexis—aided by Mr.
Espinoza—and her grandfather. I'd thought we'd won that
game. Perhaps we had. But by becoming Princess of the New
World, Alexis had started another chess match, and we needed
to be careful with our every move. Unlike a real game of chess,
there were more than two players, and we could never be sure
if we even knew about all the possible pieces participating in the
game.

"Apologize, and I'll settle for removing your privileges instead of
removing your head," Princess Alexis's voice seethed, but her mind
kept repeating that this was just a show. She kept her bare arms
flexed, and while she didn't let up on the pressure she applied to
Kendra's sternum, she loosened her grip on Kendra's neck enough
so that she could speak.

"Forgive me, Princess." Kendra spoke, looking down at
Alexis's feet. "I mistook my place."

Alexis couldn't help but smile at the apology.

*You're enjoying this a little too much,* Kendra complained. Her
unfiltered thoughts became a rash of name calling only to be
dwarfed by Alexis's unfiltered responses.

*I must take your necklace now,* Lexy informed Kendra.

Kendra's protection stone, a small Burmese ruby, had been mounted to the top arch of her silver trinity symbol pendant that held a diamond separation stone at its center. Lexy grabbed it and jerked it hard. I felt the pain on Kendra's neck where the necklace pulled tight and the chain and clasp dug into her skin before breaking.

Without the protection stone, and with Alexis pinning her against the wall, Kendra had no defense against Alexis's allure. Kendra, tense a moment earlier, relaxed, and her eyes glanced up and down Alexis's body. In nothing but a white bra and panties, she was just as covered—or uncovered—as Kendra had been when she'd worn that string bikini for me.

*Modesty is important!* Surprisingly, it was Lexy repeating Kendra's thought. *Turn around, Jake.*

*Wait, you don't care about modesty. Didn't you just say—.*

*Turn around anyway,* Jake! Lexy's mental shout cut off my thought.

I obeyed.

Princess Alexis took her hand off Kendra's throat and stepped back, removing her forearm from her sternum. Even under the control of Alexis's allure, Kendra's mind still connected to ours. I could feel her mind, but it felt numb, as if she didn't have her own will. Her own lust, yes, she had that. I felt massively jealous that her lust didn't point at me. Even harder to understand was that Lexy reciprocated it—again not pointed at me.

"Leave us," Alexis commanded, and the servants, eyes on the floor, turned and marched away.

Alexis reached out and handed me Kendra's necklace. Without having to look, I grabbed it from her. Then she tapped her separation stone, and Lexy's mind was gone. Still, Kendra's numb and controlled mind creeped me out, so I tapped the separation stone like I'd seen Kendra and Alexis do a dozen times. Nothing happened. I tapped it again and added a hint of magic. It worked that time. My mind was my own again. Partially. I could still feel their emotions coming through. Mostly lust. Ugh! It was that emotion that I most wanted to escape. Useless separation stone!

I took a deep breath and wrapped myself in an everything-seal. I didn't need a separation stone.

I closed my eyes and took a moment to count upward using prime numbers until my mind drifted from numbers to Sis and Luiz and the jeeks. I thought of my mom and what she must be going through. How did it feel to be innocently accused? What did she think about in prison? Did she wonder if my murder—well, my faked murder—and John's were connected? Did she have any hope that she'd be proven innocent?

Alexis tapped my shoulder and said, "I am dressed."

I turned around and dropped the everything-seal. Kendra's separation stone continued working for me, though. I breathed a sigh of relief that both girls' lust now seemed in check.

Lexy wore the leather shirt that covered everything from her neck to her hips. I wasn't sure if she had a trench coat or cape over it; it seemed somewhere halfway in between the two. Her black leather pants and knee-high boots seemed at home on her. Or perhaps it was Alexis who felt at home wearing them.

Alexis glanced between Kendra and me. "Lust isn't a sin unless you act on it when you shouldn't."

I blinked at her, clearly confused. That didn't sound like something Alexis would ever say, and not just because she'd used contractions.

"Those are not my words." Lexy gave Kendra a long, considering look. "Kendra keeps repeating that phrase in her mind."

I considered disabling the separation stone to hear Kendra's thoughts, but I didn't.

"Come," Lexy's voice took on a regal tone. "We must go meet our visitor."

# CHAPTER 16
# VISITOR

Keagan came up in our Trinity of Mind. Alexis's thoughts and feelings went about twenty directions at the same time. She loves him. She hates him. She wants to kill him. She wants to see him again. She hates that Kendra diagnosed her with Stockholm syndrome. She took comfort in the idea that her love for him could be a mental illness because she feels so guilty for loving the man that murdered and turned her mother. She'd blocked that murdered part out, claiming he hadn't murdered her, but that he had only turned her. When it happened, she knew that her mom had been murdered, but since her mom turned and was still around, she quickly became confused, even though her mom hasn't really been her mom since. If the creep asks her to marry him again, I think he'll get a very different response than last time. Still, she should explain to Luiz about her mother so he knows what to expect. He thinks his dad is still his dad. —Jake

We walked into the parlor in the usual defensive formation, Kendra in front and me slightly behind. The parlor was another receiving room, like the one that held the secret entrance to Lexy's bedroom, only this one was near the front door instead of near the garage. A huge bay window looked out toward the Great Salt Lake. Thick curtains were tied open, allowing the afternoon daylight to fill the room. Two highbacked chairs sat on the left. They were the snooty kind that felt like they were tipping you out of them, as if urging the visitor to stay as short a time as possible. Across from them sat a loveseat that looked too uncomfortable for its name. A piano pressed against the wall behind the chairs.

Princess Alexis hadn't requested the protective formation, but it was starting to become normal. I slipped my hood over my hideous head.

The visitor stood staring out the bay window wearing jeans and a white T-shirt that stretched around his muscled arms in a way that made me miss my muscles. I could tell he had no intention of sitting. The chairs would have tipped him out after a short stay anyway.

The man stood at least my height. His hair was as dark as mine, although my stubble was currently lighter in color. He looked younger than O'Brien. I guessed he was in his late twenties. I recognized a fellow gym rat. He worked out at least as much as I did, which reminded me that I hadn't worked out today. I needed to work out. I could no longer lift half the weight that I used to, and if I was ever going to get my muscle back, I couldn't miss a day.

"You requested an audience with the princess," Kendra spoke, her voice strangely without a hint of emotion.

"Yes," the visitor answered. His eyes glanced from Kendra to Princess Alexis. He scanned her outfit quizzically.

"What is your name," Kendra asked, not using a contraction. Alexis was speaking through her.

"Porter," he answered. "Porter Rockwell."

A wave of fear flashed from Alexis into me. I wasn't sure why a guy using a false historical name scared her. Every Mormon boy knew about Orrin Porter Rockwell. A Wild West gunslinger from the 1800s, he served as a bodyguard to both Joseph Smith and Brigham Young. Some called him the Destroying Angel.

"Yeah, right!" I cut in. "You're lying. What's your real name?"

Alexis glanced my way, head tilted in curiosity. I could tell she wanted me to disable the separation stone, but I didn't. Ha! We'd see how she liked not having the choice of reading my mind whenever she wanted. I left her to wonder how I knew this guy was lying.

"I'll stick with Porter if you don't mind." His voice had a distinct disrespect for authority.

Alexis focused on him, then smiled. "His name is Trenton Marx."

113

I watched Trenton flinch and blink his dark brown eyes at the sound of his name. He shook his head and recovered.

"Whatever." Trenton refused to confirm his name. "I have a letter for you." He reached for his back pocket and pulled out a full-sized, white envelope. He took a couple steps toward us and then extended the wrinkled envelope to Kendra, who snapped it from his hands. The envelope didn't have anything written on it and it wasn't sealed. Kendra pulled out a single sheet of paper, also wrinkled.

"It's blank," Kendra stated, confused. She seemed to have gained a bit of self-control back.

Trenton shrugged. "Not my problem. I was told to deliver it. I did." He flipped us off as he started to leave.

"Stop," Princess Alexis commanded with every ounce of her allure. I felt my protection stone hum as it protected me from her intense power.

"Nope," Trenton walked right past Kendra and Alexis, shaking his head. He didn't even look at me, which probably meant my fist to the corner of his eye was a cheap shot. Being much weaker than I used to be, he didn't crumple to the ground, but since Alexis kicked low, sweeping his feet, he still dropped face down onto the hardwood floor.

"She said stop," I said flatly. I probably wouldn't have punched him except I had noticed Carolyn and Lillian were spying on the conversation. A challenge against Princess Alexis could not go unpunished. My first knuckle had made the connection. It split and bled down my finger. Alexis became very aware of my bleeding fist.

Despite lying face down on the floor, Trenton raised his hands above his head in a gesture of surrender.

"Uh, oh," Kendra gulped as she glanced toward us. Her eyes moved left to right as she read the letter. She showed no sign that she even noticed us take down Trenton.

I looked at her, confused. Hadn't it been blank?

"Look who this letter is from." Kendra pointed to the page that had been blank, but I could now see writing.

"Wasn't the paper blank?"

"Alexis asked if I could make it readable," Kendra replied. I hadn't noticed her use magic a moment ago but punching someone could be distracting.

I grabbed the letter and started reading it out loud. I had a hard time believing the words I read. They didn't make sense.

Princess Alexis,

It has come to our attention that you are currently residing inside the Deseret Line. Your presence alone would not have been of concern had other incidents not occurred.

Your actions against Miguel Espinoza have been reviewed and determined not to be a breach of the Vatican Vampire Treaty due to article 2.1. The death of John Braen is not a breach due to the recent addendum to section 2. We have reviewed the six women Miguel Espinoza has taken and found four of them to be exempt under articles 2.2 and 2.3. However, two of them are still under review.

We are also reviewing the events that occurred last night in North Salt Lake. While distasteful, Club Exposed still resides inside the Deseret Line and, as such, remains part of the *Rockwell Addendum.* While the Haitian caplatas are responsible for the altercation, we cannot help but notice these issues began when you entered the treaty area.

We politely request that you remove yourself from the treaty area immediately. We request that Miguel Espinoza accompany you.

Any breach of the Rockwell Treaty will not be tolerated. Please understand that we have discussed the matter with your grandfather and your leader, John Kaloyan. He will not interfere should we decide to remove you by force.

The Danite Secret Seventy (DSS)

What was the Vampire Vatican Treaty? And the Rockwell Addendum? Or the Deseret Line? I looked at Alexis. "Last week, you said, 'Most of Utah is off-limits. It is not anybody's territory.' This is what you meant," I held up the letter to Alexis.

"Yes," Alexis confirmed. "It is an extension of the V. V. Treaty."

"What is—" I started and tapped Kendra's protection stone in my pocket, but Alexis cut me off and didn't tap hers.

"We'll discuss this later. She turned to the man on the floor, "Trenton, you may rise now."

Trenton rolled over, scooted away from us, and then stood up.

"Mr. Espinoza and I have no intention of leaving. The Joan of Arc addendum, added after she was sainted in 1920, exempts dhampirs. Even if it did not, section 7.1 allows me, as it does Mr. Espinoza, residence inside the Deseret Line."

"Write your own response, because I promise to do my best to misquote you," Trenton mocked.

"Carolyn," Lexy turned, calling out into the hall. "Fetch me a pen, paper, and envelope."

"One more thing, princess. The DSS are offering sanctuary to Jacob Stevens and Kendra Duncan." Trenton spoke slowly and calmly. "Sanctuary from you."

Trenton said my name. My full name. I blinked at him nervously. *Everyone* (well, almost everyone) thought I was dead. How did this man know I wasn't? Come to think of it, how did the Danites—a name I recognized as a Mormon secret society that supposedly disbanded in the mid-1800s—know about me? How did they know about Mr. Espinoza? They knew everything.

Trenton touched the corner of his eye and winced. I couldn't have hit him that hard.

"Jake, Kendra?" Trenton spoke like he knew us. "Would either of you like to come with me. We could make your lives *normal* again."

Normal. Until he said that word, I thought I wouldn't be tempted at all by an offer of sanctuary. But I gotta admit, being normal was my holy grail. The offer sounded pretty good. I considered it. I even considered making Kendra go. But what if that led to us being hunted? What if we ended up in another fight to the death, like at Bear Lake? Look what happened to my family. To Mr. Espinoza. Who else might be caught in the crossfire?

Besides, with the way I looked, I doubted normal would be coming any time soon. Any offer of a normal life now was a pipe dream.

"I'm staying." I glanced at Kendra for her answer, but she was still partially under Alexis's allure, though Alexis wasn't trying to control her, so Kendra was in no shape to answer. "So is Kendra," I added since she couldn't answer for herself.

"Your servant is back," Trenton nodded to the hallway. I glanced behind me and saw redheaded Carolyn coming with pen and paper in hand.

When I turned back around, I found Trenton pointing a .45 caliber handgun at Princess Alexis's head. His finger squeezed the trigger.

Standing close behind Alexis, I stretched my arm forward, placing it between Lexy's face and the bullet. I felt the bullet hit my sleeve the same time I heard the gunshot. The bullet deflected off the magic shield I'd placed on my hoodie. A few small gravel rocks—I always carried some now—crumbled to dust in my pocket. The bullet impacted my arm with a lot of force. The bullet couldn't penetrate my sweater, yet the momentum had to go somewhere, so my forearm involuntarily smacked Alexis in the face. Her head whiplashed, but nothing she couldn't quickly recover from, even if it had turned her irises to an angry black.

I pulled in magic and tried to decide between burning Trenton to ash or erasing him to nothing. I decided on erasing him, probably because a part of me craved the ecstasy. I started forming a magic missile when a hand touched my shoulder.

"Wait," a calm male voice spoke into my ear.

I glanced around. Lexy and Kendra stood in front of me. Lexy had pulled a rune-marked knife from somewhere on her body. Behind me, no one stood between me and the extravagantly decorated parlor wall. No one was on either side of me. Who had just touched my shoulder? Who had told me to wait?

"Wait," the voice spoke again, but this time, it seemed to come from just behind Alexis, only no one was there.

Lexy stopped and spun around, trying to find the source of the voice.

Trenton had plenty of time to fire a second shot, but he didn't. Why had he pulled the trigger once but not again? He held the gun up and seemed to be making himself an easy target.

"Come on," Trenton shouted. "You won't even let me die fighting?" Trenton's eyes glared at the air between Kendra and Alexis.

Alexis and I paused our attacks. I held my magic and she held her long knife, but neither of us attacked.

"With whom are you speaking?" Princess Alexis demanded. I stepped forward enough to notice her eyes had gone completely black.

Trenton began to laugh maniacally.

"With whom are you speaking?" Lexy demanded again.

He tried to calm his maniacal laugh, "You wouldn't believe me," he managed. He dropped the gun, and it clattered loudly on the wood floor as he covered his face. Alexis blinked, and her eyes widened. She'd plucked the answer from his mind.

"You attempted suicide by assassination attempt," she stated.

I glanced back at her. The red had mostly returned to her eyes. She lifted her left arm and twisted it so she could see her wrist. She remembered the many times she had set the blade of her knife against her wrist, and her eyes thinned.

I pressed against her separation stone and felt a part of me slip through the magic, just in time to see the most prominent of those memories.

She stood in a dark, glass-entry shower cutting her wrists. Blood in the shower had a scent far stronger than she realized. She barely had time to glance up before a tall vampire with dark skin slid open the glass door. Cutting her wrists had been a waste of time. She wouldn't die. Her grandfather would not let her.

Lexy glanced back at me as if she had detected my presence in her mind. I could see the regret in her eyes just as well as I could feel it. I could empathize with her. I'd felt that same way, once. I'd had to live with the way I was conceived for so many years, having a mother that, through no fault of her own, couldn't love me. Grandma loved me instead. At least until she died. I remember the date being July 13th. Being only eleven, I stared at her motionless body in her coffin, knowing she was gone and would never be around to love me again. I stood at her grave and watched as they lowered the closed coffin into it. Luiz left for the summer that year, visiting family in Mexico for the whole summer. My mother made life difficult for me. She told me repeatedly that she wished I had never been born.

Three times that summer, I planned to make my mother's wish come true. Twice, without her knowing it, Sis thwarted my plan by needing me. The third time, Luiz stopped by, having returned home a week early. And now, the ugly hideous thing that I was, and with the bad thought that Kendra and Lexy had shared, the one I wasn't supposed to repeat, and the effects of the shadow blades pushing me toward that direction, I felt that way again. With Kendra's mind quietly under her control, Lexy's emotions too easily mingled with mine. If I let it keep going, then . . . well, I couldn't let it. I couldn't go down the path that the shadow blades and the bad thought pushed me toward. I stopped prying past Alexis's separation stone and tapped my own.

Alexis turned away from me and stowed the knife somewhere under her cape-like trench coat. She held out her hand toward Carolyn, who quickly stepped forward to hand her the pen and paper.

Princess Alexis set the paper on the top of the piano and began writing. I watched her hand move gracefully across the paper. Back when I had barely known Lexy, she had left me a note with that same perfect handwriting. She had only signed her first name in the note for me, but this time, she finished the letter signing her full name. Why did I get the impression that, like never using contractions when speaking, her beautiful handwriting had been beaten into her?

Somehow, Princess Alexis made the act of folding a letter and stuffing it into an envelope look elegant. Even the way she offered Trenton the letter looked elegant, like a lady of King Arthur's court requesting that a knight kiss her hand.

"Go," she commanded. "Go before I change my mind and grant you the death you desire."

Trenton took the envelope with no grace and stuffed it in the back pocket of his jeans. He nodded at me as he walked past us.

"No need to show me out," he yelled as he walked the short distance from the parlor to the front door. Then he whispered, "Come on, Clarence."

Huh? Did this psycho have an imaginary friend? Probably. Then again, who's voice told me to wait? Why had I obeyed that voice so easily? Maybe his friend wasn't so imaginary.

I pushed magic into my eyes to catch a glimpse of Trenton's invisible friend and immediately regretted it. The world became agonizingly bright. So bright that I involuntarily shut my eyes and quickly slapped my hand over them too. I couldn't pull the magic sight from my eyes fast enough. Even with both my hands and eyelids shading me, the brightness seared into them like ice picks. Finally, the magical sight faded, but not before the pain forced me to collapse.

Alexis caught me and held me up.

Even though the figure had shone too brightly for me to see, between the whisper in my ear and the extreme brightness, I guessed at who accompanied Trenton. I'd just seen an angel.

# CHAPTER 17
# ZOMBIE

*I have six older brothers and sisters. You would think I could handle being with two people constantly, but sometimes, I can't. I am six years younger than Karynn, my closest sister. She graduated four years ago and left for college. Sis calls me the seventh and only child. Maybe I am a spoiled only child. Is that why it is annoying to be with Jake and Alexis constantly? I can't get any alone time. Well, I get a little with the separation stone. It is such a great gift. —Kendra*

"How did he hide a gun in jeans and a T-shirt," I wondered aloud.

Eldra stepped into the parlor. She looked at the gun on the floor. "He didn't. He took it from the drawer there." She pointed to a small desk in the hall near the entryway. It was topped with Peace Lilies sprouting from a red pot.

"I am all for the right to bear arms, but why do we have a gun by the entryway?" I asked. "And how did he know where to find it?"

"To answer your first question," Eldra offered, "Alexis is the Princess of the New World. She might have to kill someone who comes to her door." Eldra ignored my second question. "The visitor is gone, so postponing training is over. I have reconsidered teaching you sunlight."

"What then?"

"Go to your room Jake, and wait for me there," Eldra directed.

"Kendra, you and . . ." Eldra stopped. "What is wrong with Kendra?" she growled.

"Oh, Lexy, uh," I didn't want to explain it to Eldra. "I mean, Kendra's necklace broke." I pulled Kendra's necklace from my pocket. "I didn't realize she would be so out of it," I commented to Lexy. "She pretty much zoned out. I'm not sure she even flinched at the gunshot."

"I have not been controlling her," Lexy responded.

"If you're not controlling her then—," my voice cut off as I saw the last bit of light fade from Kendra's eyes, leaving them empty and vacant. Her head turned awkwardly as she looked from Lexy to Eldra, as if looking at us with her chin, which was creepily familiar.

I sensed the spell forming inside her in time to cast a containment around Lexy and myself. I probably should have included Eldra, but the wizened druid didn't need my help. Before Kendra could cast her spell, Eldra wrapped Kendra in a containment and sucked all the magic out of her.

Her chin-first face rotated toward me with an awkward slowness. Her boy-cut hair shifted on her forehead and her eyes refused to blink. Her vacant eyes would likely haunt me forever. Then she lunged at me open-mouthed with white teeth spread wide enough to bite.

Lexy stepped swiftly to intervene and punched Kendra, stopping her just as her teeth reached an inch from my throat and whiplashing her head backward. Her eyes rolled back, and she crumpled to the ground, unconscious. Lexy grinned at me, not at all guilty. The tip of her tongue slid from her left fang to the sharp point of her right, where she left it until she retracted her fangs. "I have wanted to punch her since finding out that she kissed you first." Her smile turned to an exaggerated pouting lip. "Does that make me evil?"

I stared at Alexis, a mixture of anger and mirth drowned out by concern for Kendra. The mirth belonged to Alexis, not me. I knelt and cradled Kendra's head.

Eldra walked to Kendra and took her hand. The old druid's eyes went white, like they had when she had studied me. She focused on the half-circle scar on Kendra's hand. The scar showed clearly defined teeth marks.

"It seems," Eldra interrupted, "that the caplatas have taken a part of Kendra's spirit." Eldra pursed her lips. "This bite is somehow infected. Not with a disease, but with the caplatas' shadow magic. I can see her soul slowly leaking out."

"What do we do?" I asked, but I already knew the answer. Somewhere, the caplatas had a clay jar sucking in Kendra's soul. My new goal became finding that clay jar and breaking it.

Hesitantly, I pushed magic into my eyes, nervous that the bright angel light that I had seen last time I'd used my sight would still be there to blind me. But it was gone, allowing me to focus on Kendra. At the rate her spirit leaked from her body, it would be gone in an hour or two. Once the shadow magic drained her spirit, she'd be all zombie.

"When I looked at her before," Eldra muttered, "I saw nothing."

*What changed?* I wondered. How was the shadow magic causing her spirit to leak out so quickly now and not when Eldra had looked earlier? My hand reached into my pocket for Kendra's necklace. The crystals had a dim glow. I knelt next to her and slid the necklace around her neck. Alexis had broken the last link in the necklace, so I hooked the clasp to the next link. With my magic sight, I watched both her separation stone and her protection stone burn to life.

Her spirit stopped seeping from her white scar, but not completely. Ever so faintly, I could see her light leaking, seeping from the wound on Kendra's hand like the silk strand of a dangling spider.

"It seems you just bought her a week or two," Eldra stated flatly. "I am not sure if it is the protection stone, the separation stone, or both." The way her pursed lips pulled on her frown made her look disappointed. Was she disappointed that she wasn't going to get to watch Kendra die? Kendra and I had killed her husband, a man with whom her mind had been intertwined with for well over a century. Perhaps I wasn't misreading her at all.

"How do we save her?" Lexy asked Eldra. Her voice sounded soft and concerned. Worry mixed with guilt exuded from Lexy. She no longer felt a mischievous contentment that she had punched Kendra. Instead, she blamed herself for removing Kendra's necklace.

"We find the voodoo witches," I answered for Eldra. "They'll be gathering her spirit in a clay jar. We need to break it."

"How do you know?" Lexy asked.

"That is how we fixed the zombies last night while you were passed out," I answered.

"Well, I've never seen a spirit spring a leak before," Eldra laughed. "Too bad we can't just call a plumber."

I glared at her. What was she doing, trying to be funny at a time like this? But I really didn't care about Eldra. Nothing mattered but protecting Kendra. I had to protect Kendra. My chest overflowed with the need to protect her. That need pushed out all other thoughts and emotions.

I felt pulled toward Kendra, and involuntarily, I stepped over to her and picked her up off the ground. I glared at Eldra and then at Alexis and turned to keep my body between them and Kendra.

Alexis smirked, her grin reaching her red eyes. "I am no danger to Kendra, Jake."

Had she forgotten that she had just knocked her out with a single punch? I held Kendra away from them but continued to glare back over my shoulder at the black-haired, dhampir princess and the ancient druidess.

"Keep calm, Jacob," Eldra spoke with a voice suddenly as soft and as comforting as my grandma's voice had always been. "Everything will be all right."

I believed Eldra, but maybe only because she sounded like my grandma. How she could switch emotions from moment to moment was beyond me. That grandma was insane!

"What can we do?" Alexis asked Eldra. A hint of worry slid from Alexis into me, reminding me that she cared for Kendra.

Eldra's long, gray braid swung as she turned to look from me to Alexis. "The escaping essence of her spirit has a destination. I might be able to find where it is going."

"How can I help?" I gasped out, finding myself completely out of breath. Kendra didn't weigh much, but I'd momentarily forgotten that I was not as strong as I used to be. My legs trembled weakly, my back already ached from her weight, and the muscles in my arms burned. Alexis hurried to me and lifted Kendra from my arms. Part of me wanted to protest, but despite having just punched Kendra, Alexis had spoken the truth. She was no danger to Kendra.

It was probably the wrong time to feel inadequate as a man. As a dhampir, Alexis was far stronger than me. She was stronger than me even before I burned off my muscle mass. She didn't struggle at all as she cradled Kendra in her arms.

"Perhaps it would be best to take her to her room," Eldra suggested, her voice still soft.

Lexy nodded in agreement and started toward the hallway, avoiding bumping Kendra's head on the walls. I followed her past Carolyn who had been eavesdropping on the whole incident. Alexis continued upstairs to the bedroom where Kendra had been sleeping for the past week. Since Mr. Espinoza had taken her cavern bedchamber, Lexy now roomed across from Kendra and directly above the room I stayed in. Kendra's room was not decorated. The bare walls seemed lifeless and the bed, covered by a deep red comforter, looked like a single red rose surviving in a desert.

As Alexis laid Kendra on the bed, I wondered about Sis's comment earlier. She'd mentioned that it felt like Kendra had to be invited into her own home. Where did Kendra belong? When your very existence is a danger to your family, can you stay with them? O'Brien didn't think so. That was one reason why he had faked my death. And he was right. Look what happened to my stepfather. How could we ever ensure the safety of Kendra's family? Perhaps, this room was Kendra's permanent room now.

I heard steps behind us and looked to the door.

Eldra had followed us.

"Alexis, out of your armor and go practice. You know what to do," Eldra ordered with a grating edge to her voice.

Alexis nodded, and a hint of magic touched me, and she left. I found it strange to hear her taking orders. What agreement had she and Eldra made?

"Jake," Eldra's voice switched to a tone soft and sweet. "We will find a way to help her."

I glanced between Kendra and Eldra. It was strange to see Eldra look at Kendra without hate. She seemed mellow now, but she hadn't mellowed with age; it was just by choice.

"That night at Bear Lake, you offered your life to save her," Eldra commented. "Greater love hath no man than this, that a man lay down his life for his friends."

*John 15:35,* I thought to myself. I'd memorized that scripture as part of early morning seminary. I only went because Sis always dragged me along. I hadn't expected Eldra to quote scripture to me. I watched her stare at me with awe—as if I were some kind of hero—with the same eyes that hated me not so long before. Yep. This grandma was crazy.

"You would do it again," she added. She pulled her gray braid over her left shoulder and seemed to fiddle with the end of it. "That night. The night you two killed Robin, my husband, your first magic missile hit us hard. It rattled me. When your second missile hit us, instead of defending himself, he defended me." A tear pooled in a wrinkle under her left eye for a moment before finally dropping. "Did you know that I have watched many wars of mankind in the past two centuries? Dozens of men turn and run in battle. But you," she looked me up and down, "you stayed and gave it your all. My husband sacrificed his life for me. You didn't give your life, but you were willing. You are still willing. You would die to save her even now."

I nodded. I didn't know what to say. I didn't feel worthy of her praise. I hadn't given my life. I'd been a fool. I had cast a magic missile in desperation. If it hadn't been for Alexis finding a way to help without harming her grandfather, and for Alexis's mother, Carina, switching sides and coming to our aid, we'd all be dead.

"You are a rare man," Eldra continued. "You've almost convinced me that you are worthy of the love of both these girls. I will help you save this one. But you must leave me alone with her."

"Why?" I asked.

"I am going to track her spirit. The presence of other spirits makes it more difficult."

"OK," I nodded, not sure if I really understood.

"You should go train," she added, and she threw her silver braid behind her shoulder. "Go to your room. Activate the containment and make it self-sustaining. Then I want you to cast magic missiles at the containment until you either break it or you pass out."

I cocked an eyebrow at her. Was she nuts? Did she realize that casting a mere four of them would most likely drain me thoroughly? I would burn out in a minute.

"Count them," she added.

I didn't move. I just stood there thinking. Why would she want me to do that? How did that count as training? She might as well have told me to dig a hole just to fill it in again. I guess I'd be out of her hair if I had something to do.

I grabbed Kendra's hand. Her fingers felt warm. If not for her warmth, she would have seemed lifeless. But along with her warmth, I could see her chest rise and fall. I squeezed her hand and then let go.

"OK," I told Eldra. "I'll go practice."

# CHAPTER 18
# PRACTICE

*The letter from the Danite Serenty caught me off guard. I am not a monster bound by the V. V. Treaty. I am only half-dhampir. I am exempt. Do they dare break the Joan of Arc addendum? Perhaps nobody would care. Perhaps killing me would simply reinforce that Utah, like the Vatican, is a monster-free zone. I have an idea to counter their letter. It has two parts. The first starts with Mr. Espinoza. He is not exempt, which is why I sent him to Las Vegas to find specific girls to be his thralls—girls who didn't break the treaty. Still, I may have to send him away. I will start the second part this Sunday. Won't Kendra be surprised. —Alexis*

I have this ability to poke holes in containments. I read in the druid manual that containments could be broken by hitting them with extreme amounts of magic but otherwise were impenetrable. Why could I break containments? What was it about me that gave me this ability? Did it have to do with Caradoc's blood? Or perhaps with being a protector?

I didn't want to start casting magic missiles right away, so I played with the containment, trying different things for about twenty minutes. Nothing. No poked holes at all. I failed completely.

The faint glow of magic in the wall of the containment surrounded me like a glass jar. I lit a small flame in my hand. I put my hand next to the containment and blew on the flame. It looked freaking cool to watch the flame hit the containment. The flames licked at the glass-jar containment wall, only there was no glass for the fire to darken.

126

I took a breath. Why was I hesitating to cast a magic missile? Perhaps because doing so might be addicting, and I didn't want to feel the addiction. Or was it the magic missile that was addicting? Perhaps it was the pleasure of erasing evil from existence that was addicting and not the magic missile at all. I remembered how I'd been tempted to erase Sis and O'Brien that night at the movie theatre parking lot. No, it wasn't erasing *evil* that was addicting. It was erasing *anything* that was addicting.

"*Bealustræl,*" I whispered the Old English phrase as I pulled magic into the space between my palms. I let the missile grow until I could barely sustain the amount of magic inside me. The missile neared the size of a basketball, larger than I'd ever created before. I released it at the containment.

The containment's magic seemed to flicker but never failed.

"One," I said out loud.

I created another magic missile. Again, I let the magic flow through me and into the orb between my palms. Again, it looked about the size of a basketball. Of course, it didn't look anything like a basketball. Instead, it appeared as a sphere of white-and-blue light between my palms.

For fun, instead of just releasing the missile with a thought, I raised it above my head and hurled it with both hands at the containment. It collided with crackly electricity-like noise. The containment sparked and flickered with static for about seven seconds before the sound and the flickering stopped. I expected a burnt plastic smell, like a burning out electrical socket, but there was no smell.

"Two."

As I started to create the third, I had a thought. Could I make the orb the shape of a football instead of a basketball? Don't get me wrong, I liked basketball plenty, but for me, football had something extra special. Could I shape the missile with a simple thought?

It didn't work. The orb formed in my hand, round and large, only not quite as big as the other two. The part of me that worked magic was tired. I didn't feel it in my muscles; I felt drained in my brain and my spirit. Still, I gave the missile a good toss into the containment, as if physically throwing it would make it stronger, which was nonsense, but I grinned anyway.

"Three."

I really wanted a football-shaped missile, and this time I concentrated on the shape before I even started the spell. I willed it as I cast the spell. It didn't surprise me at all to see the spell form in an oblong shape, not a perfect football shape, but close.

I'd never played quarterback, having been a running back most of my career, but I knew how to throw a football. I held my hands forward like I was going to grab the magic missile from an imaginary center lineman.

"Down. Set. Blue thirty-two. Blue thirty-two. Hike." I called out. I held the missile in one hand like a football and tossed it at the containment. I watched the orb hit the dimly visible wall of energy. The nose of the orb seemed to disappear on contact. The containment flickered as it absorbed the missile. Only it didn't absorb the whole thing. I watched the back end of the football-shaped missile pass through what appeared to be the inner wall of the containment before it encountered another containment wall, which flared to life with its own slight glow and absorbed the remaining portion of the missile. The second wall's light faded away.

I hadn't yet reached the advanced section of the druid manual, but I had an idea what it would say about containments. Containments could be created with layered patterns. Just like a bulletproof vest used layers to better stop a bullet, the Star of David containment used layers to better stop a magic spell.

The inner portion of the silver Star of David on the floor formed a hexagon. Straight lines connected the star's points, forming an outer hexagon. A circle also surrounded the Star of David at the star's points. A decorative pattern filled each sectionof the design.

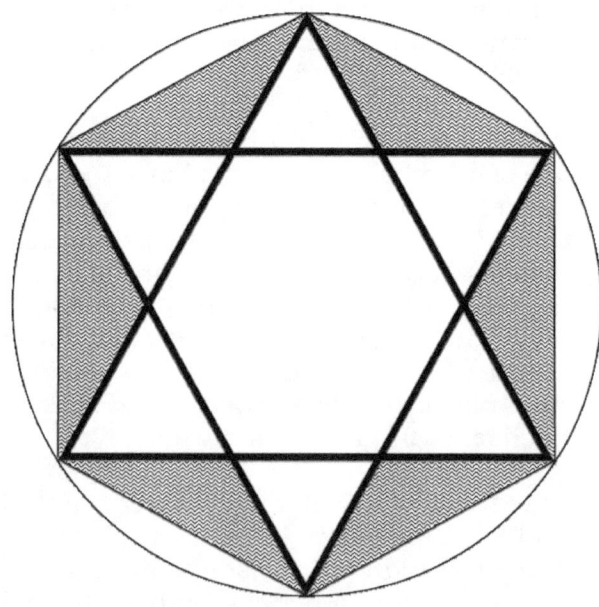

This containment wasn't any stronger than any other containment. This was just a pattern of multiple containments. Only the other containments subtly buoyed the inner containment.

"Four."

I formed another football-shaped missile, again looking more like a football than the previous, and launched it at the wall. This time, I tried to make a hole in the inner hexagon containment layer. Sure enough, the entire football slipped through the hole and hit the second level, then splashed into the inner pattern lines and broke into phantasmagoric surges of electric-like light. Another seven seconds passed before the shattered football light show disappeared.

"Five," I said, grinning.

With excitement growing inside me, I focused on each line in the pattern, slowly creating a small hole through layer after layer of the containments. I struggled through the last layers, but after a minute, I felt I'd created a small path all the way through.

I squatted down in quarterback position again.

"Down. Set. Red twelve. Red twelve. Hike," I tossed my new football-shaped magic missile through the opening. The path I'd made through the containment wasn't quite big enough. The containment edges sliced my magic like razor blades. The missile refracted as it traveled through. A small, misshapen remnant of magic shot from the outer layer of the containment and launched its way directly toward the mahogany desk. The misshapen missile hit, splitting between the edge of the desk and the large druid tome. The room shook as light cracked its way out of the expensive mahogany and the druid manual lit up like a light. The missile completely erased half of the mahogany desk and my entire druid manual.

Immediately, the pounding of feet running toward my room echoed from the hall. The door flew open. I expected Alexis or one of the servants, but to my surprise, Luiz's shocked face stood in the doorway.

"¡Diantre!" Luiz commented as he fixated on the now-destroyed desk. "Were you attacked?" he asked.

"No." I sighed, then swore with clenched teeth. Luiz walked over to inspect the damage, then he turned and gave me a quizzical look. His long nose and dark hair combined with his expression made him look more like his dad than usual, although his dad's newly red eyes no longer matched his son's black ones. Luiz stood two inches taller than his dad and had strong, wiry muscles. Before his dad turned, Luiz had been the stronger of the two by a good margin. But not now. The image of Luiz's dad in Alexis's underground room with his new thralls invaded my mind. Mr. Espinoza now looked a decade younger. Perhaps that was why Luiz looked more like him than ever.

"I was just practicing and—" "Jacob Matthew Stevens!" Eldra's icy voice froze the room. Her eyes took in the damage.

Once again, her demeanor had completely changed. Hadn't she just been extremely understanding of me a few minutes ago?

"I thought I told you to practice *inside* the containment," her cold voice continued.

"I was," I defended. "It wasn't strong enough."

"Hogwash!" Eldra shook her head, her gray braid moving left to right. She clearly believed I was lying. "That Star of David containment cannot be broken. You're obviously a fool. I assure you that you erred. You must have extended your hand outside the containment."

I scoffed. "I assure you that I didn't *err*," I tried to make my voice sound like hers. "My hand didn't extend out of the containment."

Eldra glared at me. Then she glanced at Luiz and the corners of her mouth started to rise. Then she burst into complete laughter.

"Jake sounded just like me, didn't he?" she laughed out loud to Luiz.

"*Ay sí,*" Luiz cracked a grin. "It was a good impersonation. He nailed your wrinkled old Hagatha-ness!"

Eldra's laugh elevated. It seemed Luiz had free rein to mock her. For that matter, I'd gotten away with mimicking her because of Luiz's presence. The old woman grabbed her braid, which calmed both her laughter and anger.

"Two things are important to druids," Eldra spoke like an in-charge grandmother. "Training and education. All druids complete both." She gestured at the Star of David containment. "You haven't passed out yet. So, continue."

"I don't want to destroy anything else," I argued. "I just erased the desk and . . ." I decided against mentioning the druid text.

Then stay inside the circle," Eldra shot back."

"I told you!" I challenged. "I stayed inside the circle."

"And if I don't believe you?" Her lips pursed together and nearly disappeared from her wrinkled face.

"Then you pick my target."

"Fine," she spat. "I pick me."

"What? Do you have a suicide wish?" I jeered.

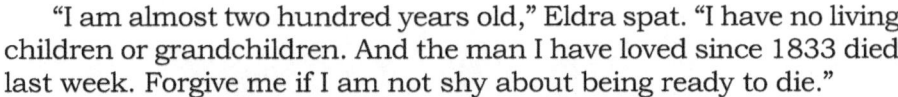

"I am almost two hundred years old," Eldra spat. "I have no living children or grandchildren. And the man I have loved since 1833 died last week. Forgive me if I am not shy about being ready to die."

"Yeah, still not going to kill you," I replied.

"If your spell makes it through, then I will block it," she almost yawned as she brought her own containment up, a single wall of magic in front of her. "Make it as strong as you can. I will be fully prepared."

"Seriously?"

"Do it," she ordered with pursed lips.

"Fine."

I made sure I stood directly in the center of the containment. I put my palms together, and with a whisper, I spread my hands apart, letting the magic rush into the space between them. I let the missile grow. It reached the football shape, but I let it enlarge until it swelled to a more rugby-sized shape. I didn't stop there. My body began to shake with the magic I held. It seemed the more I used it, the more I could use next time. It clearly wasn't related to my physical strength or else my magic would be much weaker. I finally had to stop or I wouldn't be able to concentrate on opening a pathway through the maze-like containment. My eyes focused on the containment line between Eldra and me until I'd cleared the path. I left Eldra's containment untouched. I didn't want hers to fail.

I didn't toss the missile like a football this time. Shaking with overexertion, I used every remaining ounce of my consciousness and released the missile at Eldra.

As my body began to collapse in overexertion, I noticed that I'd unknowingly made the path a little larger this time. More than half of the magic missile made it through. I hadn't noticed Eldra's face, but I could see it now, as if time moved in slow motion. Fear dripped from her aged eyes. She held her staff up, and a rune flared to life with a blue glow, creating a second containment in front of her own.

The magic missile collided with her staff-created containment first. The wall of magic flickered and the rune flashed like a strobe light before the containment shattered and the rest of the missile continued, hitting the containment wall she'd formed on her own.

Magic vibrated throughout the room, adding to my weariness. Eldra fought, pulling in more magic than she had ever pulled in her life. As I collided with the bedroom floor, Eldra's containment gave out in an explosion of magic that blasted her out my bedroom door.

# CHAPTER 19
# SCARLETT

I worry too much about other people. I know because Alexis and Kendra keep telling me so. If I hear Kendra and Alexis simultaneously say, "Stop worrying about us," one more time, I'm going to break something. Of course, they say to stop, but then I hear the other side of their thoughts that are grateful that I worry about them. Which is it? Do you want me to stop? Or are you grateful? Still, if Kendra and Alexis are listening in, I try to steer my worry toward Sis, Luiz, Mom, and O'Brien. —Jake

As I lay on the floor refusing to pass out, Luiz's lips formed some words in Spanish that I'm pretty sure would have been too vulgar to ever repeat. His eyes spread wide above his long nose and his head swung back and forth between Eldra and me, trying to figure out who needed him more.

"Her," I grunted out painfully. Then my head started to spin. I held my breath as I pinched my eyes together, fighting off my body's overwhelming urge to pass out. I thought better of holding my breath. With a deep gasp, I filled my lungs. I let the huge breath rush out of me and any chance of me passing out rushed out with it. I took a few more breaths, then opened my eyes as I raised up on an elbow and then got to my knees.

Luiz knelt outside the bedroom door, holding Eldra's mouth to his ear. His black eyes had locked onto mine and his countenance froze in fear—fear of me. I remembered the way Sis had pulled away from me not so many days ago.

A wave of disappointment rushed through me, and not just because Luiz feared me. It was more because I hadn't erased anything. I'd missed out on the pleasure of it. Some ethereal part of me itched to cast another magic missile at Eldra—to feel the immense pleasure of erasing another living being. But I knew now to expect that, and I firmly pushed the desire away. Still, I couldn't help but compare the desire to Alexis's hunger. If she could withstand her temptation, so could I.

I waited on my knees for long seconds until I felt energy enough to stand.

"She's breathing," Luiz's voice came out in a shiver. "Barely."

I hesitantly took a few steps and made sure I wouldn't fall before I continued out into the hall where my best friend held Eldra. I helped him lay her down flat on the hallway floor.

"What happened?" I heard Lexy's soft voice ask behind me.

"Uh . . ." I didn't exactly know what to say. "Training accident."

She tapped her separation stone, and since I no longer carried Kendra's, her mind joined with mine. She watched the mental video looping in my head.

*Nothing she did not deserve,* Lexy thought, but out loud, she only said, "She underestimated your power."

I nodded.

"I underestimated your power, as well. Step aside," Lexy ordered both of us.

Her mind revealed her plan to help Eldra. I mentally cringed.

*What?* she questioned. *Her immune system is adequate. She will not turn.*

Lexy knelt over Eldra and tilted her head back, opening her mouth slightly. Then she bit her thumb with her right canine. Blood beaded from the puncture in her skin. She let the beads drop into Eldra's mouth.

I counted the drops as they fell because sometimes I just liked to count things. Only eight drops fell before her thumb healed.

*She will not wake today. Perhaps tomorrow,* Lexy told me with the image of Kendra and her leaking spirit hanging in her mind at the same time.

I swore. We needed Eldra to track the witches for us. I'd just delayed that a day. Would Kendra survive a day? Anger at my stupidity flooded through me. I had nothing to direct my rage at, so I chose the wall.

*No!* Too late, Lexy tried to order my mind. My right fist landed between studs and went right through the sheetrock. Lucky me. If I'd hit a stud, I would have broken my knuckles. Still, my skin wasn't fully healed. I pulled my fist out and blood ran down my middle finger. I'd added a split on my middle knuckle to the split on my first knuckle. I had to stop splitting my knuckles punching things.

Alexis couldn't hide the fear flooding inside her at the sight of my blood. That same image flashed through her mind briefly: a man standing above a young woman strapped to a stone table. He dripped blood from his wrist into her mouth. Alexis tapped her separation stone, and her thoughts shut off.

*We're going to talk about that image someday,* I thought at her, knowing she no longer listened.

Alexis picked up Eldra, gave me a disapproving look, and then carried the old woman down the hall. Eldra was lucky to be alive and not just because she'd survived this training accident. This was the second time she'd survived one of my magic missiles. Her husband's death wasn't my fault, was it? He had been trying to kill us.

Who was I kidding? I hated what I had done. I could never make up for the harm I'd caused the aged druidess. The weight of what I had done combined with my magic's dark temptation weighed on me.

I took a few quick but deep breaths to calm down. I recognized the near panic attack that didn't come. Being shot by O'Brien and the encounter with the nightwalker had left me with post-traumatic stress that I hoped the healing stone had cured. However, the bloody cabin battle had certainly piled on more PTSD. I'd worn the healing stone the whole time I'd been unconscious, growing back my epidermis. Perhaps my mind had healed again. Of course, if my mind had completely healed, why did my thoughts lead to quick breaths at all? Maybe the healing stone had only healed the flesh. Memories can't heal. A memory must be forgotten. What happens when a memory is so bad that it can never be forgotten?

Luiz put his hand on my shoulder.

"I thought we'd hang out until papá wakes up," Luiz commented.

I looked at Luiz, which brought on a memory of Alexis's sharp teeth biting into Mr. Espinoza, followed by that of Mr. Espinoza biting into Kendra as he held her barely covered body arched above the cabin bed. Alexis had saved Kendra just in time by grabbing Mr. Espinoza's face with both hands shoving every ounce of her vampire influence into him as she commanded him to stop.

Images from Alexis's dreams burned through my mind as well.

I regretted so many things. That Mr. Espinoza had turned. How Alexis had been mistreated growing up. That Luiz would never bury his father. That O'Brien might never walk again. That Kendra's spirit was slipping away. That my mom was in jail for a murder she didn't commit. That things may never be the same between Sis and me again. That I'd burned away the druid tome. And that I had once again hurt Eldra. But there was nothing I could do about any of it now.

"Hanging out sounds great," I replied. "What do you want to do?" I asked.

Luiz took a moment to think. "Do you have any video games around here yet?"

"Not yet."

"Well, we could go check out the building where we fought the zombies," Luiz threw me a mischievous grin. "Maybe someone needs to make sure that no zombies have returned."

"You perv!" I scoffed. But his comment brought Scarlett—well, Jody—to mind. The moment she entered my thoughts, I felt my head spin. I didn't expect what happened.

Magic took hold of me. I didn't have any strength left to work magic, so I knew immediately this wasn't *my* magic. It was protector magic. Perhaps protector magic wasn't mine? Perhaps it just communicated with me.

My mind disconnected from my body.

I rose through the mansion's upper floors and roof, soaring out of the mansion and into the air. I traveled, just short of instantaneously, over the cities of Bountiful and Salt Lake. I found myself at a small, square house a good distance west of downtown. The little house had a carport but no car under it. The yellow, sun-parched grass now matched the home's fading, once-yellow paint.

I stood—well, my spirit stood—on the south side of the house between the fence and the street. I could see the sun in the western sky, just minutes from setting behind the mountains.

A red Ford Mustang, with the top down, pulled onto the cracked driveway and stopped. The setting sun reflected off its perfect red paint in a way that no other car in the rundown neighborhood could compete with. A girl opened the driver's side door and honked the horn as she stood. She wore a see-through blouse, black and flowery, and jeans that looked like she pulled them right off a runway model. But I recognized the dark hair that tapered at her chin. She was Gina, the college girl from Club Exposed that looked so very much like Alexis.

The door to the house opened and Scarlett—Jody—walked out carrying a small duffle bag over her right shoulder. She wore

135

light blue jeans and a fitted white blouse that had no sleeves but tied at the shoulders. Her red hair hung down and had a bouncy curl to it. Her face had more freckles than I remembered. Or perhaps she simply hadn't put on her makeup yet.

"Gina," Jody cheered and waved. "Thank God ya got here."

Gina remained silent. Her lips smiled but her eyes tightened. Maybe since she couldn't say anything nice, she wasn't going to say anything at all.

"Mommy," a sandy-haired boy of about eight or nine grabbed Jody's left arm. The boy wore tan shorts and a faded, blue tank top. His hair had been combed but hadn't stayed in place.

Jody turned back to her son, dropped her duffel, and scrunched down to wrap her arms around him. "I gotta get to work, baby," she said, running her hand through his sandy hair.

"But mom," he elongated the word *mom* as he hugged her back.

"I love ya, baby. I gotta go."

A short, stocky woman in her early thirties stepped to the door and put her hand on Jody's son. He let go of his mom and let the woman pull him inside.

Jody watched her son until the other woman closed the door. She grabbed her duffle, walked to the convertible, and tossed it in the back before jumping into the passenger seat without opening the door.

Gina put her mustang in reverse but only backed up about a foot when a black SUV screeched to a stop behind her. The back door to the SUV opened and three armed men jumped out. They looked like a SWAT team, only without the logo. Their all-black gear was intentionally anonymous. A fourth man jumped out the side door. The black-uniformed men rushed toward the red convertible, surrounding it.

The tallest of the men leaned in and punched Gina. Then he yanked her out of the car. On the passenger's side, the shortest but stockiest of the four men opened the car door. The other one on that side put a gun to Jody's head and forcibly dragged her to a standing position. "Let me go," she shouted in a high-pitched voice.

"We don't need her," the man dragging Jody shouted to the tallest man, referring to Gina. Tall Man nodded and coldly shot Gina in the head, letting her body drop with a smack to the cement.

The front door opened, and Jody's son came running out. He had a determined look on his face. A look that promised he could save his mother. A promise a body so small could never keep. The fourth man pointed his gun. A shot rang out. The boy spun.

My view faded, and once again, my mind traveled over the cityscape, back to Bountiful. Clouds flashed by, then the mansion roof, which I sank through.

My brain throbbed as I settled back into my body. I felt myself lying on the floor. I trembled involuntarily. I blinked open my eyes but couldn't stop the shaking. Was I having a seizure? Nope. Luiz gripped my shoulders, shaking me back and forth. Idiot friend. But hey, on the bright side, I wasn't having a seizure.

I jerked and shoved at Luiz.

He swore in Spanish, then asked, "You OK?"

I nodded, trying to stand, my adrenaline pumping.

"Why'd you collapse?" Luiz asked, grabbing my arm to help steady me.

I'd had three out-of-body experiences before. The first happened while rock climbing. I saw a vision of Kendra falling to her death. The second happened when I'd collapsed fighting the Vampire King and my mind entered Kendra's body. The third had been in a recent dream. This felt more like the first one. In that one, what I saw hadn't happened yet. I wasn't sure if it was the future or just a possible future. Either way, Kendra hadn't fallen to her death while rock climbing. I glanced out the window. I could see the sun to the west. It hung over the Oquirrh Mountains, a good hour higher in the sky than it had been in my vision. I had time.

"We gotta go!" I shoved Luiz's arms away, getting blood on his left arm.

"Alexis!" I shouted so loud that Luiz covered his ears. Frustratingly enough, she didn't turn off her separation stone.

A moment later, Alexis came strutting around the corner of the hallway, her navel showing as her white shirt flared up. She'd changed out of her practice clothes back into her Kendra-inspired attire. What type of training was Eldra giving her?

"Jake, while I'm really anxious to hear you shout my name, this is not what I had in mind." She grinned mischievously, but I ignored her innuendo.

Then her eyes met mine and her smile faded.

"What is wrong?"

"Just look," I pointed in my head. I felt hesitancy exude from her as she glanced at my bloody knuckles. She didn't want me in her head at that moment. She had thoughts she wanted to keep hidden in her mental hideaway.

Alexis took a deep breath and her eyes softened, physical clues that she was tidying up her thoughts before letting me in. With the tap of her finger on her separation stone, my vision flooded into her mind. Gone were any of her secret thoughts that I hoped to extract from her mind. She absorbed my vision and then cut off my search with another tap of her finger.

"And I had just changed back into these clothes," she shook her head. Then she grabbed the bottom of her shirt with crossed hands, and raising them, stripped it off and turned away from us all in one motion, exposing her shirtless back, covered only by straps from her white bra. She somehow managed to gracefully remove her maroon jeans in between hurried steps before disappearing around the corner.

"*Bendito, Madre de Dios!*" Luiz whispered. The size of his grin almost matched the size of his eyes. "Did you just see that?"

"Let's go," I punched his arm.

"*¿Donde?*" Luiz asked, rubbing his arm.

I'd forgotten he couldn't read my mind. His confusion remained evident in his raised eyebrows, which made his long nose even longer.

"We have to save Scarlett—er, Jody," I answered, already starting down the hall toward the garage. "She's in trouble!"

"*Aye de mi.* This day just keeps getting better!"

# CHAPTER 20
# RESCUE

*Luiz asked me how I liked going to a strip club. Jerk. Alexis, Luiz, Jake, Eldra—all of them keep rubbing it in that I am only sixteen and overly innocent. Well, I want to be innocent. I'm just in this weird place. With full access to Lexy's past, I am anything but innocent. I wish I could float away for a few years and come back when I am ready. Too bad sixteen-year-old girls can't serve a two-year mission for the church. I could use a reprieve from all this and come back when I am eighteen. —Kendra*

Alexis shifted gears and hit the gas, accelerating around the onramp. The centrifugal force urged me to join her in the driver's seat, but my seatbelt held me in place. She'd changed into her black, long-sleeved leather armor. I would have sworn it was the same outfit that she'd worn when we'd battled her grandfather, except I'd erased that one. Once on the freeway, Alexis swerved around cars, even using the shoulder if she had to. Fortunately, it was almost seven, so Salt Lake's rush hour had come and gone. Unfortunately, it was almost seven, so the sun was closing in on the western mountains, which meant that my out-of-body vision was about to become a reality.

I didn't know why the black-clad men would attack Jody, but I felt certain it had something to do with me. But how?

Alexis had to lock up the brakes to exit the freeway without rolling the BMW. Luiz kept muttering under his breath at each turn but flat-out screamed as we screeched through the sharp turn onto 35th South. The turning stopped as we headed west, the direction of the sun, which dropped ever closer to the Oquirrh Mountains.

I had a satellite map of the world pulled up on my new phone. I'd zoomed it in on Jody's small house. I found it in a very similar way to how I had traveled there. My out-of-body experience resembled the online map of the earth. I recognized Pleasant Green Park just to the north. We played a turkey bowl there with Kevin's cousin last year.

Alexis glanced at me as we approached another turn. She tapped her separation stone and there she was, a hundred percent in my head again. She split her focus between driving and the map I was looking at, but I had to blush because her background thoughts were about how attracted to me she was when I was being all protective of a stripper. Lexi's thoughts weren't PG. She intentionally used those thoughts as a shield so that I wouldn't pry at her memories.

I took notice that in her mischievous thoughts, my skin was still normal and tan. I still had the muscle that I'd burned away, and my normal dark brown hair hung to my eyes. Instantly, her image of me changed. My body thinned. Scaly-white skin and a stubbled head replaced the image of who I once was. Immediately, her provocative thoughts shattered.

Alexis made a sharp left turn, and I grabbed the car door handle to hold myself in place.

With our minds joined, she couldn't pretend that she was still attracted to me. She felt every bit as repulsed by my looks as Kendra was. She had just been so much better—practiced—at hiding it. Her mind brought up the most hideous man she had ever been gifted to. He was more of a monstrous thing than a man. Perhaps the ugliest thing I'd ever seen. He was four hundred pounds at least, with a port-wine stain birthmark over the right side of his entire body. He wasn't a vampire, but he was no longer human, either. What he was, even Alexis wasn't sure. But he was a brutal monster and assassin. He could expand his mouth like a giant suckerfish and swallow a person whole. He'd served her grandfather well and when her grandfather had gifted her to him, she hadn't once let the repulsion show on her face.

*I can ignore my revulsion for you, too, Jake.*

*Not helping!* I shouted the thought, trying to get the image of Alexis being gifted to such a creature out of our minds.

Alexis focused. She remained part of me, but somehow, she tucked everything wrong with her life inside that mental box that I couldn't penetrate. She reached into my mind and pulled up the out-of-body vision I'd had of Jody and looped over it like a video clip. She paused my vision like a movie and focused on one of the men. The man with the gun pinned against Jody's head had his arm positioned in such a way that his skin was visible between his black glove and sleeve, partially revealing a tattoo—a skull surrounded in shadow. It looked like Voldemort's dark mark only a with a surrounding shadow instead of a snake—and pressing it wouldn't call their dark overlord. Instead, they wore wireless earpieces for such communication.

*Skull Shadows.* They *are* involved. She had guessed that the scar-faced fake-cop, the one who tried to arrest Justine, was a Skull Shadow. Now she felt certain her guess was correct. If that were all she thought, that wouldn't have bothered me. A wave of fear tsunamied through her emotions and plowed into my chest, making my heart race to match hers.

*We kill them without hesitation and without remorse,* she ordered.

I'd made a promise to myself that I wouldn't let my temptation to erase people from existence win. But the addictive desire flared to life, raising high like the Rocky Mountains to the east, shoving the tidal wave of fear back like it was nothing more than a one-foot wave. I never wanted to share my addiction, but how could I have hidden it from Alexis? If my thin, scaly skinned frame weren't bad enough to horrify her, my evil addiction was. And what would Kendra think of me when she found out?

Alexis glanced at me and grinned. I hadn't expected that. Honestly, it disturbed me ever so deeply that my desire to do more than kill thrilled her so much that her fangs extended. She didn't open her mouth and show them. I just felt them extend in her mouth as if it were my own mouth. That wasn't the only physical evidence that my desire to kill turned her on, but it was the only evidence I would let my mind admit to experiencing. Her grin widened further.

Alexis braked slowly for the last turn, being careful not to squeal her tires and give us away.

I saw the black SUV first, then everything came into view. I shouldn't have been surprised to see the scene unfolding exactly like my vision, but I was. Perhaps I doubted that I had really seen the future. After all, the vision I'd had while rock-climbing, the one where Kendra had fallen to her death, had never actually happened.

As I considered the vision given to me by protector magic, Alexis struggled to prevent the virtual packing tape on her boxed-away thoughts from ripping away. I saw another painting in her memory. A man raised high, impaled by a tall, sharp log, but not dead. Hundreds of bodies lay around him. The bodies had fangs, or claws, and ravenous red eyes or brutal black eyes with no sclera. I immediately recognized the impaled man, not from my own memories, but from Caradoc's. Instead of the painting, I saw the real image. An image far more gruesome than any painter could have ever put on canvas. The impaled man was Caradoc's younger brother, William. Legions of evil had teamed up to destroy him. He had been a protector.

Alexis focused her eyes on the convertible, dragging my eyes with hers. There was no time to explore the painting of the dead protector unearthed from the depths of Alexis's mind. There was only time to do some protecting.

The tallest black-clad Skull Shadow had already lifted Gina from the car. The other two had the passenger door open, one lifting a gun toward Jody's head.

I should have thought to protect Gina, but I didn't. I completely ignored her. Jody's son was about to open the front door. Up until now, my mind had blocked out the end of the vision. But now, the way the bullet had exploded that little boy's chest became the most important moment to prevent. In fact, the need to protect Jody's child superseded the need to protect anyone else. I reached for magic.

My eyes searched for the fourth man, the one who had shot Jody's son. He wasn't where he'd been in my vision. Too late, I located him. He had his gun aimed directly at our car.

He fired. So did the gunman holding Gina.

Two bullets hit the windshield directly in front of my face. The sound inside the car cracked into my ears. A second pair of loud cracks attacked my ears right after. Fortunately, the sound barrier was all that cracked. Bulletproof windshields came standard in all cars owned by the Vampire King.

With the backdoor window still rolling down, Luiz reached out with a handgun and returned fire, acting on his own even before Alexis urged him to fire back. As I rolled down my window, I formed a small football-shaped, magic missile. I reached out the window and threw the glowing football sidearm at the shooter's chest. I ignored the fact that I had completely failed to stifle my addictive desire to erase the man. The missile flew with all the soul erasing power I'd promised myself I'd never use again.

It hit the man high, just below his neck. As Alexis brought the car to a stop, we watched the man's body and soul crack. He split into an uncountable number of molecules that all erased and absorbed into the surrounding energy, the very energy I pulled into myself as magic. I inhaled the ecstasy of it, ignoring the part of me that felt horrified at what I had done.

"First down!" I quipped. Luiz broke out in uncontrolled, maniacal laughter as he pulled the handgun inside and switched the clip.

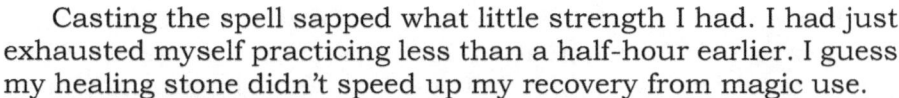

Casting the spell sapped what little strength I had. I had just exhausted myself practicing less than a half-hour earlier. I guess my healing stone didn't speed up my recovery from magic use.

Drained of energy as I was, I struggled to form another magic missile. As I did, Alexis put the car in park, popped open the door, and slid out, staying low to use the door as cover. Something shattered on the ground, thrown by a fifth man still in the truck—a vial. Magic rippled through the air. I didn't wait to find out what spell the vial contained. I side-armed another glowing-blue football at the guy with a gun pressed into the red hair above Jody's right ear.

As soon as it left me, I saw stars. My vision blurred. I imagined Captain Kirk driving my mind. "Scotty," he yelled. "Divert all power to the forward vision." Scotty's accented answer was, "There's not any power left to divert, Captain." My eyes felt a little energy flow into them, enough to give me a hazy tunnel in which I managed to watch my missile.

About a foot from hitting its target, the missile deflected toward the street and smashed against the asphalt. An area the size of a manhole blasted straight up. The debris started disappearing into nothingness as it reached its apex and evaporated completely before anything hit the ground.

"*¡Diantre!* An invisible cornerback just batted away your pass." Luiz shouted.

*Yeah, a cloaked Klingon cornerback,* I thought, still disoriented enough to see nothing wrong with mixing Star Trek and football metaphors while casting druid magic.

Alexis fired her handgun, choosing my same target. The bullet hit him in the forehead but ricocheted into the air, not even leaving a mark.

Alexis grinned, exposing her extended fangs. "Well, guns and magic are failing us." Her tongue licked her lips between her two sharp teeth. "Plan B. Join them for drinks." She winked at me and then she darted out into the open, spinning and zig-zagging her way toward them as they fired at her. Alexis dodged most of the bullets, but her leather armored torso absorbed two direct hits before a third, a hit to her left shoulder, spun her to the ground.

"No!" I shouted. Why hadn't I bullet-proofed her? But before I could finish the thought, she twisted and stood back on her feet. Her leather armor rippled with a hint of magic from where the bullet struck. Who was I kidding? She could use magic herself. Princess Alexis didn't need my protection. She'd protected herself.

I scanned the scene with my tunnel vision, which felt a bit like looking through binoculars.

The guy dragging Jody had her halfway to the SUV when I saw her son. I'd forgotten about him as soon as our presence had prevented his death. The boy plowed into the captor's legs, tripping him. Jody's captor held her tight as he fell, dragging her down with him and using her to cushion his fall. She tried to roll away, but his weight held her tight. The little eight-year-old threw his small fists at the man's face. The boy couldn't have been hitting very hard, but the man rolled away, freeing Jody, and shoved the boy backward.

I stepped out of the car and tried to rush toward them. A bullet hit me and deflected off my clothes. Yes, yes, I did have pebbles in my pockets, and I used them, as weary as I was. A second bullet hit my sleeve. I just had to hope they didn't get a head shot.

My legs didn't respond like I wanted them too. A week ago, I could run the forty-yard dash in four-point-four seconds. Now, it felt like it was taking forty-point-four seconds. The effort of trying to sprint didn't agree with my weak legs. I saw the curb. I tried to step over it. I really tried. But through my blurry and star-filled eyes, I misjudged how high to raise my foot. My toe clipped the curb and I went down. I really wanted to turn my trip into a roll, come back up on my feet and keep running, then take out the gunman before he killed Jody's kid. Instead, I fell forward. A rectangle of grass separated the curb and the crumbly sidewalk. My knees hit the grass, but my palms slapped flat on the sidewalk. I should have stopped my body's momentum before my face hit, but I didn't. Face, meet concrete. Ouch!

My hands and face bled. Pain shot from my palms up my forearms, and my face throbbed. With my skin in the state it was, even my knees, protected by pants and only hitting grass, started bleeding.

I groaned. What had just happened to me?

I forced myself to push up my torso and head. I looked up just in time to get a view of Alexis's fangs biting into the neck of Jody's captor. She held the back of the man's head with one hand and somehow raised her handgun and shot over his shoulder with her other hand, all while sucking down blood.

*Third down,* she projected the thought to both Luiz and me. I wasn't too tired to wonder what happened to second down.

Lexy's bullets hit her intended targets, but they bounced off as if I were somehow using my pebble spell on the air around them. Whatever magic the vial had contained, it protected these men. I wasn't sure why she kept firing until I noticed the guy in the SUV was staying down while she fired. The man in the van must not have trusted that the vial's magic would protect him. Lexy's shots allowed Jody to usher her son into her house without taking any fire.

The tall guy returned from behind the SUV. Had he already shot Gina in the head? I didn't see her body. Maybe he'd stuffed Gina in the back of the SUV? We'd already altered my vision. Perhaps Gina had lived too. He opened fire on Alexis, but she shielded herself with the man she fed from. The Skull Shadow didn't have any qualms at shooting his own men. His bullets didn't ricochet. Apparently, the magic didn't protect against friendly fire. His bulletproof vest did a good job, mostly, except it didn't cover his neck, arms, legs, or head.

Only one other guy was unaccounted for. I found him face down on the ground, neck broken. He must have been the second down. It probably happened while I was eating concrete. Why had Alexis not fed on him? Picky eater? She probably would have answered my mental question had she not been holding a human shield to protect herself from a barrage of bullets.

As soon as the tall guy ran out of bullets, the guy in the SUV opened fire on Alexis through the side back window that was only partially open. Alexis, still behind her bloodied, lifeless human shield, advanced on the SUV. A whack came from behind the SUV and the tall guy fell forward. Luiz moved into view and put his shoe on the tall guy's back, picking up the unconscious man's assault rifle and tossing it over his shoulder triumphantly and shouted, "Fourth down!"

"Get the girl," Alexis called to Luiz. Then she broke the SUV window with the dead man's skull and shoved the body through it. The SUV took off, clipping the front corner of Alexis's BMW. Alexis wished she had parked it closer so the SUV couldn't get away.

I looked back at Luiz. There he stood, Gina leaning into him, her face buried into one shoulder and the assault rifle he'd plundered from a dead gunman hung from the other. He had his arms wrapped around her, one high on her back and one low just at the small of her back. He had a massive grin on his face.

He pointed at Gina with his upper hand, "Touchdown."

It was a great moment for Luiz. I, on the other hand, felt useless. Alexis had taken out the two men by Jody. Luiz dropped the tall man. The last Skull Shadow got away. What had I done? I'd tripped and fallen.

*You got us here in time. You got first down, taking out a gunman. You saved Jody. You saved the boy. You made it possible for Luiz to save Gina. Gina wasn't shot in the head, so technically, you saved her too. This was all you,* Alexis answered my depressed thoughts. Then she tapped her separation stone.

"Get the bodies. If we are lucky, we can clean up this situation before the cops arrive."

Alexis lifted the tall guy from the road, onto her shoulder, and packed him into Jody's house. Luiz walked Gina past the remaining body, then sent her inside alone so he could carry the other dead man. He tried to lift the guy like Alexis had but couldn't. So instead, he grabbed the man's feet and started dragging him. I followed, staring at my bloodied hands, wishing I had the energy to help.

Even though the neighbors hadn't come out of their houses yet, I could feel their eyes looking through their windows as Luiz dragged the body into Jody's home.

Alexis stood inside, motionless. Her lips pursed. The house felt empty. It took me a second to realize it myself. The back door hung open. Jody and her son were nowhere to be seen. And hadn't there been another woman? Yes, another woman had been here watching Jody's boy.

"Where did they go?" Luiz asked.

"They were taken." Alexis glanced at the open back door. A section of the fence in Jody's back yard lay flat. Tire marks left two ruts followed by mud tracks over the downed fence.

There had been two groups? How come I hadn't known there had been two groups? I cursed under my breath. What use was my vision if it didn't tell me everything I needed to know?

I hadn't saved Jody and her son after all. Alexis was wrong. I *had* been useless. Alexis had no thoughts of encouragement for me this time.

Alexis inhaled deeply with her nose, absorbing the scents all around. If I didn't know better, I would have thought she was going to go all little werewolf Winnie on me and spout off impossible to discern details like the destination, flight number, and meal order. But Alexis inhaled, not to find out about the men who had taken Jody, but something else.

Even though her separation stone was enabled, I knew it when she knew it. As if I had pried past her protection stone, which I hadn't tried to do, I caught a glimpse of her most prominent thought.

Alexis dashed to the smaller of two tiny bedrooms and pulled open the closet. The little boy looked up indifferently but quickly turned back to his screen. He wore headphones and currently tapped at a tablet, trying to kill virtual zombies with plants as fast as he could. This kid had just gone all Mike Tyson's punch out on a bad guy and now hid in his closet completely zoned out in zombie land like nothing happened.

Alexis slid to a sitting position behind the boy, and her eyes softened. A hint of a smile made her expression almost motherly. She wrapped her arms around the boy's torso and put her hands on his chest, trying not to interfere with his arms or in any way interrupt his virtual assault on animated zombies. She just sat there with him.

I looked at Alexis with new eyes. She *was* more than just a vampire—er, half-dhampir. She cared. She knew how to fall instantly in love with a child. She glanced at me and a tear dripped from her eye. I could feel her sadness, but something wasn't right. It didn't feel like sadness for the boy. This sadness came from deeper inside of Alexis. It felt like loss—no, not loss. More like something she never had. Something missing that could never be found, and it left a huge hole in her. Did Alexis understand that emptiness? What caused it?

Then her fangs extended, and her tongue slid between them to lick her lips. Hunger lined her eyes. She'd just fed off a Skull Shadow, so she could easily ignore it, but still, she slowly removed her arms from the boy and stood up and walked out of the room. She tossed me a hard look, like the kind a guy gets when a girl catches him looking at her chest. Waves of hate that I assumed were directed toward me throbbed violently into my confused mind.

"What?" she demanded, leaving her mouth open wide with her fangs exposed, as if demanding I challenge her.

A heavy pounding on the door thankfully interrupted our exchange.

"Open the door! Police."

"*¡Esperate!*" Luiz shouted back at them.

I cringed. Why did he choose that moment to answer in Spanish? Perhaps it was wrong to assume cops were racist, but I did.

Alexis dashed toward the door. I thought she was going to open it, but instead, she sat down on the floor next to Gina, curled into a ball, and started shaking and crying. Not like the single tear she shed while holding Jody's son, but hysterical crying, with both eyes dripping crocodile tears. The two dead bodies we'd dragged inside lay in plain sight.

Luiz opened the door.

The police weren't directly in front of the door. Instead, two were on each side. The one on the right came in with his handgun steady, held straight out in both hands.

"Hands in the air," he pointed at Luiz, who quickly complied. His eyes darted to the bodies before returning to focus on Luiz.

The second policeman followed behind and pointed at me.

"Good Lord!" he shouted in surprise when he looked at me, the gun pointed at my chest. "Hands in the air." I could see the fear in his eyes.

I just stood there like an idiot. Why would an officer point his gun at me? Why was he afraid of me? It didn't make sense. I was the good guy.

*Put your hands up, Jake!* Lexy's mind touched mine. Unintentionally, I saw myself through her eyes. The very sight the policeman saw—a hideous monster. My stubbly hair did little to hide the splotchy skin on my scalp. Not for the first time, my face reminded me of a burn victim, but not quite. Where a burn victim had a rubbery, stretched scarring, my skin didn't look stretched, but instead, had hideous white-and-red splotches. As if that weren't bad enough, blood dripped down my face from my forehead, nose, and right cheek, from when I'd tripped on the curb and landed on the concrete like an idiot. I'd fought zombies that looked like normal people just last night, and now I was the normal person that looked like a stereotypical zombie. I'd seen my hideousness in Kendra and Alexis's eyes. I'd felt their revulsion, but until seeing the fear in the police officer's eyes, I hadn't realized how bad it was.

"I said, 'Hands in the air!'" the policeman shouted, elevating his voice as if trying to hide his fear with anger. Two more policemen appeared in the doorway. One was a little overweight, but the other looked solid. He looked as big and strong as I used to be.

At that moment, I wanted to die. I didn't want to exist. I hated how I looked. I hated myself. I hated what I had done to Kendra and Alexis, forcing the Trinity of Mind on them. The bad thought—the one I wasn't supposed to repeat—came to mind full force. The very bad thought that the shadow blades had found and infected.

Despite Eldra commanding me not to, I let Kendra's and Lexy's bad thought repeat in my mind.

Kendra: *Perhaps we are only connected through Jake?*
Alexis: *If he dies, perhaps the myndtiegan would break.*
Kendra: *Perhaps, then we'd both be better off.*

I added Eldra's accusation to their bad thought: the accusation that the *myndtiegan* was equivalent to rape, the guilt of which I had been trying to repress, now overwhelmed me. I wanted to try to free Kendra and Alexis. I wanted to atone for forcing them into the Trinity of Mind, and death was perhaps the only option.

On top of all that, I was a constant reminder to my mother of the worst moment of her life. She had to relive that moment every time she looked at me. Sis and mom were threatened because I existed. I'd let the nightwalkers massacre my stepdad. Kendra wasn't wrong. Everyone *would* be better off if my fake death became real.

I looked at the police officer and decided that charging him would be a good idea. After Grandma passed, Sis and Luiz had unknowingly kept me from leaving this world. Perhaps it was time I try again.

Alexis had tried to commit suicide once, so I assumed she would understand, but she didn't. Lexy's mind slammed into mine. She nudged the destitute depression out of the way and took control of my body. Not in a vampire way but more like how I had taken control of Kendra's body. My arms raised at her command, not mine.

Then the policeman moved forward and grabbed my shoulder. My skin cracked in his grip as he slammed me against the wall. My cheek, the one that hadn't hit the sidewalk, hit the wall and I felt blood immediately.

"No, not them. Not them." Alexis, back in her own mind, whimpered. Her words, quiet as they were, danced through the room. "They saved us."

The policemen paid attention. When Princess Alexis speaks, everyone pays attention. Especially when she suddenly decided to emanate her allure in full force. She had acted the hysterical female because, when a smoking-hot girl is balled up and crying, most men immediately feel a protective bond. That little bond was all Alexis needed to keep their minds from fighting back when she unleashed her allure on them. Her pumpkin spice scent filled the room.

The two officers who had entered last both reached a hand down, offering to help Alexis up. Alexis probably had them under her power already, but once she accepted their hands, physical skin-to-skin contact, there was no doubt. The policemen were now hers.

# CHAPTER 21
# SEVERED

*I felt more vulnerable than I ever had in my entire life when Jake witnessed how my grandfather forced me to feed on the family in Ecuador. I was only fifteen. Once I turned seventeen, my grandfather forced me to kill for him. I can read minds. Not usually Grandfather's, but some of his louder thoughts slip out. The last few assignments, he thought, "Die this time!" I realize now that he intentionally projected that thought, hoping that I would despair and obey him. I never despaired. I have stayed alive. Eleven times, I have assassinated my grandfather's enemies. I never fed on them. I would use a gun, a knife, a car accident, anything to avoid feeding. Jake and Kendra share my memories. Somehow, they do not hate me. I am lucky. The eleven targets were vile beings who deserved to die. What if he had sent me after a family, like the family in Ecuador? What would I have done? —Alexis*

I snapped awake when Alexis slowed down the BMW and turned into the driveway to her mansion. I sat alert, ready for anything.

The police had taken brief statements from each of us—under assumed names. The house had swarmed with police, both inside and out. Somehow—OK, it was Alexis—not a single officer asked for our identification or took pictures of us.

By the time the news vans arrived, the four police officers, fully under Lexy's influence, had us tucked away at a neighbor's

150

house. We had waited three hours—the last of which I slept—for the scene to calm down before we were finally able to leave.

Alexis brought Gina as well as Jody's son, Carl, with us. Luiz sat in the back with them. He had his arm around Gina and she slept on his shoulder—which was probably the source of Luiz's smirk. Carl's head rested on Gina's lap. The police had not called child services either. Maybe they only did that on TV, or maybe Alexis just didn't want them to. Carl breathed loudly but didn't snore. Gina didn't seem to breathe at all. I thought about bringing up Andrea to wipe that smirk off Luiz's face, but I didn't. I'd remind him about Andrea later.

Alexis pulled into the garage.

"I'm going to sleep for a week again," I mumbled. Talking pulled at the new scabs from the sidewalk-induced scrapes on my face.

"You need it," Alexis answered. "You all do."

I noticed she excluded herself. She'd fed on one of the armed men. She wouldn't need to sleep for a while. What would she be up to while we slept? How is it that she still hid secrets? If I weren't so tired and weak, I'd stay up to find out. But the healing stone didn't actually heal me; it simply urged my body to heal faster, which meant food, then sleep, then worry about what Alexis did while I slept. I couldn't forget Kendra's spirit was in danger of leaking away. Oh, and was Eldra going to kill me when she woke up?

Alexis lifted Carl out of the car and onto her right hip. His head fell on her shoulder. Luiz assisted Gina, who tried to shake off her grogginess as she exited the car.

I followed Alexis to the door into the house, hoping for an aroma of something amazing once she opened it. Surely the three servants had knocked out another awesome dinner. Alexis shifted Carl higher on her hip and easily held him with only her right arm, allowing her to reach for the handle with her left hand.

She froze. Her thumb never pushed down on the latch.

She turned to me, and with her free hand, put a finger to her lips. Then she stepped to Luiz and handed off Carl. She knew I didn't have the strength to carry the boy. I could barely keep myself standing.

As soon as Carl was out of her hands, Alexis pulled the blade sheathed at her leg.

I sighed. *Now what?* Fear, hunger, excitement—why couldn't Alexis just disable her separation stone already? What was wrong inside the house?

Oh, no! We had left Kendra here. I said a very bad word.

Fortunately, I'd had a one-hour nap, or I would have been too tired to deal with whatever we were about to face.

Alexis waited while Luiz and Gina took Carl back to the car and laid him down in the back.

"Stay with the boy," Luiz whispered to Gina.

Hopefully, if everything went to hell like it did at Bear Lake, Gina and the boy would sleep right through it. If the worst thing to happen to Carl was waking up in a strange car wondering where he was, well, compared to the alternative, that just might not be so bad.

Luiz opened the trunk of the car and pulled out a pair of handguns. He hadn't been allowed to keep the assault rifle he'd taken from the men. Alexis hadn't tried to convince the police to let him keep it. I recognized the two SIG P250s that O'Brien had used at Bear Lake. Luiz handed one to Gina. She ejected the clip, examined it, and popped the clip back in like handling a gun was second nature. Alexis nodded in approval, tapped her separation stone off, then opened the door.

Alexis flipped the switch, but the light in the hallway remained off. The darkness hung in the otherwise vacant hallway. The smell of blood hit Lexy's nose first and her fangs extended. The recognized smell of voodoo magic came second. Alexis stepped inside and tiptoed to the end of the hall before backing her lithe form against the wall so that she could see around the corner to the right. She motioned for Luiz to mirror her and look down the other way. He tried to tiptoe with Alexis's stealth, but his steps made small smacks on the hardwood. He put his back to the wall, then mimicking Alexis, he looked around the corner and then jumped back. The thirty-something maid stepped into view. Her chin dripped with blood, her once-white apron now crimson. A knife stuck out of her chest. She should have been dead. Her dilated pupils looked dead.

Hadn't it been only yesterday when I had hoped that come-back-from-the-dead zombies weren't real? That zombies were just regular humans, mind-jacked by the caplatas? I'd hoped in vain. Apparently, the caplatas also practiced voodoo necromancy by animating the dead.

The undead zombie opened her mouth, and with teeth spread wide, she lunged at Luiz.

Alexis swung the knife fast toward her neck. I looked away, but it didn't help. Through Lexy's eyes, I witnessed the way her knife severed the servant's head.

That servant hadn't been a vampire or a nightwalker. She had cooked our meals. She hadn't been Carolyn, but . . .

*Oh, please. Not Carolyn.* I added worry for Carolyn to my already huge list of worries that started with the need to save Kendra. The other servants had been reserved and withdrawn, but Carolyn had opened up to me. She'd become my friend. Subconsciously, I knew I mostly worried about Kendra, not Carolyn, but I refused to believe what happened to this servant had happened to Kendra.

Alexis led us left down the hall and into the dining room—the same one where I'd first dined with her. I recognized the long, oversized table. At the other end of it, a chair lay on its side where two more servants fed on a third. A kitchen knife lay on the hardwood floor just inches from the lifeless servant's right hand. The two hunched and feeding servants had deep gashes—mortal wounds. They were the come-back-from-the-dead type zombies, too. The sounds of their sickening gnawing and palate smacking made me cringe. Alexis, however, did not feel disgusted. Instead, she was simply on high alert. None of the three had red or gray hair, which allowed me to take a breath, knowing neither Carolyn nor Lillian was among them.

One of the two servants looked up, and her chin turned toward us. She had a cut across her nose and cheek. Blood covered her face and dropped down her bodice. When the first zombie servant started toward us, the second one looked up, also with a blood-smeared face.

*You are very squeamish,* Alexis chastised.

Alexis tapped off her separation stone for me. Alexis rushed toward them, blade in hand. I turned away in plenty of time to not look, but I still heard the flesh-slicing sound of her blade. Luiz watched. I had a morbid best friend.

"As thralls, their minds already belonged to someone else. The caplatas could not take them alive, so they took them in death," Alexis surmised. "Come. We must check on Kendra and Eldra."

Alexis's worry, which still slipped through despite the separation stone, added to my own—double the worry meant double the stress. With my recent luck, my stubble hair would grow out gray.

I couldn't avoid looking as we passed the bodies of the three servants. Women I knew. Women who had cooked and cleaned for me. Their mutilated faces, two on detached heads and one chewed on, would haunt me for quite some time. I hoped my healing stone was hard at work on my existing PTSD because this sure wasn't conducive to my mental recovery.

My overactive breathing lessened when we exited the dining hall. Alexis moved quickly through the halls, and we struggled to keep up. OK, I struggled. Luiz stayed back with me protectively. The muscles in my legs—my quads—burned. Luiz didn't breathe hard. I used to be bigger, stronger, and faster than him.

Alexis reached Kendra's room and her emotions gave me the bad news before I caught up to her. Kendra was not inside. Alexis glanced around the room, curiosity mixing into her sadness. My eyes followed hers. Kendra's bed lay empty. The blanket was tossed aside, exposing the slight crumpling of sheets that marked where Kendra's body had slept.

*She's dead.* The mental words crossed my mind. Those words weren't Alexis's or Kendra's; they were coming from my own hopeless despair. The dark pit in my mind called to me, begging me to enter and lose myself in its abyss.

*You should join her,* the despairing voice added. I considered those words. I'd been so close to just such a decision hours ago that it was easy to listen now. If I followed their advice, I would be with Kendra. In death, I'd be restored to my normal strong and handsome self—as opposed to a weak, hideous-skinned shell of who I used to be. Besides, as Kendra had thought, wouldn't everyone be better off? Wouldn't it make amends for forcing the Trinity of Mind on Kendra and Alexis?

Alexis placed her palm on the sheets.

"The sheets are cold. There is no blood. No sign of struggle."

Alexis looked at me in a way that demanded my eyes meet hers. I could see the light in her eyes, reflecting off her red pupils. Her eyes held a hint of sadness, but they also held something more. Hope. Determination.

"They took her alive," she spoke the words confidently, like they were an inarguable fact. Her words pulled me from the edge of the mental despair I nearly jumped into. "We will get her back," Alexis swore.

"Papá?" Luiz suddenly questioned, and then he bolted from the room.

"Luiz," Alexis called, but Luiz just kept going. She started to go after him, then stopped. "Do you feel that?" she asked.

I shook my head. I didn't feel anything.

She tapped her separation stone. I immediately felt what she felt. Or more accurately, I didn't feel what she didn't feel. The magic in the house had gone still, like a forest goes quiet for a predator. Why didn't the magic feel alive and powerful like normal? I grasped at the magic and pulled it into me. Once inside me, the magic came to life with its regular, vibrant energy.

I tried to ignore Alexis as she probed the thoughts that my mental pit of despair had brought up. I focused on the state of the magic around me. I sent out my mind into the house, feeling my surroundings. I could sense a direction from which the stillness had begun. I followed with my senses, my mind traveling down one story and across the mansion to the servants' wing. The stillness led me into an unexpectedly empty room.

Confused, I let my senses drift elsewhere for a minute. I focused on the third floor, but quickly the stillness pulled me back, and I found myself sensing the same servant's room once more. I urged my senses to move around the room, probing deeper. Alexis's mind, still connected to mine, felt distant, but I could still feel her worry for Kendra. She didn't seem able to follow my senses outside of my body. Perhaps I'd discovered a limitation to our Trinity of Mind.

Then I felt the void. I found a spot in the center of the room where the magic wasn't just motionless, it just wasn't there. If the magic outside that spot were like stagnant air, then inside the spot would have been a suffocating vacuum.

A containment.

This stillness had hidden the containment so well that I'd almost missed it. I focused my senses on the containment and found it impressively complete—very much like my everything-seal.

I'd never really penetrated a containment with just my senses before, but I tried it. At first, the containment held, but then I felt my senses separate as if into a trillion particles of sand and slip inside. Inside the containment, the area held no magic at all. All magic had been sucked out completely.

Three women huddled inside the magical barrier.

For a millisecond, I hoped that I'd found the two voodoo witches with Kendra, but I recognized the way the magic had been sucked out of that containment.

*Eldra!* Alexis and I thought simultaneously.

# CHAPTER 22
# SURVIVORS

My spirit can leave my body. It's called astral projection. I jumped into Kendra's body during the attack at Bear Lake. Eldra said the Trinity of Mind makes that possible, but only if a druid already knows how to astral project. Perhaps protector magic taught me how? Anyway, sharing Kendra's body was a weird experience, and not just because she was bald and naked. Being in someone else's body is different. It can't be explained. It is disorienting at first, then clumsy. You want that body to respond like your own, but it won't because it is different. After a while, you notice all the differences. —Jake

My stretched senses whiplashed back into my body, leaving me dizzy. The blood drained from my head and my vision went black.

My eyes opened a few seconds later. I was still standing. Lexy's arms wrapped around me, holding me next to her. My body reacted to her touch with a wave of lust, but with my protection stone's help, I managed to push it away and focus. Her allure still affected me, just not overwhelmingly. Never again would I beg her to feed off me. Of course, my blood would burn her like acid, which ended any concern that she'd try to bite me again.

I'd like to say we rushed to Eldra's room, but really, I stumbled slowly through the halls. When we reached the stairs descending to the servant's quarters, Alexis slipped under my arm to help me down. It must have been a full three minutes before we arrived.

I had only been to that wing of the house once—the day I had searched every inch of the mansion for Alexis. The servants' wing didn't look any less extravagant than the wing with my room. Of course, the mansion wasn't old, so it surely hadn't been built with servants in mind. These rooms were just as extravagant because they were also intended for rich occupants.

My legs burned as I followed Alexis into Eldra's room. It was similar to the room I stayed in. It had a bed against the wall under a window and a desk on the right, with plenty of space in between. A circled pentagram marked the floor, only this one wasn't made with embedded silver and was much smaller. Instead, it had been drawn quickly with what looked to be a purple, dry-erase marker.

Three women huddled inside the circle. Eldra sat in the middle, strong and sure, holding her staff upright, both hands above her head. Carolyn and Lillian each leaned into her, one arm in an embrace and the other holding onto one of Eldra's raised arms. Carolyn shivered uncontrollably. As old and gray as Lillian was, Eldra made her look young.

Even as my heart wrenched that Kendra wasn't with them, I celebrated that Carolyn and Lillian had found Eldra and survived.

Eldra's eyes met Lexy's. She took a deep breath, and then as she released it, she let go of the containment, and her body collapsed. The two servants gasped and kept her slumping body from smacking against the wood floor. The staff dropped behind them and rattled to a stop.

Carolyn glanced at me and gulped as she quickly looked away. Neither woman looked Alexis in the eyes.

"Sh-she t-told us not to l-let her hands fall," Carolyn whispered through a quivering chin. "We obeyed her," her words sounded desperate. "As you commanded, we obeyed her." The desperation in her words exposed her fear of being punished as if she'd done something wrong.

Visions from Alexis's time with her grandfather flooded into my mind. I caught a glimpse of a dark room. Two disobedient servant women hung from chains. The Vampire King stood by one of the women, his eyes black with fury. He slid his fingernails down her right shoulder, slicing her skin like a bad Freddy Krueger dream. Blood spilled down the screaming woman's arm. The Vampire King licked it.

Alexis pushed at my mind and her memory faded. Carolyn wasn't just afraid of becoming a caplata zombie, she was afraid of the repercussions of failure, of disappointing her master.

157

*I would never,* Alexis assured me. I believed her.

Alexis moved slowly yet gracefully toward them. She put one palm on Carolyn's cheek and the other on Lillian's. Alexis was not like her grandfather. Her compassion flooded through her hands and into the two shaking servants' bodies.

"Everything is going to be all right," Alexis whispered softly, her feminine words decorated with her allure. Immediately, the two women calmed down. They tilted their heads into Lexy's palms as a child would their mother's. For the second time today, Alexis proved that she knew how to show real, untainted love.

Alexis gave the two women a moment, then slipped her hands under Eldra and carried her to the bed. Alexis worried about Eldra. We needed her. We needed her to find Kendra, mostly, but we needed her for more than that. She was special. Perhaps the last living druid with power.

*She will not sleep long,* Alexis thought.

She adjusted Eldra's head on the pillow and turned back to her servants. Eldra should have still been recovering from our training accident where I'd hit her with my magic missile. I wasn't sure how she'd managed the powerful containment that both stilled the magic and hid her presence, as weak as she should have been.

"What happened?" Alexis asked the servants.

Carolyn and Lillian glanced at each other, but even after experiencing Lexy's compassion, neither met her eyes.

"I don't know," Lillian answered toward the floor. "I was tending to Eldra. I never left this room." Her eyes darted to Carolyn.

Alexis turned her eyes to Carolyn.

"We didn't know they were in the house until it was too late. I went to check on Kendra, and she wasn't in her room. I went looking for her, but before I could find her, Jennifer screamed. I ran to help her and found Kim biting her. Jennifer yelled to me that witches were in the house. She grabbed a kitchen knife and told me to run. I came down and woke Eldra. She said her magic could hide us if we helped her."

"The caplatas entered the house?" Alexis questioned. "They could use magic inside our threshold?"

Carolyn nodded. She opened her mouth to speak, but then closed it and looked at her feet.

Alexis approached Carolyn and lifted her chin with her fingers. Alexis forced Carolyn's eyes to meet hers. "What are you afraid to tell us?"

"I don't know," she started, but Alexis plucked the truth from Carolyn's mind.

*Kendra invited them in.*

Alexis dropped her hand from Carolyn's chin. The servant immediately looked down at her feet and grabbed her red braid nervously.

"I revoke your invitation to this home, Kendra," Alexis spoke out loud. "And I revoke any whom you have invited in." The words hung in the air awkwardly. I assumed that meant if the voodoo witches came back, they wouldn't be using magic inside the mansion.

Eldra stirred but didn't wake.

*Back to the car. We have to go after them,* I urged Alexis.

*We will,* Alexis answered. *But not tonight.* Her mind flashed an image of my haggard, scraped face. The healing stone had accelerated my healing, and in the short hours since falling on my face and hands, the scrapes were already thick scabs. She also tossed me an image of Eldra sleeping off her exhaustion. She hadn't even recovered from our training accident before she'd been forced to exhaust herself hiding from the caplatas.

*If we try tonight, we will lose.*

*But Kendra needs us,* I argued.

*Yes, she does. And she needs us to succeed, not fail.*

*But we can catch up to them if we leave now.*

*Catch up to them where? Which way did they go?*

She was right. I didn't know where the caplatas were headed. Did they head north or south? East or west?

*Eldra will know how to track them,* Alexis assured me. *Wait for her to wake.*

*I can figure out how to track them,* I assured myself more than her.

*You need to figure out how to sleep.*

I wanted to argue further, but I couldn't think of one argument for risking a rescue attempt tonight that Alexis didn't have a good counter for. I unhappily agreed with her. I needed food and rest, in that order. The healing stone wasn't magic—well, it was—but it couldn't create mass by magic. It just made my body speed up its normal processes. The healing stone simply made my body's regenerative system work faster and more accurately. I still needed food and rest.

"Servants," Alexis spoke. "Jake needs food."

She tapped her separation stone, cutting me off from her thoughts before pulling out her phone and dialing.

"Take Jake with you," she told Carolyn while putting her phone to her ear. I could hear the phone ringing ever so slightly. I wanted to stay and hear the conversation. Who was she calling? Why was she making a phone call? How did she manage to keep these answers from me before she enabled her separation stone?

I faintly heard a woman's voice answer.

"One moment," Alexis spoke into the phone. She raised her right eyebrow and gave me a get-out-of-here-and-quit-listening-in-on-my-conversation look.

*Seriously?*

I reluctantly followed Carolyn out of the room.

Alexis shut the door. I pressed my mind against her separation stone, trying to pry an opening. It worked somewhat. I caught her greeting.

"Mother," Alexis started.

Then Carolyn grabbed my hand and pulled me along. With her interruption, the opening I'd pried into Alexis's mind closed.

Carolyn smiled and looked me in the eyes. "Thank you for coming. You saved us."

"Did we?" I wondered, letting her drag me down the hallway. "The voodoo hags left before we returned."

Carolyn took a roundabout path to the kitchen, avoiding the hallway by the garage and the dining hall. I didn't complain. I didn't want to see the bloodied corpses any more than she did.

As I walked, I lost hope. I had believed that everything would end with Keagan's challenge. Once we moved past that, everything could go back to normal. It would take time. But eventually, I would heal. Eventually, I would build my muscle back. O'Brien would heal. I'd somehow let everyone know that I hadn't died.

But it hadn't ended. We'd been attacked twice.

I can't remember ever being demotivated to eat. But when Carolyn brought me a two-steak dinner with potatoes and vegetables, I only ate half of it.

# CHAPTER 23
# CONNECTED

*We all have nightmares now. At the same time. Eldra says that we need to disable the separation stones before bed because our dreams will help us learn to cope with the Trinity of Mind. I tried it for a couple nights when Jake was still recovering, but I can't. Not just because I awkwardly learned something new. I've never been more frightened than by Alexis's nightmares. I keep my separation stone enabled at night for now. Still, I sense when Jake or Alexis slips into a nightmare, and then I slip into my own. I replay that night at Bear Lake. I have two main nightmares. In the first, we lose the battle and ... I can't write the rest. In the second, Mr. Espinoza feeds on me. I'm alone. Jake and Alexis never come save me. I don't want to tell Luiz how scared I am of his dad. —Kendra*

Some people think that experiencing a real-life horror would keep them up at night. Maybe those people have never had such experiences. Or maybe I just react to them differently. Real-life horrors don't keep me up. They wear me out so that, the moment my head hits the pillow, I fall into a sleeping prison where I relive the horrors over and over again in my dreams. Worse, I can't wake up, because the dreams have me locked in a cell and refuse to let me out.

My dream repeated itself all night. It started with saving Kendra from the voodoo-created zombies outside Club Exposed and ended with her finding me sleeping in my room and feeding on my flesh. Of course, she invited the servants to dinner too. I can honestly say that dying in my dreams doesn't kill me in real life. Sorry, Freddy. Your story isn't true. My story is real life. Dying in my dreams just shredded my emotions and piled on the PTSD.

I could feel the connection to Kendra like I could feel the morning sun pounding through my closed eyelids, but my

161

sleeping prison refused to release me until the dream finished this cycle one more time.

I ran from the dining hall. The two zombie servants stopped feeding on the third servant to come after me. I took one look back as I rounded the corner. Great. The third servant, her flesh shredded from being partially eaten, stood up and stumbled toward me too.

I ran for my room. I ran fast too. Not that it mattered how fast I ran. In my dream, I didn't really go anywhere. Every time I looked back, the bloodied servants stumbled toward me with hungry eyes. It seemed like I ran forever before I found my room and slipped inside. No sooner was I in my room than I found myself in my bed sleeping, my head on the pillow.

My spirit left my body. I stood to the side of the room, watching my body lay helplessly on my bed. I wanted to see me hide under the covers as if that would make me safe, but no matter what I wanted, my sleeping form just breathed into the pillow.

I heard the floor creak. The same one I'd heard with each cycle of this dream. I looked and there stood Kendra. She wore the white camisole and panties she had worn the night Mr. Espinoza had tried to feed off her, only in my dream, she wasn't bald, and the front of her camisole dripped with blood that had fallen from her mouth. Her hollow eyes followed her chin as she located my body in my bed.

Kendra took awkward steps toward the bed. I watched her mouth with dread. She had bitten into my exposed face a half-dozen times in this cycling dream. I tried to close my eyes and not watch her feed on me, but try as I might, my eyes wouldn't close.

From the other side of the room, my consciousness braced against the repeating horror, as if tensing for a startling moment in a horror movie that I'd already seen.

Kendra reached my bed, and her face approached mine. Her lips parted.

Then she kissed my cheek.

Instantly, I found my consciousness back in my body in bed. I opened my eyes to Kendra. The blood had disappeared from her chin and white camisole.

"Jake." I blinked as I tried to wake up and adjust to the unexpected turn of events. My face felt noticeably not eaten. Instead, the touch of Kendra's lips lingered.

"Jake, wake up!" she shook me.

"Kendra?"

"It's me," she confirmed. "I'm not going to eat you this time, I promise."

With one hand, I lifted the blankets, and with the other, I reached for her hip and grabbed it. I pulled her into my bed with me. She came willingly. Our lips met. I pulled her against me.

I remembered everything about her. Her scent. The way her lips tasted. The way her golden-brown hair fell straight down her back. Her hair felt silky pressed between my palm and the back of her camisole. Her teeth felt smooth as my tongue slid between them.

"Wait, Jake." Kendra pushed away from me.

I tugged at her, trying to pull her back to me, but she held firm.

"Jake," she started. "As nice as this is, it isn't why I came. I need your help."

"What do you need?" I asked.

"I've tried to talk to you all night, but I couldn't stop," she paused, "I couldn't stop eating your face."

"Wait, you knew you were eating me?"

"Silly Jake. These aren't your dreams. They are mine. I tried so hard to not bite you, but I couldn't. Not until the sun came up."

My mind tried to separate what was dream and what was reality. Kendra had left the mansion for some reason, but I couldn't quite remember why. I tugged at her hip, but again, she resisted. I looked into Kendra's eyes, then I glanced down at her state of dress and back up. Her hair, long a moment ago, was now her current boy cut.

"I know, Jake." Kendra smiled. "I'll probably never be properly dressed when you are affecting my dreams. What can I expect from a silly boy like you?"

"Can you come back, Kendra? Why did you leave? Did you let the voodoo witches into the mansion?" I blurted the questions out without giving her time to answer. Her answers flashed in my mind instantly. With each answer, I remembered more of reality and asked more questions. She couldn't control her body when she'd invited the caplatas into the mansion. The witches had forced her to bite the servants they encountered, to infect them with the caplatas' magic, but when that failed, they'd killed them and reanimated them with necromancy. Kendra, under the witches' control, had left without challenge.

We'd assumed her separation stone would block out the caplatas, but it hadn't. Why hadn't we left her guarded?

"I'm in control right now," Kendra affirmed. "You have to find me before nightfall, Jake. I can be me in the daytime, at least if I fight hard enough. I can't find your mind when I'm awake, but I can find your heart in my sleep. I pulled your heart to me tonight."

"My heart?" I asked, confused.

"They are hiding me in the shadows. They hurt, Jake. The shadows hurt."

"How do I make the shadows go away?" I asked. "How do I find you?"

"You can follow me to my heart. Remember, Jake?" As she asked, the setting changed. The mansion and bed faded away, replaced by Kevin's living room. We sat on his couch.

"What do you mean?" I asked. But both verbally and mentally, she avoided giving me a direct answer, as if an unseen force actively prevented her.

Kendra had a tear dripping down her cheek and onto her lip. I'd kiss her, then she would explain it to me. I put my hand on her face and leaned in to kiss her. But just before our lips met, the sun hit me in the eyes. I tried to shield them . . .

I woke up in my bed. Late morning daylight filled my room. It was probably almost ten. The sun didn't shine directly into my window, but Alexis sat on the windowsill, purposely using her runed blade to reflect the sun into my eyes. Her mind felt warm as we connected.

Today she wore jeans with holes ripped in the knees, and smaller holes all the way up her thigh, including a hole where her leg met her hip. Her white shirt had long sleeves, and except for a rectangle of opaque material at her breasts, the shirt was mesh and see-through. It covered all but the straps of her black bra. She'd chosen a black bra *because* it contrasted with her white blouse. Despite the shirt being see-through, she still considered it a Kendra outfit. I couldn't hide my thoughts from her. I found her outfit beyond attractive.

She noticed me looking.

*Thank you for your flattering thoughts. I let you sleep a long time and—,* she stopped as my dream moved to the forefront of my mind.

I sat up and let her rifle through my exposed mind because there was nothing I could do about it anyway. I could hide nothing from her, even though she found ways to hide plenty from me.

I sat on my bed, shirtless. The skin on my chest, dry and white with wrinkled red splotches, made me cringe. Alexis wished in her mind that I still looked like I had before. Unlike the memories and thoughts in her lockbox, she chose not to hide her subconscious response to my looks. Normally she would have ended our connection, but this time, she ignored my recent self-esteem issues and replayed the last version of my looping dream.

"So that is why your mind was vacant," Alexis spoke out loud. "Your mind had left. You were inside Kendra again."

"I was?"

"When she said, 'And you can follow me to my heart,' what did she mean?"

I glared at Alexis, letting my mind lash at her for waking me just a moment too early. Why couldn't she have given me a few more seconds for Kendra to explain?

"I could not have known, Jake," Alexis defended herself without apology.

*Stop prying, Jake!* Alexis demanded, tapping her separation stone. A side thread of my consciousness had started investigating the dark parts of her mind, the parts she always tried to hide from me. I'd pulled up the image of the woman on a stone, a man dripping blood into her mouth.

"How is it you hide things from me?"

"It takes focus." Alexis smiled flatly.

She slipped from the windowsill and started toward the door. She swayed her hips, knowing I was watching her walk away. She stopped just outside the door and leaned back in.

"Eldra is awake. Get ready quickly and meet us downstairs. We need to save your girlfriend today." With that, she shut the door.

I hated it when she called Kendra my girlfriend. I wasn't exactly sure why she did it or why I hated it. Did I hate because it implied that Alexis didn't consider herself my girlfriend? Or *did* she consider herself my girlfriend, too, and she just liked taking a shot at me for having two girlfriends at the same time? Or maybe it wasn't a shot. Maybe that was Lexy's way of telling me that she understood the situation and was completely fine with it. I'd been in her mind, so I doubt she knew herself.

I walked into the bathroom and looked at the frightening creature in the mirror. It was me.

*Or maybe Alexis just isn't interested in me anymore.*

In my dream—well, Kendra's dream—I'd been normal. Kendra had still had long hair. I wished the dream were reality. I had known what I was doing when I'd used my hair, skin, and muscles as fuel. But what I didn't know is that I would survive. I had expected to die. I thought I was giving my life to save them. Giving up my life for those I love would have been far easier than giving up my quality of life.

I turned on the shower. It would take a minute for the water to warm up, so in the meantime, I got a towel and hung it on the shower door's bar. I rolled my boxers into a ball and tossed them at the laundry bin. I missed. I never used to miss.

I could feel my mental pit of despair rising again. Part of me wanted to let it take over. Everyone thought I was dead already, right? What would be different if I made their belief a reality?

I pushed those thoughts away, letting anger replace them. Stick Witch and Voodoo Whoopie had taken Kendra. They'd zombified the servants, killing four of them. My mom was in jail, charged for the murder of my stepdad. O'Brien lay in the hospital paralyzed. Mr. Espinoza had kidnapped seven girls to turn into his thralls and everyone, myself included, seemed to be fine with it. I had all that to deal with, so how was it that the one thing my self-esteem couldn't handle was my hideous skin and weak muscles? I needed to suck it up and quit whining.

I slapped my hand on the tile. All that did was make my hand sting and my ears ring. The scabs covering the scrapes on my palms were already falling off. I glanced back in the mirror. The scrapes on my face were scab free, but fresh abrasions marked where the scabs had been. I appeared so hideous still that I hadn't noticed the absence of scabs.

The sound of the water hitting the marble softened as it changed from cold to warm. I stepped under the running water and embraced the most amazing sensation in the world.

Running water was energy. Warmth was energy. A hot shower was nature's magic at its purest. I let the warmth run over me and the energy ran through me. I forgot about everything else. I let it all go. It could all matter again later, but right then, I could just enjoy it.

A few quick minutes later, dressed in pants and a hoodie, I headed downstairs.

The pounding and drilling and other power tools tipped me off that the house was undergoing construction. I hesitated to follow the sound because it came from the dining hall, but my curiosity got the best of me. There was no evidence of the mutilated servants. The massive table had been removed, and two men with hammers, having pulled up half the hardwood floor already, pounded pry bars under the next row of wood slats. Two other workers were laying new hardwood a distance behind them.

One of the workers glanced my way and gasped, causing all the men to stop what they were doing and look at me. It creeped me out.

"The new floor in here will match the new floor in the garage hallway," Alexis spoke into my ear, making me jump.

"I hate it when you do that!" I snapped.

Alexis smiled at me, then turned to the workers. "Keep working, boys." She grabbed my hand and dragged me toward the servants' quarters.

"Miguel cleaned up for us last night," Alexis explained. "The two crews arrived to finish the job this morning."

"Where was he last night?"

"Do you really want to know?"

I didn't know how to answer her, so I didn't. Four servant women had died, and they'd just been cleaned up. No cops. No funerals. It disturbed me deeply. I sighed.

We walked into Eldra's room. Luiz and Carl tossed a football back and forth. Gina sat on the bed. She wore gray, skinny jeans and a blue, frilly shirt. She glanced up from her phone and nodded a hello. I'd completely forgotten about Gina and Carl. I'd forgotten that the Skull Shadows had taken Jody and another woman. I had so many problems I couldn't even remember them all.

Eldra sat at the desk reading some sort of foreign language on a tablet.

*"Dímelo,* Jake," Luiz nodded.

"You're late, Jacob," Eldra's grating voice cut through the room.

I cringed. I'd knocked her out with my magic missile and left her near defenseless when the caplatas attacked. The reprimand was surely coming, so I braced myself for her wrinkled wrath.

"Next time you tell me you can break through a containment," she continued, "I'll believe you."

I waited for more. I waited for her fury, but it didn't come.

"Perhaps, Alexis," Eldra added, "your guess is correct."

"What guess?" I asked.

Alexis ignored me. I looked back and forth between them before I gave up.

"Hey, Carl, can I have a catch," I put out my hands, calling for the football.

He gave me one quick look, ignored me, and threw the ball to Luiz.

*"Lo siento,"* Luiz offered. "He's scared of you."

I tried to play off how deeply that hurt. Luiz didn't need to know about my inner turmoil, and Carl didn't know me well enough to care.

"Fine. Let's go save Kendra."

"Easier said than done," Eldra rasped. "Where is she? Where are we going to go save her?"

Eldra voiced what I already knew and had been avoiding. We had no idea where the caplatas had taken Kendra.

I looked at Gina and Carl. "Do you think the Skull Shadows intentionally lured us away from the mansion?" I asked.

"We discussed that," Alexis interjected. "We believe the Skull Shadow attack on—" Alexis stopped and looked at Carl. "Gina?"

Gina looked up from her phone.

"Oh, right." She hopped up and slipped her phone down her shirt into her bra. She waited for Carl to toss the ball to Luiz one more time, then grabbed his hand. "Come on, Carl," she urged, smiling and softening her voice. "Carolyn can take you rock hunting."

"Aaahh!" he whined. "Can't you take me rock hunting?" he asked.

"Can't. I gotta check in at work. Carolyn will help you find a lot of nice rocks on your hike."

"Wow. Are we hiking the mountain?" Carl asked.

"Yep. I bet you can find a prettier rock than she can."

"Probably!"

We watched and waited for them to leave. Gina closed the door behind her and it thudded loudly, reminding me it was a solid wood door.

"The Skull Shadows must be working with the caplatas," Alexis started. "The attack couldn't have been a coincidence. The primary target was Kendra; the attack must have been a distraction."

"I disagree," Eldra cut in with her grainy voice. "Caplatas don't work well with others. Perhaps they simply waited for us to leave. They knew Kendra had been infected and guessed we would leave her behind at some point."

"That's possible," Alexis shrugged. "But you forget that other piece of evidence." Her countenance stiffened, and her gaze fixed on Eldra. Why did I get the impression she was trying her best not to glance at me?

"What piece of evidence?" I asked.

Eldra and Alexis both answered at the same time, "Nothing."

"Luiz?"

"¡Diantre! Jake." Luiz exclaimed. "Don't drag me into this. I don't know anything."

"You know Gina pretty well now," Alexis teased. "They shared a bed last night."

"Eh, aye!" Luiz shouted back at her. Then he glanced at me, but embarrassment didn't allow his eyes to stay on mine.

168

Alexis had said that to distract me. I shouldn't have let her distraction attempt succeed, but I did. I had some seriously mixed emotions.

Luiz eyed me, waiting for me to decide on my reaction.

I opened my mouth, but nothing came out.

"I think we need to focus on finding Kendra," Eldra interrupted. Then she held up a hairbrush and pulled a golden-brown strand from it. "Jacob, Alexis, you might want to focus on how I cast this spell. No better way to learn a spell than to experience it firsthand."

Eldra stood and walked toward Alexis and me, the strand of hair in her palm.

"Place a hand under mine."

Alexis put her hand palm-up against Eldra's hand, and I put my hand palm-up against Lexy's. Skin-to-skin contact with Alexis usually stole all my focus, even if it wasn't overwhelming. I was aware of her soft skin and way the back of her hand curved ever so slightly between her wrist and knuckles. Still, I managed to focus on Eldra's spell.

"This spell detects Kendra or other essences of Kendra," Eldra explained. "We present Kendra's hair to our magic and use it to detect any similar entity."

I listened, and like always, I put a scientific spin on learning the spell. "So we tell our magic what DNA pattern to look for?"

"I'd never thought of it like that," Eldra blinked. "We had a few druid scientists before . . ." She didn't say it, but I knew she was thinking of The Day of a Thousand Deaths. "Anyway, I suppose your idea may be spot on."

"So, if Kendra had a twin, this spell could find her twin?" I asked.

"As a matter of fact," Eldra nodded, "it would. I once used a twin to find her sister. Now enough with the questions."

Eldra closed her eyes and took a deep breath. The magic in the room started moving toward us and flowing into the aged druidess. Alexis tapped her separation stone, removing the barrier between her mind and mine.

*This way, we will learn far more quickly,* Alexis thought.

"Feel the magic around us," Eldra commanded. "Breathe in the power, and let it flow through you to your palm."

Luiz jumped up on the bed to watch us, causing a mild distraction. The bright window behind him seemed to frame him like a picture.

"Silence!" Eldra growled at him.

"*¡Mía culpa!*" Luiz raised his hands as if Eldra had pointed a gun at him.

"Now, push the magic into Kendra's strand of hair," Eldra continued as if the interruption hadn't occurred.

The magic filled the long strand of hair. I could see the blue glow as the power intensified.

*I wish I could see magic like that,* Alexis mentally voiced her jealousy.

The corners of my mouth lifted. It felt good that I could still impress Alexis since I no longer had the looks. Alexis's mind agreed that I was hideous, even though she tried to ignore that and focus on the spell.

"Wait until it is so intense you can't push anymore," Eldra forced her gravelly voice through gritted teeth as she strained to compress her magic into the single hair.

"*Sécan,*" she spoke an Old English word to invoke the spell.

I watched the magic spread around the strand of hair in a perfect, glowing, blue sphere, and then one part of it pointed south and a little west. For some reason, I had expected it to point east, though I didn't know why, and a part of me felt disappointed in the direction the spell offered.

The sphere writhed, undulating and moving from oblong back to a sphere multiple times, then it intensified. Eldra's hand started trembling. I felt the aged druidess drawing energy from Alexis and me up through our palms to keep the spell alive. I could clearly see the sphere pointing south by southwest. We had a direction. I wasn't sure what more Eldra needed. But she strained further, the trembling in her arm increased.

"Aaauggh!" Eldra ripped her hand away, dropping the hair from her palm, ending the spell. She let loose a string of cursing that somehow reminded me of old western movies, and when one of the phrases mentioned Billy the Kid, Luiz broke out in laughter.

"*Vieja,*" Luiz laughed. "Papá told me you were approaching the two hundredth anniversary of your first wrinkle, so tell me you actually knew Billy the Kid, because that would be *chingón!*"

Eldra looked at Luiz. She started off with fierce eyes, but they didn't last. Eldra broke out laughing.

"So, the spell pointed that way," I pointed mostly south but a little west. As soon as I thought about the direction, I realized I was pointing toward West Jordan.

"Bah!" Eldra spat. "The magic found traces of Kendra at her house but otherwise found nothing."

Worry flooded through me. Did something happen to Kendra?

"Calm down," Eldra groaned. "The caplatas have her hidden. A common containment wouldn't be strong enough to hide her. The silver Star of David containment could hide a person, but only if the caster had spirit magic, which caplatas do not have."

"Are they not syphoning her spirit?" Alexis asked. "That sounds similar to spirit magic, does it not?"

"Not the same," Eldra answered. "Spirit magic is from inside yourself, from your own spirit. The caplatas, however, are using voodoo to control someone else's spirit."

"So they've hidden her?" I interjected.

"They must have. We know little about it. Perhaps their shadow magic can hide her?" Eldra continued. "We know far too little about voodoo. And any attempts to learn more have been met with extreme resistance."

*"They are hiding me in the shadows. They hurt, Jake. The shadows hurt."* I remembered Kendra's words from her dream. Before I could share them, Alexis's phone rang. She looked at the number, tapped off her separation stone, and then answered it. We listened to her give one-word responses for a minute before she hung up.

"O'Brien's third surgery went well yesterday. Earlier this morning, he woke up and demanded to speak to you, Jake. Supposedly, he went crazy and tried to get out of bed. They sedated him, but the doctor was hoping you could be there when he wakes up again."

"Sorry, no," I immediately refused. "I'm not doing anything else until I locate Kendra."

"Perhaps," Eldra cut in, "visiting O'Brien and finding Kendra are not separate tasks. O'Brien has an uncanny ability to find whom he seeks. He is a *Finder*. His advice would be most welcome."

I started to protest then stopped. I had nothing to say.

# CHAPTER 24
# O'BRIEN

*Kendra is amazing. She loves so easily. She forgives everything. She trusts everyone. At least, she once trusted everyone. That is changing. And yet her mind is so naïve. The opposite of my mind. She was pure until my memories corrupted her. Wearing a white bikini for Jake is what she considers her most rebellious and daring act. My grandfather gifted me for pleasure and sent me out as an assassin. The actions I have performed in my life are corrupt beyond anything Kendra ever wanted to imagine. For a while, I have considered my most rebellious and daring act to be my attempted suicide. To Kendra, my most rebellious and daring act is staying alive. —Alexis*

I t seemed like a lifetime since I'd been to see O'Brien, but it had been just yesterday morning. So much had happened in one day. He needed a haircut, which I hadn't noticed yesterday. Yesterday, I'd been too busy noticing his atrophied legs and the tubes in his nose and mouth. Today, he didn't have the tubes. Every now and then, his face contorted, and the vein at the corner of his eye bulged, showing that even asleep and on drugs, O'Brien was not free of pain.

A few weeks ago, I didn't have a problem with hospitals, but now I couldn't stand the smell. And the constant beeping picked at my nerves worse than I picked at the white flakes on my skin.

O'Brien's room had only two seats, so Lexy sat by me. She surprised me and held my left hand—the hand that didn't have two split knuckles; one from punching Trenton, and one from punching the wall. I liked her hand in mine. She also put her head on my shoulder.

172

I couldn't decipher Lexy's emotions toward me. I couldn't get a read on her. When she looked at O'Brien, she exuded gratitude and pride. He had impressed Alexis. She'd treated O'Brien as disposable, a pawn to use against her father. But he survived. She saw him as more valuable now, as if he were a pawn that was upgraded after reaching the far end of the chessboard.

An hour passed. I wasn't sure what to say to Lexy, so I said nothing. She didn't seem to be her usual talkative self. She didn't tease me or brashly flirt. She just sat there holding my hand, and off and on she'd lean her head on my shoulder. It was a very different experience than any we'd ever shared before.

The only emotion coming from her was comfort. She still wore the mesh, white blouse and skinny jeans with small holes that went high on her thigh. She didn't flaunt it, though, and she could have. She could have tormented me with her state of dress, but she didn't. Perhaps she was getting all the attention from me that she needed.

I kept my hoodie pulled tight and my right hand in my hoodie pocket. I kept my disfigured skin as hidden as possible.

I was just about to take a bathroom break when O'Brien finally stirred and blinked open his eyes. Lexy lifted her head off my shoulder but kept a hold of my hand. We stood and leaned over O'Brien's bed.

Another two minutes ticked by before he was fully awake. I should have taken the bathroom break.

Alexis dropped my hand and took O'Brien's hand in both of hers. Her touch sparked energy into O'Brien. His eyes opened wider and he took slightly bigger breaths.

"Charles," Lexy whispered softly. "Jake is here to see you."

That was only the second time I'd heard someone use O'Brien's first name. This time was much less creepy than the first. Lexy's voice was far smoother and softer on the ears than a nightwalker's. Still, hearing her call him Charles felt awkward.

"O'Brien," I smiled.

He whispered something that I couldn't hear, so I leaned down close.

"Alexis is the Vampire King's granddaughter," O'Brien whispered. "You can't trust her."

I chuckled a little.

"Yeah," I replied. "I know."

"Are you yourself?" he asked. "Or are you hers?"

I glanced at Alexis. *Was* I hers? I was pretty sure I was myself. I remembered how I had felt the first time I'd been exposed to her

173

allure. I'd offered myself to her. I'd begged her to drink my blood. I didn't feel that way now, but I did love her. Was loving her just another way to be hers without being controlled by her allure?

"I think so," I replied. "I mean, I feel in control."

"Be wary of her," his eyes stared at Lexy.

"Yeah. I'll *always* be wary of her," I answered and then smiled at Lexy.

"Kendra is the other magic user," O'Brien continued.

I could tell he didn't remember what had happened. He'd forgotten the events at the cabin.

"What is the last thing you remember?" I asked.

"The nightwalker," he answered. "How did we survive the nightwalker?"

"A magic missile," I answered.

"You?" he asked. I felt a bit of déjà vu. It seemed we'd had this conversation before.

"He must have hit me hard," O'Brien coughed. "I used bones of steel."

"The nightwalkers are gone," I assured him. "They won't bother us anymore."

"Kendra is the other magic user," O'Brien repeated. "At the cemetery. The magic. I didn't know who used magic because nobody did." He took a moment to swallow. "The magic came to life on its own."

"I know," I replied as dots connected in my mind. How could I have been so foolish? How did I not think of this before? That was how I shared her dreams all night.

"You two are connected," he added. "This happens sometimes between potential pairs, who," he coughed and swallowed, "fall in love before they're discovered and trained."

Connected. Kendra had told me; I just hadn't understood until now. *"You can follow me to my heart. Remember, Jake?"* I remembered, finally.

"You have to find her and hide. Don't let Alexis take her. Don't let them get you."

"I won't," I assured him. "I'll find her and save her."

I straightened up and turned to Alexis, about to tell her what I'd just remembered. But O'Brien grabbed my hand.

"What is it?" I asked. He needed to hurry because I really needed to find a restroom.

"Do you know of the Skull Shadows?"

I nodded.

"They're here."

"Yeah, we ran into some of them yesterday," I told him.

O'Brien's eyes widened.

"No. They're behind you. Run!"

Alexis and I whipped around. Behind us, two men in dark suits stepped past the large window about to reach the hospital room door. Our eyes met theirs. They both reached under their suit coats for their handguns.

Alexis snatched the chair she'd been sitting on and forcefully launched it legs first into the doorway, then she darted forward, following the chair. The chair hit both men, but only one of them took the brunt of the force. The chair knocked him backward and he lost his balance and went down.

The other one shook off the attack and fired at point-blank range at Lexy's torso. He hadn't fully raised his gun. Lexy's body twisted, but she continued forward, grabbing the gun as it fired a second time. That bullet whizzed past my ear and hit the window, shattering it.

Alexis broke the man's wrist, took the handgun, and smacked him behind the ear with the base of the gun's grip. He collapsed. The other man scrambled to pick up his dropped gun. Alexis and the attacker fired at the same time, but I kicked his arm just before his gun went off. His shot hit the wall. Lexy's bullet hit him in the neck, and he dropped to the white tile floor. Blood poured out onto the floor.

Screams rang out through the hall. Nurses ducked into rooms or behind counters.

Lexy turned back to me. Blood soaked an area around her stomach, covering the entire right side of her once-white, see-through blouse. Had the blood splattered on her? She took a step toward me and then fell to her knee. No, the blood was hers.

I rushed to her.

Sirens blared throughout the building, attacking our ears. Emergency lights flashed from where they were mounted at various intervals along the walls.

"We cannot stay here," Lexy whispered, wincing.

"Get out of here," O'Brien rasped as loud as he could from his bed. He was trying to get up but couldn't. He'd had to be restrained after going berserk the last time he'd woken up.

"Stay there, O'Brien!" I shouted back.

I put my arm under Lexy's shoulder and tried to stand up. I couldn't lift her myself.

"You're going to have to help," I told her.

She stood, cringing in agony. I could feel both her pain and her desire to feed seep into me. The sclera of her eyes streaked with red.

I helped her stumble toward the elevators.

175

"No," Lexy tugged at me. She screamed in pain. "The alarms. No elevators." She nodded toward an exit sign next to a door with a stairway sign.

The spinal trauma floor at the University of Utah hospital took up most of the seventh floor of their new facility. Even with my help, Alexis wouldn't make it down seven flights of stairs. Would I make it down seven flights of stairs without help? It took considerable effort just to help her reach the door to the stairwell. I let go of Lexy to push it open, and she dropped to her knees.

"Jake," Luiz shouted, just climbing the last set of stairs. He rushed to Alexis and ducked under her arm, cursing in Spanish at the blood staining her stomach. He had on his West Jordan High Chess Master shirt. He loved that shirt. Lexy's blood would surely ruin it. The door closed and dulled the blaring alarm. I could still hear it, but as background noise.

"I need blood," Lexy muttered. Her fangs had extended. I could feel her hunger. She wanted to feed on Luiz but fought the desire.

I slipped back under Lexy's other arm, opposite Luiz. As weak as I was, I am not sure that I helped much, but we started down the stairs. My leg muscles burned after descending a single flight of stairs. Only six more to go. I could feel the pain of Lexy's gunshot wound like it was my own. Or perhaps I just had stitches in my side already.

I heard steps slapping on the stairs coming toward us. Three security guards rounded the stairs to our floor. Their navy blue uniforms contrasted against the white walls and light gray stairs. The first guard had a dark, bald head that reflected the lights. He looked three feet taller than the other guards, but that was probably just because he was also a couple steps ahead of them.

Alexis stopped and straightened. Luiz slipped from under her arm and moved back. Her allure hit me in full force. My protection stone hummed warmly at my neck.

"Help me," her soft feminine voice echoed powerfully in the stairwell. I'd thought that with the protection stone, her allure couldn't take control of me, but it almost did. It had never been this strong before. Her pain and desperate situation augmented it. I had to focus my mind to fight it off. Luiz and the three guards had no chance. They took full notice of Alexis and lost themselves to her.

I tapped Alexis's separation stone for her and pushed magic into it. It worked. Our minds joined. Lexy's pain and hunger flooded into me, but I became part of her, unaffected by her influence. She clung to a thread of control over herself. She didn't want me in her mind but accepted me anyway.

Her mind wasn't normal. It was primal. Hungry. How she controlled her desire to feed, to rip Luiz to shreds in hunger, was beyond me.

The tall guard reached her first.

"Are you OK?" he asked, with a hint of a southern Louisiana accent. He reached a hand toward her and she took it.

*Not you,* she thought. *Wrong blood type.*

"Go upstairs," she ordered him. "You will find two gunmen. A black .45 is in the hall." Lexy paused and grimaced in pain. "Tell everyone that it was you. You wrested the gun from them and shot them. You are a hero." She let go of his hand. "Go!" she ordered, and he took off up the stairs.

One of the other two guards had a mustache. He was strong and looked to be approaching fifty. The other was a thin blond man who couldn't have been more than a few years older than me.

*I need A positive compatible,* Lexy thought. She could smell their blood types. Until that moment, I had no idea that blood types mattered to vampires.

Alexis held out both hands. Each officer took one. She smiled with her fangs exposed at the younger officer. His green eyes showed no fear but instead welcomed the predator.

She wanted to pull him close and rip into his neck. She wanted to shred him and bathe in his blood. But she didn't.

Lexy turned over the policeman's wrist, slid back his sleeve, and bit into his radial artery. I could feel her satisfaction as Lexy sucked at his blood, breathing it into her lungs. To Lexy, the man's blood felt like a breath of air after nearly drowning. She held his wrist to her mouth for a long time.

*Lexy,* I shouted at her mentally, urging her to stop.

Her ravenous red eyes flashed at me, reminding me of the painting of the impaled protector and warning me to back off. I didn't back off. I grabbed her arm and tugged at her. She'd used all her will power. The predator in her had taken over. She couldn't stop without help.

*I need to help you stop.* My thoughts didn't work. Despite our joined minds, she couldn't hear me. The primal predator and the instinctual desire to feed dominated Lexy's mind.

"You're already healing," I shouted at her.

She jerked her arm away from me and shoved me. I fell back against the wall and then rolled painfully down a few steps before

I stopped myself. I felt blood on my wrist and left hand where they'd hit the stairs.

Neither Luiz nor the older mustached security guard had moved. I wasn't sure if they were able to.

"Stop her, Luiz," I shouted.

Luiz looked at me, blinked, but did nothing.

With no other recourse to stop her from killing the young security guard, I grabbed at the magic around me. I created a magic missile. Immediately, my addiction kicked in and I almost cast it at Alexis. But instead, I dropped my magic. I couldn't attack Alexis. I couldn't erase her. I loved her. Still, I had to stop her. A drop of blood dripped from my left hand. I looked at my bleeding left wrist. I couldn't attack her, but I could singe her.

I flicked my hand at her. A few drops of blood hit her. Two small drops hit her left cheek.

She spat out the guard's wrist as she jerked backward, her hand reaching to her face. Guilt flooded into me. I'd hurt her. She sat on the steps in pain as my blood burned into her.

I managed to get to my feet. I shoved the young guard.

"Move," I told him. I kept shoving him past Alexis. Then I reached back and grabbed the older guard, pulling him past Alexis as well.

"Go!" I ordered them.

The older guard started up the stairs and didn't look back. But the young guard hesitantly took a step. Then another before stopping. I could feel Alexis calling to him in her hunger. I pushed him again, and he took two more steps. Then he turned and gazed longingly at Alexis.

*Let him go,* I urged her.

I pushed the side of his face, turning his head to point back up the stairwell.

"Go! Go! Go!" I yelled.

Alexis could have ordered him back to her, but she didn't. She stood frozen, her mind trying to fight the predator inside. But this allowed him to decide for himself. He finally started upstairs. He made it to the top of the current flight, glanced back one final time, and then continued up the next flight of stairs and out of sight.

I turned just in time to see Alexis, eyes black with rage, look up at me. She lunged at me, arms outstretched. I put my hands out to stop her. She grabbed my hands to push them away.

"Aaeeeee," she blasted out a high-pitched scream that echoed through the stairwell and rang in my ears. She jumped down the stairs away from me.

My blood had burned her again. Smoke rose from her palm. Crouching like an injured tiger, she glared at me. Then her stance softened, followed by her eyes. She looked at me with pained, sorrowful eyes that were now damp and red as normal—normal for Alexis anyway. The all-consuming predator inside her faded away and her mind returned to me, as did her shame. She tapped her separation stone, too embarrassed to let me in, too ashamed of how she'd lost control.

"Thank you for stopping me, Jake," she offered. I noticed she thanked me but didn't apologize. I wasn't sure what to do with that.

"Feeling better now?" I asked, irritated.

"A little," streaks of red were already returning to her sclera. "I am still hungry."

"Pretend you're fasting," I countered.

Alexis grabbed the bloodied mesh bottom of her shirt and ripped it away, revealing her bloodied, bare abdomen. She also revealed the bottom half of her black bra. I felt a little ashamed for noticing. Why is it that, even in a situation like this, guys still notice things like that?

"I am also still injured."

"Let's get out of here!" I suggested. "Then we can fix you up."

Alexis used the mesh to wipe the blood off as best as she could. The wound had started closing. It looked almost sewn together by thread, but the strands were not thread, they were skin. Her body was stitching her wound, healing in a medically intelligent way.

"You still need Luiz under your arm?" I asked.

She grinned at me and started running down the stairs two at a time. Luiz started moving the moment she did. She reached the bottom floor before I reached the third floor. She had to wait for me as I stumbled down the last two flights of stairs holding my aching side and heaving in big breaths as if I'd just run a mile. I also still needed to find a bathroom.

"Would you like Luiz under *your* arm?" Alexis mused.

I didn't find it one bit funny. I flicked my left palm at her, the one that had blood on it. She cringed, but this time, no blood got on her. My scrape had stopped bleeding. She giggled a high-pitched giggle like I'd done the funniest thing in the world. Luiz laughed too, a strange and abnormally forced laugh for him. The laugh was nothing more than him responding to Lexy's allure. Under her allure, a person could be as much a zombie as when under a voodoo witch's power.

We pushed open the stairwell door letting in the full sound of the blaring alarms. I plugged my ears as we rushed into the lobby. No police cars had arrived yet. A single security guard hid behind the security desk, his revolver shaking in his hand. If he had to use that gun, he'd probably shoot the wrong person.

The lobby appeared empty otherwise. Everyone must have left when the alarms started ringing. I kept my fingers in my ears as we made our way to the front entrance.

Behind us, I heard some doors open. I glanced back in time to see a man and a woman. The man wore jeans and a sports jacket over a yellow, button-up shirt. The woman wore a knee-length, black business skirt with a purple blouse and carried a handbag. Both gave us startled looks before pulling out guns and pointing them at us as we rushed toward the entryway. I dove headfirst at the ground and slid on the smooth tile almost the rest of the way to the entrance. I crawled the last few feet.

Alexis shoved Luiz to the ground, and he crawled toward the doors too. Alexis sprinted ahead of us, and if I saw correctly, she dodged the first four bullets as if she were Neo trying to make Morpheus proud, before the fifth caught her shoulder. I'd tried to push magic into her mesh shirt, to make her bulletproof, but maybe I was too late. She fell into the glass doors, pushing them open. Pain seared her left shoulder. Luiz and I crawled after her. The gunman had ignored us initially. But once Alexis exited the doors, a bullet hit my hoodie and ricocheted off it. Yay, the bulletproof spell still worked. Once outside the doors, I rolled to one side and Luiz rolled to the other, and we both swung the doors closed.

Outside, to my surprise, Lexy's BMW raced toward us. Loud smacks echoed as bullets hit the glass doors and windows behind us. The windows must have been thick because the first few bullets didn't make it through. We rushed along the sidewalk to the valet parking area. Was Lexy's car driving itself? How was it coming toward us? That didn't make sense.

The BMW wasn't slowing down anywhere near soon enough. I stopped rushing toward it, wondering if it had gone all Christine on us and wanted to run us down. Then the front tires turned, the car screeched and spun a one-eighty, leaving black streaks on the asphalt, before coming to a stop.

The driver's side window rolled down to reveal a pair of pink sunglasses with plastic-gem trim. The big lenses in the gaudy frames covered half of Eldra's face.

"Get in, kids!" she shouted. That was the first time I'd ever been glad to hear her gravelly old voice. We each reached a car door at the same time; Alexis, the front passenger side, Luiz and I, the opposite rear doors. Eldra started driving before we were even in the car. We had to jump in or get left behind.

A bullet hit our back window. The impact left a mark, but the bulletproof glass didn't shatter. I heard two more gunshots, but neither hit our car.

We'd escaped.

Our only concern was O'Brien, but he now had an Alexis-assigned officer protecting him, and the sounds of sirens meant a swarm of police officers would be on their way.

# CHAPTER 25
# ROPE

I spend a lot of time listening to Kendra's and Alexis's background thoughts. Girls are very judgmental. They criticize each other. I can't tell you how many times I've been told that girls dress the way they do for boys. That is a lie. They dress the way they do for other girls. They care about what other girls think more than they care about what guys think. Dressing is a competition and Kendra and Alexis both want to win. My opinion only matters because it helps decide the winner. When I like both their outfits the same but in different ways, they tell me I've cheated them. —Jake

Safely in the BMW, far from the Skull Shadows, I closed my eyes and focused on the emotional bond between Kendra and me. I felt it ever so slightly at first. I felt the connection strengthening.

"I need blood," Alexis informed Eldra, interrupting my focus. The thread that connected me emotionally to Kendra weakened.

"I see you managed to tear half your shirt off. I suppose you were injured?" Eldra's question seemed more of a reprimand.

"We're only complaining about her injury," Luiz grinned. "We like her half-shirtless."

"You have a terrible mind, boy!" Eldra told Luiz.

I could feel Alexis's honey-scented hunger mix with her annoyance at the conversation. She wasn't up for Luiz's and Eldra's banter.

"Hey, can we focus on Lexy?" I cut in.

Eldra thinned her eyes at me. I tried to ignore her Medusa death stare as well as rip away my focus from Lexy's annoyed hunger. I tried focusing on Kendra. With O'Brien's help, I'd figured out what Kendra meant, about how I could follow our emotional connection to her. I just hadn't been able to try while people were shooting at me.

I imagined Kendra sitting with me on the couch in Kevin's living room. I imagined our first kiss and the connection that flared up between us. The thread between Kendra and me thickened. It began building in my chest.

Then the connection snapped into place. I could feel it. My mind followed my emotions down our connection as if it were data passing through the air to a Wi-Fi access point.

*Jake,* Kendra's mind shouted from what seemed a long way off. Something kept me from reaching her, something not unlike a wall. I hit it and recoiled. Pain seared through my soul as my soul whiplashed back to my body in the car.

"Where are we going?" Eldra asked.

Lexy and I answered at the same time, but with different destinations.

"East," I said as Alexis said, "Home."

"Which is it?" Eldra growled.

Lexy tapped her separation stone. Her pain hit me full force. Her stomach wrenched in agony as it remained only half-healed. The second bullet throbbed in her left shoulder. Carolyn and Lillian were the only remaining servants, and Alexis needed blood. She also wanted to change into her leather armor. For a moment, her hunger abated. At least for her. I felt it as if she'd pushed all her hunger into me, because, well, she had. I looked at Luiz and for half a second, I considered biting into his wrist.

*How did you let a bullet through your shirt twice?* I demanded while Alexis probed my mind for why I wanted to go east.

*This mesh shirt couldn't hold the magic,* she thought back.

*Modesty is important,* Kendra's words flashed in both our memories.

"I need to make a stop at Gina's work," Lexy explained after perusing my memories, "then we will go east." She licked her lips in anticipation. I sighed. Gina was about to get a surprise visit at work. Alexis was seriously considering turning Gina into one of her thralls.

*I have never bound a thrall,* Alexis thought to me. She had taken temporary control of many people. She had meddled with plenty of minds. But binding a thrall went beyond that. It was a blood bond. Total servitude. Total obedience. Carolyn and Lillian

183

were thralls, but not Lexy's. Their master did not want to be named, so even Alexis didn't know who the two surviving servants belonged to or if their master was friend or foe, or even if they shared the same master. The two women were enthralled with the purpose to serve whoever lived at the mansion. Were they loyal to us? For now. Alexis stopped pushing her hunger into me and her mind went hazy except for one singular focus. Blood.

The desire was all-consuming. I could feel its potency. Even Alexis, who had refused to feed for blood for long periods of time, would never muster enough willpower to shake off this desire. She'd lost control feeding from the officer, and she was about to lose control again. Her will had long since broken. All she could do now was keep herself from trying to feed on Luiz and Eldra.

*Mr. Espinoza fed on Luiz far too long,* Alexis thought to me. Luiz was in great shape, and that hid the fact that his body was recovering from a large blood loss from just a week ago. If *I feed off Luiz now, he could go into hypovolemic shock.* I didn't know what that was, but Alexis did. If she fed on Luiz, his heart might not be able to pump enough blood to his body, causing his organs to shut down.

*Eldra is not my blood type.*

Alexis regretted the thought the moment she had it. This was another fact she had been hiding from me, despite the Trinity of Mind. Vampires have blood types. They were just as tied to the blood chart as any human who needed a blood donation. This was a secret that only vampires knew. Even many vampires didn't know it. Some of the older ones had eschewed science and hunted by scent and desire alone. Feeding on individuals with blood types that didn't smell right often led to a few nights of fever-like symptoms.

Having A positive blood type meant Alexis could feed on the vast majority of people: anyone A positive, A negative, O positive, or O negative. That included almost ninety percent of the country.

*And usually Bombay blood type, too,* Alexis added. *Except your blood makes the symbiotic protists in me burn.*

That same image of a man standing over a woman on a stone table, dripping blood into her mouth, stood out prominently in Alexis's mind until she tapped her separation stone.

I swore. What was this girl hiding from me? I would have dwelt on it longer, but I had plenty of other concerns, and that included finding a bathroom. The visit from Trenton had left Alexis disconcerted. The Vampire Vatican treaty had a section called the Joan of Arc Addendum that defined a dhampir as a human for the purposes of the treaty, but only if they abide by human law.

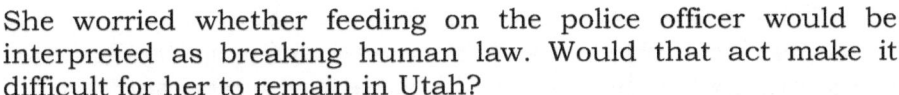

She worried whether feeding on the police officer would be interpreted as breaking human law. Would that act make it difficult for her to remain in Utah?

One thing was certain. There was a whole ocean of secret politics in this world, and all I'd done so far was dip in my toe. A wave of increased hunger flooded from Alexis. She twitched, almost going after Luiz, but stopped herself.

"Go faster. Alexis needs blood soon," I warned Eldra.

Eldra glanced at Alexis, who writhed in agony, confirming my statement. Eldra accelerated. Over ten minutes of hungry, pained anguish passed. For half of it, the car sat unmoving at the various red lights of downtown Salt Lake before we finally headed to the industrial district.

Eldra pulled into the back of Club Exposed. I wasn't prepared for the way my breathing increased when I saw the parking lot where Stick Witch and Voodoo Whoopie attacked us. Images of their shadow blades and the voodoo zombies crashed down on my mind. I remembered everything so clearly.

Alexis didn't wait for the car to stop. She popped the door open and spun gracefully out of the car, twisting smoothly into a sprint. Blood covered her back where her shirt didn't. Lexy sped to the rear entrance at a speed that would have earned her a gold medal at any Olympics. I watched her, impressed by both her finesse and dexterity. It distracted me enough that I forgot about the near panic attack.

"¡Madre de Dios!" Luiz swore. "Your second girlfriend has skills."

I glared at him, but he just grinned back wider under his long nose.

Eldra finished parking, and before we could argue, Luiz popped open the door and went rushing to the club's door.

"I'll get him," I offered. Maybe I could find a bathroom inside, too.

"He doesn't need you to get him," Eldra responded. "He is of age. He can make his own decisions."

"He's not eighteen yet. And I think you have to be twenty-one to go in there."

"Neither the law nor a birthday decides when a man is a man," Eldra growled. "Throughout history, a man becomes a man by their actions. If you and Luiz weren't men before the Cabin Battle of Bear Lake, you're sure as hell men now."

She'd just tossed me a compliment. I should have just accepted it and kept my mouth shut, but I had to ask, "The Cabin Battle of Bear Lake? Did you name it?"

185

She glared at me through the rearview mirror.

She was about to answer when her phone rang. It caught me off guard, seeing the aged druid swipe her screen and put the phone to her ear.

"Hello," Eldra answered. I could hear the hum of someone speaking on the other side of the phone, but I couldn't hear the words. "You've got her." More humming. "Uh-huh." I tried to focus, but it didn't matter. "It has to be today?" Eldra asked. She uh-huhed into the phone a few more times before finally saying, "We are close. We'll be there in under ten minutes."

Eldra caught me off guard by pulling out of the parking spot. "Uh?"

"Relax. This is important. Alexis and Luiz will be a while. We'll be back before they have to wait long."

I couldn't relax. I really need to use the bathroom. Oh, and Skull Shadows had just made an attempt on O'Brien's life.

Fortunately, we didn't drive more than five minutes north before Eldra pulled into Woods Cross High School. I'd played against them in football the past two years. It was close to two years ago. We won thirty-four to thirty-one. Last year, we annihilated them forty-two to nothing—one of my football team's two shutouts.

We pulled right to the front doors. Brown brick surrounded dark glass windows. Above the entryway, a block letter sign read: "Home of the Wildcats."

I busted my brain, trying to figure out why we would come here. What could be so important that we would ditch Alexis and Luiz and delay rescuing Kendra?

Eldra opened her door. In her current floral blouse, she looked so much more like a grandmother than a druidess. I pulled on my hood, making sure it covered the majority of my hideous face and followed her inside.

Eldra made a beeline for the office, which wasn't far from the front entrance.

I had to tap her shoulder and point at the restroom to get her to stop. A few minutes later, relieved and hands washed, I found myself back in the school's hall where Eldra waited for me.

"Feeling better?" she asked.

"Yes, grandma. And now I know, don't wait to go," I quipped. Perhaps Eldra hadn't babysat kids recently like Sis and I had, so Eldra didn't catch my joke. Instead, she ignored me and turned back toward the office.

I wanted to pester the old hag for answers, but I'd spent my opportunity making a joke. Perhaps this was something to do with druid politics and we were discreetly meeting someone who happened to work here.

I tried to shake off the odd sensation of being in a foreign high school in the summer. The halls of my own school, West Jordan High, gave me an odd feeling during the summer, but somehow, the silent foyer of Woods Cross felt worse. Perhaps it was the complete lack of life in a building that nine months out of the year had more than a thousand kids. It was almost a relief to walk into the office where there were people instead of the creepy, quiet emptiness.

A counter separated us from three adult women. Two were older, perhaps Lillian's age, but the third couldn't have been much older than twenty-one. They all three looked up at us from a mix of computer and paperwork.

The room smelled like grandma perfume that I was certain came from the two older women. One of the older two women with long gray hair and a grandma's roundness to her form smiled at Eldra. Eldra wore a cream-colored blouse with flowers on it over dark maroon pants that matched the center of the flowers. Her soft black shoes looked comfortable. She fit right in, and a casual observer might confuse her for one of the ladies that worked in this school office.

"Mrs. Locksley, I suppose?"

"Yes," Eldra answered.

The other two women returned to their duties. The one in her twenties smacked the stapler so loud that I twitched involuntarily.

"Oh, good. I'm Mrs. Hallsworth. We spoke on the phone several times."

Was Eldra's last name really Locksley? I'd never really considered asking. I wasn't sure why. I hadn't known O'Brien's first name had been Charles. I'd promised myself that I would do better, that I'd take better care to get to know those around me and to be less self-involved. Perhaps I hadn't yet learned to fulfill that promise. Then again, perhaps with the barely cordial relationship Eldra and I shared—I had killed her husband after all—we had chosen to avoid talking to each other except when necessary.

"There is a lot of paperwork to fill out," the gray-haired women continued. "You say you have three students transferring into our school?"

The younger woman banged on the stapler again. I jumped. She had a whole stack of collated papers. Each time she smacked her hand against the stapler, an image of being shot in the thigh flashed in my mind.

"That's correct," Eldra answered.

"Wait," I interrupted. "You're registering us for school?" I glanced flabbergasted from Eldra to the three women. "I thought," I started, but there was nothing I could say in front of an audience.

The three women seemed to notice me for the first time. Until now, they had just ignored me, assuming I was just another teenager oblivious to the world around me. But then came the looks. They noticed my abnormally white and scarred skin. Almost in unison, they gasped and covered their open mouths with their hands. At first, they were horrified, which I probably should get used to. But when their eyes softened, their horror changed to pity. That made me feel worse.

"Your schooling is extremely important," Eldra turned to me and glared. "This is going to take a while. Why don't you have a seat while I fill out this paperwork, please?" Eldra sounded so nice, despite her gravelly voice. This must have been the first time she had ever said please to me. Of course, it was all fake niceness, as evidenced by her unpleasant look that included wrinkles pressed together as tightly as her pursed lips. Other wrinkles seemed to shoot out of her eyes as part of the death-ray stare that accompanied her words.

I sat down on a plastic chair against the office window. I felt like I was in trouble and waiting to see the principal. I pulled my awesome new phone out of my hoodie pocket. I hadn't really had time to play with my new toy much yet. I needed something to distract me. The evil voodoo caplatas had taken Kendra somewhere to the east and the need to save her pounded on me with all the stress in the world. Not to mention the Skull Shadows had just attempted a hit on O'Brien.

Smack, smack. That stapler sounded way too much like a gunshot. There was only one thing that could keep me from going insane right now. Earphones. And I had to find a version of *Madden NFL* that I could play on my new phone.

# CHAPTER 26
# MUNDANE TASKS

*Alexis is a gifted dancer. She has moves. I probably shouldn't be pulling up her dance memories because, well, let's just say she wasn't dancing for drill team. But I can't stop dipping into those memories because she is so good at dancing. Just sharing her memories is making me a better dancer. If she danced on drill team, she could be one of the best on the floor. I'm five foot six, and I am considered tall for drill team. It is difficult to be much taller and be able to dance with enough grace to be on drill team. Alexis is five foot ten, yet she has a fluidity to her dancing that goes above and beyond grace. —Kendra*

**W**here did you and Eldra go? Alexis jumped into my head just as I threw a virtual pass to a virtual Luiz. I'd created both Luiz and me as characters in *Madden*. Since Utah didn't have a pro football team, I always played the Arizona Cardinals. I'd spent so much time setting the game up, that I'd just run the first play of the game.

Alexis didn't want the first image that came with her question to be Gina and the two other exotic dancers who had each donated a pint, or that Luiz was having way too good of a time, but such images escaped her mind anyway. Perhaps her mental barrier was slipping. But then again, she wasn't trying to hide these memories behind her mental barrier.

I didn't have to answer Lexy's question in words. She perused my background thoughts and misgivings about attending school. What I thought in the forefront of my mind was, *I love my new phone,* and I meant it. Even if playing *Madden* was the primary reason.

*Of course, you two have to finish high school.* Alexis ignored my video game delight and laughed at my shock at having to finish high school. *I will be there with you,* she offered as consolation, but her worry as to whether we'd get Kendra back made her thoughts not so consoling.

*Somehow, I thought you had already graduated,* I answered, sharing her worry about Kendra.

Alexis had never been to school. Her mother had home-schooled her until her thirteenth birthday. After that, well . . . I tried not to delve into those thoughts, even though Alexis assured me that I was welcome to any of them.

*Do you still have a clear direction on Kendra?* Alexis steered my thoughts.

*She's still somewhere east of here.*

*Hurry back. We need to find her before nightfall.*

I looked at the all-too-familiar, round, white school clock on the wall. The hands pointed to eleven-thirty. Where had the morning gone? Oh, yeah. Our visit to O'Brien in the hospital had resulted in thwarting an assassination attempt against him, a gun chase, and a getaway. We'd left O'Brien with three security guards, at least one of which was Alexis-influenced, to protect him from a follow-up attack. By now, police were surely swarming the place. It was probably on the news. I paused my game and checked. Yep, it was. The news headline was "Shooters Thwarted at Hospital." I didn't click the link. I went back to *Madden*.

The attack had come as a surprise. Yet after a gunfight last night, why wouldn't I have expected a gunfight this morning?

Sacked! I wasn't focusing on my game, and I got sacked by the Patriot's defense. They had Luiz triple covered. It was tough to play *Madden* on my phone and focus on communicating with Alexis at the same time.

"Eldra," I interrupted. Three other mothers had also entered the office to work out registration issues with their children, so all three women were busy. To my great relief, the younger woman had stopped the gunshot-like stapling. One mother sat waiting. She kept giving me pity looks. "Alexis says she's ready."

Mrs. Halls-something-or-other, I forget her name, also gave me a pity look and answered for Eldra. "This will only take a few more minutes." She seemed accustomed to pacifying teenagers.

Alexis didn't disconnect from my mind, but she started having a girl chat with Gina and one of her two coworkers. As my mind could access Lexy's vision, I was glad she and Luiz remained in the back rooms. All the women were covered, at least where it mattered, and Lexy and Luiz weren't watching the lunch performance.

I tried to ignore their conversation. Gina's friend liked to drop the f-bomb a lot, as if every sentence was incomplete without it.

*I bet you could influence her to not swear every other word,* I suggested to Alexis. *Come on. Just do it.*

Alexis seemed to ignore me, but the next time Gina's friend spoke, she never once added her favorite, four-letter interjection.

*Maybe you subconsciously used my influence for me?* Alexis suggested. Surprise mixed with annoyance spread from her to me. She didn't like to be used by anyone.

*Or maybe you subconsciously obeyed me?*

*Which is more likely?* Alexis snapped. *That a guy used me against my will or that I obeyed him? Occam's razor suggests the former.*

*That was a little harsh,* I answered, somewhat hurt.

Alexis had not meant to be that harsh to me. But she'd never really been treated right by a guy in her life. I was pretty much the first, and her mind didn't know exactly how to deal with a guy who genuinely cared for her.

*I'd never use you against your will,* I assured her.

*Except for forcing the Trinity of Mind on me,* she retorted but instantly regretted it. *Forgive me. You saved our lives. Just because I have a thought, does not mean that is what I truly believe.*

I could never explain what it felt like to share someone else's every thought. People have a lot of thoughts. People think thoughts that they don't believe. I found that all three of us often have internal debates. We think about many sides of an issue before we really settle on an opinion. So many of our thoughts are ones we discard. Until my thoughts were laid bare to Kendra and Lexy and theirs laid bare to me, I had never fully understood this.

Despite her apology, I felt the guilt of forcing the Trinity of Mind on the two girls. Eldra's accusation came to mind. "Forcing a permanent *myndtíegan* is worse than rape!" she had said. It affected me more than I let on. I tried to push away Kendra's and Lexy's bad thought.

Alexis continued to console me mentally. She was not successful. Fortunately, Eldra's next sentence caught my attention.

"Being on the drill team is extremely important," Eldra affirmed.

"I'm so sorry. Drill team tryouts happened last spring. The girls have already completed all their fundraisers and purchased their four dance outfits for the year," said Mrs. . . . oh, right, Mrs. Hallsworth.

"Perhaps I could call the drill instructor and speak with her. Could I have her phone number?"

"I don't think she'd like me giving out her number," the woman answered curtly, no longer smiling, as if the matter were closed.

I felt magic move in the room. I couldn't exactly tell that the magic came from Eldra. It just moved as if her magic were just air and a breeze had happened to pass through.

I looked up from my game. The woman's eyes froze. Though nowhere near as wrinkled as Eldra, the older woman had crow's feet stretching out from the corners of her eyes. People blink every second or so, and their eyes normally move a few times here and there in between blinks. Even the wrinkles on their skin move. So, when a person doesn't move their eyes at all for a few seconds, it's extremely obvious.

After a moment, Mrs. Hallsworth finally snapped back to life with a series of quick blinks.

"I think we have everything we need," she spoke. She looked around as if confused or lost in thought. "Oh, wait. Let me just get that number you asked for. The drill instructor is Katie Spinwell. You'll just love her. She will be so excited to hear about your two girls."

*I did not know she could do that,* Alexis shared my awe. *I thought vampires had the exclusive on mental influence.* Alexis couldn't hide her thrill—for school.

*You* want *to go to school?* I accused. *And you want to be on the drill team almost as bad as Kendra!*

*My mother has worked it out with Grandfather. Since Keagan's challenge failed, my status as Princess of the New World will not be challenged again until I finish school. If my mother can get him to word it in such a way that college is included, we could have five years of peace.*

She let me peruse her memories about vampire leadership challenges. They made the best MMA fights look tame. Such fights were usually to the death. In some rare instances, if the winner was unusually adept in mental dominance, they took ownership of the loser's mind and made them thralls. Vampires could control other vampires, as Alexis's grandfather had for so long controlled her.

A dim light of hope lit inside me. I would attend my senior year of high school. College remained a possibility. I still grasped at some semblance of a chance for a normal life. That line of thinking boosted my spirits.

I took a deep, audible breath. I breathed so loudly that I drew the attention of the mother sitting in the chairs waiting her turn. Her pity look obliterated any trace of the hope I'd just had.

I swore under my breath. I was going to experience my senior year in a new high school with no friends while looking like a thin, albino freak.

# CHAPTER 27
# DRUID CACHE

*Grandfather gifted me more times than I can count. Jake and Kendra are virgins. They had an interesting point of view. They asked if I had been forced every time. Perhaps I was. They claim that being forced doesn't count. They believe that if I was never a willing participant, then technically, I, too, am still a virgin. —Alexis*

We swung by and picked up Alexis and Luiz. Alexis wanted to go home and get her leather armor. We hoped to find Kendra before nightfall. But since we planned to take on the caplatas, we needed some extra magical supplies. Eldra made Alexis choose. We had time for one place. Alexis conceded that the druid cache held more importance. The druid cache consisted of a mostly empty storage unit with a shelf of liquid spells captured in glass vials. Hopefully, Eldra could help us find some vials we could use. She didn't seem to mind that O'Brien had picked through them recently. We discussed our attack plan as we drove.

After I indicated which storage unit was the right one, Eldra parked. I recognized it because it was the only storage unit with a combination padlock. The rest used keys.

I remembered coming here with O'Brien. My memory bordered on photographic. As we all got out of the car, I replayed that first visit in my mind. I could hear O'Brien as if he were repeating the words to me. I spoke the words I remembered. "The druids have caches hidden around the world. Every capital city has one, including Salt Lake City. They are hidden in plain sight, and even most druids don't know about them."

"Sounds like they follow a similar principle as my grandfather and his mansions."

"A mansion in every capital city is way cooler than a storage unit," Luiz chimed in.

"Well, the mansion and its contents are far less expensive," Eldra explained. "There is usually an item or two in the druid's cache that could buy the mansion and everything in it."

I went straight to the padlock and bent down to enter the combination: 3-27-18. I tugged, and the padlock popped open. I smiled. I love my awesome memory. As I looked at the numbers, I noticed they were all variations of three. The first number *was* three. The second number, twenty-seven, was three times three times three, or three to the third power. Eighteen was three plus three multiplied by three. Also, three to the fourth power is eighty-one, which, when flipped backward, made eighteen.

*I am starting to understand why Kendra calls you a geek,* Alexis mocked my mental math. She'd connected just long enough to get the combination. Perhaps later, I'd suggest to Eldra that she change it.

With the loud sound of wheels rolling on metal, I raised the garage door. Inside, I flipped on a switch and heard the hum of electricity leaving the solar panel battery. I flipped a second switch and two lights came on.

Luiz and Eldra followed me inside, but Alexis hung back with a hint of apprehension. Perhaps she wasn't sure if there were magical protections to keep her kind out. Alexis had left Club Exposed wearing a black, long sleeve, button-up blouse— actually, the buttons were snaps—with a pink cowgirl hat and oversized sunglasses. Her blouse also had pink thread that matched the hat. Her charcoal jeans hugged her bottom half as tightly as her usual leather pants did, except where the jeans had intentional holes.

Alexis had tried to choose a leather outfit. However, while Gina had offered plenty to choose from, they either didn't cover much or didn't fit Lexy's five-foot-ten-inch figure.

Her choice of long sleeves and a hat wasn't just by happenstance. I didn't understand it yet, but despite making her stronger, feeding made her more susceptible to sunlight. Even had her mesh white shirt not been ruined, she would have needed to change.

On her left cheek, she also had two brown spots, a large freckle and a smaller freckle just under it, where drops of my blood had burned her. I assumed the marks would go away soon enough. My blood had burned her palm, too, but her palm showed no such marks.

I repeated what O'Brien had told me again. "This place is solar-powered." I gestured toward the battery. "A lot of the new caches are equipped with solar power instead of lamps and oil."

"Lamps and oil?" Luiz raised his eyebrows at me.

"Druids were old school," I answered.

"They still are old school," Luiz pointed at Eldra, "This hag's wrinkles were old school when lamps and oil were still in."

Eldra unexpectedly chortled loudly. I chuckled more at the way she laughed than at Luiz's joke.

As I walked toward the lone wood shelf in the back, I could smell the dust as easily as I could see it. Footprints marked the dusty floor. I recognized the military boot pattern. O'Brien and I had left these footprints. This is where I'd first learned to cast a containment. Where I'd first learned that I could see magic even when other people couldn't see it.

I could sense the containment surrounding me as surely as I could see the four walls. "The storage unit has a containment spell around it," I continued explaining. "You can cast magic inside it without worrying about someone outside sensing it.

*"Está vacío,"* Luiz muttered to himself as he pulled a chair from against the wall and set it up.

"Are you coming inside?" I called back to Alexis.

"Am I invited?"

*"¡Hay, no!"* Luiz responded before I could answer. "You don't want to come inside this oven. *Hace demasiado calor!"*

I shook my head at Luiz. A bead of sweat had already formed on the side of his temple and it dampened his short black hair. I didn't feel the heat. Was I subconsciously controlling my body temperature?

"Yes, you're invited," I replied. I felt guilty for not thinking to invite her earlier. I'd noticed her lingering.

"I would prefer an invite from Eldra."

"Just come inside," I groaned, but she ignored me and looked to Eldra.

"Alexis, please join us inside," Eldra offered.

She came inside without incident and joined me at the back by the solitary wooden bookshelf. She slipped off her pink cowgirl hat and sunglasses and set them on top of the bookshelf. Without her sunglasses, the two brown burn marks that I'd given her stood out more prominently.

"That didn't heal?" I asked, pointing at her cheek.

"Hey, you can't just take your hat off like that!" Luiz complained. "You need to work a pole if you're going to take off your stripper clothes."

Luiz could get away with joking with Eldra, but would he get away with what he just said to Alexis? She was going to tear his head off. Except, the only emotion I could pick up from her left me staring with my mouth open. It was not the anger or even mild annoyance that I expected.

"Do you see a pole?" she asked with a smooth, emotion-hiding voice.

Luiz glanced around, then jumped up and grabbed the copper ring that stuck out from behind the bookshelf. I'd used that copper ring to help learn to cast my first containment.

"How about this," Luiz extended the copper ring to Alexis. "Can you spin a hula-hoop?"

Alexis gave Luiz a hard stare. The copper ring hung in the air until I was sure Luiz was going to apologize and put it back, but he just kept holding it.

Finally, Alexis grabbed it from him, and in one swift motion, she snatched her hat and slipped it back on while simultaneously flipping the ring over her head and down to her hips, which were already rocking in a smooth rhythm.

Her movements demanded the full attention of our eyes, making it impossible to look away. The copper ring gave off a slight metallic wisp as she spun it around her hips. Her body moved as if the most gifted Hawaiian hula girl and the hottest Latina salsa dancer had a baby who was now all grown up. Even Eldra watched, mesmerized by Lexy's hula hoop dance.

It didn't last long. She completed a full circle as she moved, removed her hat, and spun a few times. Then she put the hat on the shelf without missing a hip movement or letting the copper ring even alter its pattern, then she flipped it back over her head and extended the copper ring to Luiz the same way he had extended it to her.

Luiz grabbed the copper ring and stumbled backward, overexaggerating his reaction. He fell onto the folding chair he had set up, dropped the copper ring, and fanned his face and neck with his hands as he said, *"¡Hay, Dios mío!"*

A part of me wondered if we should be wasting time. With Kendra captured, shouldn't we be focused in our efforts to reach her? Shouldn't we have a sense of urgency? But only part of me felt that way. The other part of me had just had a moment of pure fun. It had been less than a minute. But it was a minute so enjoyable I would never forget it. That single moment of fun stripped layers of stress off me. The muscles in my shoulders loosened. Sure, Alexis had given us the half-minute dance, but Luiz had started it all. This proved why I needed Luiz as my best friend.

The still-healing skin around my mouth pulled as I smiled what was probably the biggest smile I'd had since before this all started.

"Mercy from heaven," Eldra interjected, "that's as rare as Billy the Kid at church on Sunday," bringing everyone back to the task at hand.

"What?" I asked.

"A teleportation vial," Eldra spoke, and her voice held a quiet reverence, devoid of its usual gravelly sound. She pointed at a clear vial with a phantasmagoric display of swirling colors. She reached for it, but then stopped and didn't pick it up.

"If it's so rare, why is it here?"

"It makes sense that we put one here," Eldra surmised. "Utah is off-limits. If a druid overstepped the bounds of the treaty in this state, it may take such a spell to escape." By treaty, she meant the Rockwell addendum of the Vampire Vatican Treaty, which I'd just learned about.

"How can we use it against the caplatas?" I asked.

"We can't," Eldra replied. "Besides, this spell is too valuable. With this one vial, I could buy a dozen of your grandfather's mansions. It takes nearly fifty years to make a teleportation vial."

"Fifty years? Ah, man!" I complained. "So once I master magic, I can't just *disapparate* all over the world. Next, are you going to tell me I can't catch a portkey to the Quidditch World Cup?"

"Don't confuse fiction with reality," Eldra responded. "In the real world, teleportation requires enough energy to bend the fabric of time and space and create a portal—a wormhole, science calls it now—that you can step through. And usually, the other side of that wormhole is days or weeks into the future. Not to mention that the earth is moving in its rotation, as is the solar system, as is the universe, as is the multi-verse."

"I thought most druids weren't scientists."

"The way we learn astrology and the way scientists learn astrology are quite different, but we both still learn."

"Well, we could use the vial to send the caplatas to the bottom of the ocean next week." I laughed.

"Or the portal would become a giant faucet for the bottom of the ocean. The energy from the ocean would keep it open indefinitely. You could end up flooding Utah with a giant ocean."

"I get it. Drowning the caplatas, good. Refilling Lake Bonneville, bad."

"No, this spell needs to stay right here," Eldra continued using a soft voice that paid homage to the rarity of the colorful vial.

As Eldra perused through the other vials on the shelf, I couldn't help but want to ask her about each of them. Somehow, I stayed silent. There would be plenty of time for her to teach me. We needed her so desperately. I needed her to train me. To help me.

I needed to protect myself. The attacks would never stop. The caplatas attacked even after Keagan fled. They attacked again last night. The Skull Shadows were after my family. Why had they tried to take my sister into custody? Why did they attack Jody? They knew more than I did. Did they know I was a protector? Did they know that Jody was chosen to be protected? Lexy's mother, Carina, had warned me, "If anyone finds out what else you are, nothing will slow the legions that will hunt you." If they knew, then they were hunting me. I needed Eldra to help prepare me for when the legions found out. I took a quick breath as the image of Caradoc's impaled brother came to mind.

"Truth," Eldra grabbed a vial.

I remembered when a truth vial had shattered in O'Brien's jacket. He had suddenly become overly talkative. After he had shared too much, in anger, I'd lit our beater truck on fire while we were still sitting in it. Fortunately, we got out with only minor singes before it burned down to a blackened metal skeleton.

What would we do with a truth vial?

"Sight," Eldra grabbed another vial.

"What? So that the blind can see?" Luiz asked.

"No. Sight allows the drinker to see magic. You can also see everything else better," Eldra replied.

"I can do that already," I answered.

"Maybe this is for Luiz," Eldra replied. "And you would do well to take care when using your sight. There are things that should never be seen. Things that can never be *unseen*."

Eldra took two other vials.

"What are those?" I asked.

"Just trifles," Eldra answered, intentionally answering my question with a non-answer.

"There isn't much here," she complained. "We have all we can use." With that, she sauntered toward the storage unit's garage door.

I looked longingly at one of the four remaining metal boxes on the bottom shelf. Thousands of dollars filled each, and I didn't have a dime to my name. Tempting.

I noticed three more vials of disguise. I'd used one to attend my own funeral. I wondered if disguise could hide my hideousness. More tempting.

I glanced back. Eldra lifted the storage unit's garage door with the loud rattle. Alexis was trying to teach Luiz to keep the hula hoop above his hips. I grabbed a disguise vial and quickly slid it into my sweatshirt pocket.

"Jake," Eldra called. "Since you can sense which direction to go, you drive."

# CHAPTER 28
# DRIVING EAST

Alexis likes to torment Kendra and me. She jumps into our head when we are using the bathroom or in the shower. She still thinks our views on modesty are laughable. Kendra now wears her separation stone in the shower. I have no such luck. It isn't Alexis's fault. Her grandfather made her this way. —Jake

Nobody cared that I didn't have a driver's license. So, I drove us east.

If I were to choose an eighth wonder of the world, I would choose the Wasatch Mountains. The mountains stood like a granite wall. This year, even in August, the very tops had patches of white snow that somehow never melted. I-80 curved into Parley's Canyon as if it were a secret passage through the otherwise impassible granite megastructures. The world seemed just a little different as I drove east.

I wasn't used to being in the driver's seat. I gripped the steering wheel a little more tightly than I probably should have. I didn't dare follow the emotional bond all the way back to Kendra because, last time, a dark barrier had knocked my consciousness back with a great deal of pain. Probably not safe to do while driving without a license. Our bond pointed east to Kendra as assuredly as a compass pointed due north. But better than any compass, our bond provided far more than just a direction. It gave me a sense of distance. It also assured me that Kendra was still alive.

Alexis sat to my right, blocking me from her thoughts. Eldra slept in the back. She hadn't fully recovered from either my magic missile or the hiding spell she'd held in place long past her point of endurance. Luiz also sat in the back, texting Andrea. She'd called him while he waited for us at Club Exposed with Alexis. She asked where he was. He lied. Perhaps guilt had caught up with him. Eldra had said he'd reached manhood now and could make his own choices. Becoming a man might mean that he was old enough to make his choices, but it didn't mean that he would always make the right choices.

Luiz had been my best friend for as long as I could remember. Did his night with Gina change that? I didn't think so. My church leaders had constantly bombarded me with the idea of choosing good friends that shared our same values and avoiding friends who didn't. Then these same church leaders would tell me on another occasion that I needed to make friends with peers outside our faith. The statements appeared contradictory and mutually exclusive. Which statement should I follow?

My peers outside my faith didn't share my values. Luiz drank alcohol at parties. He preferred to have his father turned than to bury him. He preferred to watch when Alexis decapitated our zombified servants, while I looked away. Had he really slept with a college-aged stripper?

Alexis didn't really share my religious values either. She didn't dress anywhere near modestly. Though it was no fault of her own, she had been with hundreds of people since age thirteen. She drank blood. She had killed, also only when forced by her grandfather, at least until Mr. Espinoza.

Who was I to judge them? I wasn't even sure I believed in these values. Though my mom raised me in the church, I'd never been a churchgoing boy. Even when Sis dragged me along, I mostly sat out in the foyer. I hardly listened during seminary courses, which Sis also dragged me to way too early in the morning. I didn't always make the right choices. I'd been past second base with a girl. I probably would have gone all the way with Alexis in the Druid Grove if our moment hadn't been cut short. But those weren't even my worst sins. Oh, no. I had done far worse.

Do you know what it is like to kill? I don't just mean killing and sending a spirit back to heaven. I mean killing a man so dead he doesn't have a spirit left to return to heaven with. I'd committed the unpardonable sin of erasing men from existence. Sure, they'd shot at me. That probably justified lethal self-defense on my part, but did it really justify erasing them from existence?

*Am I evil?*

I'd also let O'Brien fake my death. I let my mom and sister give me a fake funeral. I let the nightwalkers kill my stepdad. I let my mom take the rap for it. I'd done nothing to help exonerate her. I hadn't even told her I was alive.

*Am I as ugly inside as I am out?*

I glanced at Alexis. She looked out the window contentedly as we passed Park City. She noticed my eyes on her.

"Have you ever been to a movie in Park City?" she asked, interrupting my thoughts.

"Why would I see a movie in Park City? I have two Megaplex theatres not far from my house."

Alexis had never been to a movie. She'd hardly even watched TV. You could give her the most obvious movie reference in the world, like saying, "I'll be back!" in a guttural, Arnold Schwarzenegger accent, and she'd have no idea what you were talking about. So, the fact that she even mentioned movies caught me off guard.

"Hmm. I heard that Park City was the place to see the *crème de la crème* of movies."

"Oh, you mean the Sundance Film Festival. I thought you just meant regular Hollywood movies." I shook my head, wondering how I'd misunderstood her question. "Yeah, this is where you can come and see a bunch of independent films. I've never been. Supposedly, it's pricey."

"After we get Kendra back, the three of us should all go," Alexis suggested. "I would enjoy doing something that normal high school friends would do."

"Sounds fun," I answered. I didn't want to say yes or no. If I said no, she'd feel bad. If I said yes, how would I pay for it? I didn't see how I could afford it. As Princess of the New World with a grandfather richer than Warren Buffet, Alexis probably didn't have any issues buying the tickets, but I didn't really have access to cash. In fact, if she didn't provide my clothes, feed me, and give me a bed to sleep in, I'd be homeless, wearing rags, and starving. Sis currently lived with Kendra's parents. She was an inch away from becoming a foster child, but I was about to turn eighteen. Maybe now wasn't the best time to realize that on top of being an evil monster, as ugly on the inside as I was on the outside, I was about to start out my adult life as a jobless, penniless mooch.

I'd tried to give my life to save Kendra and Alexis at the Cabin Battle of Bear Lake. I'd failed to both give my life and to save them. Fortunately, Alexis and Carina had pulled off the win after I went down. Now, to save Kendra, I had a chance to try and give my life for them again. *This time, I won't fail.*

"A year of high school," Alexis smiled. "I never imagined it would be possible."

About twenty minutes beyond Park City, I-80 started heading north to Wyoming. North was the wrong direction, but being on a freeway in the middle of nowhere, I had to drive about five miles further to find an exit that let me turn around.

The emotional rope tugged me east, not northeast. If anything, it was slightly south. Alexis pulled up her map. We needed to take Highway 40. I'd been on that road twice recently. Once on a wakeboarding trip with Dylan and again when O'Brien had circled the Wasatch Mountains trying to hide our tracks and make it look like we were heading east out of Utah.

Highway 40 went too far south. As we approached Heber, my bond with Kendra still pulled me east, but now it also pulled me a bit further north. Highway 40 kept going south for quite a while. It didn't feel right.

"The map shows a road leading northeast into the mountains," Alexis suggested, looking at her phone. "Turn left at the light at the bottom of the hill."

I turned left. We followed the south side of the Jordanelle Reservoir for a while. I thought about the wakeboarding trip. Dylan asked Sis out for the first time on that trip. Dylan wasn't such a bad kid. He'd bullied me when I was younger, but he grew out of it. His parents were cool. His mom knew how to load up the meat on a sandwich, something that someone who eats as much as I do would never forget.

"Alexis, this is where I first saw that scar guy," I noted.

"Who?" she questioned. She went to tap her separation stone but then didn't. It was distracting for me to drive with her in my mind—mostly because her mind was a horrible backseat driver.

"Vertical scar guy," I explained. "Remember Officer Connelly? The Skull Shadow."

Alexis nodded.

I had to admit, having a verbal conversation instead of a mental conversation was kind of fun. Sharing thoughts removed all the anticipation.

"I saw him here at the lake."

"Just now? As we passed the lake?"

"No, not now. Months ago. It would have been the Saturday before, well, before O'Brien shot me and faked my death."

"That was only two weeks ago tomorrow."

"Seriously?" I exclaimed. "Has it only been two weeks? It seems like a lifetime ago. These have been the longest two weeks of my life."

"You showed me that memory. You saw Officer Connelly at the reservoir during a wakeboarding trip."

"Well, he didn't say he was Officer Connelly then, but it was him," I added. "He was flashing Caradoc's photograph around, asking if anyone had seen him." A Caradoc memory caught me off guard, but it was short. Caradoc and O'Brien stood in a rented room high on the mountain east of the reservoir. They watched me with a telescope. I went to run a hand through my hair and found only stubble on top of my not-so-smooth scalp. I'd almost forgotten that I was hideous.

Alexis didn't have a follow-up comment. She seemed deep in thought.

"Do you think the Skull Shadows are responsible for the Day of a Thousand Deaths, for killing all the druids?" I asked her.

"The Skull Shadows are highly trained and extremely secret. But in the end, they are mercenaries and assassins. The Skull Shadows surely played a part in the Druid Genocide, but they wouldn't have orchestrated it. Someone else hired them."

"Are you sure?"

"Jake, Carina has confirmed three groups were involved: Vampires, Nightwalkers, and Skull Shadows. I asked her if more secret societies were involved. She didn't answer. It could not have been easy to plan and execute over a thousand assassinations on the same day."

"So, your grandfather hired them?"

"Maybe." Alexis didn't seem so sure. "My grandfather may have been hired, too."

"OK. All of them were hired to kill all druids. That includes O'Brien and Caradoc. Caradoc disappeared. Are they still after O'Brien?" I didn't ask if they were still after me, because I didn't want to bring it up.

"And you, it seems," Alexis sighed, bringing up exactly the topic I wanted to avoid. "They tried to arrest your sister. They want to flush you out."

"Flush me out? They had me right there."

"Did they know you were you?"

"What do you mean?"

"Jake, Kendra's mother did not recognize you."

The truth of her words hit me hard. I'd hoped that, as Alexis's General, I wouldn't be hunted anymore—that everyone assumed I was dead. I'd hoped that those that knew I was alive believed me to be little more than one of Princess Alexis's thralls. But after the continued attacks, it had become clear that wasn't the case. *Nothing would stop the legions from hunting me.* The nightwalker, Alexis's grandfather, the caplatas, the Skull Shadows; how many different groups were after me? The caplatas met with my biological father in my dream. He'd reprimanded them for failing to find me.

Had my father orchestrated it all? Did he want me dead? Was the only reason I was alive because my revolting albino skin and thin body disguised me? I touched the vial of disguise in my pocket and realized I'd wasted my time taking it. I was already disguised.

My breaths heaved out too quickly. They sped up and didn't slow down.

Alexis grabbed the wheel, saving us from a head-on collision with a big, black Ford truck. She slid her leg around the gear shift and hit the breaks for me. I would have stopped the car on my own, but I was busy hyperventilating. I hadn't noticed the panic attack coming on.

Alexis removed her sunglasses and put both hands on my cheeks, forcing me to look into her red eyes. Her mouth moved but I couldn't hear her. The full power of her allure pushed against my panic. But my body didn't react to it. Other voices sounded in the background, but I couldn't make them out.

If the dream where the caplatas were reporting their actions to my biological father was real, and I sensed that it was, then my biological father was after me. Now that he found me, he wanted me. This wasn't just about me being a potential druid. This was personal to him. Perhaps at the start, he'd sent the nightwalker after Caradoc and O'Brien, but once I'd been found, I became his target. He sent the voodoo witches for *me*. The caplatas had taken Kendra to get to *me*. All of this was my fault.

My body shivered. The air conditioning in the car brought goosebumps to my albino skin. I wanted to pull my hoodie over my head, but I couldn't move due to my shivering and lack of breath. I needed more air.

"Jake," Alexis's voice sounded numb through my terror. I felt her soul pry open my panic attack. Fighting it off for me. Taking my experiences into herself and absorbing the emotions that came with them.

*Jacob Matthew Stevens,* Alexis squeezed her way into my mind and used my full name. Hearing my full name made the warmth of the magic all around me vibrate. It caught my attention completely.

Suddenly my chest inhaled deeply. The air that I so desperately needed filled my lungs even as Alexis's mind filled mine. The sense of her soul combined with mine warmed me like the soft blankets in my room at the mansion.

She leaned in close, her legs still straddling the gearshift in the center console. Her pink cowgirl hat bumped my forehead. I noticed the two brown dots still marked her cheek. Would they be permanent? Her warm hands felt comforting on my cheek. She didn't have the usual calm face that I'd come to expect from her, at least, when she wasn't tormented by hunger. No, her eyebrows raised high above eyes—eyes that had turned white in fear. I could smell her fear like an icy fog. In my mind, she'd latched onto the dream of the caplatas and my biological father.

"Holy hell, Jake!" Alexis swore out loud. She'd never sworn out loud before. "The Unforgiven."

# CHAPTER 29
# HANNA

*Alexis and I took a trip to Aeropostale to get her normal clothes. It was a lot of fun. Except she intentionally picked all the clothes that I said were too immodest. I'm jealous a little. She picked a bunch of cute outfits I would like to wear, but they just weren't up to my church's standards. I found myself recommending them to Alexis instead of telling her to be modest. Sharing Lexy's thoughts is altering a lot of my beliefs. —Kendra*

T he Unforgiven?" Eldra spat from the back seat.
Alexis let go of my cheeks and leaned away from me as she disconnected from my mind. She turned and looked to the aged druidess as if begging for help.

"Why are we talking about a *maldito* Metallica song?" Luiz blasted the question raucously.

"It is not a Metallica song," Alexis started. "It's a—" "It's nothing," Eldra cut Alexis off, her gravelly voice loud and final.

"It is, too, a Metallica song," Luiz started singing with his best imitation of James Hetfield's metal voice. "New blood joins this earth."

"Luiz," Eldra cut in. "Not now."

"And quickly he's subdued," Luiz lowered his head, feigning shame, but he couldn't hide the smile at the corner of his mouth. Then he added, "That last line sort of fit the moment, didn't it?"

Eldra kept her lips thinned. The absence of her normal laughter toward Luiz staled the air in the car. She fixed her eyes on Alexis as if saying with her eyes, "We'll talk about this later."

Alexis nodded.

I rolled down the window and breathed in the clean mountain air. Normally, I wouldn't have let something like this go. I'd harp on what was going on. But I had just recovered from another full-blown panic attack; the first since I'd woken up from a coma. I'd hoped my mind had healed, but who was I kidding? My mind had hinted to me on numerous occasions that the healing stone wasn't fixing it. Panic attacks are not about the physical. Sure, there is a psychosomatic reaction, but panic attacks are about memories and thoughts. And as I've suspected before, memories can't heal.

I had to suck it up because my number one priority was saving Kendra, and I'd die before allowing another night to pass without saving her. The clock in the car read just after three o'clock. In August, the sun set around nine. We were in the middle of the Rocky Mountains following back roads that I'd never been on. We could wind on these roads in the mountains for hours and still not find Kendra. Why had I chosen this moment to have a debilitating panic attack?

"Sorry," I apologized. I felt embarrassed. Inadequate. If Alexis hadn't taken control of the car and brought us to a stop, I could have crashed and killed us all. She still straddled the gear shift, pressing her left foot on the brake.

"Jake," Alexis kept her voice smooth. Her white eyes faded to pink before settling back to red. "How about I drive, and you focus on Kendra?" She tapped her separation stone and her mind opened back up to mine, allowing her to feel the emotional string pulling me toward Kendra.

I nodded and exhaled choppily as if finishing a sob. I opened the car door to get out.

"So, Alexis," Luiz started, "Angelina Jolie's got nothing on you!" He pointed from the back seat to the stick shift between her legs.

"Wait till she gets in the driver's seat," I replied as I stood up. "We'll be gone in sixty seconds."

As I walked around to the passenger side, I experienced Alexis's weird euphoria at recognizing a movie reference. She had seen only a handful of movies on rare occasions in her life and that was not one of them. However, I was a connoisseur of movies. I usually only slept for four hours and so I watched a lot more movies than the average person. She'd used my memories, not hers, to catch the reference, but she loved the feeling.

Alexis also felt my jealousy toward Luiz. He pulled humor out of nowhere and rescued me from my embarrassing moment again.

As I played a compass pointing toward Kendra, Alexis drove. We wound our way east. We found Highway 35 and followed it for miles. Kendra still felt distant. We started climbing the highway over Wolf Creek Pass. Maybe it wasn't just the Wasatch

Mountains that should be the eighth wonder of the world. Maybe it was the entire length of the Rocky Mountains. The mountainside looked like Christmas-tree land, only without snow. We rolled down the windows to let the pure air fill our car. As we rose higher on the mountain, white-trunked quaking aspens replaced the spruce trees. Lexy could also smell the difference, not just the different trees, but the thinness of the air as we ascended in elevation.

My bond with Kendra now pulled east and possibly north. I couldn't be sure until we crested the peak.

I had a map of the area up on my phone. I couldn't find any roads leading northeast. If we backtracked forty minutes and took Highway 150, we'd end up going to Wyoming long before we made it far enough east. We had to keep going to a small town called Hanna, and then, we could head north on Highway 135. Or maybe it wasn't a highway. It looked on the map to be a dirt road.

"I have hunger," Luiz called from the back seat. "We skipped lunch."

"We're in the middle of nowhere," I answered. "But we're approaching a small town."

"Does it have food?"

"Doubtful," I answered, "but I'll look."

I pulled up nearby restaurants on my phone. I should have brought up that there wasn't time for dinner. We needed to find Kendra. I don't know why I didn't. I just searched.

"There is a bar or a dude ranch."

"Are you sure the dude ranch has food?"

"It came up when I searched restaurants," I answered.

"We will try the bar first," Alexis cut in. "Bars always have food."

"Yeah, but will they let us in? We aren't twenty-one," Luiz questioned.

"Seriously?" Alexis looked in the rearview mirror at Luiz and raised her eyebrow. "You will rush to follow me into a strip club, but you have concerns about whether a bar will let you order an early dinner?"

"Oh, right," he lowered his head sheepishly.

Eldra chortled.

Hanna wasn't a town like you typically think about when you think of a town. Hanna consisted of two buildings across the road from each other: on the north of the road, a country store with a gas station, on the south, a bar and restaurant.

Alexis parked in front of the bar and restaurant. She slipped out of the car, then reached back in and grabbed the pink cowboy hat. Luiz raised her eyebrows at her. "So that I fit in," she laughed.

As Luiz walked toward the bar, he grinned.

"Eldra, this bar looks like you. Old and worn out."

Eldra smacked him in the backside with her staff. "Be careful," she grinned so wide even her wrinkles grinned with her, "or I'll tan your hide till it's old and worn out."

*"¡Hay de mi!"* Luiz jumped. "You're old enough to know how to literally tan hides!" Eldra laughed again.

Since the place was both a bar and restaurant, we had no problem walking in and sitting down at a booth. We sat at a booth on the left by the window, one booth away from the entrance to the bar. Alexis slid in beside me, with Luiz and Eldra across from us.

The décor, the tables, and everything else about the bar, except the liquor bottles, looked at least three times my age. They even had a picture of the same old cowboy everywhere. I recognized him but couldn't place him. Longhorns, real ones from a bull, jutted out at the top of the wall to the right. Orange wood paneling covered the walls. The wood looked old but had been stripped and retreated recently with a poor choice in color. The ceilings hung too low for my liking. A dozen other patrons sat at other tables. Another dozen or so middle-aged people hung out in the bar, a separate room to the left.

"They are obsessed with the Duke," Eldra laughed.

"Who's the Duke?" Luiz asked.

"John Wayne," Eldra pointed with her staff to the nearest picture on the wall. "The most famous country western star of all time."

"I thought Clint Eastwood was the most famous country western star of all time," I countered, but at least I remembered where I'd seen the old cowboy before. I watched a lot of movies, but I'd never watched a John Wayne movie. My enjoyment of westerns hadn't gone that far in the past yet. Perhaps a few John Wayne movies would be something to watch when I next got a free night. I hadn't had a free night to watch movies until the early morning hours in over two weeks.

A blonde woman in her forties came over and looked at each of us, pausing for a moment on Alexis, then focused on Eldra. Another thin woman, also older, worked behind the bar. Tattoos covered the better part of her thin arms.

"Glad y'all could come in. Do you want something to drink?"

"We are in a hurry, young lady," Eldra stopped her. "Would you be good enough to take our order now?"

"Sure, what can I get ya?" The waitress glanced at me, swallowed nervously, and tossed her yellow hair back.

"Bring us four of your largest steaks, two medium rare and two as rare as you can legally not cook them."

"The sides?"

"Veggies and mashed potatoes for the sides. Add an American Bacon Burger Meal and a chicken salad."

"You know us so well," Luiz grinned.

She'd ordered the four steaks for Alexis and me. I always ate a lot—extreme consumption. Lexy's extreme consumption started recently. We'd also enchanted her protection stone to be a healing stone, and she needed a lot of extra food and energy to keep her skin from getting sunburned.

"Drinks?" The waitress asked. She glanced my way nervously again.

"I'll have your house beer, but these three are too young and too Mormon," Eldra answered.

"Hey, I'm Catholic," Luiz complained.

"Too young," Eldra countered.

The waitress stood there as if waiting for something, but she kept glancing at my face under my hoodie and forcing herself to look away.

"That's all. Go on and put our order in, honey," Eldra shooed her away.

"Thanks, Eldra," I offered.

She nodded. I hadn't had to tell her that we needed to hurry, or that I didn't want the waitress to look at me. Perhaps Eldra really didn't hate me. Or perhaps she cared for me just enough to fight against her hate for me. Once again, I realized how much we needed her and how important she was to us.

Alexis took my hand under the table. A hint of worry rolled into me from her touch that matched my worry. We both wanted to save Kendra. Her nerves fretted about taking time to eat before finding Kendra, too.

Alexis and I didn't talk. Instead, we listened as Luiz quizzed Eldra about Billy the Kid. I could have been wrong, but her stories sounded embellished.

Our food arrived fifteen minutes later, and I devoured my two steak meals. Alexis somehow managed to eat demurely while at the same time keeping my pace. I'd have teased her that her fangs gave her an advantage at eating rare steak, but I didn't want to talk, and she kept her mind hidden behind her separation stone.

After our meal, Alexis and I made our way to the restrooms. I came out first and sat down. Alexis came out a few minutes later. As she walked to our table, I heard the restaurant door open and a slight breeze wafted inside; a breeze noticeably imbued with magic. I would have just ignored the gentle magical zephyr if not for the way both Alexis and Eldra immediately turned their focus to the door.

A man had entered. He wore a blue-and-white, plaid cowboy shirt and a white cowboy hat, but he wasn't a cowboy. The Ute tribe and its reservation surrounded the nearby area. A few Utes went to West Jordan High with me, but I only knew one of them. Kelly Chapoose started as a lineman on my football team. Or was it *my team* now? I tried not to dwell on the fact that I'd be going to Woods Cross and likely not playing football. The guy in front of me didn't look anything like Kelly, though. He stood a few inches shorter than me—making him average height. Two braids, one on each side, touched his shoulders. Gray hair weaved throughout his braids like veins in the walls of a silver mine. His thick nose seemed to have no end as it turned into two deep grooves that bracketed his flat mouth.

A Caradoc memory caught me off guard. Caradoc had spoken to this man or perhaps a man that looked just like him: The man was named Chief Wah-kara.

Caradoc sat across a fire from Chief Wah-kara. The chief wore a tan, leather shirt with beaded threads like I'd seen hanging from dream catchers. He had a fur blanket over his shoulders and covering his lap. The small, almost smokeless fire crackled in the center of the dirt floor where it separated Caradoc from the chief. The small fire provided the only light. Shadows danced across the chief's face as the flame flickered in different directions.

Two others sat across from the chief, a middle-aged man and woman.

"The governor requested this rendezvous," Caradoc began. "He sleeps little. He worries that the chief stands with the Coyote. It haunts his dreams. He wants you to stand with him in the treaty's addendum."

"Coyote gives to Nuchu. Coyote takes from Nuchu," answered Chief Wah-kara. "Coyote is our history. Bear and Rabbit and

Porcupine are our history," the chief continued. "The wind blows over the land. Us Nuchu, we cannot stop the wind. Coyote is like the wind. Us Nuchu, we cannot stop Coyote."

"Then you want no part of this," Caradoc stated.

Chief Wah-kara shook his head and stared into the small fire. The flames reflected from his eyes.

"The governor will be unhappy. You will displease him," the middle-aged man added. The moment he spoke, I recognized him as Eldra's husband. The woman who looked to be in her thirties was Eldra. Matching the young and smooth wrinkle-free face to Eldra's current visage took a bit of imagination.

"The white man follows the path of the coyote. Sometimes he takes the path as friend. Sometimes thief. Sometimes enemy. The Coyote changes his mood with the sun."

⚭ ⚭ ⚭

Eldra lifted her staff protectively. Her movement grabbed my attention, pulling me from Caradoc's memory. Her lips pursed, and her eyes stared thinly at the man who had entered the Hanna Restaurant and Bar. Surely she remembered meeting this man, too.

"He's not . . ." I was about to say Chief Wah-kara, but I didn't because he must have died well over a hundred years ago. "Who is he?" I whispered the question as I let magic fill me. If she had her staff ready, I needed to be ready too.

"I don't know," Eldra answered in a raspy whisper.

The Chief Wah-kara lookalike sat down at a table that faced us. We'd have to walk past him to leave.

"Caradoc—I had a memory," I whispered back. "You were there." I moved my head gently to gesture to the man, "He was there. In a teepee."

"Chief Wah-kara died over a century and a half ago," Eldra continued to talk quietly. "This man looks just like him."

What did she mean? That it was his grandson or something?

Alexis reached our table but didn't sit down. She kept the Native American in her line of sight.

"Let's go," Eldra growled and stood.

*Who is he?* Alexis asked. I offered her Caradoc's memory as my only answer.

The man who looked exactly like Chief Wah-kara smiled at Eldra as we walked past him. He moved to follow her, but I cut him off, and we bumped into each other.

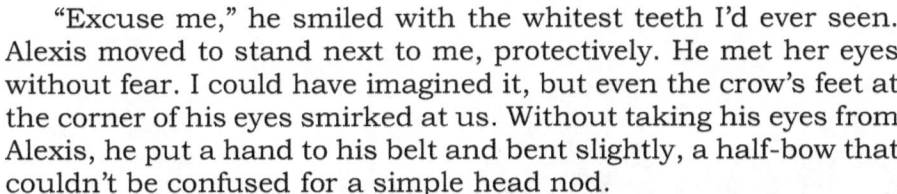 

"Excuse me," he smiled with the whitest teeth I'd ever seen. Alexis moved to stand next to me, protectively. He met her eyes without fear. I could have imagined it, but even the crow's feet at the corner of his eyes smirked at us. Without taking his eyes from Alexis, he put a hand to his belt and bent slightly, a half-bow that couldn't be confused for a simple head nod.

*He bowed. Does he know who you are?* I wondered to Alexis.

*I do not know,* she answered.

Neither of us believed his bow was a coincidence. This man knew that Alexis was a princess, and neither of us doubted it. Alexis tossed him a warning smile. She didn't extend her fangs, but if he knew to look, as I did, he would have seen the sharp points of her canines anyway.

We walked out to a changed sky. Solid blue had dominated the sky when we entered the bar. It now had a cavalry of clouds charging eastward over the Wolf Creek Mountains, as if chasing us. Our dinner break had allowed the clouds to catch up. I hoped that the caplatas didn't know we were coming. If they did, they probably conjured the threatening storm. But I doubted they had weather-shaping magic, if there even was such a thing, and I doubted they knew we were coming. I hoped to surprise them, shatter the clay bottle that held part of Kendra's spirit, and get Kendra back. Their shadow magic would be useless in the daylight. The clouds worried me, though. Would they cover the setting sun and hide its light earlier than expected?

*We will find her,* Alexis answered my concern.

I couldn't hide my doubt from her as we all crossed the road to the country store.

# CHAPTER 30
# WARNING

*I am an only child. I did not have any brothers or sisters. Jake and Kendra are the first people around my age whom I have interacted with for longer than a week. My grandfather does not keep children around except one a generation. He picks a woman, kidnaps her, and has a dhampir child. If the mother survives, he lets her raise her child for a time, but eventually, he kills her. Sometimes, he will turn her. He did not pick a woman this generation because my mother, the prior generation's dhampir, had me quite unexpectedly. Dhampir women, like vampire women, are not supposed to be able to give birth. —Alexis*

Eldra wanted us to stock up on snacks in case our search lasted all night. After stocking up with a dozen bags of jerky and some junk food—including a bag stuffed with those mini crumb doughnuts that I love so much—we piled into the BMW and set off toward the compass-like pull of Kendra's emotions.

After gauging the direction and distance, I picked a road that wound on for almost an hour. It felt like we should be fleeing the approaching clouds, but they gained on us ominously. Lexy could smell the coming storm. Still, we continued on.

The food combined with the long ride pulled at my eyelids, begging them to close. Alexis glanced over from the driver's seat and noticed my dropping eyes.

"You should sleep for a few minutes," Alexis suggested.

"No, I'm fine," I lied.

"We have the direction for now," she assured. "I can wake you when we get closer."

I looked one more time at the map on my phone. The map showed only one road, and we were already driving on it.

"I guess we have about an hour," I conceded.

Falling asleep in the car wasn't something I was used to, but it was starting to become a habit. I wasn't supposed to need much sleep.

"Use your seat belt to rest your head on."

I lifted the seat belt so that it held the side of my head. My hoodie provided just a bit of cushion. I closed my eyes and listened to the hum of the engine, the grind of the dirt road, and rustle of the wind passing by.

I didn't fall asleep right away. Luiz spotted an elk and asked Eldra about animals in the 1800s. I listened to the first part of her story, about seeing a hillside where a heard of elk covered two square miles. The men in her party killed dozens of them for sport and left most of them to rot. Luiz didn't have a witty comment for that. She moved on to the freshness of the land. Its beauty. The raw wilderness that existed before the settlers filled the valleys.

I'm not sure at what point I fell asleep. But a rough, washboard patch in the dirt road rattled the car and woke me up for a moment. I didn't stay awake long. I drifted back into my partial slumber.

Kendra inevitably returned to my dreams. This time, they weren't Kendra's dreams; they were mine.

🔺   🔺   🔺

I moved to the door and opened it. A much younger version of Kendra stood in the doorway.

"Hey, Jake," she smiled.

"What are you doing here?" I asked.

"A sleepover."

"With Sis?"

"No, silly," she laughed. "You invited me for the sleepover this time.

This dream was a repeat of the first dream I ever had about Kendra. I was only fourteen. It was one of those weird dreams where nothing made sense. We ended up sleeping in weird locations in Sis's room. For some reason, I had to sleep with my legs under Sis's bed. In the dream, Kendra and I made out until Sis interrupted us. Somehow Sis had never left the room, yet she didn't catch us kissing. At fourteen, a make-out session was about as steamy as my dreams got. However, the dream continued beyond where it had ended at fourteen, and not in the way I would hope.

215

"Kendra," Sis interrupted. At her interruption, Kendra suddenly lunged at her, with hollow eyes and mouth agape. She tore at Sis's cheek first. Then she moved to her throat and bit down. She turned and looked back at me, and I saw Alexis instead of Kendra. Alexis's fangs extended, blood dripping down her chin. She bit into my sister's carotid artery again. I stood there and did nothing, not because I didn't want to stop her, but because I was trying to move, and for some reason, I couldn't.

She finished with Sis and turned her bloody face toward me. I tried to back away, but chains caught my wrists. A dungeon surrounded me. The dungeon where Alexis's Grandfather, the Vampire King, had forced her to feed on the family in Ecuador. To my left, the family hung from chains as dark silhouettes, their naked bodies robbed of dignity.

I heard the Vampire King's voice. Now instead of hanging from chains, I stood by him.

"Feed on the woman first. Then the children in order of age," he commanded. "I want him to see his family leave this world in the order they came into it."

I looked, and instead of an Ecuadorian family hanging from chains, it was Sis, Kendra, and Jody's son Carl. Even though Alexis had fed on Sis earlier in the dream, Sis now hung from the chains alive, whimpering in fear. Alexis stepped forward to Kendra. Kendra thrashed against the chains.

"Jake," she yelled. "Save me!"

Numbness prevented me from moving. I took slow steps toward Kendra, but I never reached her. Something blocked my path. A barrier, perhaps? No longer did I hang from chains, but I was no less confined.

The barrier reacted like a containment, only it was active. Aggressive. It pushed back against me, holding me a distance from Kendra, preventing me from rescuing her. The dungeon disappeared, as did Alexis, her grandfather, and Jody's son.

Darkness took over. It engulfed Kendra, swallowing everything around her. In the darkness, I could see only her. Nothing else existed. Just me, Kendra, and the darkness holding me away from her. Try as I might, the darkness wouldn't let me by. It seemed to be mist, ethereal and easy to walk through. But when I tried to rush through it, it knocked me back like an oversized linebacker.

Three times I rushed it, and three times it knocked me backward, leaving me staggering to the ground.

I stopped trying to rush at it. Instead, I approached it cautiously. A face formed in the darkness. A tight-skinned monstrous face. The elongated head had obsidian skin pulled tight around the muscle. A cloak covered the rest of the creature.

I formed a magic missile in the shape of a football and hurled it at the nightwalker. The glowing, elongated orb traveled in slow motion. The nightwalker opened its mouth and the glowing football slipped between its rotted teeth and disappeared. The nightwalker didn't crack with light. Not this time. This time the missile fizzled and went away. By swallowing my magic, the nightwalker seemed to deal me a draining blow far stronger than when I had rushed at the darkness. Weakness rushed through my body, and I stumbled down.

Then I remembered Alexis's spell.

*"Dæg leoht,"* I shouted.

Daylight collided with the darkness, but the darkness absorbed it. It consumed the light.

The sunlight wasn't getting through. The darkness contained it. It was not a containment, but it was similar. I could poke holes in a containment. Could I poke holes in this? Instead of pushing against the darkness with my brute force, I slid a million little pinpricks into it. The light spilled passed the darkness.

Kendra turned and looked at me.

I let myself become part of the light and I followed the rays of my daylight inside.

I seemed to float just past the darkness for hours. My dreams faded to nothing. I didn't dream at all. Only peaceful contentment remained. A deep, dreamless slumber.

❧ ❧ ❧

*Jake!*

My peaceful slumber ended. I opened my eyes, but the darkness remained. Hadn't I conquered the darkness in my dream?

*Jake,* Kendra's mind danced in momentary excitement, hiding the sheer terror that had consumed her since the moment the caplatas had taken her.

I touched my face. I felt Kendra's hand on Kendra's cheek. I'd traveled to her body. Like the night at Bear Lake, I'd astral projected myself into Kendra. We'd shared our dream through our emotional connection, but now we shared our consciousness because my spirit shared her body.

*Do you have to take control of me like this?* Kendra complained. She didn't like being pushed aside. It augmented her vulnerability. Now, not only was she captured, but she couldn't move her limbs. She couldn't blink her own eyes. She shoved at my mind, but it didn't budge.

*Sorry,* I replied. I didn't know how to give her control of her body back. I tried to think it, hoping to make it happen, but it didn't.

*Where are we?* I asked. Kendra's bare feet molded the damp earthy floor into shape. It wasn't mud, but it wasn't dry dirt either. I lifted one foot and felt a thin film of damp earth clinging to the bottom of it.

A complete absence of light made the darkness absolute.

*A cave. A mine.*

I couldn't feel magic in the room at all, but I did feel a sense of corruption. A curse that wanted to make itself known but instead hid impotently a distance from us, unable to function without magic to fuel it.

*It feels icky here,* Kendra thought, concerned. She wanted a shower and imagined herself washing her body clean. We awkwardly tried and failed to pretend I didn't share her imagination.

*Can't we just walk out of here?* I asked, to chase away the awkwardness.

*There's nowhere to go. They did something to the entrance. We're in a sealed room. There's no way out.*

I tried harder to find magic. I just wanted a little magic to cast fire light so that we could see. Like the tainted curse, the magic seemed to be just out of reach.

*The caplatas' shadow magic prevents me from casting a spell,* Kendra lamented.

*Stick Witch and Voodoo Whoopie,* I cursed. *Where are they?*

Kendra's mind exploded into a million thoughts at once. I couldn't catch one because there were so many. I saw images of Kendra walking into a rock wall and continuing through it. Other images of Kendra huddling without a seat in the back of a black hearse. Atabei had taken Kendra's necklace, both her separation stone and her protection stone. Her spirit still leaked into Atabei's clay bottle.

*She has taken almost all of me,* Kendra's spirit whimpered.

I couldn't see Kendra's spirit with my eyes, but I could see it with my mind despite the lack of magic. It was thin and fragile, like the see-through shirt Alexis had worn this morning.

*I hate Alexis!* Kendra's mind cursed, but another part of her mind contradicted her and said, *I love her as much as I love you, Jake.*

If Kendra had control of her cheeks, they would have been flushed with embarrassment. She didn't want her mixed emotion

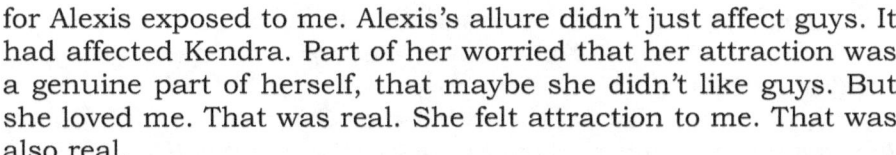 

for Alexis exposed to me. Alexis's allure didn't just affect guys. It had affected Kendra. Part of her worried that her attraction was a genuine part of herself, that maybe she didn't like guys. But she loved me. That was real. She felt attraction to me. That was also real.

Although, due to my thin frame and ugly skin, her attraction had waned significantly. She liked guys. She tried to hide from me how she enjoyed it when she and Sis practiced kissing, but again, her thoughts were laid bare before me, thoughts that made her self-conscious. Unfiltered thoughts scattered about her mind, but Kendra deserved much more than for me to judge her for the thoughts that flitted in and out of her head. She deserved credit for her continued effort to choose the best thoughts and discard the rest.

*I know you love me,* I mentally formed the words, but I couldn't hide from her the truth. Part of me felt that since I was no longer muscular and attractive, our love was lost. Still, I cleared my mind of unfiltered thoughts and formed the words, *I know you* were *attracted to me.*

Those words comforted her swirling emotions and let her mind calm. With a calm mind, she was able to focus.

*I need to warn you.* The warning became her primary thought, and the kaleidoscope of other thoughts dimmed as this moved to the forefront of her mind. *The caplatas are preparing a spell. They've been working on it all day, Jake.* The spell brought back Kendra's fear. It wrapped her like the cold of winter. *They know we are connected, Jake. How do they know?*

I pulled at her thoughts, nudging out what she knew of the spell. It should have been easy, but like my mind, Kendra's mind struggled with PTSD. She didn't want to talk about what the spell would do to us. She wanted to block this all out. Without my help, her diminished spirit couldn't fight off her debilitating fear.

*Their spell kills the three of us, Jake. They've used it before to kill those who are connected. The Trinity of Mind links our minds. The spell pulls the minds out of your bodies and into mine.*

I saw the next image in her mind before she formed the sentence in her thoughts.

*Then they are going to cut my heart out.*

*So we all die,* I thought back. I couldn't help but wonder if that would be so bad. *Maybe you are right.* I reminded her of her bad thought. *Maybe death is better. You and Lexy would be free of the Trinity of Mind in the next life, right? And, perhaps then the Skull Shadows would stop going after Sis. The charges against my mom would probably be dismissed. Surely the Skull Shadows had planted the evidence against her. Perhaps if I died, everyone would be better off?*

*No, Jake,* Kendra reprimanded me. *Of all the stupid, dumb, horrible things you ever thought, that is the worst yet!*

She tossed a bunch of thoughts at me to show me why life was worth living. A bunch of those thoughts included images of herself. One of which included her in a wedding gown, standing beside me while I wore a tuxedo. Another was of her standing in front of me in a pure white negligee on our wedding night.

*I know marriage is a long time off, but that is how I think about you,* Kendra defended herself. *That's how I've always thought about you.* She tried to end her thoughts there, but her mind continued almost against her will. *Before you became ugly,* her thought finished. *Sorry. I don't mean that.* She fought verbally against her thoughts. *We must get out of this alive. Your skin healed so quickly, maybe the scarring and splotchiness will lessen with time. And surely, you'll get a tan. You might be yourself again someday.*

Kendra was too young to be ready to deal with me being disfigured for life. She wasn't shallow, so much as she was just sixteen. She was trying so hard to convince me to not want to die, and she only made it worse. It wasn't her fault. She had given so much already. She'd given up her family. She'd given up her dream of being head of the drill team. It seemed like a petty dream, but to a sixteen-year-old girl on the drill team, that had been her whole life up till now.

I thought of how Eldra signed us all up at Wood Cross High and had made certain to get the drill team instructor's number.

Kendra exploded with joy at the possibility. Until that moment, she'd been fighting off painful thoughts that drill team was over. She had worried that she'd never dance in front of a half-time crowd again.

*My dreams are possible. Your dreams are possible,* Kendra assured me. *Go back to your body and save me. Save us!*

*Do they know we're coming?* I wondered.

*I don't think so. They think they've blocked you from me.*

I *did* need to go back. I probably should have gone back a long time ago. I didn't know what time it was. Surely Alexis would have woken me?

Except, could she even wake me while my spirit occupied Kendra's body?

*How did you get out of my body last time?* Kendra asked.

*I don't know. I just went to sleep.*

*I've been sleeping all day,* Kendra worried. *There's no way I can go to sleep now. Especially not with you in my head.*

I was stuck. What would Alexis and Eldra do when they couldn't wake me? I imagined them trying to wake me and failing. I imagined Alexis panicking even though she never panicked. Eldra and Alexis would discuss the best course of action. They would decide to drive home, hoping to try again tomorrow. They wouldn't know tomorrow would be too late. The caplatas would finish the spell tonight. Unless I figured a way out of Kendra's body and unless I led us back here in time to stop the spell, Kendra, Alexis, and I would be dead by morning.

# CHAPTER 31
# WAKING

Kendra is missing. I can't think of what to write this morning. I had nightmares again last night. Something else is happening. Something not related to the Voodoo witches. I don't know what it is, but I can feel it. Perhaps I can recognize protector magic now. If so, it is a warning, but also a calling. Whatever it is, I know it is my job to stop it. —Jake

I couldn't be sure how long we sat in the dark, thinking together. We thought of football and drill team. Sis. Alexis. Our families. Marriage (like, way in the future). We discussed magic. We communicated at the speed of thought, so we had a lot of conversations during what felt like hours.

I also experienced the extreme discomfort of being cold and damp while wearing a pushup bra. Because the humidity in the cave dampened Kendra's clothes, her bra had begun to irritate her skin. Having taken the driver's seat in her body, I felt the irritation nag at me while Kendra, pushed aside by me, couldn't feel it.

*I'm taking it off,* I repeated for the millionth time.

*Don't you dare!* Kendra repeated.

*It is pitch black. I'm not going to see anything.*

*I don't want you touching anything, either,* she countered.

This time, I ignored her. I tried to reach the strap at her back to unlatch it. I could feel where the bra latched, but no matter how I twisted my arm—Kendra's arm—I couldn't unlatch it.

Kendra laughed at me. It wasn't an audible laugh, but more like a tickle of emotion from her spirit. I watched her provide me a mental image of how she would remove her bra while leaving her shirt on. She would first slide the shoulder straps out her sleeves and pull her arms through. After that, she could push her bra

222

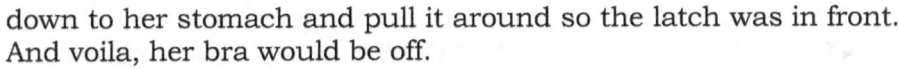

down to her stomach and pull it around so the latch was in front. And voila, her bra would be off.

*Fine, you do it,* I offered.

Just like that, I gave her control of her body. It was unexpected but a big learning moment. Not that I planned on astral projecting into Kendra's body often, but next time, maybe I could let her keep control of her body or at least give her control back sooner.

Unfortunately, giving her control wasn't such a good idea. She didn't have much of a spirit left, and when she was in control, she wasn't *in control.* Kendra was a voodoo zombie. Maybe I should have considered that before letting her take control again.

Voodoo shadows lashed at my spirit. My spirit retreated away from Kendra. I slipped from her body out of self-defense. I felt myself stuck in the shadows. But I'd passed through them once, I could do it again. I let my soul slide through as tiny particles which reformed and traveled back to my body at the speed of light.

I opened my eyes. *My* eyes, in my own body. My head lay on Alexis's lap in the back seat of the BMW. Her palm held my stubbly-haired head. The dots on her cheek hadn't faded away yet. Apparently two permanent freckles now? She looked down on me with her red eyes.

"Jake!" Alexis exclaimed. "Eldra, Jake woke up." She sounded so happy and celebratory that she could have been celebrating a surprise trip to Disneyland.

"*¡Por fin!* Where've you been?" Luiz demanded, glancing in the rearview mirror from the driver's seat.

I jerked to a sitting position. My ears needed to pop. The pressure in my head made it throb.

The intense darkness outside had turned the windows into mirrors. Darkness. We'd failed to find Kendra before nightfall. The car's engine purred more than usual, and the slight tilt of the car suggested we were climbing uphill. A light rain tapped on the windshield.

"Where are we?" I demanded.

The window wipers pushed the rain away. Outside, the bright headlights illuminated the two-lane road and confirmed that we were climbing a huge mountain. We were headed back over Wolf Creek Pass.

"On our way home," Eldra answered. "I assumed the caplatas captured your mind."

"We can't go home!" I exclaimed.

"We can't find Kendra in the dark," Eldra stated.

"Yes, I can," I assured her, my voice cracked with urgency.

"We will find her tomorrow," Alexis promised.

"They won't kill her until they use her to get to you," Eldra surmised.

"They are going to kill her tonight," I shouted, causing my ears to pop, releasing pressure from my head even as my worry pressurized it some more.

Luiz stopped the car. Alexis slipped into my head, got the instant download, including the part where Kendra imagined our wedding night. Oops. That cut at her heart. As soon as she had the info she needed, she tapped out. I had to explain the situation verbally to Luiz and Eldra, but I refused to say anything until Luiz turned the car around and headed back toward Hanna.

Eldra listened intently as I explained the important details, but Luiz kept interrupting. Eldra had me go over the spell two more times, asking me questions that I didn't know the answer to.

"I've never heard of such a spell," Eldra frowned. "Are you sure?"

"Kendra is certain."

"I haven't dealt with caplatas before," Eldra mumbled. "Caradoc handled any voodoo issues directly."

"Perhaps it is a trap?" Alexis wondered.

"Jacob," Eldra focused on me. "Is it a trap?"

"With that spell, they can kill the three of us from anywhere. Why would they hide so far away in the mountains if they wanted to lure us into a trap?"

Alexis glanced at Eldra. I caught the hidden message in a look, which left me wondering what they were hiding from me.

"Luiz?" Eldra turned to my friend, who until now had remained unusually silent in the driver's seat.

"It's a trap. I'm with Admiral Akbar on this one!" Luiz quipped.

"Who?" Alexis asked.

Eldra continued, ignoring them both. "Jacob and Alexis face death whether we attack tonight or not. But you and I do not. If we have the element of surprise, we can snatch Kendra and run. If it is a trap, we cannot defend ourselves against their shadow magic. We will all die."

"I say we call in *papá* just in case."

"That may not be wise," Alexis explained. "The caplatas have a powerful mind magic that almost took control of me. They failed, but I remained near-catatonic while fighting for my mind.

A newly turned vampire, like your father, might end up being their puppet."

"He looked unaffected the other night," Luiz challenged.

"When you shot at the caplatas with a shotgun, and they ran?" Lexy used the question to win the argument.

"I'm going tonight no matter what," I affirmed. "But Luiz, maybe we drop you off and have your dad come and get you."

"Or Gina," Alexis winked at him.

"Or Andrea," I countered.

"*¡Espérate!* You want to leave me out of this?"

"Luiz, I . . ." What could I say to make him happy?

"Didn't I help at the cabin?" he challenged. He knew we planned to leave him out. It wasn't his choice.

"You did help," Alexis spoke. "However, at the cabin, I expected to have more days to prepare. I had no intention of including you in that fight."

"Still, I kicked *culos* and took names!"

"What names did you take?" Eldra questioned, a grin fighting through her forest of wrinkles.

"Can I at least wait at the car?" Luiz begged. "If you get trapped, maybe they won't expect you to have backup—someone who can sneak in and rescue you. Or maybe I charge in guns blazing. I bet these caplatas die from bullets just like everything else. They ran from my shotgun."

"I survived two bullet wounds just this morning," Alexis reminded him. "They could have eyes on the car. If they capture you as soon as we leave the car, then we'll have to save you, too."

"*¡Qué brujas malditas!*" Luiz shouted in frustration.

"If he hides in the trunk, can he get out?" I asked.

"I could take the key; it has a trunk button," Luiz offered.

"These modern gizmos aren't keys. Still, we need it to drive," Eldra countered.

"No spare?" Luiz hoped.

"Actually," Alexis pointed to the center console. "There should be a spare in the center console."

Luiz popped open the center console and pulled out an oblong piece of technology. The first time I'd tried to drive this car, it had taken me a good ten minutes to start the BMW, and yes, I did have to read the manual in the glove box.

"We'll likely be hiking," I explained. "Once we are on foot, how will you find us?"

"The GPS on the phone locator app," Luiz answered, throwing his hands up as if to say, "Duh!"

We discussed the plan as we drove. Deep down, I worried it was a trap, but I hoped it wasn't. I wanted to believe we could surprise the caplatas, shatter their clay pots, and escape with Kendra. It should be easy. Maybe if they aren't looking, I could erase them with the most epic magic missile yet.

We stopped and stashed Luiz in the trunk. We moved some of the guns and boxes of bullets to the back seat so that he could fit. We also moved any exposed blades so that he didn't get cut. Alexis took the driver's seat.

It took us a little over an hour and a half until we crossed Rock Creek headed toward Moon Lake. We drove until we reached a campground loop. Today being a Friday night in the summer, the campsite didn't have any spots left. It appeared the rain had convinced one family to start packing up. Perhaps the rain scared them off. Still, we didn't wait for them to leave. We left the campgrounds and made our way northwest until we found a dirt road that moved in the general direction of Kendra. We followed the dirt road until it ended.

I could sense Kendra nearby. I estimated she was within a mile or two at most when we parked and exited the car. There were no more roads. Just dirt and pinion trees and hills that rolled up to the Uintah Mountains.

The rain continued to drizzle, almost noiselessly. It smelled clean. The small, plentiful raindrops danced onto our clothing. I didn't have a raincoat, just my hoodie, but the hood wasn't over my head. My stubbly scalp already felt damp as I slipped the hood on. The cotton material would soak through soon enough.

This was my first time standing in the rain since I could use magic. It doesn't rain much in Utah in July or August. This was a rare occasion. The rainstorm shimmered with energy that I assumed I could pull in for a spell, but when I tried, the raindrops washed the magic out, preventing it from taking any controllable form.

"Uh," I started, unsure how to share the bad news. "I'm not sure if it is the rain, but I've lost Kendra."

Alexis's face went still with concern under her pink, cowgirl hat. Eldra pursed her lips and scowled.

"What do we do?" I wondered.

"Wait," Alexis raised her eyebrows ever so slightly. "It rained the whole last hour. When did you lose her?"

I didn't answer. Instead, I opened the passenger door and slid into the seat, out of the rain. I tried to feel Kendra, searching for some part of the emotional rope that bound us together.

"Nothing," I commented. I had lost her. Why would I have lost her? If it wasn't the rain, then perhaps . . . Oh, no! Had the caplatas killed her? I froze for a good thirty seconds.

"Jake, what is wrong?" Alexis read my worry in my wide, unblinking eyes.

"I can't feel her!" I whispered, too afraid to say it out loud for fear that would make it more real. Would we die because of the rain? Would the caplatas spell go uninterrupted because we couldn't find them?

"Your hair is wet. So is your face." Alexis suggested. "Perhaps—" I pulled my hoodie off. I had a black t-shirt on underneath that almost came off with it, but instead, wadded around my neck. I quickly pulled it back down, but that still left my white, splotchy arms exposed. Though Alexis claimed she didn't care that I was ugly, her thoughts had constantly contradicted her. Of course, those thoughts were unfiltered. Still, I was glad her separation stone wasn't off.

I wadded my hoodie and used it to dry my hair. Then I waited. Still nothing.

I relaxed and focused on my memories of Kendra. I glanced at Alexis. I knew what memories to think of. I wouldn't make the mistake of choosing poor memories this time. I thought of the day we went rock climbing. She had made sure to sit by me in the car. Later that day, we had gone on a date to the Gateway Mall. She'd tried on a shirt, and since she had worn a swimsuit under her clothes, she'd pulled me with her into the changing room. After that, we'd hit the splash pad. My memory followed that day's events to when Kendra had almost left crying. I'd been trying to *not* like her since she was my sister's best friend. But Sis had assured me that Kendra was not off-limits. Those words had brought such joy. I had rushed upstairs to Kevin's front room, where I found Kendra crying and where I'd first kissed her salty, tear-dampened lips.

The emotional connection between us flared to life. I scanned the darkness toward a faint outline of hills that preceded the mountains. I knew which direction to go.

"That way," I pointed and started to get out.

"Wait," Alexis put her hand up and stopped me from getting out of the car. "I can see farther than you in the dark." She slid into the passenger seat and sat on my lap. She turned her head and kissed my cheek.

"Look," she pointed. Do you see that hill with those two little knolls on the right of it?

227

"No."

She tapped her separation stone. Her unfiltered thoughts hit me pretty hard. She had kissed my cheek to remind me that she loved me every bit as much as she was repulsed by me and every bit as much as Kendra loved me. The magic emotional bond between Kendra and me caused jealousy to spill out of her like blood. Her thoughts about Kendra still contradicted each other. *Someday, I will have to kill Kendra. If you marry her, you'll have to marry me, too. I know how to make her disappear forever. I can marry you and Kendra, too; that is legal now.* Alexis imagined cutting off Kendra's head with a runed blade.

*I am quite jealous. It will pass. Kendra's head is safe,* Alexis assured with the conscious forefront of her mind.

The conscious forefront of my mind believed her. The rest of my mind, not so much. I had some unfiltered thoughts myself—mostly bad, but at least one of the thoughts would be fun.

"Do you see the hill and the two knolls," she spoke verbally.

"Yes," I answered.

*I like that fun thought,* Lexy's emotions warmed. *When this is over, we should do that.*

*Kendra would kill me if she ever knew I thought that.*

*I will make sure to remind you about it then the next time she is around.*

Alexis slipped from my lap and from my mind, before moving to the trunk. I followed her. Once again, the rain lightly danced over me. This time I felt it on my bare arms, too. Again, the rain's energy felt powerful, and again, my access to magic felt interrupted. I lost my connection to Kendra. This time I didn't panic.

"We will head toward the first knoll closest to the hill," Alexis told Eldra, then she tipped her pink, cowgirl hat at the trunk and added, "There was an umbrella in here."

She opened the trunk.

"Are you letting me out or did you want to join me?" Luiz smiled up at Alexis. He lay in an awkward position on his right side and already held up a flashlight, anticipating our needs.

"Thank you," Alexis took the flashlight and handed it to me. "I also need that umbrella behind your hip," Alexis indicated. "Can you move?"

"I can move my hips for you anytime," Luiz quipped.

"Is now good? Here, let me help," she reached for him. Her fingers brushed the skin at his hip as she grabbed the top of his pants. Luiz's dark eyes widened, making his long nose look longer. Alexis lifted his midsection with one hand, then reached

228

under him with the other and pulled the umbrella out. Then she dropped him.

"Thanks," Alexis smiled. She popped the umbrella open.

Luiz didn't answer. Lexy's touch had put him in a fugue.

Alexis also grabbed a runed blade from the trunk. It had a small sheath and a strap that she wrapped around her right leg. The leather seemed very out of place wrapped around her charcoal Wranglers with holes.

"We will be back in two hours," Alexis told Luiz. "If we are not back by then, I think guns blazing is better than sneaking in and getting captured yourself." Then she shut the trunk.

Alexis tossed her pink hat into the front of the car—no need for sun protection at night.

"Make sure to put your cellphones on silent," Eldra suggested. "We don't want them to give us away."

All three of us put our phones on silent. It took me a second to figure it out. It was my first cellphone, after all. I was probably the only geek in the world who was a month from turning eighteen before he got his first phone.

Eldra and I moved to walk on either side of Alexis. I put my hoodie back on. Alexis kept me covered but tried to share the umbrella with herself and Eldra as we walked toward the hill and two knolls.

We walked for twenty minutes before we passed the knolls. I fidgeted with a coin in the pocket of my hoodie. I hadn't remembered having a coin in my hoodie pocket. We continued in the same direction for another while longer. The red mud stuck to our shoes, making it difficult to walk easily. Alexis kept glancing down at her shoes, annoyed. Not only did she not have her usual leather armor, but she didn't have her usual leather boots on. The mud had already ruined her white shoes. Her shoes had matched her also ruined sheer-white blouse.

Eldra struggled the most. She didn't act like her age affected her at the mansion, but her staff wasn't just for the magic show. She leaned on it, needing its help for every step.

We reached a barbed wire fence. An old No Trespassing sign lit up from my flashlight's beam. We ignored the warning. I pushed one wire down and one wire up. A barb poked into my palm, making it sting. If I'd still had calluses on my hands from weightlifting, it probably wouldn't have drawn blood, but I didn't, so a drop formed. Alexis noticed. Once across the fence, I pressed my hand to my hip, letting the damp bottom of my hoodie act as a Band-Aid.

"We are outside the line," Alexis told Eldra, who nodded back in understanding. We crossed into the Ute and Ouray Indian Reservation. I understood Alexis to mean that we were no longer inside the area protected by the Rockwell Addendum of the VV treaty.

It made sense why the caplatas had come all this way. They wanted to perform their spell outside the boundaries of the treaty.

I kept the flashlight pointed slightly downward, forming a circle of light a few yards in front of us. I couldn't feel Kendra anymore. I'd tried to stay under the umbrella, but the rain shifted with the wind. Alexis did her best to keep me dry, but my hoodie was already damp from trying to dry myself off. Alexis chose another landmark in the same direction, so we simply headed toward it. Once we reached it, I would cover myself fully with the umbrella, dry off and try to reestablish the emotional bond with Kendra.

I found myself staring at that circle of light made by the flashlight, lost in thoughts and worries, fidgeting with the coin, as we walked toward the next landmark. I should have looked up sooner, but I didn't. We almost walked right by it, but my peripheral vision caught a multicolored shimmer to my left. I turned my head.

"Wow!" I exclaimed.

# CHAPTER 32
# RHOADES

*I am sixteen. Jake is turning eighteen in a month. Alexis is already eighteen. The age difference is evident in how we think. Jake is clearly two years older than me. Alexis seems ten years older. She became an adult at thirteen. It's funny. I want to be an adult, and Alexis wishes she could be a kid again. —Kendra*

**"D**o you see that?" I asked.

"What do you see," Eldra questioned.

About a football field away, in the shape of a thick figure eight, magic glimmered off a section of a crag that jutted up only fifteen feet or so. The magic seemed to come from the rockface itself. Each stone within the figure-eight shape held a faint glow.

"Magic," I answered.

I hadn't told Eldra that I could see magic, even faint magic, clearly. Most magic users can't see magic unless a massive amount is used. The figure-eight radiated with a substantial amount of magic. Perhaps other magic users were far more limited in their ability to see magic than I expected.

"Neither of you see it?" I asked.

I changed direction, leaving the protection of the umbrella and moving my mud-heavy feet toward the shimmering section of the cliff face. Alexis turned toward me, spinning the umbrella slightly with her movements. The centrifugal force flung rainwater from the tips of the umbrella to my face as she shook her head while mouthing, "No."

The rain dampened my stubbly scalp again. Utah is normally warm and dry in the summer, and this summer had been unseasonably warm. But the dark mountain air, damp with the rare summer rainfall, left me shivering. I did my best to pull at the energy around me to regulate my temperature, but

231

something about the rain kept me from providing warmth consistently. Goosebumps stood up on my flawed albino skin. I shivered.

I marched with my heavy, mud-laden boots. The scene danced with color in front of me.

"Enhance your sight," I finally suggested to Eldra.

"You can't use magic in the rain," Eldra growled.

*Have you been using magic in the rain?* Alexis's mind lurched into mine.

*I've been trying. Keeping myself warm has been flaky in the rain. The umbrella helped.*

*Jake, in the rain, neither Eldra nor I can feel magic, let alone try to use it. And for us, the umbrella did not help.*

Honestly, I wished, not for the first time, that I couldn't use magic at all. That everything was back to normal. That O'Brien had never discovered my potential. That Alexis hadn't pulled me deeper into the darker subcultures of our world. I'd be asleep in my bed, wondering what the jeeks and I were going to do tomorrow after our unofficial morning football practice.

Alexis scanned my memories of seeing the color of magic. When I'd created a containment at the druid cache, the magic had glowed a clear gray, like a bottle. I had learned to detect a magic user using this ability while cooped up in a hotel room. Alexis had used magic the first time we'd met. I saw the magic faintly as she used it. I'd seen it when teaching Kendra to use magic at the Bear Lake cabin. At the druid cache, the vials of magic were different colors to me. To Alexis, the vials all appeared the same color: a clear liquid. She hadn't been able to see their colors.

With less than a dozen yards to go, I realized what type of magic the twisted image was made of. Illusion. The magic was shaped like a figure eight because the illusion covered a figure-eight-shaped opening into the small cliff face.

Was this the cave where Kendra was being held? It had to be.

When I reached the opening, I could almost see through the magical mirage. The illusion made the cave opening look like part of the crag. Nobody would know a cave entrance existed here unless they tried to touch the wall at this exact point.

I hesitated, unsure if the cave was safe to enter. I noticed the coin in my pocket was digging into my palm because I'd made a fist around it, squeezing it nervously.

*Is it safe?*

*Ask Eldra,* Alexis suggested.

I turned to Eldra and gestured to the opening, too afraid to speak in case my words traveled the length of the cave and warned the caplatas of our arrival.

"I know of this mine," she whispered, a worried look on her face. "Go inside, but whatever you do, don't take anything. If you see gold, leave it. Don't even touch it."

"Why, is the opening going to turn into a tiger's maw and clamp shut on us?" I whispered back. I wasn't Luiz, but I could attempt humor, too, right?

"It's a mine, not the Cave of Wonders," Eldra replied, a hint of a grin stretching her wrinkled cheeks. "Let's move inside. Be quiet. Be wary," Eldra added.

I couldn't tell if her whispered warning had to do with the cave or the caplatas.

*Perhaps both,* Alexis suggested.

I drew an arrow in the mud with my foot, pointing at the cave wall. I pulled out my phone and swiped up the location app. Even out here in the middle of nowhere, the phone had service. I texted Luiz my exact GPS location right before we disappeared into the cave. Sis had tried to call three times in the past five minutes. She would have to wait.

I took a deep, damp breath. The cold rain air chilled my lungs. Then I stepped through the illusion and into the entrance of the mine.

I felt two things about this mine immediately.

First, this was a place of power. The mine exuded the power like Sis's deadbeat dad exuded alcohol—her real dad, not John. It came from everywhere. I remembered my biological father asking the caplatas in my dream if they had found the place of power and if it was outside the line. They had answered yes.

Second, I felt the familiar way the mine made my muscles move—like a physical layer of some unknown substance undulating between my muscle and my skin. Evil. I sensed the caplatas, but this was far worse than last time. This evil pulsated from the mine like the tunnel was alive, a long demon worm that we were walking into, or more like a millipede with thousands of demon legs—legs that crawled around my albino, goosebumped skin.

Alexis mentally shuddered. *Your millipede-caused, undulating inner skin is so much more disturbing than your hideous outer skin,* she insensitively thought as she shared my ability to sense evil for the first time. She generously gifted me a full mental movie montage of my hideous body in various states, as she and Eldra had treated me the days after the Cabin Battle of Bear Lake. Then she imagined slicing her runed blade through my neck, so she'd never have to deal with my hideous skin again.

I pictured the freckle-like dots my blood had left on her cheek and mentally imagined cutting myself and flicking more blood on her, causing her skin to boil. It was an unfiltered thought, a retaliatory reaction to her thoughts. But I brought that thought to the forefront of my mind and enhanced it. I imagined bathing Alexis in my blood till her skin peeled from her body.

Alexis's eyes flashed black. She pulled the runed blade from a strap on her leg. She envisioned ramming it through my heart. Nothing in her mind suggested that she was having an unfiltered thought. No, she planned to bury that runed blade deep inside me.

*Save me,* a voice whispered in my mind. It didn't sound like Alexis's mental voice, but I assumed it was her. She held the upper hand and intended to kill me, why would she want me to save her?

Just as Alexis started to move, Eldra grabbed her shoulder.

The image of the knife buried in my heart shattered in Alexis's mind. We both turned to Eldra. She mouthed the words, "This mine is cursed." Eldra forced a smile that looked more like a grimace caused by a tug-a-war between her cheeks and her lips, with her wrinkles caught in the middle. "Smile."

Eldra's smile was in no way contagious. I couldn't make my cheeks even try.

Alexis, however, was more adept at smiling in the midst of vile corruption. Her smile showed her teeth, and she blinked until the smile reached her eyes. Her smile included happiness, beauty, and the power to change our curse-caused emotions. The corruptness in the tunnel fled from it. Her smile was so powerful I expected to see beams of magic emanating from it. But her smile didn't need magic. Her smile transcended magic and trumped it.

*Smiles are far more powerful than magic!*

I smiled back and any corruption from the cave's curse fled from me as well. In my perception, Eldra's smile changed from a wrinkly wrestling match to a warm, grandmotherly grin.

*Save me,* I heard again.

*Who are you?* Alexis asked, but no answer came. *Jake?*

*I don't know.* My smile almost dropped, but I forced my lips wider.

I took a few steps deeper into the tunnel, nervously letting my smile lead the way. I could stand up straight in the tunnel but just barely. I only had to crouch a couple times to keep my stubble-haired scalp from scraping on the carved ceiling. My arms only had a couple of inches to spare on either side.

The tunnel started out straight with a downward angle that continued to steepen for a good thirty feet. Then it ended with another shimmer of magic—a second illusion, dimmer but more intricate than the first.

Alexis didn't like the tunnel. It reminded her of the underground jail cells in Ecuador, from memories neither of us wanted to relive.

I scanned the walls. There wasn't any sign of gold anywhere. The mine walls looked cut. A part of me hadn't made the distinction between cave and mine. I'd never been in a mine before, but I'd been to Timpanogos cave. The juxtaposition of this mine and Timpanogos made the differences obvious. Caves are natural; mines are manmade. Caves are shaped over centuries by water, with stalactites hanging from the ceiling and stalagmites rising from the ground. Mines are cut out, with carved walls and noticeable tool marks.

As I ran my hand along the wall, I noticed writing. A name. Caleb Rhoades.

Wait a minute. I'd heard of this mine. How had I not realized this sooner? I rubbed the coin in my pocket with delight. We'd traveled deep into mountains east of Salt Lake City, past Rock Creek, and were now hiking in the hills around Moon Lake. I'd seen the No Trespassing signs. We had crossed onto the Ute reservation. Eldra had just said not to touch any gold. I shouldn't have needed century-old cave graffiti to spell it out for me.

Alexis had never heard of this famous mine, but she followed my thoughts.

This mine was a legend among legends. Of all the gold mines in the west, it was perhaps the most talked-about and most sought-after mine. Rumors of this mine's existence had started well before Brigham Young reached the Salt Lake Valley and said, "This is the place."

I turned back to Eldra and Alexis but kept the beam of light on the name scrawled in black on the mine's dark rock wall.

I almost shouted it out, but at the last moment, Alexis reminded me to keep quiet.

"The Lost Rhoades Mine?" I mouthed to Eldra, not using my vocal cords at all.

"One of the mines," Eldra answered, also moving her lips but not making a sound. "Be wary," she urged. Again, her warning ambiguously targeted both the cave and the caplatas.

I started geeking out. I mean, I was exploring the Lost Rhoades Mine. Or one of them, as Eldra said. Were there multiple mines? I'd never heard that, but I wouldn't call myself an expert on the lore. I'd heard the myths and legends at scout camps, just like all the other boys had. Supposedly, gold from this mine was used to mold the Angel Moroni that stood at the top of the Salt Lake Temple. The church has never provided an answer as to whether that was the truth or just a myth. But you'd be hard-pressed to find a Utah boy who hadn't heard the story. Most assumed it to be at least partially true.

The air in the mine didn't smell the same as the air outside. The strong scent of rain had dissipated as we descended, and an equally moist but slightly unpleasant mustiness replaced it. Alexis found it to be far more pungent than I did.

My hoodie remained damp, so I removed it. Subconsciously, I slipped the coin into my pants pocket. The inside of my hoodie wasn't damp. I used it to dry my stubbly hair, then tied it at my waist.

I focused on my memories of Kendra and conjured the smallest possible thread to connect our emotions. After a few brief seconds, the pull of our emotional connection followed the cave opening almost to the end, but the connection's trajectory veered just a little left and intersected with the mine wall about five feet from the second illusion.

My soul leaped inside. *Kendra is here!*

The cave floor had a six-inch-wide stream of water only a half-inch deep running down the middle of it. I scraped the red mud from my boots and let the water clean the soles. Eldra's soft black shoes looked like a cross between flats and tennis shoes. The red mud had stained them, but there weren't any clumps of mud on her shoes. Due to the rain, she wouldn't have been able to use magic to shed the mud from her shoes until we were in the cave. I never felt her use magic. *This grandma's got skills!*

Alexis took her flats off one at a time and scraped the mud away. I expected her to lament the loss of an expensive pair of shoes, but she had already lamented enough during the hike. Now, she lied to herself, claiming not to care at all that the red mud had stained and ruined her four-hundred-dollar designer flats.

*I am not a material girl.*

*Nope, you are way hotter than Madonna.*

She grinned, and her mental mood lightened. She hadn't intended her comment to reference Madonna, but at least she knew who Madonna was. I had now succeeded in making both Eldra and Alexis grin. If I were a Dungeons and Dragons character, my humor points would have just leveled up.

Once I finished cleaning mud off my shoes, I put my hands in the little stream, palms down to wash them, then I wiped my hands on my hoodie around my waist. Alexis dried her hands on my hoodie as well, shamelessly grabbing my butt in the process.

With our shoes lighter, we headed toward the second phantasmagoric illusion. The mine curved to a dead end in a way that would have looked completely natural if I couldn't see the magic at work. I stepped forward, intending to walk through the illusion until Eldra grabbed my hand and stopped me. I turned back to her, tightening my eyebrows questioningly.

She mouthed something. I wasn't sure what she said. I only made out the first syllable, "Boob." I must have read her lips wrong.

*She said, "Booby trap,"* Alexis informed me.

Kendra would have reprimanded me hard for that mistake, but Alexis didn't care. There couldn't be two girls whose minds worked so completely opposite of each other. I missed Kendra. I wished she were here to snap at me and tell me I was being a stupid boy.

"Booby trap." I mouthed back to Eldra. That made so much more sense.

*You should be better at reading lips.*

I ignored Alexis and shrugged toward Eldra. "What kind?"

"Not sure," Eldra mouthed. "Let me look." She gestured to herself, then to her eyes, helping me along with makeshift sign language.

Eldra tried to move past me. I put my back to the wall and so did Eldra. Even still, to fit past me, her body smashed against mine. I cringed as she dragged her grandma breasts halfway across my stomach and then stopped, stuck. Lexy's mental laugh resonated harp-like in my mind so loudly that I briefly thought she had laughed audibly and risked tipping off the caplatas to our presence. Eldra had to suck in. She put her right hand on my shoulder—even more awkward—to push me and pull herself past me. Her runed staff caught my shin—ouch—as she finally made it past me. Alexis didn't stop her musical mental laughter until Eldra began probing the illusion with threads of magic that were almost too thin to be seen.

Usually, magic creates a ripple effect, but Eldra formed the magical threads so thin and fine that they didn't cause a ripple at all. One of the threads changed from a light blue to a deep red. Then other threads shifted. Slowly the threads worked around a section of the illusion until they completely wrapped around a spider-web-like section. The threads tightened, shrinking that section of the illusion until it disappeared. Caradoc knew this spell. His memory instantly taught me how to cast it. Sharing my mind, Alexis learned it, too.

Alexis, not for the first time, pried at my mind, trying to find Caradoc's memories but came up empty. I couldn't pull up Caradoc's memories at will either. They seemed to be triggered only by outside events.

"Turn that off," Eldra mouthed, pointing to the flashlight. "Look with *sight.*"

*The third eye,* Alexis thought.

*I've heard it called that before, but isn't that term reserved for fiction?*

*No, that term is used in real life as well,* Alexis assured me.

I turned off and pocketed the flashlight. We both pushed magic into our eyes and the darkness disappeared. The mine came to life. Elements look vastly different with enhanced eyes. I could faintly make out the different elements in the rock, each separated ever so slightly in color. An earthy part of the mine wall revealed brighter spots inside—gold maybe. Some were long and thin and of various lengths from one inch to the largest being about a foot. They moved.

*Worms,* I thought, identifying the wriggling creatures.

Alexis reprimanded me. *We are in a gold mine and you are excited to find worms. Boys.*

*I thought you weren't a material girl.*

*What girl does not love gold?*

Eldra, now in the lead, stepped through the second illusion. I followed behind the aged druidess. Alexis followed just behind me.

The tunnel turned right in front of us. The original miners hadn't cut straight forward. They'd cut through to the left. The third eye revealed why. The light dimmed, and the rock's texture increased in density. We'd encountered a column of thick, dense material, possibly granite. The miners had chosen to cut through the weaker, red sandstone.

The tunnel circled the column of granite until it turned left to continue the same direction as the entrance. After thirty-three steps—I counted—it curved slightly to the right, and the wall began to dance with flickering shadows—something provided a flickering light just ahead.

*Torchlight,* Alexis confirmed.

With sight, I could see through the earth enough to discern what we were approaching. Around the next right curve, there would be a straight, five-foot tunnel before what was clearly a cavern entrance. I'd stopped paying attention to the evil-detecting undulation between my skin and muscles, but a sudden increase warned of a deeper evil.

Despite looking through solid earth, my sight revealed seven shapes of light—all human-shaped silhouettes—occupying the cavern. One murky silhouette stood exceptionally tall and thin. Stick Witch. I quickly located a short and thick silhouette—similarly murky—that could only be Voodoo Whoopi.

Who were the other five? Probably voodoo zombies—regular humans that I couldn't kill. And they'd be unnaturally strong, which put me at a disadvantage.

None of the human-shaped silhouettes looked like Kendra. Could I really tell? Looking at a person's light through solid earth, even with sight, was probably as accurate as recognizing someone from behind at a distance. But I'd known Kendra my whole life. I recognized every curve of her body, the way she stood, the way she walked, everything. I was pretty sure I could tell.

Other non-living light sources glowed around the room. Stationary objects that outshined the living souls. Some looked like pillars, but I couldn't tell what the rest of them were.

We'd spent plenty of time talking about our surprise attack strategy while driving. Now it was time to implement it. We had two plans, one if they expected us and one if they didn't. To me, it seemed they didn't expect us. Eldra lifted one finger, and then pointed at the cavern with two fingers, indicating she also thought we had the element of surprise.

Energy surrounded us. I let it fill me. Why hesitate to erase them? Two magic missiles. Erase these witches from existence.

*I am completely fine with that,* Alexis assured me. *Why would you feel guilty about that?* she wondered, confused at my moral view of magic missile self-defense.

We took hesitant steps to the opening of the cavern. The room came into view so bright that it hurt. We had to wait a few seconds for our eyes and our sight to adjust to the brightness.

A stone altar stood in the center of the room, surrounded by nine pillars. A circle of small candles burned inside the hollow underside of the altar and various other candles lined the walls around the cavern. I half expected Kendra to be lying on top of the altar, but she wasn't. She wasn't anywhere in the room.

239

Instead, the altar held a stone basin, wide and shallow. Stick Witch, thin and tall like a burnt-out lamp post, stood over the basin, her arm outstretched.

Voodoo Whoopi stood a few steps back, her fingers fidgeting and her lips moving as if reciting Hail Marys like Luiz's mom always did, only instead of a rosary bead necklace, she held shrunken heads on a cord. In the minimal light, her black clothes hung from her like a priestess's robes, dimming her soul's murky light.

The texture of the cavern walls looked designed and architected, as if this were a room in a Central American ruin and not a mine cavern. Was this a mine or a tunnel to an underground Aztec temple? The ceiling curved above us about twelve to fifteen feet high. Two large round disks hung from the ceiling. Because those disks were too bright to look at directly, I assumed they were made of pure gold.

The other five figures—two women and three men—stood motionless. The small torchlight cast shadows over their faces as much as it illuminated them. The caplatas had picked up some new voodoo victims here on the Ute reservation. All five of them had tans far darker than mine. The women had long black hair. One woman wore a white blouse. The darkness obscured the other zombies' clothes.

*The reservation is outside the line and not part of the treaty,* Alexis reminded me. *They have not broken it.*

*But they attacked us in North Salt Lake,* I argued.

*They attacked a dhampir and two potential druids,* Alexis answered, making it clear that the treaty didn't cover us.

Alexis stretched magic into a containment around me, allowing me to start forming a pair of magic missiles. Her containment made it so that my magic wouldn't ripple out like a beacon announcing our presence. I just needed a few seconds to power up the missiles.

That is when my new smartphone made a very loud ding.

# CHAPTER 33
# CAVERN

*Thralls do not make good friends. I wrote about not ever having a friend before. Occasionally, Grandfather brought thralls that were my age into his mansion. These girls never kept secrets, and they do not live very long. Two of them stand out in my memory. I spent a few days with them. Perhaps I thought I was forming a friendship. One betrayed my secret hideout to my grandfather. Grandfather had Dane drain the other of blood in front of my eyes because I had befriended her. Grandfather said that I should not make friends with my food. —Alexis*

When Sis had called me a few minutes ago, my phone hadn't made a noise. When she decided to text me because I hadn't answered, well, my phone chirped as loud as a morning magpie. I'd missed a mute setting, but now wasn't the time to pull out my phone and figure it out.

We froze in a pregnant pause as seven sets of eyes turned toward us.

*What the hell, Jake?*

My two magic missiles finished powering up during that pause. I released them. They lanced through the air toward the caplatas, casting a blue light into the dim room and illuminating the caplatas' faces. Shadow blades swung up from the darkness and caught the missiles, sending them to the cavern walls, each erasing a large section of wall.

On the bright side, I exposed two huge piles of gold. And by *bright*, I mean with sight, exposed gold is as bright as halogen spotlights. We had to shut off our sight because the two exposed

241

sections of gold blinded us. Unlike the disks hanging above, they weren't dimmed by an inch of dust. The gold didn't look like nuggets or a vein in the mountain. It looked misshapen, like it had once been jewelry or goblets but had been partially melted and smashed together like playdough.

I didn't really have time to further analyze the gold because a dozen shadow blades sliced away Eldra's containment seconds after it was formed.

The caplatas hadn't reacted quickly enough to form the shadow blades themselves. Their defenses had already been there. The caplatas had prepared the cavern with protective spells.

"It's a trap." We should have listened to Luiz's Admiral Ackbar quote.

Eldra smacked the top of her staff into her left palm and multiple carved runes lit up like the Salt Lake Temple at Christmas. Four lightning bolts shot out, two at Stick Witch and two at Voodoo Whoopi. A static hum filled the room.

The shadow blades intercepted three of them. The third hit Stick Witch's outstretched hands. The lightning shook her body, and her bones flashed with blue-tinted light providing us an x-ray. Her skull, her backbone, her ribs, her pelvis, and her arm and leg bones all flickered in and out of view. The static hum faded in and out too, matching the rhythm of her pulsating bones.

*"Brecan glæs,"* I pushed magic at the jars at Voodoo Whoopi's' waist.

She opened her mouth and showed me the length of her blackened tongue. A choking sound followed. No, not a choking sound.

"Did you just laugh at me?" I questioned, dumfounded.

"Atabei," Voodoo Whoopi referred to herself in the third person, "be not fooled again by the albino. My ouangas," she shook the jars at her waist, "are fireproof plastic, hah!" They hadn't shattered nor would they. I've read stories where modern, manmade materials like plastic couldn't be imbued with magic. Well, this was real life, and in real life, magic is just energy, and energy affects anything, including plastic, just in different ways. I considered testing the jars' resistance to fire, but I had to defend myself. Atabei gestured and a shadow blade tried to spear me. I wasn't sure what would happen if the tip of a shadow blade impaled me, but I wasn't about to find out. I twisted and brought up an angled wall of magic, deflecting the shadow blade from my chest.

Eldra's spell finished. Stick Witch looked ready to collapse but didn't. Instead, her bones flashed twice more, and then the same

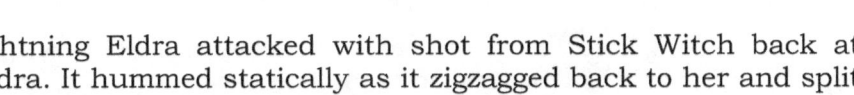

lightning Eldra attacked with shot from Stick Witch back at Eldra. It hummed statically as it zigzagged back to her and split into three, hitting Eldra's face, chest and stomach.

Eldra staggered backward and went down behind a pillar, dropping her staff.

The five voodoo zombies walked toward us, their ominously hollow faces made even creepier by shadows created by the cavern torchlight. Once again, they were living people, spirits trapped by the caplatas, who now controlled their bodies.

*Alexis, Eldra needs help! Why aren't you fighting?*

*I am,* she answered. Voodoo Whoopi pressed at Alexis's mind, fighting to take possession of her body. The witch somehow used Lexy's spirit to hijack vampire microbial lifeforms in Lexy's body. Those microbial protists refused to allow her body to move as if unsure who to obey, Alexis or the caplata. They had made the same attempt during our first encounter, but I hadn't understood then that Alexis had been in a mental and spiritual battle with them. If only she could turn off the communication between her spirit and the microbial protists.

Voodoo Whoopi's shadow magic not only attacked Lexy's vampire side, it somehow augmented her allure and reversed it into herself, attacking her human part. If the Hagathas gained control of Alexis, could Eldra and I survive?

I took my eyes off Voodoo Whoopi and glanced back at Alexis. Usually when I see magic, I see color; but instead of color, a black haze surrounded Alexis. I pushed a containment around Alexis and shoved my will into her mind, releasing her from her catatonic standstill. Once released, she lurched forward with a speed quicker than humanly possible and swung her fist at my face. I ducked. Her fist punched into the zombie behind me.

I swept at the zombie's legs as he reeled backward, and he went down. His long black braid swung to the side as his head hit the bottom corner of the stone altar.

*First down.* I hoped the man suffered only a concussion.

Alexis continued past me, rushing at Stick Witch, her runed blade raised. Three shadow blades launched like darts at her. She moved so quickly that I lost the containment I had on her. I tried to bring it back up. Too late. The three blades speared her from all directions. My containment cut the shadow blades off from their source and they faded away, leaving no outward mark of their attack. Still, Alexis fell, her momentum carrying her forward till she crumpled at the feet of Stick Witch.

*Jake!* Alexis screamed.

I wanted to help, but I had to back away from two zombie women. My back hit the cavern wall. There was nowhere to go unless I ran back toward the entrance. I considered just erasing them and being done with it. The older woman's hair hung to her mid-back, and a few long strands caught on her outstretched right arm. The younger woman looked to be half the age of the older, perhaps only a few years older than me. She had short, straight hair that stopped at her neck, an A-line cut. Her face held the same high cheekbones and curvature of eyes as the other woman. Mother and daughter. Despite the heightened temptation, I couldn't erase them. I could never do that to a mother and daughter.

But what could I do to them?

I wrapped them both in an everything-seal. They stopped moving and the color returned to their eyes. I stepped between them as they stood, disoriented.

Alexis needed help. Both Stick Witch and one of the two zombie men stood over her. They pried into her mind, trying to control her, not kill her. Stick Witch joined Voodoo Whoopi in the attack on Lexy's mind. She was now losing the battle. Only our Trinity of Mind kept her from succumbing.

I dropped the everything-seal on the women behind me and took three quick steps and launched into a perfect form tackle. My shoulder hit the zombie left of Alexis just above the belt buckle and I kept running through him. He dropped backward, his head hitting the floor with a loud thud.

*Second down.*

I would have celebrated, but that is when I felt it. The shadow blades. Two of them slid through my torso, both through my back.

I screamed.

The shadow blades' paralyzing fear included a taint of despair similar to the nightwalker's fog—similar but not the same. The shadow blade magic tried to take over the mind but didn't destroy one's sanity. Mentally, I could defend against it by making like Peter Pan and pulling up my happy thoughts. But unlike the nightwalker's scream, the shadow blades also attacked my spirit, pulling and stretching and tearing as it sapped it away. The agony, even though it wasn't physical pain, reverberated throughout my body.

I wrapped myself in an everything-seal and the pain ceased. But the shadow blades didn't stop. They flickered around me like flames flicker around a log, and with each movement, they weakened my seal. I didn't have much time.

*Help us, and we will help you.*

The voice wasn't Lexy's. It wasn't Kendra's. It wasn't Caradoc's. I surely didn't need another voice in my head. But it wasn't just one voice. Many voices hummed that thought.

Whoever or whatever this hum of voices came from, it communicated to me mentally, mimicking the way Alexis and I had communicated through the Trinity of Mind. It also mimicked my emotional connection to Kendra to show me where it was. It didn't want to be misunderstood. I considered rushing to the voice's source to see how it could help me, but right then, Eldra stood up and used a rune that shot light at a shadow blade, erasing it.

*Of course!*

Despite the Trinity of Mind, Lexy's mental battle prevented my thoughts from getting through to Alexis. Using both my mind and magic, I slammed back at the voodoo magic that fought to take control of her vampire side. I battled just hard enough to get my thought through.

*Cast daylight the instant I free you!*

"Eldra," I yelled, "hit Voodoo Whoopi with lightning."

Then I offered Alexis all the magic I had as well as all the magic I could pull in from around me. I formed an everything-seal around her, knowing it would only last a second or two because my actions left me unprotected. The shadows blades took me.

"*Dæg leoht,*" Alexis shouted. The cavern lit up like a sunny day at the beach. The shadow blades disappeared, erased by daylight. The zombies stopped moving. Thanks to Kendra, I knew that the zombies couldn't be controlled in daylight.

Eldra palmed her staff and a rune lit up. Lightning crashed into Atabei, who still held the shrunken head version of the rosary bead necklace. The witch couldn't defend herself; she was already stretched too thin, trying to control the zombies and restore the shadow blades. The lightning lashed into her without remorse. Her body lit up with electricity until her eyes rolled back into her head and she collapsed, convulsing.

*Third down.*

Alexis, still glowing like the sun, delivered a spinning back roundhouse to Stick Witch's face. The tall woman's head whiplashed to the side and back as she dropped to the ground.

*Fourth down.*

Alexis dropped the daylight spell and the cavern became darker than night. No, the candles still flickered their meager light, but our pupils had shrunk and needed to adjust.

As our eyes adjusted, the room filled with candle-caused shadows, but they were harmless, not shadow blades. The three remaining zombies woke, and following previous orders, started back toward us.

Alexis and I simultaneously decided to destroy the plastic jars—ouangas—housing the spirits. However, before we could act, Kendra joined our minds. She had been physically approaching since the battle began. But her mind didn't have any thoughts. I felt her magic reach out to me, pulling on me, using me to help her cast a spell. I wasn't sure what spell she planned to cast because her vacant mind offered no such answers.

Then three blue lights the size of marbles appeared down the tunnel. The magic missiles floated above Kendra's hand, illuminating her in their glow. Did she intend to stop the three remaining zombies? Had she lost too much of her spirit to know that she would kill them? They were still human.

"Don't!" I shouted while Alexis said, *Kendra, no!* to her mind. We both willed her to stop.

But she released the three missiles anyway.

Too late, I realized our mistake. We had no defenses up. The three, marble-sized magic missiles hit their marks: Alexis, Eldra, and me.

# CHAPTER 34
# ROPED

Alexis and Kendra mentally argued over clothes and fashion for well over an hour. At least they weren't arguing over me. They paused now and then to mock my terrible fashion sense. I mean, they mocked what I used to wear, not the dark hoodie I wear now. I can't imagine ever discussing clothes and fashion for an hour with the jeeks. For Alexis, though, fashion doesn't hold top priority. Alexis refuses to wear anything but leather when acting as the Princess of the New World. She must dress in armor for every fight. —Jake

Caradoc sat across from Chief Jake Arropeen and another Ute, who went by either Nuch or Blackhawk. He wore no weapon, but the way his cheeks flexed in the midday sun coupled with his careful, ready eyes gave him away: He was a seasoned warrior.

The suspicion in Arropeen's expression proved that this rendezvous would be less amicable than the one they had shared a decade and a half earlier. Caradoc had been right to come alone. Bringing other druids would have been interpreted as hostile.

"My condolences on Chief Wah-kara's passing. Would that I had returned before Chief Wah-kara died. Still, as is my word, I have returned with the solution," Caradoc explained. "I can release the Trapped Ones."

"The moon came. The moon went. The curse remained." Chief Arropeen answered.

"Yes," Caradoc agreed. "I had hoped to find the solution with far more haste. I sailed from England the moment I had the answer."

"Too many white skins have sailed from England," Chief Arropeen frowned. "We share our lands. We share the wind. But they take our land. They only share war."

"Even the Mormons have turned against you?"

"The white man learned well from Coyote," Chief Arropeen confirmed. "Hunger came. White man didn't share the land. The land gifted its corn, but the white man took it all."

"I'm sorry," Caradoc lowered his head.

"I will free the Trapped Ones and remove the curse."

Chief Arropeen shook his head, "We dare not free them."

Caradoc looked back, confused. He had put years into this effort. The druids placed a high priority on eliminating cursed land. Especially when it involved trapped souls.

"Why not?"

Chief Arropeen shrugged. "Coyote is part of us. His reasons are like the night, difficult to see." The chief's eyes began to glow, but he didn't move. The background faded from outdoors to become the bar in Hanna. His face changed from that of Chief Arropeen to that of Chief Wah-kara.

A new voice entered my mind—as if I didn't have enough of them. "Many summers have passed since the coyote danced the shadow dance. Use the coin. Summon Coyote to the underworld, Jake Stevens!"

I snapped awake as other voices echoed through my mind.

*We are the Trapped Ones. Release us!*

I felt a rope pinching my bleeding wrists and ankles long before I opened my eyes. My shoulder ached from lying on it. The hard floor didn't give my body any cushion. My legs were bent behind me, and when I tried to move them, the rope pulled at my hands. I couldn't move.

*Welcome back to the living,* Alexis thought. *Interesting dreams.*

Alexis shifted on the hard, stone floor as she considered where the voices that woke me came from. Her back, along the shoulders, brushed against mine. We lay on our sides, back-to-back. Rope tied my hands and feet. It was also tied to Lexy's hands and feet. As to whom the Trapped Ones were, her guess was as good as mine.

I was just happy to wake up. Three figures, the zombies that we hadn't dealt with, stood like statues, soulless and without a purpose. As painful as it felt to wake with bleeding wrists and ankles, it was much better than not waking up. We could have been eaten by the zombies. Had the zombies' orders been to capture, not kill? Or perhaps they had stopped when Kendra had knocked us all out?

My head rested just inches from one of the thick, towering pillars. One dim candle remained lit. Shadows, fortunately not voodoo ones, shrouded the cavern. I tried to avoid thinking about Kendra, which I couldn't hide from Alexis, but she humored me anyway.

*Eldra has not woken.* Alexis glanced at a dark lump a few feet from us before moving to two other shadowy lumps. *Neither have the caplatas.*

*Atabei didn't die?*

*Unfortunately, no. Both caplatas are breathing,* Alexis confirmed.

*Who tied us up?*

*Kendra or the zombies?*

I located two other forms that I assumed were the zombie men that we'd knocked out. Were they alive?

*They also still breathe,* Alexis assured.

*Who tied us up?* I asked again as I tugged at the knots at my wrist. I couldn't free my hands. I reached for magic and—*Don't,* Alexis warned too late—the ropes and knots tightened painfully. I felt a drop of my blood run down from my wrist to my palm. I stopped. I tried again, and again the ropes tightened. The second drop of blood followed the same path, then dripped to the floor.

*I already tried. If you use magic, the rope will constrict. Grandfather has used these before. The rope is enchanted. It will rip through your wrists and ankles.*

*Enchanted?* Cinderella, the Disney version, came to mind. *Interesting word choice.*

*Interesting? What word should I choose?*

Instead of answering, an unfiltered thought entered my mind where I imagined I pulled in enough magic to burn everyone in the cavern to ash and let the ropes sever my hands and feet.

*Not the best idea,* Alexis mocked me.

*So, where is Kendra?* I asked.

*I do not know.* She savored the memory of punching Kendra when she had first turned zombie on us back at the mansion. She hoped to do it again.

*Kendra got you back. You knocked her out with your fist, so she knocked you out with a magic missile. When are you going to stop it with the catfighting,* I jested.

Alexis had a few unfiltered thoughts. Some toward Kendra. Some toward me. I ignored them.

*Do you know which tunnel she went into?*

*She was not here when I awakened.*

Before I'd woken up, Alexis had tried for a while to find a way out of the rope. She shifted her shoulder and the cords pulled at my hands. She hadn't been able to locate her runed blade. Her belt buckle had a hidden blade, but she had no way to reach it.

We tried to fray the rope by rubbing it against the floor, but the ropes tightened again.

A shadowy form sat up, startling me. My jolting body jerked Alexis as well, making my wrists bleed more. Alexis couldn't decide which frightened her more, the caplatas or my blood.

Voodoo Whoopi moved over to Stick Witch.

"Manouchka," Atabei shook the other witch's dark form until Stick Witch groaned.

We hadn't found a way to escape. It was too late. I couldn't think of a way out of this. Alexis remained calm but not without a great deal of effort. She could panic at any moment.

Manouchka sat up and twisted her long body. The flickering candlelight reflected off her black eyes as she stared toward me. She stood without taking her eyes from me.

"Our new puppet be strong," Atabei added. "She knocked three druids into dreams. She will make a powerful caplata."

Atabei's black eyes turned toward us.

"Kill the cancerous one," Voodoo Whoopi hissed.

"Hey," I challenged. "That's offensive to people with cancer. They only get bald, not hideous."

The witches ignored me. I glanced at the three zombies expecting them to move, but the candlelight reflecting from Stick Witch's eyes extinguished, and it was she who approached me.

*Free us. We can protect you,* the Trapped Ones hummed their offer again.

The offer enticed me. In my dream, Caradoc planned to free them. I could finish the job he started. However, Lexy's gut said not to free them. I didn't know how to free them anyway. If I had known, I'd have freed them the moment Stick Witch unsheathed her skull-hilted dagger. Shadows crawled up and down the blade like black tongues of flame.

Despite the large cavern with nine pillars, Stick Witch needed only five steps to reach me. She raised the blade. My fear mingled with Lexy's. I tried to pull at magic but the binding on my wrists tightened, stopping me. Was I willing to give up my hands to save my life? I probably should have been.

Stick Witch pointed the dagger at me as she knelt. The blade headed toward my ribs without mercy. I pinched my eyes closed and looked away. I cried out in my mind with different threads of consciousness. I gave a mental shout of goodbye to Alexis and Kendra, while part of me ached that I would never see my sister again.

"He's the protector," Alexis spit out as quickly as she could. Despite Alexis's unprecedented use of a contraction, she hadn't spoken fast enough. I felt pain lash at my body and mind from a slit near my ribs. My rib cage tensed in agony, and I tried to move but doing so cut me more.

"No," Alexis shouted. She couldn't see me, but with our minds as one, she felt the blade bite into one of my ribs as if it were hers.

A trickle of blood trailed from the wound down my belly. I fought against my desire to thrash my body, to try to roll away, or do anything. Movement would cut me more, so Lexy stopped thrashing, too. There wasn't anything I could do. I soon wouldn't have to pretend to the world that I was dead anymore because I would be.

Except, Alexis's fear calmed. Seconds ticked by and I wasn't dying. The pain ended at my rib, not deeper.

I opened my eyes. Stick Witch knelt over me. I still lay on my shoulder, back-to-back to Alexis. The blade embedded in my side, just below my chest and in front of my bicep. Only most of the blade remained outside the frame of my body. She'd hit a rib. She probably would have pushed harder or perhaps pulled the blade out and stabbed again if not for Alexis's confession about me.

Stick Witch's body twisted back toward Atabei, giving me an unwelcome view of her tangled hair.

"He is the protector. The one whom the Unforgiven has been looking for," Alexis added.

"You be lying," Atabei accused. "The protector be strong. A muscle boy with tanned skin."

"No," Alexis continued. "He is not an albino. His skin is healing. He . . ." she struggled to find a way to explain quickly. "A spell damaged his skin. It nearly killed him, but he survived."

Neither Atabei nor Manouchka moved.

Alexis didn't have anything more to say. While I had heard Alexis's words, I was more interested in her thoughts. Much of the knowledge that she'd hidden from me about protectors now resided at the forefront of her mind—thoughts I could pick as easily as I picked apricots in July.

*I am a protector.* A protector had existed in every generation since not long after mankind began on this earth. Most protectors didn't live long. Many prior protectors were well-known historical figures from different religions. From the Bible, there were confirmed protectors such as Moses, King David, and Samson. Many believed the protectors to have godlike power or to be the offspring of gods. The Greeks wrote of Hercules, Achilles, Jason, Perseus, Theseus, and more. All throughout history, protectors have lived and died, fighting to save the world from evil. A higher power had placed us here to fight for the weak, to protect men and women from evil unleashed on the world.

Lexy's vampire background included unique and very pagan myths and legends. According to those, some evil force altered humanity, creating vicious subspecies that turned on their own kind; meanwhile, an opposing force, a good force, altered a single human bloodline to protect it. As a Mormon, I believed in God. I believed in Christ. I also believed in Lucifer and hell. But I'd never heard of a *protector*. Who created us? Did God create us? Perhaps it didn't matter. Perhaps I'd never know.

Alexis's knowledge triggered my latent Caradoc memories. Caradoc's brother had worn the protector's mantel. As had his nephew. And his nephew's son, and so on for three generations. The last protector was the boy I'd seen in my dreams. The one that looked so much like me. My biological father. *How could a protector possibly have turned into someone so vile?*

As a protector, we feel compelled to aid those in need of protection. Sometimes, we only need to protect them once. Sometimes, we are compelled to protect them for life. This small glimpse of knowledge awoke inside me an awareness of those whom I had already chosen to protect for life. The list of my protectorates burned inside of me. I felt bound to these protectorates with a power more compelling than the magic in the ropes that bound my hands.

Sis. The jeeks: Luiz, Ethan, and Kevin. O'Brien. Alexis. Those all made sense. My mother's absence from the list concerned me. Why not Mom? The list contained others that didn't make sense at all. Jody. Why? What made her special? She was just a stripper, right? Some higher power put a high importance on her, so who was I to argue? Her son, Carl. And Caradoc. Wasn't he dead? How could a dead druid be on my list? But he wasn't the most confusing person on my list.

That was Manouchka. Even as she stood and moved away from me, the urge to save her grew inside me. But save her from what? I didn't understand. Especially since she had just stuck a knife a half-inch into my chest. She had just tried to kill me, and I had been fully intent on killing her first.

Or had I?

I had chosen to focus my attacks on Voodoo Whoopi and not Stick Witch. Perhaps that hadn't been a coincidence.

*Free us first. We can help you save her. And not just her, all your protectorates.*

I had no idea if the lost ones were good or evil. Too much evil spread throughout this mine already. Were they part of it? Could I free them? Lexy's gut initially said no, but their new offer appealed to me on an instinctual level. As a protector, I felt compelled to free them, but not to protect them. I didn't understand the compulsion.

*What do you think?* I asked Alexis.

*Could freeing them put us in a worse situation than we are already in?* Alexis considered. She had a point. Voodoo Whoopi could kill us or take our soul at any time. How could things get worse?

*OK, Trapped Ones. How do I free you?*

We could feel them holding back their glee as they told us.

# CHAPTER 35
# DREAMSPEAK

*Justine is my best friend. I have known her since we were babies. I felt closer to her than any of my brothers and sisters. With the Trinity of Mind, it only took a couple days for me to know Alexis better than I know her. Is Alexis my best friend now? Or maybe I should say frenemy? I don't include Jake because I see him as something other than a friend, assuming he doesn't pick Alexis. —Kendra*

Alexis wriggled at my back. We needed a distraction, but hog-tied, we couldn't move much. Magic wasn't an option. "I see you be thinking to each other," Atabei challenged. "You be careful with your words, or I be hearing them," she laughed. "My new prize be sharing all your details with me," she gestured toward the left. Through Alexis's eyes, I could see she pointed toward a shadowed tunnel.

*Now we know where to look for Kendra after we kill you,* Alexis thought at the caplatas.

*We can't kill Manouchka,* I thought.

*You cannot. I can,* Alexis challenged.

"Manouchka and I think to each other, too." Atabei approached me as she spoke. "We share the dreamspeak. The Unforgiven awaits us. He be wanting us to dreamspeak. He be wanting to know about you." She grinned, her hideous black tongue visible between her teeth. In the dim flickering candlelight, her dark, rotund form stooped over me.

She planned to do something to me. I expected magic until Lexy smelled the sweet scent. I waited for it. But for a long moment, Atabei didn't move. She looked down at me like I was a three-dimensional poster and if she looked through me long enough, she could see the real me. Or perhaps she was considering disposing of me instead of delivering me up to the

254

Unforgiven. How could she hold so still staring at me? Her creepy motionless stare made me want to scream.

Her hand shot at my face.

I flinched but the ropes pulled at my feet and hands, which in turn tugged at Alexis.

She shoved a cloth over my nose and mouth. I tried not to breathe, but I hadn't had time to hold my breath, so my lungs started burning almost immediately.

*Alexis,* I called for help but there was nothing she could do. Her anger flared to life. Her violent thoughts shocked me while her violent thrashing shook me.

My lungs burned. I had to take a breath soon.

My bodily instincts took over. I breathed.

*Free the Trapped Ones,* I pleaded to Alexis, knowing she couldn't use the magic necessary.

"You be joining us in the dreamspeak again," Manouchka cackled.

And I did.

Lexy's anger trailed after me into my drug-induced slumber, as if she refused to let me go alone to whatever dream world the caplatas were taking me to.

🔺 🔺 🔺

The colorful shack—the one I'd blown up with a propane tank during my prior dream visit—looked completely undamaged. It stood exactly as I remembered it. Instead of bright sunlight, a dark, starless sky hung ominously over me. A chain ran through cast-iron manacles at my feet and hands. Atabei pulled a second chain, connected to a fifth manacle at my neck. If I didn't move with pull, the chain cut off my air. I followed Voodoo Whoopi into the shack.

A tall, shadowy figure already stood inside, clothed in black and hooded, like the grim reaper. As my eyes adjusted, I realized it was Stick Witch. She wasn't wearing a hood, it was her hair, long and full.

I struggled to make out the shapes in the darkness. I found the spot under the three-burner stove where the propane tank had been vacant. I had nothing to blow up the shack with this time.

Atabei's eyes focused behind me, then widened.

I didn't need to glance back to know that Lexy stood behind me. She hadn't been pulled into the dreamspeak as I had. She wasn't manacled. She had come into this dream free.

She stood behind me. Her red eyes demanded they be looked at. A silver crown wrapped around her head. A large black diamond rose at the front of the crown, trimmed with smaller red rubies. The combination looked like a heart dripping blood. Her hair hung below her shoulders. A cape, like her grandfather had worn, hung from her neck and flared around her bare arms. Her black leather bustier tied up the front, coming just short of her matching pants that stretched around her hips and thighs like another layer of skin. I would have called her knee-high boots combat boots, except they had four-inch heels, which put her an inch taller than me. Her regal confidence also rose up tall, as heightened by her outfit as was her stature.

Even without her allure, I would have wanted to bow in her presence. Her look and confidence combined with her allure, as powerful as I'd ever felt it. I dropped to my knees. It wasn't just me. Atabei and Manouchka also bowed to the Vampire Princess of the New World.

Bowing, Manouchka looked like a tall stick that had broken in half. Perhaps she should have tried a curtsy instead.

In my dream state, I felt confused. I shouldn't have been affected by her allure. My hands reached for my protection stone. It wasn't there. Had I lost it? But this was a dream, wasn't it? If I wanted it around my neck, it would be, right? I reached for it again and found it there.

Immediately, Lexy's allure dimmed. I stood up.

"Remove his shackles!" Alexis ordered.

Atabei fell to her knees. I heard a clink as she unlatched my feet. The chain rattled as she stood, the top of her head not even near my chin. I shuddered when her clammy hands touched mine. Another metallic clink freed my hands. She grabbed the manacle at my neck, her fingers touching my skin below my jaw. My shuddering doubled.

She didn't unlock it. I looked down at her face. It trembled. No, it vibrated unnaturally. Then she shoved me away, grabbed the chain hooked to my neck, and jerked. My head yanked toward Atabei as my body continued away from her. My neck broke. I collapsed.

If this wasn't a dream, I would have died. But I refused to believe my neck was broken. I willed it to be fine when I reached my hands up to check. It was.

Alexis shouted something at Voodoo Whoopi, but I missed it.

"You have no power here, child!" the short witch cackled. Shadow blades flared to life, lashing at Alexis. The dark knives cut away her cape. Another knocked away the crown. Both the cape and the crown disappeared into nothingness. The blades didn't stop there. They slashed at her laces, both those of her shoes and those of her bustier. The black knives lacerated her leather armor, piece by piece, until it was gone, leaving only the shadow blades themselves covering her. The blades surrounded Alexis, cutting at her body, leaving lines of dripping blood.

"No!" I screamed.

The shadow blades sliced off parts of her body in gruesome chunks until she disappeared. My heart sunk. She was gone. They'd killed Alexis. How could this be?

In anger, I pulled at my magic, but the manacles clamped down around my wrists again, and like the ropes I'd been tied with, they constricted when I used magic. The pressure increased, threatening to crush my bones. I dropped the magic, but not before the pain almost woke me. I came close enough to wakefulness to feel Alexis still lying on the rocky floor behind me, still alive. The shadow blades had done no physical damage to her but had only pulled her out of the shared dream.

"She be not dreamspeaking with us!" Voodoo Whoopi spat and licked her white teeth with her black tongue. "Look, he is here."

I turned, knowing who she spoke to behind me.

I knew that face because, except for a hint of gray and age lines at the corners of his eyes, it could have been my face. My biological father had seen me in our last shared dream. He hadn't recognized me because my dreams weren't just dreams. They were nightmares where my skin not only never healed, it looked worse. Ugly, wrinkled, colorlessly white, except for splotches of scabs all over my body. I found myself in boxers, my hideousness even more exposed. I wanted to die, to give up this life rather than live it as a repulsive creature so retched and vile that neither Alexis nor Kendra could stand to stay with me much longer.

I heard my voice, except it didn't come from me, and it sounded lower in tone.

"You dare bring the albino thing to me again!"

Again, we stood in the room that looked very similar to the dining hall at Lexy's mansion. I recognized the way the texture in the dark wooden table had lighter tones than the table in Lexy's mansion. I noted the three chandeliers provided less light than I remembered.

The chain at my neck rattled as Atabei tugged at it.

"He be not just the albino," she seemed almost gleeful as she cackled the words. "This be him. The protector. He be disguised. Cursed by his own magic."

My biological father's eyes focused on me. I felt the touch of magic brushing against me. Then more forcefully, the magic pushed inside me, probing me. I recognized the same spell Eldra had used, only harsher. I felt far more violated than when Eldra had used it. I could tell the creep knew how I felt and didn't care. What did I expect? This guy had violated my mom. He had no qualms against violating my mind.

Alexis and Atabei had called him The Unforgiven. I didn't know exactly why, but I could guess. I hadn't forgiven him for what he did to my mom, and I doubt that even ranked in his top ten worst crimes.

"It's him!" he smiled. "After all this time, you've found him. Bring him to me," he ordered.

"And the girl princess?"

"Bring her to me as well. With her gone, perhaps our friends of the night will rejoin our ranks." He glanced at me, sensing my worry for Alexis. He flashed me a wicked, knowing smile. "A vampire girlfriend?" he questioned, raising an eyebrow.

"She's not a vampire," I answered defensively for Lexy. "She's only half-dhampir."

"That won't do," he shook his head. "A vampire and a protector? Together? You don't know yet, then?"

My confused look answered him.

"Just bring her head—" "No," I shouted.

"—and dump her body outside in the sun."

Atabei nodded.

"Go!"

A gust of wind blasted into me. I shut my eyes. When I opened them again, I stood alone. The yellow shack had replaced my biological father's dining hall. I wondered how long I would stay there when the pain at my ankles and wrists pulled me awake.

I opened my eyes to see Manouchka stepping over me with a long blade, looking down at a point just behind my shoulders—Alexis's neck.

# CHAPTER 36
# RELEASED

*Eldra is going to register us for school. Kendra exploded with excitement when I told her. She had worried that she would not continue school. I have spoken to my mother, and she is working on getting my grandfather to make the decree. Sometimes, my mom acts like she was never turned. Do I dare hope? Kendra thinks I could be on the drill team with her. I had three high schools nearby to choose from, but how could I pass up the irony of attending Woods Cross. —Alexis*

I had about three seconds to save Alexis's life. It is times like this when pain just doesn't matter. Even death doesn't matter. John 15:13 jumped into my head, perhaps because Eldra had mentioned that verse recently. "Greater love hath no man than this, that a man lay down his life for his friends." Could I use magic until I die? Until I let the magic ropes kill me? I could, but actually, the ropes wouldn't kill me. They'd cut off my hands and feet. I'd not be giving my life; worse, I'd be giving up more of my quality of life. Could I do that for Alexis?

I could.

As I reached for magic, another idea slipped into my mind. Like a thought, only not in my voice. The thought didn't come from Alexis, Kendra, Caradoc, or the Trapped Ones. Perhaps it was divine inspiration? Did I believe in that? With Manouchka standing over Alexis, ready to chop off her head, now was not the time to delve into how strong, or not strong, my religious beliefs were.

I focused on the ropes. I didn't draw in magic yet, I only focused. I chose a point on each knot of rope. No, not a point, more of a line of molecules. It took intense focus as there were two knots, one on our hands and one around our ankles. Instead of reaching for magic, I chose all the molecules in those two lines. Then I tried to convert those molecules to magic.

The ropes tightened the moment I started. I felt the molecules dissolving even as the ropes tightened. The molecules didn't dissolve fast enough, or perhaps my imagination couldn't focus on both points of the rope at the same time.

The rope at our wrists snapped, but the rope around our ankles lasted longer. Something cracked at my right ankle, but it wasn't the rope. The pain suggested that the rope had cracked my ankle bone. Then the second rope severed and fell away just before the pain made me lose all focus. Had I been able to free Lexy?

As if in answer to my question, Alexis rolled back on her shoulders, twisted, and kicked Manouchka in her left thigh. The witch's leg lurched back, and Stick Witch fell, dropping her skull-hilted blade. It clanked as it bounced on the rock floor and skidded to a stop a few feet away. Alexis rolled toward the knife and snatched it up, but before she could use it, the shadow blades took her.

I sat up and slid back. I screamed out some word, I don't know what. I couldn't be sure whether I screamed in pain or in fear that the shadow blades would shred Alexis as they had in the dream. I fought aside the pain and wrapped her in an everything-seal. The shadow blades licked at the containment like flames, unable to penetrate it, but their force took its toll.

The three remaining zombies reanimated. All three focused on Alexis.

I slid backward on my backside past the pillar, dragging the leg with the throbbing, cracked ankle bone. Too many thoughts fought for my mind's focus. One of them involved freeing the Trapped Ones. I knew exactly where to go and what to do. More shadow blades launched at me. I shielded myself, but now I had to hold two containments, all while forming a third spell.

Manouchka recovered. She pulled a second knife from inside her long robes, but it was much smaller, a two-inch blade. She jumped toward Lexy's back and stabbed.

"Lexy!" I warned.

Alexis turned and ducked slightly, so the blade caught her high on her shoulder, near her neck. She let out a high-pitched gasp. She elbowed Manouchka in the face, likely knocking her out; her last act before my containment gave out. The shadow blades hit her. Alexis stood frozen, once again in a mental battle to control her vampire side.

Maybe she could have fought off the shadow blades at least to a stalemate, but the three remaining zombies reached her. They bit at her. I felt the soul-stealing magic pulling away her soul. I watched as her soul wisped into a plastic container at Voodoo Whoopi's hip. Atabei turned Alexis into one of her zombies. For the first time in a while, my mind was alone. If only I had time to think about all the things that I didn't dare think about with girls in my head.

We should have taken the time to go back to the mansion and get Lexy's leather armor. We'd been in too much of a hurry. We hadn't found Kendra before dark anyway.

I needed just a few seconds without fighting shadow blades. That is when music started playing throughout the cavern. I recognized the beat of Maná. I smiled.

Atabei turned away, staring down the entrance to the cavern, confused.

I continued to slide on my backside, one hand now on the wall, one on the floor. I followed the wall past another pillar. When my hand felt the magically hidden, fist-sized hole between two stones, I stopped. I pushed magic around my wrist to keep the booby trap from cutting off my hand as I reached in. I grasped the secret latch and pulled. Unfortunately, it didn't move.

*Yes, free us!* the Trapped Ones shouted into my mind.

I pulled harder, but the latch still didn't budge.

Voodoo Whoopi moved to the opening of the cavern, and began sending her zombies, Alexis included, into the cave to investigate the music. With Alexis zombified, did Luiz stand a chance? He'd die helping us.

I used the distraction to create the largest magic missile I could muster. Then I released it. I hoped that since the missile wasn't targeted toward Voodoo Whoopi, the shadow blades would let it hit its target. The missile collided with the altar, confirming my hope. The altar exploded. Before the dust and shards hit me, they erased into nothing. Water splashed from a black hole below where the altar had stood.

*"Maiku ma-nook päh-gär måsoge såp cåck maá-pa-ni,"* I spoke the Nuchu words the Trapped Ones had taught me, directing them into the hole in the floor.

The black surface bubbled and splashed. They were trapped under the altar in a well? In water? I'd expected the Trapped Ones to be some type of benevolent spirits. But the water threw me off. Why water?

Voodoo Whoopi turned and stared at the hole in the middle of the cavern, eyes wide with surprise.

"You be killing us all!" she spat. Then she grabbed her necklace of shrunken heads. "Return," she shouted, calling back her zombies.

As Maná continued to echo through the cave, the first thing—a Trapped One?—splashed out of the water. An emaciated corpse of a five-year-old girl grabbed the edge of the stone floor and started pulling herself out. Scratch that, an emaciated five-year-old mermaid? Caradoc's memories told me that it was a water baby—a freshwater mermaid believed to be nothing more than Native American lore. She had black hair that seemed to be falling out, gray colorless eyes, and sharp teeth. I preferred my mermaids with red hair, blue, oversized cartoon eyes, and dressed in seashells.

One of the knocked-out zombies, the man with the long braid, lay close to the water-filled hole in the floor. The girl crawled with creepy speed to the zombie and didn't hesitate to bite into the flesh.

Too late, the questions that I should have asked before freeing the Trapped Ones came to mind. Who trapped them and why? I'd let the fact that Caradoc planned to free them influence me. What did he plan to do with them when he freed them? Caradoc's memory answered me. Help his protector nephew kill them. It would have been nice if his previous memory had been more complete.

It wasn't like I hadn't sensed the enhanced evil. I'd known the evil in this place wasn't only coming from my Voodoo friends. Did I just call the caplatas my friends? I guess the enemy of pure evil is my friend.

I tried to stand, but the sharp pain of the cracked bone in my right ankle rattled me to my very core, and I fell back down on my backside. I couldn't save the man whom the water baby fed on. It was too late for him. Perhaps it was for the best. If I tried to save him, then the deal I'd made with the Trapped Ones would be off. They'd kill us all.

The second water baby jumped out. She had more hair than the first one—very purple hair that hid its face. It—she? —moved quickly on its hands and tailfin around a pillar to the far wall, as if hiding. I noticed other differences between the first water baby and this one. Before I had time to consider those differences, a third splash drew my attention.

The third water baby had no hair, just a long forehead that stretched from its hollow black eyes. I could see its skull where its nose should have been. The hollow black eyes turned to me;

its hunger visible in its gaze. To this creature, I was food. It turned away and started toward another passed-out form.

Oh, no. Eldra.

"Not her," I shouted.

I pulled at the magic, not sure what I would do with it. Both the water babies turned toward me and hissed. They sensed my magic. They recognized it and hated it. Blood covered the first water baby's face, and the hiss exposed the chunks of flesh in its teeth. I expected to smell the blood, but Alexis wasn't in my mind. All I could smell was the stale-water scent of the now-exposed well.

The third creature turned away from me but didn't change its target. It still went for Eldra. Alexis jumped out of the cavern opening. As the water baby bit Eldra's hip, Voodoo Whoopi tossed Alexis a bone-hilted dagger. She caught it, and in one motion, she lopped off the creature's bald head. The body collapsed, and the head fell, tumbling off Eldra's hip and rolling a few feet before coming to a stop. However, Eldra's blouse had been ripped open on the side, and she had a noticeable chunk of her hip bitten off that filled with blood. The bite shape almost blended in, as if it were just another of the maroon flowers on her blouse.

Two more water babies lifted themselves out of the dark well. They joined the first water baby and hissed at Alexis.

The other three zombies moseyed into the room, walking more slowly than Alexis. They stomped to the edge of the watery opening and began to kick at the rising water babies.

Voodoo Whoopi lashed at the first water baby with her shadow blades, but the creatures absorbed the shadow blades with no damage done. Stick Witch reached into her robes and pulled out a blowgun. She lifted it to her lips and shot a water baby with a dart. She reached into her robes again and pulled out a small cloth doll and began pretend-fighting with it like she was a little boy with an action figure. The water baby she'd shot matched the figurine's movements, fighting against its neighbor. Creepy, yet funny.

One of the two water babies that surfaced pointed my way. Was this one a little boy? Something about the shape of the eye sockets looked distinctly masculine. The sockets, vacant, eyeless holes, sunk into its skull. The nose looked wide but flattened. It opened its hungry mouth revealing sharp teeth, where the teeth weren't missing. The tight, thin skin didn't do much to cover its child-like skull. Worse, the skin around the neck had sucked in so tightly I could see the shape of the hyoid bone and the small but sharp Adam's apple. Even without eyes, it saw me. Did it know who freed it? Because just like the other one, it considered me to be a food source. Worse, it saw me as weak and injured. As a predator, it chose me over the more able humans in the cavern. A creature in a starved frenzy probably wouldn't even remember any such promise of protection until after it had its fill.

Why had I made this fool's bargain again? Well, things had been dire. Kendra had taken what should have been an easy win against the caplatas and turned it into a near-death experience for us. I'd almost died by a knife. Alexis had almost died by the same knife and now obeyed Atabei as a vampire—I mean half-dhampir—zombie.

The water baby charged me like a sea lion, teeth bared, using its hands and its tail fin to propel itself forward.

I went to the old faithful. I'd already pulled in plenty of magic. *"Bealustræl,"* I whispered. My missile hit it as it reached about five feet from me. The creature cracked into light and broke into pieces that my magic consumed. I'd almost forgotten the ecstasy of erasing a creature from existence.

Three more of them surfaced. And the one that Alexis had decapitated, the one that had bitten Eldra, had somehow pulled its head back on, and it just sat there very still.

*Seriously? Healing from decapitation?* I swore.

The first one, the one that had fed on the knocked-out Ute man, now engaged with Alexis. Only it looked nothing like it had when it pulled itself out of the watery prison. It's hair, once thin and falling out, now hung long and full. Its skin from waist up had a healthy tone, the same color as the man's it had eaten. The tailfin had split into two long fins. Even as I watched, the scales were fading. Still on hands and fins, it now moved with an agility that it hadn't had earlier. Alexis couldn't seem to hit it with her blade, but perhaps that was because Atabei directed her movements, leaving them slow and awkward. Neither Alexis nor the creature matched the beat of Luiz's blaring music.

The water hole had an unlimited supply of these creatures. No more than three could surface at a time, but three more waited behind those.

Sitting on my backside, I shimmied backward as fast as I could toward Eldra. It took a good few seconds to get to her. With my good leg, I kicked the *recapitated*—pretty sure I just made that word up—water baby as hard as I could, sending her back into the black pit of water. It slowed a couple of the things from resurfacing too. Hopefully, Eldra wouldn't be bitten again.

*"¡Madre de Dios!"* Luiz shouted as he entered the cavern with a shotgun at his shoulder, his body moving to the beat of Maná.

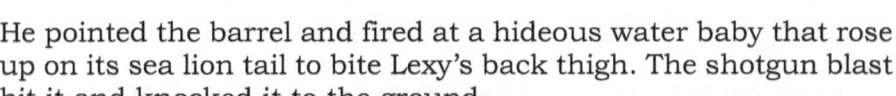

He pointed the barrel and fired at a hideous water baby that rose up on its sea lion tail to bite Lexy's back thigh. The shotgun blast hit it and knocked it to the ground.

"Get back," Luiz yelled behind him.

Had Luiz brought someone with him? A girl with glasses, her hands covering her ears to protect against the loud sound of gunfire, stepped into the cavern.

*Andrea?* I swore. How did she get here?

Luiz's girlfriend took one look at the scene and screamed. Whatever she thought she would be getting herself into, it hadn't been this.

Alexis retreated as three of the things flapped toward her. Luiz fired at one of them, and it dropped to the ground. Unfortunately, the other one that he had shot earlier raised up on its hands and tailfin.

Water babies swarmed and pulled down the last of the three zombies. The five zombies' fallen clumps provided a bloody buffet. As a protector, I should have reacted more harshly to the creatures eating the braided-haired man, but I didn't. The deaths of the mother and daughter, however, stirred in me an insatiable, righteous anger. Not protector anger, just my own anger. I pulled magic into me, using my anger, using my failure to save them, to hold more and more power. I spread my hands, fingers out. An apricot-sized magic missile formed above each finger. I released them all with my failure-fueled anger. Ten water babies erased. My body shuddered. Half of me wanted to pass out from the massive exertion. The other half of me wanted to revel in the most satisfying moment of pleasure that my magic had ever delivered. If I hadn't been addicted to the ecstasy of erasing living beings from existence before, I was now.

Despite the pleasure, I collapsed onto Eldra's chest, and she puffed out air.

Another shotgun blast rang throughout the cavern.

"Get off me," Eldra shoved. I'd unexpectedly awakened her. She sucked in a breath of pain and touched her hip. Her hand came away covered in blood.

For being bitten, it didn't take her long to assess the situation. She sat up, stretched out her hand, and her staff launched itself into her palm as if it were a lightsaber and she were a Jedi. If I weren't too busy realizing that erasing ten water babies hadn't even made a dent, I would have geeked out. It was one of the coolest things I'd ever seen.

A rune lit up in the staff, and a blast of electricity hit the water. The three water babies climbing out fell back in. The splashing went crazy, but no more water babies tried to climb out.

Regrettably, I counted fifteen that had already climbed out of the water. Stick Witch now held two dolls, one in each hand, and controlled two of the creatures. Voodoo Whoopi pulled in a massive flow of magic. Sweat dripped from her dark forehead. Again, she multitasked, throwing shadow blades at water babies and controlling Alexis, but neither of those required the extent of magic she pulled in. I wondered at her purpose for all that magic until the five zombie clumps convulsed, shaking off the water babies. Each sat up. Necromancy. The Undead zombies grabbed at the water babies that moments before had been feeding on them.

I tried to make ten more magic missile marbles but couldn't. I only made one. I fired it and almost passed out. Luiz shot another water baby, but the damage done by the shotgun pellets wasn't having much of an effect. Andrea huddled behind him, too afraid to help, but too afraid to run away alone either.

"Where is Kendra?" I shouted at Voodoo Whoopi.

"She be safe," Atabei answered.

The effects of the electric blast must have worn off because three more water babies splashed out of the cursed well. Eldra blasted the water with lightning again, but it didn't have the same effect that it had the first time. The next three thrashed some in the water but only for a few seconds.

"Free Kendra. We need her help," I pressed the witch.

"There be no help for us," she answered. "We be fighting to the death. Coyote warned us. Free them and we be dead."

Coyote.

What had Chief Wah-kara said to me when my memory turned into a dream? *Use the coin. Summon Coyote to the underworld, Jake Stevens.*

Did he mean the Native American's legendary deity and trickster, *Coyote?*

Amidst the melee, I reached into my pants pocket.

My hand slid around the large coin. Where had that coin come from again?

# CHAPTER 37
# COYOTE

Alexis keeps tormenting Kendra and me by suggesting that we roleplay certain situations. Kendra's cheeks turn beetdigger red every time. She wants me to ask Lexy to stop, but I told her that she's put up with Luiz for years, she can put up with Lexy. —Jake

I pulled the coin from my pocket and pinched its edges between my finger and thumb. The pure silver coin caught the candlelight, revealing a coyote's head. When had I picked up this coin? I remembered fiddling with it but couldn't remember where it came from. But my dream suggested that, with it, I could summon Coyote.

I hesitated. Did I really want to summon him? Freeing the Trapped Ones hadn't been a good idea. I'd done that blindly. Perhaps I should think this through.

I looked up from the coin and into a water baby's emaciated face. Its sharp teeth and long, sparse black hair reminded me of when I'd unclogged my bathroom sink, pulling out a black, corroded mess of Sis's hair.

I reached for my magic, but the creature lunged at me. A shotgun blast knocked it to the side. Andrea screamed. Or was that just my ears ringing from the shotgun blast?

"Uh, Coyote," I said, fidgeting with the coin. "Help please."

I didn't know how to summon him, but that didn't work.

"Coyote, I summon thee?" I said it like a question. Perhaps he couldn't hear me over the blaring beat of Maná and the mermaid melee.

The water baby Luiz had just shot stirred. I pulled in magic to erase with a large magic missile, but I struggled. I needed to

267

pace myself. I needed to use way less magic. I smiled at the idea that popped into my mind.

With the hand not holding Coyote's coin, I made a single small magic missile, smaller than a marble. With a whisper of *bealustræl,* I launched the glowing orb at the water baby's head. The top of her head lit up with glowing cracks and erased everything above her lower jaw from existence.

I could save a lot of energy by only erasing half their heads.

Yet the scene in front of me nearly sapped me of all hope. A dozen water babies lay on the ground but almost all of them were stirring. Another few hung feeding on the zombies who, despite being partially eaten, fought back. Atabei's voodoo necromancy magic still divided into three focuses. Stick Witch now only controlled one water baby, but she had her blowgun out to retake a second. Three more water babies slipped from the abyss and more came behind them. Alexis lunged at two, kicking one back into the water and stabbing the other. Knife wounds didn't seem to slow them down at all. Luiz handed the empty shotgun to Andrea and pulled out a couple handguns. He fired both guns at the same time, twice. He missed everything. So, he put one gun in the back of his pants, aimed a single pistol, and took a water baby in the forehead. Eldra defended herself from a circle of water babies with small taser-like shots from her staff.

"Free Alexis, she'll fight better!" I yelled at Voodoo Whoopi.

If she heard me, she didn't show it.

I pushed magic into my voice, trying to augment it. "Free Alexis, now!" I spoke, but the words came out louder than gunfire. It vibrated the whole cavern. Everyone, including the water babies, put their hands on their ears.

Atabei reached to her side and opened one of her plastic containers. Alexis's spirit didn't want to go back into her body at first, but Atabei whispered something and the spirit wisped its way to Alexis.

Giving Alexis her spirit back almost got her killed. She staggered, disoriented. Two water babies tackled her. As if I weren't in enough pain, I felt their teeth dig into Alexis's shoulder as if digging into mine. While long-sleeved, the black cowgirl shirt didn't protect her at all. Why didn't we take the time to go back for her leather body armor?

I had a small magic missile ready, I didn't dare hit its head, for fear it would erase part of Alexis's shoulder, so I launched it at its lower back where its fin began. An oval-ish area on its back shattered into light and disappeared, leaving the creature in two pieces. The top half didn't let go of Alexis.

Luiz took aim at the second one. Alexis had her hands around its neck, but it managed to twist its jaw, almost snake-like, and bite her forearm near the wrist. Its hands thrashed at her, ripping the front of her shirt, unsnapping all of the snaps, and scratching her ribs. Luiz fired and hit it in the jaw, just missing Alexis's wrist. The water baby's jaw let go. Alexis stood up, grabbed the creature by an arm and a leg, and tossed it at the watery hole, knocking the next three rising water babies back in with a splash.

Alexis reached around her shoulder and pulled at the head of the one I'd cut in half, but it bit harder. She pulled harder and ripped off a huge chunk of her shirt by the shoulder, revealing a bloodied, bitten mess. She tossed the head at the water babies that were once again rising from the well, but this time only knocked one of them back in.

*Welcome back to the living,* my conscious mind said, but my unfiltered thoughts added, *I can't believe my girlfriend was momentarily a vampire zombie.*

*If only we had time to roleplay that,* she answered suggestively.

I might have blushed if I weren't injured, sitting on my butt, and fighting for my life. I tossed three more marble-sized magic missiles and three more water babies went down with their heads erased. Even using small missiles, the spells sucked away my energy.

The water babies that fed on the Ute zombie corpses had begun to transform. They now had legs. The water baby that I'd first erased the head of had reshaped itself into a smaller water baby. I glanced at the bottom half of the water baby near Alexis's feet and the three I just hit. Would they reshape too? Were these water babies or shapeshifters?

Alexis reached down and grabbed the water baby's bottom half, a sea-lion-like tail, and tossed it back into the watery hole.

Adding magic to my voice had been quite effective. Perhaps it would work to summon Coyote. I still held the coin in my right hand. We didn't have much time. We were about to be overwhelmed.

"Cover your ears," I yelled over the sound of Maná.

Staring at the coin, I pushed magic into my voice and called, "Coyote!"

I wasn't sure if the summoning worked, but an ear-cracking, magic-infused shout sure was attention-grabbing. Every single water baby stopped what they were doing and turned to me. In a way, it helped. Alexis still had the long, bone-hilted knife that Atabei had tossed to her, and she decapitated the distracted water baby closest to her. They didn't fight back as she decapitated a second one. The rest didn't seem to care. All of them focused on me.

Alexis shook her head. *Just when I become the center of attention, you steal the show.*

The horror-movie version of mermaid children charged at me like sea lions—both the half-changed, morphing ones and the dead and corroded ones. The two most-transformed creatures stepped awkwardly toward me, still figuring out their new legs.

I couldn't stop that many with magic missiles.

*"Fyr Leoht!"* I yelled, bringing up both palms.

A torrent of fire launched from both my hands. The surge of water babies slid to a stop. The heatwave threw the closest two to the ground and engulfed them in magic flame. They dragged themselves back as quickly as they could. Steam, faint in the dim light, rose off them, but they didn't look burned. The things had just gotten out of the water and had been dripping wet. All I'd done was dry them off.

The two of them that now had legs turned and attacked Alexis. Luiz kept shooting them, but unless he hit them in the center of the head, his bullets didn't do much damage. Even the ones he did hit in the head only slowed down for a minute.

Most of them still came toward me.

Luiz's music stopped mid-song. The water babies turned their hollow eyes my way. The noise level dropped so dramatically that the cavern became deceptively peaceful. I could hear water dripping off the creatures onto the stone floor. My sister had a soothing app on her phone she used when babysitting. The dripping sounded exactly like that.

A coyote howl broke the silence. It echoed through the cavern, long and loud.

It also drew away the water babies' attention. Yay! I wasn't the center of attention anymore. A huge sense of relief washed through me when they looked toward the tunnel entrance. What can I say? A bunch of Crypt Keeper mermaids staring me down in a dark cavern had me freaking out in fear.

We backed up, forming a defensive circle, shoulder to shoulder. Why did we let Voodoo Whoopi and Stick Witch join our group? I guess I'd answered that earlier. The enemy of pure evil is my friend. I considered reaching over with my bone-hilted blade and slitting Voodoo Whoopi's throat. Wait, I wasn't holding a bone-hilted blade. That hadn't even been my thought. It had been Lexy's.

We could hear someone coming. The distinct sound of cowboy boots on the entrance to the cavern echoed their way to our ears. Or maybe just to Lexy's half-dhampir ears.

The seconds ticked by. At least the swimming dead weren't attacking us.

Then Coyote walked into the cavern. He stood proud, if not tall, and looked exactly like he looked a couple hours earlier when he'd walked into the Hanna Restaurant and Bar. A spitting image of Chief Wah-kara, according to Eldra. A man that had died in the mid-1800s.

In his cowboy boots and plaid, Western shirt, he looked like he didn't have a care in the world. If the dozens of sharp-teethed water babies bothered him at all, he didn't show it.

He looked at me directly with a mocking grin.

"I see that you've been lured like a rabbit to a snare. Welcome to Carre-Shin-Ob, where the Trapped Ones dwell."

# CHAPTER 38
# ONLY ONE

*Jake is a boy. I've learned things about boys. Things I shouldn't know until I am married. I don't want to talk or write about those things yet. Eldra says I should, but I just can't. Each time I learn something new about boys, Alexis laughs at me. When I get embarrassed, she calls me a prude. I am not a prude! Am I? Jake doesn't defend me. Worse, he has done things that I shouldn't know about. Things I'm mad at him for. I know I should forgive him, but forgiveness is hard. I know even the worst person, even murderers, can be forgiven, but that doesn't make forgiveness easy. —*
*Kendra*

Coyote turned away from me and looked at the water babies.

"My grandchildren," Coyote frowned. "Hundreds of seasons you have been trapped away. With each change of the season you have been given a chance to change. Have you?"

He wasn't speaking English. I didn't know what language he spoke, but magic flowed with Coyote's words—magic that carried a perfect understanding of what he said no matter the language he used. Only, the magic flowed with such subtleness that if I hadn't noticed his tongue giving off a barely visible magic light as he spoke, I wouldn't have detected it myself. We stood—well, I sat—in the presence of a being thousands of years old. Perhaps older. He'd had plenty of time to perfect the way he spoke. And his speech was perfect.

"Do you remember your crimes?" He asked. "Long have I missed my daughters whom I brought with me to this world. They chose to live among the water babies that were once native to the lakes and rivers of this land. They mated with them, spawning you. You killed many of my daughters, your own mothers. You drove the water babies to near extinction.

272

You tricked entire tribes of the Nuchu and Diné, drowning them for nothing more than the thrill of watching the way they thrashed under the water before their bodies went limp. Men, women, children, even babes. Your crimes brought a protector to this land. Your punishment should have been death. But I bargained with the protector to trap you instead, to give the seasons you needed to dwell on your atrocities and change."

When he mentioned the protector, Alexis began concentrating on counting the water babies to hide her thoughts from me. Hadn't I already garnered everything from her mind? *What else could she be hiding?*

"I ask again, have you followed the seasons and changed?"

Many of the Trapped Ones lowered their heads, their skull-like faces pointing regretfully to the floor. All those with legs, any that had fed on the voodoo zombies, and others that had attacked us most aggressively, hissed at Coyote, glaring with pure hate. It was difficult for Crypt Keeper mermaids to look scarier, but somehow, they pulled it off. Except the ones who had fed weren't just gaining legs. They were starting to take on the features of the people they had fed on.

Coyote glanced at the five corpses of the voodoo zombies. They lay motionless, now little more than fed-on corpses that would have been much more gruesome were the light not so dim. Voodoo Whoopi wasn't holding her shrunken skull beads, but instead, she eyed Coyote in fear.

"Did you feed on these Nuchu?" he growled low and angry, pointing to the forms of the Ute man and the Ute mother and her daughter. An angry power flowed within his voice.

I felt responsible for the voodoo zombies' deaths. Could I have protected them? Probably. I *should* have protected them.

*Why not them?* I asked the protector magic. Once again, I hadn't expected an answer, but the protector magic answered, showing me the zombies' past. Again, it wasn't my magic, but protector magic from outside of me, as if some intelligent force was aware that I was new to being a protector and was answering me as a mentor answers a novice. Scenes from their lives made up of foreign memories, like a montage of reasons they weren't worthy of being protected. The braided-haired man was a deadbeat dad and a drunk who often beat his wife. Had he lived, he would have ruined his three boys' lives. They would have turned out just like him. Without him in their lives, they'd grow up better. The second man could best serve this world by leaving it. As a meth dealer, he spread his product around the tribe to the best of his abilities. The woman and daughter were addicts whom he'd trapped into cooking meth for him. But the mother and daughter were different. They weren't meth dealers, just addicts. Unlike the drug dealer, they had retained a possibility of redemption. The last man served as the meth dealer's muscle. He'd lost his humanity with his first murder. The caplatas chose these five because their poor life choices put them on a dark path, making themselves easy prey for the caplatas' controlling, zombie magic.

Coyote's eyes moved back to mine and bored into me. As the protector magic faded away, I realized all the creatures in the room had sensed it. Coyote had already known who I was, but the water babies hadn't. Until now. I might as well have posted a giant sign with a flashing neon arrow pointing at me, reading: Protector here.

"They lost their way, but they are still Nuchu, Protector," he commented on my visions of their lives.

He turned back to the water babies. "Did the many seasons in your watery snare teach you nothing? Did you only ferment your hate?"

The very first water baby, who had also fed first, now had dark hair and looked more and more like the Ute meth dealer. He stepped forward and answered Coyote. He spoke with a series of clicks and tones. The clicks reminded me of dolphins, but the tones I'd never heard before. Unlike Coyote's words, I couldn't understand the language this creature spoke, but the harshness of the clicks and the cacophony of the tones made it clear that whatever it said, it wasn't nice.

A second water baby, also now with two legs and starting to look like the Ute meth dealer, chimed in with similar clicks and tones and equal anger. In fact, over a dozen of them were all transforming into clones of the five former Ute zombies.

Coyote looked like he was about to say something, but a third set of clicks and tones echoed from the back, behind the far pillar. These clicks and tones echoed soft and slow, contrasting with the harsh ones from the Ute clone.

Coyote's eyes focused behind the pillar. Could he see perfectly in the dark? A few seconds passed before a water baby sea-lioned around the pillar into view. I recognized the full, purple hair. She was the second water baby to exit the watery prison; the one that had rushed to the back and hidden itself. She slapped her tail forward, steering clear of the watery hole and other water babies.

Should I be concerned that, while Coyote stood there doing nothing to help us, more water babies continued crawling out of their watery prison?

A few water babies hissed at the purple-haired water baby as she cautiously made her way toward Coyote. One of the Ute meth-dealer clones lunged at the purple-haired water baby. Coyote moved quicker than lightning. He threw an obsidian knife—no idea where he pulled it from—at the lunging water baby. The blade shot like an arrow and hit the water baby low by the navel. The water baby dropped to the rock floor just before colliding with the purple-haired girl. A small spot inside the fallen water baby began to glow. The water baby began to shake until it split apart at the molecular level, separating into a mix of elements, water, and (for lack of a more chemistry-like word) goo.

The purple-haired water baby continued forward. Her hands, human-like but thin and bony, aided her tail in moving her forward. While the tail was the shape of a sea lion's, its color and texture looked more like otter's fur. She stopped in front of Coyote and bowed her head.

She clicked and toned at him, and he listened.

*"The seasons have changed you?"* Coyote asked, incredulous eyes opened wide, stretching his deep wrinkles. "You? The first? You, the coldest winter. The one who taught the others to kill, who led them down this trail. You brought this curse on all of them."

Knowledge of his words' meaning continued to travel over subtle magic, aiding our ability to understand him.

"You didn't feed on these Nuchu? You, who suffered here longest. Winter has thawed into spring. You have woken like a bear after winter, the hungriest. How do you withstand your hunger?"

She looked up at him. Her face looked less skull-like than the others. She could have been a little girl in the dim light.

"Of all of these," he gestured to all the water babies that were now filling the nine-pillared cavern, "yours is the one life that is not mine to return," Coyote told her.

Coyote turned his eyes to mine again. I couldn't look away when he did that. His gaze held mine. If he gave me an order, I'd likely obey it. Still sitting on my butt, I felt the need to stand. So with great pain and effort, I stood—mostly on one leg.

*Help keep me strong,* I asked Alexis.

"Only the protector can remove your death sentence. I've used all my tricks to delay it. I'd hoped to delay it longer, but this generation's protector, Jacob Stevens, is here now."

*And Coyote knows my name, too. Of course, he does.*

"As a protector, you—" "I haven't shared with Jake his duties as a protector, yet," Eldra cut Coyote off.

Coyote's eyes met Eldra's with recognition, and he grinned. She did not grin back.

"If you don't warn the rabbit about the coyote, the rabbit will be eaten."

Eldra glared at him, not answering. Alexis had shared what she knew of a protector with me, what other secrets were there?

"Very well. Still, he must decide."

He looked back at me. I really didn't like the way the power in his eyes affected me.

"Do you remove her death sentence?"

I shrugged. I wasn't sure what to do. Coyote kept his stare, clearly not accepting my shrug as an answer. I didn't feel any desire to protect her. But neither did I feel a desire to kill her. I didn't get a vision of her past like I had with the five Native American voodoo zombies. I tried, but her past appeared blank as if the seasons had eroded it away. All I knew was what she had done since she left the watery prison. She had hidden. She had chosen not to fight us. She may not have chosen our side, but she chose the right side, which was the equivalent of our side.

"Sure, she can live," I answered.

Coyote nodded, but he seemed disappointed, like he hoped I had left the death sentence in place. His eyes lost focus, clearly deep in thought.

The purple-haired water baby clicked and toned at Coyote.

"No," Coyote cut her off. "I cannot give my forgiveness. But you can earn a place with me when this world ends. Serve this generation's protector. Protect him. Keep him alive, and I will take you with me and my few remaining daughters when this world ends."

I wasn't sure if he meant for us to have the knowledge that came with his words, but the knowledge came anyway. The magic didn't just translate his words into English. It carried knowledge surrounding the words, including the background information that may have been missing. From that knowledge, I learned that Coyote wasn't thousands of years old. He was far older. Older than our world. He wasn't a god. He wasn't a man. Wherever he came from, his species had evolved in such a way that they never grew old, and unless killed, they never died. He'd evolved on another world. Earth wasn't his second world. It wasn't even in his first ten. Each time a world died, he moved to another. He measured his life not in years, but by the number of worlds he'd lived on.

He was an ancient alien. If only Giorgio A. Tsoukalos were here to meet him. This was hair-raising.

The water baby nodded to Coyote, then sea-lioned her way over to us. I guess she was on our team now; my personal, purple-haired Ariel sworn to protect me.

Coyote turned and started walking back through the tunnel.

"Wait," I called. "Are you just leaving? Aren't you going to help?"

"My job is done. I tried to save my grandchildren. I saved one. I killed one. I gave you more help than you will ever need."

He had intentionally withheld the magic from his voice in that last sentence and had spoken it directly in English, to hide the meaning in his words. What was he hiding?

"What about the rest of them?" I asked.

"If you haven't lifted their death sentence, then do your job, Protector. I'll not interfere again, but they are still my grandchildren. I will not help you kill them. Nor will I stay and watch them die."

He turned and continued walking away. Some of the water babies clicked and toned at him sadly, while others chattered at him with hateful hisses.

He looked back at the water baby that had joined us. "Do not seek my few remaining daughters in the great waters. They fled this land because of you and now hide from man in the deep. They will kill you."

He turned to the other water babies. More than fifty of them had crawled out of the water. "I leave you like a group of rabbits trapped with a coyote."

The two water babies, both now clones of the Ute man who'd been a meth dealer, shouted again at Coyote with their tones and clicks.

*Get some clothes!* I complained. *Gross.*

*This is not a movie,* Jake. *This is real life. Creatures who shapeshift do not magically have clothes,* Alexis chided me.

Coyote listened to their shouts and answered. "It is the protector's job to enforce your punishment. Killing him will only delay it."

They clicked and toned one more time.

"If you kill the protector and escape, I won't interfere unless you feed on man again. But that will only delay your punishment for a season. When this world ends, you will not ride the red sun with me to the next world." With those final words, Coyote disappeared into the tunnel and was gone.

I probably would have gone after him, but at that moment, Stick Witch tried to stab me. Alexis saw it coming and knocked the skull-hilted blade from her hand just before Voodoo Whoopi kicked her behind the knee. Alexis dropped to the stone floor, grabbing at Atabei, but the caplata slipped free of her grasp. Alexis rarely let anything slip through her grasp. I tried to help, but Stick Witch shoved me. I went down easily— back on my backside. I did have an extremely painful, cracked ankle bone, not to mention weak legs in the first place.

When I sat up, Voodoo Whoopi and Stick Witch stood in the midst of the water babies.

"We be offering to help kill the protector in exchange for our lives," Voodoo Whoopi shouted. "You must all swear by the skulls," she held up her shrunken head version of a rosary bead necklace.

The primary clone of the Ute meth dealer, who appeared to be their leader, clicked and toned at Atabei. I felt magic bind their agreement. My agreement with the Trapped Ones had not been magic bound. That was a mistake that we'd have to avoid in the future—assuming we had a future.

The caplatas had just joined sides with the Trapped Ones. All that stood between them and us was one of the nine pillars. The water babies charged us at the same time the shadow blades lashed at us.

# CHAPTER 39
# SPIRITS

*Jake and I are now not so different. His skin is hideous. He is quite ugly, and he knows it. Yet he is beautiful on the inside. I am similar. My skin is flawless. I am beautiful, and I know it. Yet I am quite ugly on the inside. My beauty is not even me. As a half-dhampir, I am a carrier of the vampire virus. It gives me the craving for blood, and it combusts in sunlight, but it keeps my skin and hair and everything else about me nearly flawless. The addiction to blood leads to killing, which corrupts the soul. I have avoided killing for blood whenever possible. Unfortunately, my grandfather forced me to kill, corrupting my soul anyway. I am jealous of Kendra. Extremely jealous. She is beautiful on the inside and out. —Alexis*

We had beaten the caplatas a few times, right? They ran away the first time. I escaped their dream the second time. Alexis killed their dead zombie servants the third time. We even beat them in this cavern. Sure, Kendra caught us off guard, but that was after we'd incapacitated the caplatas, so that didn't count. Technically, we could boast a 4-0 record, right? We could beat them a fifth time, couldn't we? With over fifty water babies on their side? Yeah, probably not. The caplatas had captured us a few minutes ago, with only Kendra's help. They still had her help. The last thing I needed was voodoo zombie Kendra hitting me with another magic missile.

Where was Kendra anyway?

No time to wonder. While sitting on my behind, I had to fend off a dozen voodoo shadow blades with a containment while at the same time casting fire through my magical shield to protect my injured body from multiple charging versions of the Ute meth dealer, two fully cloned versions of the meth-dealer's hired muscle, a couple half-cloned versions of the mother and daughter and the other man, a bunch whose transformation was too early to tell who they'd be, as well as untransformed water babies.

The pillar forced the attackers to come at us from the right or left, but so far, they only came from the right.

Luiz aimed his handgun and fired a single shot at the closest water baby. The bullet hit it in the chest, knocking it back. Andrea screamed. Again. That was probably all she'd be good for. Alexis tossed Atabei's belt my way with a thought. *Free Kendra.* Alexis hadn't uncharacteristically let Atabei slip through her grasp; she had successfully removed Atabei's belt of *ouangas*.

*You're awesome!* I thought, raising the belt to examine the plastic jars.

Then she lunged forward and stabbed a nearby water baby in the navel, exactly where Coyote's obsidian blade had struck a mortal wound. But this water baby didn't separate into goo. Instead, the fish girl pushed toward Alexis and snapped her sharp teeth. Alexis dodged its teeth and swiped through its neck, sending its head falling.

My fire had kept them at bay last time. It worked again. The water babies retreated from the yellow flames. I tried to hold the fire with one hand while with the other I fiddled with the belt Alexis had thrown at me. I had to figure out which jar held Kendra's spirit. As I analyzed the belt, my wall of fire died down.

Eldra grabbed the belt from me.

"Hold them off," she ordered.

I held up both hands, close together, palms out, and restored the wall of flame on the right side of the pillar. Of course, that forced the water babies to discover that the pillar had a left side. I spread my arms in a V, sending half the flames to the left side of the pillar. I somehow managed to keep control of the two walls of flame. The downside, neither flame completely blocked the path to us anymore.

Luiz fired his handguns over and over. Thank goodness the pistols had sound suppressors or our eardrums would have shattered in the enclosed cavern. The shots were still loud because, in real life, sound suppressors are by no means silent.

Eldra opened the first plastic container. The spirit just left. It didn't try to go find its body. Instead, it wisped away at a slight upward trajectory. It danced almost happily as it floated up past the golden discs before disappearing through the cavern ceiling.

"Wait," I yelled to Eldra, hoping it hadn't been Kendra's soul that had just flown off to . . . well, heaven? Hell? Who knows? "I saw Voodoo Whoopi use a spell to—" A clone of the Ute man crawled slowly through the flames on my left. Fire wrapped around him as he came at me. He ignited, but he seemed unaffected by using his epidermis as a human torch. No, I was wrong. This wasn't a clone. He wore bloodied clothes, and I could see the guts hanging down from the gnawed opening in his torso. *Ugh!* Voodoo Whoopi had pulled out her necromancy skills again. My flames lit his dangling entrails like candle wicks. The undead zombie fell flat.

Alexis protected us to our far right. The pillar protected us straight ahead. Luiz shot his handgun at any water baby that tried to take advantage of the incomplete flame walls. Eldra fiddled with the belt of ouangas. She'd pried open another container and was controlling the spirit with a yellow cloud of magic.

The undead zombie managed to stand, now a human torch after plowing through my magical fire, his jeans steaming and his shirt, well, his entire torso and head on fire. I considered dropping my walls of flame to blast him with a magic missile, but if I did that, we would be overrun by water babies. The fire flicked around him, but his body opened a passageway through my wall of flame, and a few water babies braved the path.

In two seconds, he had moved to within a few feet of me. I wanted to call for help, as I was a sitting duck—literally sitting—but all I managed was to yell, "Ahh!"

He opened his mouth and leaned forward as if to fall on me and bite me. Then the butt of the shotgun crashed into his face, knocking him to the left of me.

Andrea screamed in a mix of fear and delight. "I got him," her voice came out a billion octaves higher than normal. She *had* managed to make herself useful for something other than screaming. Of course, she still screamed.

"Hit that one too," I pointed at a water baby that had followed the zombie through the flames. It flapped its sea-lion tail and hands quickly toward my legs. I feared the water baby's bite more than the zombie's. Perhaps it was the sharp teeth.

Andrea switched to a hybrid baseball-golf swing. The shotgun butt connected with the water baby's skull-like head.

"Fore," I yelled as the water baby landed in the midst of my wall of magical fire. The creature shook, dazed, and thrashed before erupting in huge flames that blocked the left side of the pillar for me. It was a good thing, too, because I needed a break.

"He isn't dead," I gestured to the burning undead zombie who now crawled toward me. The smell of his burnt flesh made it hard to breathe.

Andrea grabbed the zombie's foot—his foot wasn't on fire yet—and pulled, but he was heavy, and she couldn't move him well. At least she stopped his progress. I jerked my hurt right ankle away—Ow! —to keep the zombie's fire-engulfed mouth from biting me.

Alexis appeared next to me. With a quick swipe of her blade, she took off the burning zombie's head.

Luiz stopped shooting for a moment. *"Fútbol,"* he called. He kicked the head through the flames at Voodoo Whoopi. The severed head hit her in the chest and knocked her backward. She stumbled and fell, almost falling into the well that the water babies still climbed out of.

Alexis grabbed the headless zombie's leg from Andrea and swung the burning corpse into place on the opposite side of the pillar as the burning water baby. Now both sides of the pillar had a burning body helping to block the water babies' path. My magical output decreased to almost nothing. Augmenting fire was easy, like reading leisurely, whereas creating the walls of flames with only magic and air for fuel had been like running sprints at the end of football practice. I could read all day, but nobody could run sprints for long.

I took a deep breath.

Many of the water babies that Luiz shot were slowly getting back up. The bullets made holes in their skulls or torso but didn't cause any lasting damage.

"How do we kill these things?" Luiz asked.

"They can grow back heads," Andrea pointed to one that was reforming its head on the other side of the flames.

"I stabbed one exactly where Coyote's knife had hit," Alexis pursed her lips. Sweat dripped from her cheek, which meant the battle took so much of her attention that she no longer subconsciously cooled herself. She wiped hands on her charcoal jeans, one leg of which was shredded.

Another glowing spirit shot away from Eldra. It found the gnawed-on corpse of the Ute daughter. The spirit seemed confused as it tried to enter her body. Instead, more bits of spirit seeped from the body. Slowly, the spirit took on the image of the Ute daughter. She turned to us and gave us a look of utter sadness. Then she faded downward, as if melting into the floor, and was gone. I did not like that. If I ever died, I hoped my spirit would wisp up happily, not fade downward.

A water baby launched itself with its tail through the fire at Alexis. A second one readied to launch too. Alexis caught the first one and spun with it. As the second water baby launched, Alexis threw the first one into it. They collided in the air above the burning Ute man. I focused the fire's heat on them, and both caught fire before they could escape. They screamed as they added fuel to the pungent odor of burning flesh.

With three bodies burning at the right side of the pillar, the heat beat at me, but I just used it as energy for magic. Luiz, on the other hand, had sweat dripping from his forehead down his long nose.

With the additional fleshy fuel on the fire, I felt free to strengthen the containment around us. Just in time, too, because Voodoo Whoopi stopped controlling her zombies and joined Stick Witch in throwing shadow blades at us. The dark ethereal knives sliced at us, colliding with the containment and flattening into giant showy tongues, licking to feel for a weak spot.

"Found you, girl," Eldra shot out the words, flashing her wide smile at us.

"¡Dios, mío!" Luiz shouted. "That wrinkled smile is the scariest thing in the room," he turned and shot a water baby trying to get through the flames then turned back. Despite my painful ankle and my soul weary from magic use, I found my own smile, reenergizing me. Thank you, Luiz.

The light of Kendra's spirit expanded to full size, but only her face showed detail, the rest of her was just a silhouette. Her spirit glowed brighter than any of the spirits we'd seen before. Her spirit had an overwhelming beauty to it. It even distracted some of the water babies. A few stopped and stared.

"Uh, oh," Eldra growled.

"What?" I demanded, the word coming out louder and more abrupt than I intended; a little preoccupied to worry about keeping my temper.

"Her spirit is fighting me," she grumbled. "I can't hold it long."

"Let her go back into her body," I shouted, thinking the answer was obvious.

"She is trying to go upward," Eldra growled back. "I don't think she intends to go back to her body."

"Then send her back to her body."

"Her body isn't here," she grimaced, showing the strain.

"Put her back in the bottle then!"

"I tried. I can't."

I shouted a very bad word. I couldn't lose Kendra. Where was her body? I pushed magic into my eyes and looked toward the cavern where she had come. The room exploded with light. I couldn't see anything. Gold encased the entire room, which lit up like the sun with my sight. It hurt my eyes. I couldn't look.

I almost turned off my sight. But instead, I found a safe place to look. The shadow-blades were not light. They were utter darkness. I focused on those shadow blades, which barely made the light around them bearable. I felt my pupils shrink. My eyes, both physically and magically, adjusted to extreme light. In a few seconds, I could look away and scan the area near the entrance to the cave. At first, I only saw the light of the cavern, almost every bit of it formed of gold. Then I saw the water babies and learned that I had to keep my sight to fight them.

*Alexis?*

*Saw it,* she answered.

As I searched for Kendra, I could see how the mine became a cave and traveled into the earth. I could see more than I ever expected. The tunnel wasn't just a cave. It was a volcano tube. I followed the light miles underground to the center of the dead volcano which spanned upward many square miles. Many tubes shot out, making it look like a giant tree. A tree that, with my sight, glowed with gold. Enough gold to make the metal no longer rare.

A sense of greed greater than anything I'd ever felt in my life swept over me. It felt all-consuming. I thought it would overwhelm me. I wanted the gold. I had to have it.

With great mental effort, I remembered that my focus was not gold. It was finding Kendra.

My eyes adjusted further. I could see more detail. Down the tunnel, I made out an area of light that didn't match that of the gold. An anomaly of light. Kendra?

"I'm losing you, girl," Eldra spoke to Kendra's spirit.

"There," I pointed. I hoped.

"Where is—" Eldra started to ask. But Alexis put her hands on Eldra's cheeks and looked into her eyes. Alexis used her vampiric telepathy to share what I saw with Eldra. It only took a half-second, and Alexis had to turn back and kick at a Ute woman clone who wanted to bite her.

Eldra pushed at Kendra's spirit. Urging it toward the anomaly of light that stood out from the background of gold. I watched the spirit flow to that spot, enter it. Then the anomaly collapsed.

"It worked," I shouted. "She—."

I'd lost focus on the containment and it came crashing down. The shadow blades lashed at us.

# CHAPTER 40
# CERTAIN DEATH

Learning magic is the greatest benefit to the Trinity of Mind. Eldra planned to teach us to cast daylight, but she might not need to. Alexis cast daylight at the Cabin Battle of Bear Lake. I experienced casting it through the Trinity of Mind. I'm sure I could cast that spell now. I've already cast spells from Caradoc's memories. —Jake

A shadow blade hit me with the same despair of a nightwalker's mist.

Alexis shouted, *"Dæg leoht!"* and stretched out her arms.

Sunlight erupted from her body. Unfortunately for Luiz, Eldra, Andrea, and the one pardoned water baby on our side, the shadow blades had already stunned all of them, and they dropped unconscious to the cavern floor to my right. Only Alexis and I had maintained consciousness long enough to witness the sunlight obliterate the shadow blades.

*Hit them fast,* she told me.

Already on it, I formed a baseball-sized magic missile and hurled it at Voodoo Whoopi. Without her shadow-blades, how would she defend herself?

Atabei grabbed a water baby and used it as a shield. My missile hit the creature instead. The primary clone of the Ute meth dealer clicked at the water babies that hadn't transformed, and they flippered their way in front of the clones, creating a protective wall. A second wall of water baby pawns formed in front of Atabei and Manouchka. Stick Witch had to duck down low for the wall to be effective for her.

I formed three marble-sized magic missiles and hit three water babies in the wall in front of Atabei. With my sight still active, I hit them in the right spot. It wasn't so much their brain as it was their source of existence—their lifeforce. I could best describe it as a glowing, three-dimensional splatter half the size of my fist. Each hid their lifeforce in a different part of their body. They were hybrids—only half water babies, a cryptozoological creature thought only to be a Native American myth. Their other half was a regenerative species as old as the galaxy. Since they could change their shape, they could choose where to store their lifeforce. These creatures' very existence would rock the scientific world, and yet here I was erasing them with utter glee.

I formed three more small magic missiles, but this time I had to use them for defense. Two water babies launched at us, one on each side of the pillar. I flicked a marble at the source of life of the one to the left and erased it. The one on the right lurched toward Luiz's leg, but Alexis grabbed it by the neck, lifted it, and buried the bone-hilted dagger into its source of life, all while keeping the daylight spell going. The goo plopped to the stone floor, and damp particles splatted and splashed. Luiz's left shoe took the most of it; the rest ruined the leg of Lexy's holey Wranglers that wasn't shredded.

Eldra and our new purple-haired friend rolled back to consciousness and sat up. Andrea and Luiz remained stunned.

I started to manufacture marble-sized magic missiles in my left hand as fast as I could, flicking them at their targets with my right index finger, then reloading and repeating. Perhaps magic use was like running, and I'd just hit my second wind because earlier, I'd struggled.

We held them off that way for a good twenty seconds. Alexis had access to plenty of magic this time. I poured magic into her sunlight spell as fast as I could. No magic-draining containment surrounded us, and we weren't using our clothes, hair, skin, and my muscles to power the spell. We had infinite access to magic. The only limitation was Alexis's magical stamina. Her physical stamina could have held this spell indefinitely, but magically, she was tiring fast.

We were getting weaker, not stronger.

Alexis strained to keep up her spell, but holding daylight drained her too quickly. She dropped the spell, and the room went pitch black for everyone. Everyone except me. I still had my sight up. With it, my vision didn't change.

I brought the containment around us the moment the light disappeared. Just in time, too. Voodoo Whoopi had her shadow blades giving it a tongue lashing immediately.

Seeing Eldra knocked down had reminded me that I could do some crazy things with my magic missile. Especially when I created it the size and shape of a football.

I stood up, putting all my weight on my good leg. I formed the magic missile, the same way I'd done when Eldra had challenged me while practicing. I let it build up to a football, then beyond to a swollen rugby ball. I hadn't really played with density of my magic missile to this point, but I did. I urged the photons of the missile's blue light to squeeze together.

A part of me worried this was a waste of time and energy, as it had been when I'd cast it at Lexy's grandfather. If I used this spell, would it fail and leave me too drained to save my friends? Even if it did work, could I fight off the rest of the water babies? I didn't know. But I hoped. Sometimes, you must act on hope because it is all you have left.

I threw the glowing blue football at Atabei like a quarterback trying to fit a bullet pass in between two linebackers.

Atabei lashed a shadow blade at the missile, trying to catch it. Like I had done with the Star of David containment, I imagined the shadow blade was a containment and tried to force a hole in it. The magic missile football blasted through the ethereal knife and continued toward its target. Atabei's eyes spread into large white circles, and her jaw dropped to reveal her black tongue resting on her bottom teeth. Just before colliding with her chest, a water baby who was part of the wall leaped in front of Atabei.

It didn't matter. The football-shaped missile spiraled through the water baby, leaving a gaping hole of nothingness. The shadow blade and the water baby had absorbed much of the missile, leaving it about a third its original power, but that still left the magic at least twice as powerful as the missile I'd used to kill the nightwalker. It hit Atabei right in the numbers—well, between her bosoms, anyway.

Voodoo Whoopi exploded into nearly infinite molecules that evaporated into pure energy that shot in waves away from the epicenter of the blast, rocking the entire cavern. The blast threw Stick Witch hard against a pillar and threw the wall of water babies toward us. Stick Witch's head whiplashed off the pillar, and she fell in a clump. The water baby clones of the Utes tried to keep their feet, but the blast blew them to the ground. Water splashed out of the well and spread on the floor. Fortunately, the water stopped before reaching the flames protecting us.

The blast knocked me back against the cavern wall with plenty of force.

The tide had just turned. With Atabei erased, and Manouchka unconscious, we could pick off the water babies one by one. There was no stopping us.

We'd won.

*You did it,* Alexis cheered in my mind. Maybe it was because I'd just thrown a football to win the day, but I imagined I was on the football field and she was on the sidelines in a cheerleader outfit.

*Oh, we are definitely roleplaying that someday,* Alexis winked at me.

"Why is the water glowing?" Eldra broke our revelry with her gravelly voice.

I didn't know why the water was glowing, but a foreboding fear rumbled through me. Had I just made the cardinal mistake of celebrating too early? Like the players who poured Gatorade on their coach while the other team still had a chance?

A half-dozen Ute clones, some clones of the Ute men, some the mother, some the daughter, stood up and smiled, watching the water.

I knew something terrible was going to come out of the water, I just didn't know what.

Time seemed to stop as we waited.

Then a hand appeared. It raised out of the water and slapped down on the wet stone floor. Water dripped from the wrinkles on the aged hand, a hand that looked very familiar. When it first lifted from the water, the hand glowed, but within seconds of leaving the water, the glow faded away.

A second wrinkled hand grabbed the edge. A glowing form began to pull itself out of the well.

I recognized the aged face. The harsh wrinkles. Eldra's wrinkled, grandma body crawled out of the well like Samara from The Ring, only naked and with long grey hair. The areas where water clung to her—her wrinkles—held their glow the longest. By the time she took two steps from the well, her glow faded and was completely gone.

I remembered kicking the water baby—the *re*capitated one that had bitten Eldra—back into the well. Maybe that hadn't been such a good idea.

I tried to pull at the magic, but there was nothing. I'd felt this before. At the Bear Lake cabin.

"I don't just look like her," the naked version of Eldra spoke, her gravelly voice a perfect match to Eldra's. "I got her knowledge and her skills, too." She looked directly at me. "Feel free to burn away your skin to make magic. I'll be ready for it this time," the Eldra clone cackled.

Luiz chose that moment to wake up. He looked up and saw the naked Eldra and cringed.

"*¡Dios mío!* That's gross. Put some clothes on *vieja.* Those are the saggiest—" he stopped midsentence when he turned toward me and saw the real Eldra fully dressed and holding her staff. His mouth hung open. For once, even Luiz couldn't finish his thought or find something else funny to say.

Water baby Eldra lifted her palms and lightning lashed at us. I searched desperately for some magic, but there was none. I cringed and closed my eyes, preparing for the pain of death by magical electrocution. I heard the hum of electricity, but the pain never came. Instead, only a small static shock flashed through me, like touching a doorknob after walking on carpet with socks all day, only over my entire body.

I looked up.

Eldra, the real one, stood next to me, her eyes focused on her staff, one of the runes glowing. A dome of light surrounded us, blocking the electricity. After a few seconds, her clone dropped her attack, and the real Eldra dropped the white dome.

Her staff stored magic like a reservoir. Wow! I wish I'd had that at the Bear Lake cabin. I could have avoided burning away my skin and muscle and going from a two-hundred-pound high school football phenom to an ugly, hundred-and-fifty-pound, dermatologically challenged horror show.

"We can take you—I mean her—right?" I asked Eldra.

Without looking at me, she shook her head.

"Well, at Bear Lake—."

"Dane was incompetent," Eldra growled. "And I fought against his control."

I didn't have much time to consider that. If things weren't bad enough, the water babies regrouped and charged us. There was no flaming barrier on either side of the pillar keeping the water babies away. The burning bodies now only smoldered, and I had no magic to bring back the flames.

Alexis hadn't been distracted. During the pause after the exploding magic missile football, Alexis had found her rune-covered dagger and now held a dagger in each hand. She stepped forward to meet the charge alone. Her shredded, bloody shirt and exposed bra provided no more armor than did her ripped-up Wranglers. She used my sight to see where to strike. Her runed-blade in her right hand flashed from one water baby to the next, as her left hand slashed the bone-hilted dagger back and forth, driving the water babies back.

Luiz moved behind Eldra. He dropped something to the floor, and it clinked. "Last clip," he noted as he slapped the magazine into the handgun.

Lexy's mind latched onto Luiz's. She still had the ability to use her vampiric allure to control him. By controlling him, she could show him where to shoot and help improve his aim. Still, even if he pulled an O'Brien and never missed, twelve bullets were not going to be enough. Of course, even with Lexy's aid, he wasn't O'Brien. Missing his first shot proved that. An unchanged water baby hung from each of Lexy's legs, further ripping into her jeans. Three fully changed Ute clones—a mother, a daughter, and the meth dealer's hired muscle—came at her at once. She couldn't concentrate on helping Luiz aim.

I had to find a way to help. As I pushed myself up, palms on the stone floor, I realized that I had access to plenty of magic. And not from my hair, skin, and muscles. My palms felt the rough cavern floor under my hands. The elements that touched my palms called to me, offering to give up their existence to provide me the magic I needed.

I hadn't needed a staff to store magic. Had I just touched the floor with my palms at the Bear Lake cabin, I could have kept my skin and hair and muscle. I ignored that realization. Instead, I focused on converting the matter under my palms to magic.

I filled my body with pure, vibrating energy.

I formed my football-sized magic missile and chucked it, spiral and all, at the naked Eldra clone.

"Jake, no!" Eldra shouted, too late.

As my missile approached bad Eldra, it seemed to stretch before all the magic that formed the missile was sucked like smoke into a lightning blast that came at us exponentially more powerful than the first one.

Eldra defended us again with her staff, the rune once again flaring to life. When the lightning hit, the dome shuddered and shrunk, losing at least eight feet in diameter, leaving Alexis fighting outside the dome. The lightning hit both her and the water babies she fought. Her back arched and she threw her shoulders backward as electricity poured into her.

She screamed. I screamed with her.

Then, still pulling magic from the floor with my palms, I pushed my own containment around her. She stumbled backward. Luiz caught her and pulled her into the protection of the white dome. The two unchanged water babies and the three fully changed Ute clones that had been fighting Alexis turned to molecular mush. If Naked Eldra was concerned about collateral damage, she didn't show it.

Eldra's strength surprised me. She was stronger than I expected. Uh, both of them, but the water baby clone was stronger.

"We are tired. I am tired. But my doppelganger has already fed on my hip and appears to be at full power," Eldra noted. "There is only one way we can win."

Alexis lay at Luiz's feet, unconscious but not dead. I could feel her through the Trinity of Mind, just as I could feel Kendra, but for the moment, both remained unconscious, leaving me alone in my mind. Normally, that would have been a moment of heaven. But now, I needed them with me.

Eldra, the good one, reached one of her wrinkled hands down and placed it in on my shoulder. Still sitting, I looked up at her wrinkled face as she offered herself to me.

She projected a thought through her touch. *Myndtiegan,* the magic spell I'd used to form our Trinity of Mind. The word came along with her offer, as did a mental image of her plan.

"No way," I shrugged her hand off my shoulder.

I already had two girls in my head and Caradoc's memories. I wasn't adding a fourth and turning our Trinity of Mind into a Quaternity of Mind. But was that really the reason? Or was it her plan?

The lightning came again. Again, Eldra blocked it. A different rune lit up on her staff, the other having been drained. Her protective dome shrank further. Luiz grabbed Alexis's ankles and pulled her to me.

"Grab Andrea," I nodded to Andrea's catatonic form and used my hands to shift myself closer to Eldra, dragging my right leg with the cracked ankle.

Luiz spun and leaped toward the girl. He grabbed her by one leg and pulled. A jolt of electricity zapped through her as Luiz pulled her inside the shrinking dome. It zapped Luiz, too. It must not have been too much electricity because instead of killing Andrea, it woke her up. Andrea's scream echoed through the cavern as the lightning stopped. Luiz wrapped his arms around her to calm her down.

*How is she even here?* I wondered.

*Later,* Alexis's mind answered. She knew because she controlled Luiz, so I knew instantly, but I didn't have time for that problem.

The water inside the well glowed again.

"Oh, you've got to be kidding!" I was about to say some very bad words but Eldra beat me to it. Her two hundred years of cussing experience trumped my almost-eighteen, naïve years.

Another figure climbed out of the water.

Well, I had no question who was coming out of the water. When these half-water-baby, half-ancient-cosmic-species bit someone, they could turn into them. So, there were no surprises when an exact copy of Alexis splashed out of the well with all of Alexis's grace and stepped to Naked Eldra's right. She'd be easy to tell apart from the real Alexis because she didn't have any tattoos.

However, I did have one question. Wasn't Alexis bitten by two water babies?

The water hadn't lost its glow. A second set of hands splashed onto the edge of the well before another Alexis clone launched out with one motion, splashing water everywhere. She landed on one knee with one hand touching the ground. She stood and stepped to Eldra's left.

"Evil Eldra," Luiz shouted, "you're ruining a perfect double-mint moment!"

That joke lasted for only half a second because the entire cavern of water babies formed a line. The water babies that looked like the Utes took position next to naked Eldra and the two Alexis clones. The leader, a clone of the Ute man, whispered something into the ear of the Alexis on the right.

"Protector," the Alexis on the right spoke. "Pardon us, and we will let you live."

Hey, that sounded great to me. We came here to get Kendra and deal with the witches. I erased Atabei from existence. Manouchka hadn't moved since she'd been blasted against that pillar, alive but unconscious. Kendra lay unconscious down the cavern. I had no beef with these water babies. Coyote could clean up his own mess.

I opened my mouth to answer in the affirmative, but the words wouldn't come out. Instead, a thousand future lives flashed into my mind. No, not just lives. Horrible deaths that were gruesome ends to innocent people at the hands of the creatures in front of me.

*You cannot free them,* Alexis remained unconscious, but still, her thought stirred in my mind. *You are this generation's protector.*

*You have to protect us all,* Kendra somehow added despite remaining unconscious.

Perhaps they were speaking to me from their dreams. If I could stall until both girls woke up, maybe I could . . . nothing came to mind. I couldn't see a way we could win even with both of them awake. We couldn't win this fight.

"It is not a difficult decision, Protector. Make your decision." the Alexis to the right of Evil Eldra urged.

"How do I know you won't kill me the moment I pardon you?" I shouted back, hoping to buy us some much-needed time.

The Ute man and the Alexis on the right whispered to each other.

Luiz and Andrea moved to Alexis. Andrea lifted Lexy's head onto her lap and tried to wake her.

If Evil Eldra attacked with lightning again and Good Eldra's protective dome shrank anymore, we would all be dead. I didn't dare ask her how much magic she had left in her staff for fear the water babies would decide to attack.

*Kendra, Alexis,* I pushed at both girls with my mind. *I need you.*

I felt them move closer to consciousness, but whatever power allowed them to speak to me from their dreams left. I couldn't tell how close they were to waking.

The primary Ute clone of the meth dealer whispered quiet clicks again to Alexis on the right. She translated for him. "Killing you would only condemn us of a new crime."

They had a strong argument. A part of me wanted to pardon them and walk out of here right now, so why couldn't I do it? Why was it my job to protect future people? I didn't ask to be a protector. I didn't ask to be a druid. This had all been forced on me. All I'd gotten out of it was a magical plastic surgery from hell. I could dress like Freddy Krueger for Halloween and all I'd have to do is put on a hat and a razor-fingered glove—no mask or makeup needed.

I opened my mouth to pardon them again, but a second time, the thousand gruesome deaths that I'd seen before flashed into my mind again. A protector's foresight.

The compulsion rising in my chest changed. I needed to protect everyone in the room. All of them were under my protection. Alexis, Luiz, Andrea, Kendra down the tunnel, and for some strange reason, Manouchka. Why I couldn't let her die was a problem for another time.

I had to protect everyone here.

Wait. That wasn't true. I hadn't named one of the people here. I didn't feel the need to protect Eldra. I glanced at her. She put her hand on my shoulder again. *Myndtiegan,* she magically offered herself to me though her touch once again, the details of her plan repeated with the magical offer.

"Do it. It is the only way," she spoke. A clever phrase. I knew what she meant, but the water babies should assume she was convincing me to pardon them.

"Kill them," both the naked Alexisises shouted at the same time. Nope, they weren't fooled. Their mouths opened and their fangs extended.

I took Eldra's hand. I let Eldra into my mind. We became one, joined in a temporary *myndtíegan*. At the same time, she lit up two runes on her staff.

Time slowed to a crawl. I remembered the magic vial that had slowed the nightwalker. Time slowed similarly now. I could see Evil Eldra preparing to cast lightning. The two Alexisises appeared to hang mid-step as they had begun to charge us behind the rest of the water babies.

*No. This is different. Time didn't slow down,* Eldra explained. *Our minds sped up.* As she spoke, the image of the sundial rune on her staff dominated her mind.

I didn't have to ask how she sped up our minds. I knew because she knew.

*I can save us,* Eldra confirmed. *I'm old and death is at my door. You'll not have to suffer my mind long.*

*I can't. I need you. You are the only one that can teach me to be a druid. To be a protector. You are the only one that can teach me to protect Sis and Kendra.*

*You must. It is the only way.*

*But love is a requirement,* I reminded her.

*Am I not here to die with you?* Once again, John 15:13 flashed through my mind. *Make the* myndtíegan *permanent,* she offered. Her two-hundred-year-long life hung behind her consciousness like an impending tsunami. All its memories.

*If you are to survive, you will need this.* Eldra released her memories at me, like a reservoir released by a collapsing dam.

Her entire life hit me all at once. Every memory. Every thought. It took me what felt like years to process it all. I saw her parents. I saw her home in England in the early 1800s. Her father never returned one day. Her mother sold everything they owned for passage on a ship to America. Trying to heal her sick mother on that ship was the first time Eldra had used magic. She killed the cholera virus, but it hadn't mattered. The virus had damaged too much of her mother's body. The crew tossed her corpse unceremoniously overboard. The crew treated Eldra worse than a slave until their arrival at Ellis Island.

She hadn't taken but a few steps off the dock before she met Locksley, her future husband. He had sensed her magic. He taught her to be a druid. They spent their lives together. I watched them live. I shared the struggles of her first nine-month pregnancy. She gave birth to her first daughter. She had eleven children in her life. Three died at birth or shortly after. She watched the rest of those children grow old and die, except her seventh daughter, turned druid, who was assassinated on the Day of a Thousand Deaths. On their last anniversary, Dane drugged them, weakening their minds. Then in their most vulnerable state, he took control of them—until I freed them. But in the process, Kendra and I had killed Eldra's love. I shared the pain of her husband's death.

She had chosen to show me everything. More importantly, she knew how to show me everything nearly instantly. Eldra had shared herself with Locksley for a century and half. Neither Kendra nor Alexis knew how to be this open—yet. In time, we would share with each other the same way, but not for many years to come.

I'd just lived all two hundred years of Eldra's life as if it were my life. In my mind, it had even felt like two hundred years, but in reality, it had been less than a second. Lightning still formed in Evil Eldra's palms. The two Alexises had only just completed their first step and were halfway into their second.

She could execute her plan now. I could still stop her. The choice was mine. Only *I* could cast the spell.

Eldra pushed her magic into me but I didn't let it in. Not yet.

*In heaven, will you say hi to my grandma and tell her I miss her?*

I let her magic in.

Time returned to full speed. Good Eldra tossed her staff to me, and I activated the protective dome just in time to intercept the lightning. With my palm against the floor, pulling magic from the elements in the rock floor it touched, the domed containment expanded, filled with more power than ever. The staff recharged almost immediately.

It worked. I told you I had enough love, Eldra thought to me. She voiced her last words for all to hear. "Greater love hath no grandma bitch than this, that she giveth her life for the bigamous bastard who killed her husband."

Her body lit up with a white glow and rose into the air toward the top of the cavern. If my mind weren't joined with hers, I would have had no idea what spell we were about to cast. But I knew. I had to cast it after all.

*"Maniġe wæpenstræl sylfum,"* I shouted.

Eldra's body ripped itself apart. I felt the pain like nothing I'd ever felt before, an immense sharpness, like a million long needles being simultaneously shoved all the way through my body. Her body split into still smaller pieces. Her clothes, skin, muscle, and organs—all but her bones—dissolved into magic to provide the energy that the spell needed. The vials she'd taken from druid cache also dissolved, adding to the spell's power. Even the lightning from Evil Eldra was absorbed into the spell. Good Eldra's every bone separated. Her ribs straightened. Her femurs split long ways into a dozen shards. Her skull cracked into pieces.

The Ute clones, the unchanged Crypt Keeper water babies, and the two Alexises—the entire nudist colony—stopped charging us, perhaps too mesmerized by the gruesome scene that shredded the real Eldra.

The final step of the spell was left up to me. I could see the lifeforce of each water baby. The fear on Evil Eldra's cloned, wrinkled face meant she recognized what was coming. I targeted them all with a thought.

The bones, now arrows, darted toward their targets with O'Brien-like accuracy, piercing the lifeforce of each water baby. The Ute clones spun toward the well, hoping to dive in, but bony projectiles made from Eldra's skeleton hit them in their lifesources.

The two Alexises tried to dodge, with a grace and fluidity that surpassed the real Lexy's. The Alexis clone on the left had hidden her lifeforce at her right hip. The one on the right had hidden hers at the base of her spine. One spun away and jumped toward the well. The other ducked, twisted and slid behind a pillar. The missiles sought them out anyway. I watched Alexis die twice.

Evil Eldra dropped all other magic and concentrated fully on defending herself from the magical bone-formed arrow that targeted her. She managed to deflect the missile a few inches. Enough that it missed her life force, but it still hit her, low in her gut.

The room went silent. But Evil Eldra had survived.

I was already mouthing the word that activated the rune in the staff.

*"Ligetu."*

Eldra's lightning spell—now mine—lashed at her doppelganger. It hit her with the force of my pain. The pain I'd felt as Eldra's body had split apart. The pain I'd shared experiencing Eldra's two-hundred-year life. And the pain I felt at losing her.

She brought up a containment and the lightning struck it with an echoing thunder as loud as the shotgun blasts. I held the lightning as the containment flickered. She grimaced with her wrinkled face, trying to augment the containment. Trying to survive. But I held the lightning a moment longer. Her containment collapsed. The lightning collided with her aged body, and she stretched out like the Vitruvian man, her old, naked body shaking violently as the electricity flowed into her. The spell tossed the clone into the watery abyss.

I took a breath, but something moved in the water. There may be more down there. I raised the staff and pointed at the water. Either a magic missile or fire light used to be my go-to spells, but now, I had almost two-hundred years of practice with lightning, and it was now my go-to spell. *"Ligetu."* I brought forth lightning again and lashed it at the water.

I didn't let up. I kept the lightning pouring into the water for as long as I could, pouring it into the well. Attacking any water babies still in the dark well.

Protector magic rose inside me. This protector magic felt different. It didn't feel like it came from an outside mentor. It still felt more like knowledge than energy, but it felt like *my* magic. I could sense each remaining water baby that had been condemned to die. I felt their deaths as a tremble, and then, as emptiness. I held the lightning until the moment that the last water baby, hiding deep in the well, died.

I cut off the lightning. I'd used too much magic. Blood rushed to my head. I collapsed, holding the staff just long enough to keep me from hitting my head as I fell. Luiz rushed to me. He lifted my head into his lap. He shook me to keep me from passing out. I think he asked me a few questions before I finally heard one.

"*Diablo*, Jake. What happened?"

"Eldra saved us all," I whispered with a chin quivering like my sisters. "Now, she's gone."

# CHAPTER 41
# EXITING

*I miss my mom. I want to go back home. Alexis told me that she had difficulty controlling my parents, so instead of controlling them, she's altering their perception to give them what they want most. Suggestion can be just as powerful as control. My parents were desperate to get all the kids out of the house. I'm a bit hurt. It turns out that my birth, six years after they thought they were done having kids, was a surprise. Alexis used their desperation to convince them that I am grown and out of the house and attending school elsewhere. I don't think I am ready to be on my own. I already miss my parents. But I can't put them in danger. Alexis already saved them last week. If Alexis hadn't come with Luiz and Mr. Espinoza to rescue us, they would have been ripped to shreds by the nightwalkers, just like Jake's stepdad was. I'm afraid if I go home, that might happen. But I am afraid to be away from home, too. —Kendra*

I'd like to say that I rushed to Kendra and stayed by her side until she woke up. Nope. Luiz helped me to a cavern pillar where I sat against it in pain, chanting *hælan min ancléow*, augmenting my already abnormally fast healing and focusing on my right ankle.

The pungent smells of death, burnt flesh, and water baby goo hung in the air. Smoldering bodies and a candle provided the only dim light in the cavern.

I didn't stop chanting until Alexis woke up. I felt her hunger as she joined my mind.

*How did we survive?* I gave her an instant download of what happened, only I didn't press Eldra's memories upon her like a tsunami as Eldra had done to me. Alexis took a moment to digest all she learned. After which, she stood and assessed the situation.

*Kendra.* I said only her name, unable to focus enough for a whole sentence.

*I will go get her, but first, nobody has tied up Manouchka?*

I hadn't even thought about Stick Witch. She was alive. My protector magic told me that much. Alexis could see her and smell her. She'd been badly injured by the blast that had smashed her against a pillar. She might not wake up for hours, but she'd live. The protector magic suggested I ignore the witch. I could sense that without Atabei, Manouchka would return to Haiti on her own. She was no longer a threat to us. Someday, we would cross paths again.

*And Ariel?*

*Our little mermaid is just sitting over there, doing nothing?*

"I haven't been stalking you," Andrea's voice rose from the tunnel toward the entrance.

"OK, you were Nancy Drew-ing me to prove Jake was alive then," Luiz answered.

"I saw him alive at the mall. You were meeting with him and lying to me about it."

Luiz and Andrea had been talking, arguing, and laughing for some time now.

*I will silence them,* Alexis assured me, then she tapped her separation stone, cutting her mind off from mine.

"Luiz," Lexy's voice resonated down the hall. "I will be quite vexed if I have to kill Andrea because you shared more than you were supposed to."

"Alexis," Luiz rushed back into the cavern followed by Andrea. "Is that a promise? Will you really kill my pain-in-the-*nalgas* girlfriend for me?" He glanced part accusatorily and part mockingly at Andrea, who looked downward guiltily. "Because that would really save me the trouble."

Alexis ignored them. She rummaged near the cavern wall for one of the extinguished candles, and once found, she lit it from the only candle that remained alight. Then she walked into the tunnel where Kendra lay. A minute later, after I'd dodged a barrage of questions from Andrea, Lexy carried Kendra's unconscious form into the cavern. She cradled her carefully in her arms, as if she cared for Kendra more than she cared for herself. I pretended that it didn't bother me that I couldn't be a man and go get Kendra myself.

Alexis laid Kendra next to me and knelt beside her. She unclasped her necklace, with both her enchanted stones and clasped it around Kendra's neck. Her boy-cut hair didn't even get in the way. In the smoldering light of the cave, Alexis didn't need the healing stone's added protection from the sun, but she did need healing. Neither the bite on her shoulder nor the bite on her wrist had fully healed. Her Wrangler jeans, shredded below her thighs, allowed a clear view of bite marks on her legs. Her separation stone was on the same necklace, so her mind opened back up to mine—especially the full effect of her emotions.

*How are you not crying?* I asked.

Lexy checked her surroundings again to fight off her emotions. Ariel sat against the wall not far from us, her tail in front. She seemed afraid to move, as if we would kill her the moment that we noticed her.

Alexis considered the pros and cons of removing the last remaining water baby's head. Manouchka still lay unconscious. Alexis could sense her pulse from here and smell the dried blood on her temple. Even in the dim candlelight, she found the witch's carotid. She didn't act on either thought.

*Where's Kendra's stone?*

Alexis perked up. She darted around the room, searching. If Atabei had it, I'd surely erased it. Near the well, where the altar had stood, Lexy found a leather satchel that must have belonged to the witches. She pulled Kendra's necklace from it and clasped it around her neck. Her hair hung just long enough that she had to move it out of the way.

Alexis shut me out. She smiled at me, but it was fake. With the necklace found, her melancholy emotions returned, and I could feel them despite the separation stone.

Luiz kept the conversation lively until, sometime between 3 and 4 A.M., I fell asleep. My dreams were cloudy for the most part. No, not exactly cloudy. Jumbled. I couldn't decide whose mind to dream from: mine, Kendra's, Alexis's, Caradoc's, or Eldra's. Instead, I dreamed in a kaleidoscope of thoughts from different minds that changed every few seconds.

Coyote appeared in my dreams for a brief word—a few seconds where my dreams were crystal clear.

"I didn't tell you," he said. "The gold of Carre-Shin-Ob is protected. If you take any, a big ugly frenemy of mine will kill you." He winked at me and my dreams returned to a confusing fog.

Did Coyote really just use the word *frenemy?*

I woke a few hours later. I stretched my stiff neck.

"Luiz," I called. "Put it all back."

"What?" he asked defensively.

I shared Coyote's warning with him. He gave me a pained look then frowned at Andrea before they both started emptying their pockets.

"Thought so," I shook my head.

Sometime later, I sensed Kendra stir next to me. I tapped Lexy's shoulder. Alexis disabled her separation stone. We mentally agreed to clear our minds so we wouldn't overwhelm Kendra. Then we waited together until Kendra's mind fully awoke.

*Kendra,* we both mentally shouted her name as she shifted her shoulders and sat up.

"I see you managed to get your shirt off," Kendra complained to Alexis.

"My shirt is still on," Alexis defended.

"You call those shreds a shirt?" Luiz laughed. "Your bra covers more than those shreds do."

"Hey," Andrea elbowed Luiz, who was eyeing Lexy with a grin.

Kendra and Alexis started their background catfight. But it was low, white noise, much quieter than usual.

"It is OK. I can *own* shirtless." Alexis grabbed the remaining shreds of her shirt and ripped them off, wincing in the process. She gestured to her black bra and added, "I am still more covered than some are when wearing a white bikini." She winked at Kendra.

"Hey!" Kendra pouted back. She opened her mouth as if to say more, but instead, she gently touched the bite mark on Alexis's shoulder. It was not healing. She needed to either feed or to get her healing stone back. Kendra, on the other hand, was dirty, but otherwise looked fine. Kendra gave up her pouting and lifted Alexis's necklace off and offered it to her. "We can trade back."

The mental white noise of their catfighting paused noticeably as they swapped necklaces.

"You might as well cut those into Daisy Dukes," Kendra suggested, pointing to the shreds that remained of Lexy's pantlegs. Lexy grinned and pulled her runed dagger and started cutting denim.

"What happened? Where is—?" Kendra stopped. Our minds answered her questions with a vision of Eldra's sacrifice.

"She saved us," I repeated the same phrase I had said to Lexy.

Her mouth opened slightly, quivering. "No." The tears came immediately, and she buried her face in my shoulder. Once she'd absorbed our memories and answered all her own questions, she shut us out. Alexis shut me out too.

Everyone remained silent for a few minutes, letting Kendra cry.

"Jake," Kendra started, as she wiped at a tear. "It wasn't just Eldra." She leaned over and hugged me. "You saved us, too!

Without you, we would all be dead." She tightened her hug, then moved back to look me in the eyes. She glanced at Lexy, then continued. "Don't listen to our unfiltered thoughts. Listen to our words now. You saved us! You are important to us."

Kendra leaned into me and kissed me full on the lips. Her hand grabbed the back of my neck. She ignored the flaky and hideous skin. She didn't care. She just wanted to show me that I was important. The kiss lasted a good three seconds before she pulled away.

"We need you," Lexy added, with a smirk instead of the expected jealousy toward Kendra. "You saved me from fighting a nightwalker. Without you, we would have never survived the Cabin Battle of Bear Lake."

I nodded. It had been foolish of me to let my outward appearance affect my self-esteem. I had stupidly listened to their unfiltered bad thought. Unfiltered thoughts are abundant, and most were a waste of mental space. These past few days, *I* had been the one choosing the wrong unfiltered thoughts, not Kendra or Alexis. They had cast off the bad thought while I had dwelt on it. I elevated that thought from fleeting and meaningless to life-affecting. I determined to put a stop to that right now. I could still feel the shadow blades' effects working against me, so I couldn't say that my self-esteem was completely cured, but this moment of enlightenment, inspired by Kendra's kiss, was a great start to healing.

"So, Kendra," Luiz cut into our serious moment with some humor, "are you letting Alexis corrupt you? I hear you went all zombie bad girl."

"Shut up, Luiz," Kendra mumbled through her tears.

"See," he nudged Andrea, "now she's saying bad words like 'shut up.' Corrupted. You're winning her over, Alexis."

Instead of responding, Alexis jumped up and darted full speed to crouch in front of Manouchka, her eyes inches from the witch's face. Alexis put her palms on the caplata's cheeks and turned on the full power of her allure. Pumpkin spice almost hid the stench of burned flesh. When the witch opened her eyes, Alexis already owned her.

She mentally interrogated the witch for the better part of ten minutes. What she learned answered a lot of questions and had us raising our eyebrows in enlightenment.

"Go back home to Haiti. You are free from Atabei. She is gone. You are no longer magic-bound to your mistaken oath. Take your place as the family Mambo."

Manouchka blinked and nodded. Alexis let her go. The Haitian witch walked out of the cave without even acknowledging the rest of us. I'd see her again someday. I'd protected her from her immediate danger, but she still had a future need for me to protect her. From what, I didn't know.

Lexy's allure didn't affect Kendra or me, other than improve our moods slightly. Luiz and Andrea succumbed, however, ready to worship the ground she walked on. Alexis dialed it down but didn't turn it off. The princess of the new world had no qualms against being worshipped.

Her red eyes moved to Ariel. She hadn't been affected by Alexis's allure.

"Do we kill you?" she asked. "Or take you home with us?" Alexis liked the idea of a creature whose future depended on keeping me alive.

She clicked at us, pointed at her tail, then clicked some more.

Alexis made a hand gesture and a shrug, making it clear she did not understand.

Ariel looked directly into Lexy's eyes as if offering for Lexy to read her mind.

"She cannot be away from the water long in that form," Alexis explained.

"If you bite any of us, we will kill you," I warned Ariel, worried she might try to take a bite of one of us to change form.

"Take one last dip." Lexy offered. "We are going for a two-hour ride."

# CHAPTER 42
# HEADING HOME

*Jake does not know everything about being a protector yet, but he knows now that he will be randomly called up to protect certain people. He will not know who he must protect until he feels the call. Even then, he may never know why. Knowing this much seems to have satisfied his curiosity. Perhaps he will stop prying for more of what I know. If not, Eldra's training can hopefully help me keep the rest of what I know hidden from him for now. Jake is not ready. —Alexis*

As we left the Lost Rhoades Mine, I wondered if anyone would ever enter it again or if it would be lost in time to all but the ancient Coyote and his big, ugly frenemy. I used my sight to look at the tree of gold one more time. Its trunk circled one mile in diameter and stretched down through the crust of the earth for as far as I could see. Golden branches extended for miles in many directions. The mountains in this part of Utah ran east and west and rose high to the north. However, unlike the tall, sharp mountains in Salt Lake, these mountains had rounded tops, like the top of a treasure chest large enough to cover what must be the greatest unknown treasure in the world.

The walk to the car seemed farther than it had taken to walk to the cave. I hobbled the distance, leaning on Eldra's staff and staying off my right ankle as much as possible. The rain, no longer falling, had left the ground muddy, but none of the mud stuck to my shoes. Eldra had been an expert at small but practical spells. However, mud covered Ariel's tail and hands.

Andrea and Luiz jumped into Andrea's white Volkswagen Beetle and drove away. She'd secretly installed a tracking app on his phone. That solved one mystery. Luiz *had* been lying to her about where he was going. She'd been more curious than jealous, at least until the tracking app reported him at the strip club twice. And now she knew I was alive.

Alexis grabbed Ariel under her armpits and lifted her while Kendra poured the contents of a water bottle on her tail. It not only helped get the mud off before letting her in the car, but the water made Ariel feel much better. Her eyes brightened. I couldn't tell if Ariel's eyes were brown or lavender.

I sat in the back of the BMW with Ariel. I grabbed our stash of snacks. I offered a bag of jerky to Ariel. She tilted her head, raised an eyebrow, and clicked. I didn't know what she said, so I just dropped the bag of jerky in her lap, ripped open my own bag and took a big bite of a large, square piece. Ariel copied me. She devoured two large bags of jerky and started on a third by the time I had eaten one. As we drove, her hair went from purple and stringy to a thick, shining lavender that extended down to her waist. The skin on her face and torso thickened and her complexion cleared. Her lashes extended, surrounding eyes now as as lavender as the early August twilight. From the navel up, she was indistinguishable from a seven-year-old girl. However, the sea-lion-like tail covered in otter-like fur was a dead giveaway that she was more than just a girl.

We stopped at the country store in Hanna. It seemed like weeks since we'd stopped there, but it had only been last night. I couldn't walk very well. Alexis wore only her bra and daisy dukes and Ariel was a seven-year-old mermaid wearing only her purple hair. So naturally, Kendra went into the store alone and came back out with two cheap T-shirts and a brown blanket.

"They're terrible, but they are the best they had." She handed the blanket and the red shirt to Ariel. The shirt had the words "I have reservations" above an offensively stereotypical Native American woman dressed in leather holding up her hand. The brown blanket had the image of a moose on it. The black shirt she offered Alexis had a curvy, country woman busting out of a tied plaid shirt and pointing a rifle over words that read, "No. I taught *him* how to shoot." Kendra had a noticeable grin as she handed the shirt to Alexis. There had clearly been better options.

"The shirts are fine," Alexis assured her. Alexis found it fun that Kendra had tried to pick the worst shirt in the store for her.

As Alexis put the car in drive, a jacked-up Dodge Ram pulled in front of us and blocked our path. The dark-gray truck had lights on the roof—not flashing—and the letters BIA on the side. *B*ureau of *I*ndian *A*ffairs. A man stepped out. His dark hair and complexion gave him away as a Ute. His uniform also had BIA written on it.

Great. He'd surely arrest us because of Kendra's terrible taste in T-shirts.

He walked over and knocked on the driver's side window. Alexis's allure filled the car well before she rolled down the window.

"Move your truck out of our way," she ordered.

The BIA officer turned and took a few steps back toward the truck before stopping, shaking his head, and coming back.

"You almost had me," he laughed. "You are good. It took me a second to keep my wits." He glanced in the back at Ariel and me. Luckily, she'd slipped into her shirt and had wrapped her sea lion tail under the moose blanket. "A friend told me that I'd find an older woman with you. Eldra? We thought she could help our boy here. He caught a fever a week back but isn't sick."

Hearing her name so soon from a stranger was tough. My eyes watered, but I fought off the tears. Kendra couldn't fight them off, though, and tears dripped down her cheeks.

"Oh," the BIA officer took in our reaction and put it together with our post-battle state. He could easily guess that we'd just left a fight.

I glanced at the truck. A boy sat in the passenger side. Two long braids surrounded his thin face. I checked him as a potential. Nope. I sent a sliver of magic his way. It slipped inside without effort. The boy shuddered, reacting to the magic that I'd pushed into him.

"What do you need?" Alexis asked curtly.

The BIA officer hesitated.

"You need a new medicine man for the tribe," I answered Alexis's question on behalf of the BIA officer. "You lost yours on the Day of a Thousand Deaths." So many more than a thousand had died that day. Only the prominent and well-known victims had been counted among the thousand deaths. Some, like the tribe's medicine man, had not even been reported.

The officer blinked in surprise.

"That boy already took the step that you hoped Eldra would help him take," I added.

The man looked at me as if unsure whether to believe me or not. "He has no medicine man to teach him."

"We don't either," I answered. "We'll be doing a lot of reading." Again, the loss of Eldra cut painfully throughout my chest. Without her, we had no one to teach us. Or did we?

"Our ways are not written down. We have some stories, but they will not teach him what he needs."

"For now, he will be safer with you than with us," Alexis added.

He offered Alexis his card and she took it.

He glanced in the back again. The first time, his eyes had glanced over Ariel. This time he paused on her, really seeing her. His eyes widened. He let out a curse, took a step back, and drew his gun, pointing toward the back seat—directly at Ariel.

"No," I shouted. I stretched my hand out toward him and willed my thoughts into his mind. I willed him to put his gun away. He slid it back into its holster.

*We are friends!* I forced the thought into his mind.

He stepped back to the window, leaned in, and said, "Friends, do you know what that is?" He pointed at Ariel.

"Yes," we all answered at the same time.

His eyes filled with a mix of fear and hate as he stared down the little girl that sat next to me. Ariel smiled innocently back at him.

"Stay away from my people."

"I will," Ariel answered in clear English with a melodic, seven-year-old voice.

My mouth fell open.

"She's in my custody," I added, trying to hide my surprise. Lexy hadn't reacted at all. She easily hid her surprise.

The BIA officer nodded, satisfied.

"As soon as I get my hands on the type of book you are looking for, I will send a copy of it your way," I offered. If only I hadn't erased my copy.

"That would help," he agreed. He gave me his business card, too, as if he didn't think Lexy and I could share the card he had given her. With that, he nodded and went back to his truck. He drove away as Alexis pulled the BMW onto Highway 35, headed west.

I closed my eyes as we started the trip home. It felt like I opened them only a second later, and yet, we were already pulling into the garage at Lexy's mansion. Maybe it wasn't a good idea to sleep and leave Ariel unsupervised in the back seat, but it happened, and she didn't bite me. She still had the blanket wrapped around her waist, but she stepped out of the car with little seven-year-old, perfectly human feet. Perhaps the beef jerky had given her the energy to change. Thankfully, she hadn't changed into a cow.

As I exited the car, I used Eldra's staff to stand without putting weight on my leg. The door to the house opened. I expected Carolyn or another servant. Instead, Gina stepped into the garage. A small hand grabbed at her jeans and a boy pulled past her.

Carl.

He read the way my mouth dropped, and the smile evaporated from his face. He looked at each one of us and didn't find who he was looking for.

"Mom?" He questioned. He didn't cry. His face went slack. Emotionless. He yanked his hand away from Gina's and pushed past her into the house and ran off, probably to a closet.

The Skull Shadows had abducted Carl's mom, Jody. We had brought Carl to stay with us. The boy expected us to rescue her. How had I forgotten?

My heart thumped in my chest. I swallowed. Protector magic rose in my soul. My spirit left my body, traveling toward a future vision of Jody. Stars decorated the night sky. When my spirit arrived, it entered a warehouse where a figure dressed all in black—a Skull Shadow—held a gun to Jody's head and pulled the trigger.

My body needed to rest. It needed time to heal. But none of that mattered. I needed to save Carl's mom. I had only until dark to do so. Righteous anger grew inside me. I'd save Carl's mom, or I'd die trying.

# THE END

# &

# THANK YOU

You make it possible for me to write. Without you, my books are just words. With you, the characters and their world come to life. I hope you enjoyed this book and found it as fun and exciting to read as it was to write.

You'll know that you liked this book if you can answer yes to at least one of these questions.

- Are you excited to read the next book?
- Are you excited to tell someone about this book?
- Did this book keep you up at night reading?
- Were you anxious to get back to reading it?
- Did you enjoy the characters and the world?

If you answered yes to one of the above questions, then this was a 5-star book for you. Please let me and others know by reviewing the book at:

- www.amazon.com/dp/B083F2GK7S
- www.goodreads.com/book/show/50843347-breaking-glass

# SPECIAL THANKS

I am not sure that I could possibly thank my wife, Michelle, enough. She has had to put up with me while I've been working full-time, finishing a Master's of Computer Science (Yay! It's done), and writing a novel, all at the same time.

I'd like to thank all my fans who kept urging me to finish this book. Their excitement helped fuel this book's completion.

I would like to thank Sarah Bylund for her excellent editing job. She helped knock off a lot of rough edges in my book. I appreciate her feedback even when some of it was tough to hear.

My proofreaders have been great. Sara Bylund kicked it off with a proofread edit after the first content edit. Heidi Elder is extremely professional and has mad skills. She found plenty of copy-editing issues. Family members also helped, such as Jacob Barneck and Linda Barneck. An old friend, Vernie Chapoose, chipped in to help me find errors. These wonderful people are the reason this book is error free.

LaRae Roberts, a wonderful photographer, provided me with the amazing skyline of Bountiful, Utah at dusk for my cover.

Thank you all.

*J. Abram Barneck*

# About the Author

J. Abram Barneck lives with his wife and kids in West Jordan, Utah. He has been writing science fiction and fantasy since he

was sixteen. He grew up next to a creek with land to run on. He also grew up with a computer to game on.

He graduated from Brigham Young University with a degree in English and an emphasis in Creative Writing. He also completed a Master of Computer Science through Utah State University.

At BYU, he took the Sci-fi and Fantasy creative writing course taught by David Wolverton (David Farland). He also participated with Leading Edge Magazine for almost three years where he became the Assistant Fiction Director.

He currently works full-time as a Principal Software Engineer and is a father of four. He writes as much as his family and work will allow him, and he loves every minute of it.

For a more complete bio, please take a moment to visit his website at: http://jabrambarneck.com/about.

# TORCHED HEART

## TRINITY OF MIND
### BOOK 3

### WRITTEN BY
## J. ABRAM BARNECK

# CHAPTER 1
# SCARLETT RESCUE

*I don't know who I am. Eldra's memories are dominating my mind. Add in Kendra's, Lexy's, and Caradoc's memories, and I think I'm losing myself. —Jake*

"**W**hen I pull this door open, all hell is going to break loose," I spoke verbally instead of mentally through the Trinity of Mind because Luiz and Ariel had refused to be left behind.

I panted quietly as I hung on the rusty metal handle of the heavy warehouse door. We had parked a half-mile away at a church and ran through alleys halfway here before changing to a stealthy walk. My ankle, partially crushed before sunrise this morning by a voodoo witch's magic-preventing rope, throbbed in agony despite my near overdose on ibuprofen. Why was I the only one out of breath? I ignored the obvious answer.

Lexy stood just left of the doorway, red eyes locked onto a thick-but-short Polynesian man who stood guard at the door. She wore a black leather top and pants that, as usual, stuck to her like another layer of skin. Over her top, she wore a leather vest that acted as body armor. She had a blade strapped to each thigh—her runed dagger on her right and a skull-hilted blade on her left that had once belonged to a tall voodoo witch. Wearing thick-soled, knee-high combat boots, she stood much taller than the Polynesian. He wore a button-up Hawaiian shirt, damp at the armpits, gray shorts, and black river sandals. To Alexis, he smelled like he'd been sweating in the heat all day. Lexy's pumpkin spice allure hid his smell from the rest of us. Her allure—an enticing scent that could short-circuit almost anyone who smells it—had taken control of him and prevented him from sounding the alarm.

Lexy forced the Polynesian's black eyes to meet hers and read his mind, which proved fruitless as he hadn't been allowed inside the warehouse. She put a hand on his cheek—the skin contact increasing her allure's controlling power—and ordered, "Sit down." Mesmerized by Lexy's allure, he sat down on the weed-ridden asphalt and leaned back against the brick building.

Ogden used to be the armpit of Utah. Recently, both the city government and the Church of Jesus Christ of Latter-day Saints had put deodorant on that armpit by updating certain areas. The abandoned warehouse was not in one of the areas where deodorant had been applied. Rust splotched the doors. The asphalt had crumbled, and tall, dried weeds had popped up in random patches. Weathered-gray plywood boarded over the few windows. The August sky, orange from the setting sun, illuminated the graffiti on the dilapidated brick building.

My legs wavered and almost gave out. My thick denim pants rubbed my road-rashed legs. My new Kevlar armor under my black hoodie weighed me down. Of course, Luiz didn't even notice the extra weight of his Kevlar. Using both the door and Eldra's staff to hold myself up, I hoped to hide my physical weakness like I hoped to hide my hideous face. The Trinity of Mind—a permanent mental connection between Kendra, Lexy, and me—prevented me from hiding either. Kendra and Lexy shared my thoughts, so despite my efforts, they knew that I'd grabbed the door not to open it but to stay on my feet.

*He is not OK,* Lexy thought to Kendra, nodding at me.

*He's tough,* Kendra answered, tossing her head as if she still had long hair instead of the boy-cut she'd managed to grow the past week. *At least he used to be,* she added.

It didn't matter that I could hear Kendra's and Lexy's thoughts. They mentally talked about me as if I weren't there.

"Why are you wobbling?" Luiz teased under his breath. "Too lazy to work out?" He grinned.

I yanked the door, hoping that opening it would shut all three of them up. Except it didn't open. Locked.

"If the door is too heavy," Luiz continued his quiet mocking, "I can help you out."

Alexis and Kendra each stifled their laughs. I usually enjoyed it when Luiz lightened the mood, but at my expense? Not helping.

I reached out with magic to unlock the deadbolt, but it needed a key on both sides. Eldra's favorite spell to magically twist the thumb turn on the other side wasn't an option. That trick had

2

never failed me—er Eldra—before, so she'd never learned to pick a lock with magic. I could magically slide the pins in the lock, but that didn't mean I knew which key pattern to use when doing so. I made a mental note to research lock picking later.

I'd already filled both my body and Eldra's staff with magic, and now was the time to use it.

"Can *you* do this?" I whispered my comeback to Luiz. "*Hætan!*" *Heat.* Eldra knew this spell well. Kendra and I gulped, thinking of her sacrifice. She should be with us. Our hearts hadn't stopped aching since early this morning. None of us were OK enough to be here. But Scarlett—er, Jody—needed us. No, she wasn't *just* a stripper. She was Carl's mom and a good mom, too. Carl needed her. If we had to give our lives for her, she was worth it.

I used the pain of our loss to augment the heat, focusing inside the deadbolt. The red glow of melting metal illuminated the door jamb. The heat radiated outward, warming my hand, but I redirected it back to the deadbolt, not letting it burn me. Alexis had taught me how to control heat with magic. She could touch anything hot without getting burned. The smell of burnt metal, plastic, and paint permeated the air, causing Alexis to wrinkle her nose.

The protector magic had provided me a vision of this moment. In it, local gang members with handguns stood on the other side of the door. I nodded to Luiz and Kendra to step to the right side. I poured magic into my new Kevlar armor, making me double bulletproof. We'd checked all the trunks of the various vehicles in the mansion garage and had found two men's Kevlar vests. Some of the druids killed on the Day of a Thousand Deaths had worn Kevlar, and it had failed to protect them. Kendra and Lexy pulled at my magic to make their leather body armor bulletproof as well. They weren't double bulletproof. Earlier, Luiz and I had tried to chivalrously give the vests to the girls, but they didn't fit well, so the girls refused. Alexis made a call and special ordered Kevlar vests to custom fit their feminine figures, but their order wouldn't arrive for weeks.

Kendra stepped next to Luiz. Lexy, however, left the Tongan in a daze on the left side of the door and tiptoed to stand directly in front of the door as if to offer an easy target, testing if they dared shoot at the Princess of the New World. Ariel stepped in front of me, dressed in a coral camisole, gray shorts, and Converse shoes that matched her hair. Yes, a seven-year-old girl with lavender hair planned to use herself as a human shield to protect me, which is not something I would normally allow. In fairness, she was thousands—maybe millions—of years old, but doesn't remember much of it, which is probably good since she used to be evil. We'd only met Ariel earlier this morning. She was Coyote's hybrid granddaughter, half water baby—a freshwater mermaid thought to be a Native American myth—and half ancient alien shapeshifter. She swore an oath to Coyote to protect me, then fought with us against her own kind—all of whom seemed to have kept their memories. After we survived that battle, she transformed her sea-lion-like mermaid tail into the legs of a seven-year-old girl. She joined our operation, code-named Scarlett Rescue, to fulfill her promise to Coyote. I wasn't sure if I could trust her, but her willingness to stand in front of me as a human shield was a good start.

*We've got this,* Kendra added, posing motivationally in a half-T position by standing with her shoulders back and pressing her fists together above her chest so that her forearms formed a straight line. She always posed like that and spoke that phrase before her drill-team performances at half-time. Luiz teasingly copied Kendra, first cupping his pecs with his hands as if he were a girl adjusting her breasts, and then mimicking Kendra's fists-together stance.

I grinned, grateful Luiz could ease my stress, this time at Kendra's expense. I yanked the door a second time. This time, the red-hot deadbolt collapsed, and the door swung open.

Only darkness presented itself on the other side of the entry. Lexy could see inside fine, which gave me the quarter-second I needed to dive—more of a fall with my weak legs—to the right side before the machine gun spit bullets that would have ripped me apart. Three bullets hit my pants. I'd tested the bulletproof spell with the expectation that it would stop a few shots, not thirteen massive rounds per second.

Why hadn't the protector magic showed me a machine gun in my vision?

After taking a couple bullets yesterday, Lexy had dressed more prepared today. But like me, she hadn't expected an AR-15 illegally modified to be fully automatic. She side-stepped out of the way, but not before a line of five bullets hit her leather body armor, right above her heart. Without magical assistance, the first bullet would have torn through her chest, but the bulletproof spell stopped all five before she'd shifted out of the doorway—actually, four and a half. One of the rounds hit near her right hip. It had stopped, sort of. A half inch of the bullet stuck out of her

4

leather armor. She could already smell her own blood. She pulled the projectile out and looked at it. Her blood dripped down from a very sharp point. Armor-piercing rounds. The scent of honey—Lexy's hunger—mixed with her pumpkin spice.

"We got 'em!" a young man's nasally voice shouted with nervous glee after the machine gun stopped. Then he swore. "We killed a little girl!" his young, nasally voice changing from glee to panic.

I found myself on the asphalt to the right of the door at Luiz and Kendra's feet. My palms bled, scuffed, again, from diving to the asphalt. Eldra's staff rolled to a stop a few feet away. I reached for my lower right hip to see why it hurt worse than my ankle and found nothing wrong. Lexy's hip hurt, not mine. The Trinity of Mind had its flaws, such as the difficulty distinguishing her injuries from mine—both hurt.

Ariel had taken the worst of the bullets. Her seven-year-old body lay mangled on the aged asphalt. Blood oozed from a hole in her forehead. A dozen more holes splotched her chest, coloring her coral camisole in crimson. One of her legs had almost been severed. It bent awkwardly, held together by the outside flap of skin, the separated bone visible. She lay motionless—corpse-like—her lavender-brown eyes just empty glass, staring directly at me. I couldn't believe she'd died the very same day that she promised to protect me. Her eyes looked so lifeless. A pang of regret that I would never really know Ariel pinched at my heart.

To continue, order the book here: https://amzn.to/3rJ8T41

www.ingramcontent.com/pod-product-compliance
Lightning Source LLC
Chambersburg PA
CBHW021309250626
47155CB00002B/446